BLONDE
to the
BONE

BLONDE
to the
BONE

Mike Johnson

Dedication

For Doris

You would have loved this one. But then you would have loved anything I wrote. I wish you could have read it. Then again, you already know. Can't wait to see you again. But if you don't mind, it'll be a while.

ACKNOWLEDGMENTS

Many thanks to my first draft readers, Lisa Simpson and Cheryl Faith, for their great encouragement, and especially for Lisa's comment, "I've never read a book like that." Made me feel like I'd accomplished my goal.

1

From somewhere through the murmuring crowd mingling around the lighted Olympic-sized swimming pool, Daniele walked up with a handsome thirty year old man in tow and without so much as a hello demanded, "Where's Father?"

"So you came after all?" Michele asked, her smile instantly disappearing. She literally looked Daniele's date up and down and said, "You actually found someone who would go out with you?"

"Paid him," Daniele said, scanning the scene.

"Does he have a name?"

"Jack," said Jack, his broad smile revealing teeth looking whiter than they really were against his tan. He'd just returned from a midsummer escape to the Bahamas, skipping town the moment his gruesome three-year divorce had become final. He'd developed the strange habit of shaking his head like he was saying "No" for no apparent reason as he replayed the events of the previous eight years over and over in his imagination. Most of the "wobbly brain syndrome," as he put it whenever someone at work would find him staring off at the ceiling and draw attention to it, was in wonder at how there could be so much baggage – and expense – from only a five-year marriage. *And the lies she would tell!* he would think to himself going wobbly. The huge clash in his mind was his son. Five years old now, and totally controlled by *her*. You'd think as a lawyer he'd be able to at least get joint custody, which he did have on paper, but not in practice. She often broke the terms of visitation, and as much as he tried in court, it just didn't go his way. He'd actually begun to believe that his status as an attorney was costing him, with mediators, lawyers and even judges inclined to take her side. The

Bahamas trip was intended to be celebratory, but turned into more of a convalescent wound licking – and trying to get the vacillation out of his neck. But his wallet was still in agony, as he was forced to resort to a credit card to pay for his retreat. Jack extended his hand.

"A pleasure," Michele said, taking a quick, short breath before sipping on her Champaign and darting her eyes toward the strings of white twinkling party lights and tiki torches surrounding the grounds. She swung so sharply that her black velvet cocktail dress with the dark blue flower patterns flung feather-like around her knees. "You should feel honored," she said without eye contact, "she gave up on men years ago."

"Wow," Jack remarked, lifting his empty hand to his hair and scratching the way you do when you're trying to hide a handshake snub. Repeatedly glancing from Michele to Daniele and back again, he said, "You really *do* look alike."

"It's the twin thing," Daniele stated blandly, her thin straight nose with the cute little uplifted roundness on the end making the slightest little ski-jump silhouette against the lights as she idly searched through the guests. "Remember? I warned you?"

"Well, yeah," Jack said, shoving his hands into the pockets of his gray slacks, pushing his matching suit coat back and leaning forward onto the balls of his feet, "but if it wasn't for your hair I don't think I could tell you apart."

"That's why I'm brunette and she's blonde," Daniele said dryly, "so we know which one is the dumb one."

"So what're you doing here?" Michele asked, her identical nose glistening in the lights.

Jack couldn't help but stare from one to the other at their slender noses. Slim, snobbish, seductive. And after further study of their contours against the background lighting, concluded that the girls were thirty-four C's of exceptional proportion. He sighed unconsciously thinking that Michele's silky long blonde hair definitely worked better, pinned up on her right side and flowing down over her strapless shoulders to side-by-side lazy curls laying strategically in haphazard tufts upon her bare chest like contented kittens. Her long dangling earrings - dripping with tear shaped glowing sapphires laced in white gold - ended with diamonds, swinging and flashing like prisms. It was as though he was seeing Daniele once again for the first time; only his gaze was fixated on Michele.

"Father practically begged me to come," Daniele complained. She and Jack had just come from work, and she was still dressed in her navy blue pants suit, her brown hair hanging in places from her updo revealing small diamond studs. Jack realized for the first time that Daniele's hair was actually as thin and wispy as Michele's, but the darker color made it look thick. Tiki flame shadows danced across her soft white cheeks. "Where is he?"

"Haven't seen him yet," Michele said, taking a cursory look around. "Martin!" she called, waving with one hand, and with the other setting her empty champagne flute down and snatching another from the tray of a passing waiter. She smiled as Martin took short quick steps through the middle of a small cluster of people huddled next to the pool.

Martin Jackson did a little skip as he broke through and returned the smile. "Hey girl!" He smothered her in a bear hug as she all but disappeared into his colorful outfit that was either a traditional African tribal look or something from a toga party. "You were great tonight!"

"Thanks!" she said exuberantly. "But it would have been absolutely *boring* if it hadn't been for the streamers you had on the runway. And that lighting! It was just *brilliant!*"

"Oh no," he chuckled, shaking his head. "It was all Michele Calvet. The designs, the models. You really knocked 'em dead."

"You really think so?" Michele asked in a high-pitched voice full of true humility and curiosity.

"Absolutely," Martin said with sincerity, "we're ready."

Michele's smile grew, "Oh, I am *so* excited about Paris!"

"Me *too*," Martin said, "and it's going to be even better than tonight's show. Just watch, girl. You know those French models are all that!"

"Sounds like your little talent show went well," Daniele said.

"It was a *fashion* show," Michele said exasperated, "and I'll have you know it was really good." She turned to Martin for support. "Wasn't it Martin?"

"Sure was," Martin agreed, nodding like a woodpecker.

"You don't have to be such a bitch about everything," Michele said, her pecan shaped light blue eyes piercing and sparkling from the strings of party lights. The girls' features were uncannily similar, right down to eye color. They were the bright blue of the sky on the horizon on a sunny day. Not the deep blue of the overhead sky, but the whitened blue of the low distance, washed thin by the atmosphere.

"A bitch?" Daniele said with mock surprise. "All I did was ask about your stupid little show..."

"See, there you go," Michele said.

"So are you true blondes or true brunettes?" Jack asked with a lame smile that he considered cleverly suggestive, hoping to diffuse what appeared to be a growing argument.

Michele smiled, "I doubt you'll ever know," she said, then turning toward Daniele added with a snicker, "then again, I s'pose you probably will. Surprised you don't know already."

"Jack's with the public defender's office," Daniele said, ignoring Michele's slights and hoping to pull Jack up from the gutter and give some credibility to this guy who'd bugged her for two years for a date.

"Oh how interesting," Michele said, her brow furrowing. "Is that like military or something?"

Daniele rolled her eyes. "It's not the hair color Jack."

"I'm a lawyer," Jack said, looking down at her from a full head higher.

Michele laughed, taking another look up at his eyes. "Oh. Well, very nice to meet you Jack," she said, saying the "k" a little extra-hard.

"Maybe I'll go find a drink," Jack said, breaking her playful stare and escaping toward the house past a small group of young women who were giggling about something, most likely due to the free flow of Champaign.

"Doesn't get the waiter thing, huh?" Michele asked with a grin as she took a lingering look at Jack's athletic frame hopping the few steps up the patio toward the French doors at the rear of the mansion. His brown hair was thick and neatly groomed, just touching the top of his collar. "And what's with the negative nod?"

"Calls it wobbly brain syndrome," Daniele said absentmindedly. "Picked it up from his ex." Her face suddenly glowed with a subdued smile that pulled gentle half-moons in her cheeks down from her crinkled nose. "Father!" she said enthusiastically as Leon Calvet emerged from behind another huddled group of chattering businessmen and their wives, looking dapper in his white silk sports jacket and black slacks.

"Hello girls," Leo said brightly. "Good to see the two of you together for a change!"

Michele turned and brightened instantly. "Daddy!"

Leo grabbed one girl per arm and gave them each a squeeze. Michele leaned pliantly into his slightly rounded belly, while Daniele leaned back onto his arm and kissed him on the cheek.

"Well, you know I'm always here for you, Father," Daniele said into his ear.

Leo grinned. "I'd rather hoped you'd be here to show some support for your sis."

She stepped back. "I'm sure she needs it, but from what I understand her little show didn't bomb."

Michele let out an audible snort against her father's chest before letting go.

"It was wonderful," Martin reiterated.

Leo nodded a greeting. "Martin."

"Hello sir," Martin said.

"Oh Daniele," Leo said with a smirk. "Why can't you two just bury the hatchet and be friends again?"

"We were never friends," Michele said with disgust.

"Of course you were," Leo argued, "at least until college."

"Not really, Father. You don't know the half of it."

"So tell me," Leo said, crossing his arms and leaning on one leg, "and we'll put whatever argument you two have in the past."

"Oh, what difference does it make?" Michele asked. "We're better off this way. Daniele gets to go play lawyer and be a big city girl in her downtown penthouse, and I get the run of this house." She waved her arm gaily at the huge back yard, full of trees and shrubs, stone walkways with a Japanese bridge over a winding pump-driven stream that meandered off into a jungle-like mass of vegetation in the far left corner, and what must have been two hundred people dressed in the over-priced casual attire of the rich.

"At least I can pay my own way," Daniele said with a soft sneer that turned her thin upper lip to the side.

"Oh really?" Michele asked, raising her eyebrows. "And to think our taxes actually pay for you to lose cases." She sniffed. "I happen to know Daddy is paying your rent."

Daniele raised her voice, "That's not true! And I'll have you know in most of my cases I've gotten convictions!"

"Ha!" Michele laughed, pushing the right side of her hair over her ear. "How many would that be, one?"

"Better than playing dress-up with a bunch of bimbos."

"Stop it!" Leo said harshly. "The both of you." He held each of their shoulders and looked from one to the other. "I was hoping I could talk to you and convince you to get over your differences, but I guess not." He let go and sighed heavily. "Hopefully one of these days you'll both grow up and realize that you need each other, just like I need you. Hopefully something will happen that will make you think, maybe even work together for some goal that will bring you back together again."

Daniele and Michele stood silent. The small orchestra playing moderately insipid renditions of 1970's rock and roll songs suddenly seemed louder. Crickets filled the air with chirping mixed with the babble of the guests.

"Come with me for a moment, Daniele," Leo said, taking her by the elbow and tugging lightly. "Let's talk for a minute."

"Oh Father," Daniele said, drifting off with him to the row of lounge chairs by the pool. "Do we really need another lecture?"

"Lecture?" Leo asked, surprised. "I haven't lectured you since you were in high school."

She crossed her arms and faced him when he stopped. "Okay, fatherly discussion."

Leo smiled. "Just a concerned father."

"And…?"

"I see you brought a date," Leo said. "Handsome guy."

"Yes he is."

"Just tell me the truth. Is he here for my benefit, or are you really dating?"

Daniele looked across the pool and didn't answer.

"Well that's original," Leo said sarcastically. "I just wonder where you find these guys whenever we have a little get together. What's going on with you? You're so unhappy, and all you do is work. Don't you want to settle down, have a husband, a family?"

"Someday," she said distantly. "I'm just very busy."

"You've been very busy for years," Leo said. "What happened that changed you?"

Daniele looked at him. "What do you mean?"

"Between you and Michele, or just you, I guess. I don't know, and you won't tell me."

"There's nothing to tell, Father," she said with a grin. "And I'm fine. I'll get to all that romance stuff when I'm ready. Besides, look at you."

"Me?"

"It's been fifteen years since mom died, and I don't see you dating anyone."

"Don't turn this around and make it about me," Leo gently scolded. "I'm not the one who's missing her youth. Your mother and I had wonderful times together."

"So you think I'm wasting my life?" Daniele asked defensively.

"You can be so difficult sometimes," Leo said. "I know you're unhappy. You've distanced yourself from your family, from your sister and me, and I don't know why."

"It's a very busy job," she explained.

"You know I love you," Leo said, "and I'd do anything to see you happy. But you're almost thirty, and as far as I can tell you're going to be alone and unhappy for years to come unless you deal with whatever it was that happened."

"*Nothing* happened," she said earnestly.

"Then what's up with you and men? And why are you and Michele almost enemies?"

"You've certainly heard of sibling rivalry," Daniele said. "Just take it for what it is."

"Sibling rivalry is what happens to small children. The two of you were over that by high school. But somewhere along the line things changed. *You* changed. I just want to help. But you're hiding something." He took a deep breath. "One of these days, one way or the other, I'm gonna find out what it is."

"Why can't you just leave it alone?" she asked. "If I wanted your help, I would ask you. Really."

"Not good enough," Leo said, shaking his head, and then tilting his head to the side added, "Let's go back over. I want to talk to the both of you."

They joined Michele and Martin again, with Martin still reminiscing about how wonderful the show was. Jack emerged from the crowd with two flutes and handed one to Daniele who accepted it without a thank you. She didn't even offer to introduce Jack. Leo just took a glancing look at him and focused on his daughters.

He put his hands on his hips. After a momentary gaze at each daughter, he pointed his finger in the air and looked first to Daniele and then to Michele. "Remember this," he said. "Listen." When he was sure he had their attention, he slowly said, enunciating each word, "The late Benz gives you twenty twenty vision, but the upside-down Benz will get you there if you follow the second one."

Daniele's eyes furrowed while Michele stared dumbfounded with her mouth slightly open. The cricket noise swelled through the pause.

Blinking twice, Michele asked, "Which Benz?" After all, Leo had six here at the house. "Did somebody wreck one of them?"

Without giving them time to inquire further about his cryptic statement, Leo went on, "Why don't the two of you visit the Washington Monument? Go up to the top. It'd give you a chance to get together and do something carefree."

The band started up another song. After several measures Daniele was the first to speak. "Sure Father. We'll do that sometime."

Leo looked at Michele.

"Oh yeah, Daddy. I'd love to," Michele said, then shot a quick glance at Daniele but didn't catch her eye. Daniele was gawking at Leo.

He continued, "Take a map. You never know what you can see from there."

Daniele eyed her father suspiciously. "What, um, uh, Father? What in the world are you talking about? And what does that mean about the late Benz?"

Leo ignored the questions. "Just remember you two, if you put your minds together you can do anything."

He walked off without another word, leaving Daniele and Michele silent as they watched him with a bounce in his step weaving through the guests, extending cheerful greetings along the way as he circled the pool toward the back of the yard.

Daniele finally broke the trance. "That was pretty weird."

"Yeah," Michele agreed. "What was that weird Benz thing?"

"No idea," Daniele said. Then suddenly, "So why did you have to go running your mouth off again?"

"Me?" Michele whined. "You started this just like you started every other fight we ever had."

Martin said softly, "Hey. Why don't you two just knock it off for a while? You've already upset your dad, so why not just give it a rest?"

"I suppose you're right," Daniele said, taking a sip.

"I will if she will," Michele said and took a glance around. "Hey, have you seen Rick?"

"Not so far. Have you two set a date?" Martin asked.

"Not exactly," Michele said vaguely, her left thumb stretching unconsciously under her middle finger to fiddle with the ring.

"Well com'on, girl!" He said with an elbow to her side. "What's it been, six months since the engagement party?" He made a singsong voice. "Everybody's waiting."

Michele didn't respond. Instead, her expression turned bright. "Oh there he is, on the other side of the pool talking with Daddy." She waved but Rick didn't turn.

"Who's the girl?" Daniele asked, following Michele's gaze.

"I'll bet *she's* a real redhead," Jack remarked.

Daniele looked at him sideways again. "One track mind, 'ey Jack?"

Jack smiled, "It's a guy thing..."

"I've never seen you quite so...um...relaxed."

"I've never seen you anywhere outside the courthouse," Jack countered. "Or the office. Lunches at McTierney's Pub don't count."

"Look," Michele said, "isn't she holding Daddy's hand?"

"Who?" Daniele asked, looking back toward Rick and Leo. "The redhead?" She stepped aside for a better vantage point. "Oh, so she is..."

They all craned their necks as Michele added, "She's cute. Do you know her?"

"Can't say that I do."

The crowd seemed suddenly louder as the song ended, and Leo Calvet could be heard laughing from across the pool. They were standing in front of three short plump trees trimmed like French poodles. Rick was listening intently, pushing his fingers through one side of his sandy blonde hair, and the redhead had a pleasant smile with her head cocked slightly sideways staring into Leo's eyes.

"But she obviously knows him," Daniele observed.

Rick and the redhead laughed as Leo clapped his hands once and rubbed them together, the sharp smack echoing across the pool. The three of them began looking around the yard until Leo's eyes first, followed momentarily by Rick's and the redhead's, found Michele and Daniele. The redhead smiled, waved a little wave, said something to Leo and then to Rick, and then turned and disappeared down the path behind them into the bushes. Leo smiled and said something to Rick while still looking at his daughters and then did something that made them both raise their eyebrows. He flashed them a peace sign with his fingers. Then he slipped away after the redhead. Rick turned to watch Leo leave before wandering slowly around the pool toward the girls.

"Is Daddy all right?" Michele asked as Rick approached. She approved of his dark blue suit, and thought the solid silver tie against a powder blue shirt stood out nicely in the festive lights. He had serious but gentle blue eyes that were always either in deep reflection or intent on some task at hand. Right now they seemed unusually playful.

"What'd'ya mean?" Rick asked. His puzzled look made four deep V-shaped creases between his thick brown eyebrows. He turned to Daniele, the lines on his forehead smoothing out while similar deep lines formed around the edges of his smile. "Hey Danny!" he said pleasantly.

"It's Daniele," Daniele said.

"I mean he said some weird stuff before just walking off," Michele said.

He chuckled at Daniele and then shrugged back at Michele. "Dunno. Seemed fine to me."

Daniele looked off toward the bushes in the back. "Pretty weird."

"Mm-hmm," Michele agreed, the two of them looking like a mirror image as they each pondered Leo's exit.

2

Michele's heart sank. "Is this where we're doing it?" She'd just arrived in Paris in one of Leo's jets and was standing at the top of the escalator taking her first glimpse of the venue for her show. Twin pinkish metal doors – the kind with the long handles that you push from the inside to open them – were propped wide by rubber-footed doorstops. With all the rushing through the airport, a brief stop at Leo's chateau, and a mad dash in one of Leo's Benzes so that she could arrive on time, even wearing her pastel purple tank top she was perspiring in the July heat. She stood there frozen, barelegged in white shorts and tennis shoes.

Josette gave her a puzzled look. "But of course," she responded in her charming French accent. "Where do you think we will be?"

Michele smiled, hoping she hadn't hurt Josette's feelings. But she didn't need to worry.

Josette was unfazed. She was a petite woman in her early thirties, with nippy precise motions as she flitted from here to there, her willowy hands always occupied with something – with words even, when she spoke. She walked briskly around the chairs surrounding the runway and skipped onto the twenty-centimeter high stage, followed by Michele who fell behind taking short unhurried steps as she perused the room. At the rear of the low platform were the curtains that formed the small hallways on either side of the entrance from the dressing room, with a solid wall center stage that the models would walk around to enter from stage right and left. Josette sashayed stage right around the wall. Michele shuffled along, studying the room for a moment before Josette's head leaned around. "Are you coming?"

Michele fumbled in her purse for her satellite phone. "I really need to call Daddy," she said earnestly. "Just give me a moment, please. He's expecting me."

Josette disappeared saying, "Yes, yes, but you must hurry. Here the models are. Come, come, we have much to do."

Michele strode to the back of the room where she felt she wouldn't be heard and dialed Leo's cell. It rang until his voice mail came on. She didn't even listen through his message before stabbing the off button in irritation and speed dialing his office.

This was Michele's first fashion show in Europe, made possible by a business venture with Mercedes-Benz, also arranged by Leo. The show in the Galeries Rouquet was a dry run, a dress rehearsal; mainly for tourists who attended the free program so that they could say they'd been to a Paris fashion show – and to sell the modeled garments in the departments on the lower floors. The marketing agreement was for the production of a Calvet-touched line of convertibles and sedans with customized interiors designed by Michele Calvet herself, a project that she'd been working on for the past year with a team of twelve designers and engineers provided by Calvet and Benz. The companies were set to share client lists and advertise jointly, and the car manufacturer had agreed to sponsor the real show, to be held a week later in the much more prestigious Gustave Eiffel Room on the first floor of the Eiffel Tower.

This show was on the seventh floor of one of the two massive buildings that comprised the famous department store, well known for its first floor collection of every perfume imaginable. The store spanned two blocks with a narrow, busy street between the buildings. A second floor bridge over the café-lined lane connected the two halves.

Two oversized photos of the female-targeted cars, a red convertible and a blue four door sedan, were mounted on either side of the runway where photographers could capture them along with stills of the models. But that wasn't what had distressed Michele when she'd walked into the room.

The room was small with a normal ceiling rather than the raised, chandeliered ceiling that she'd had in Washington for her initial practice show where her designs - other than the Benz line - were modeled. This room seemed dingy, like the converted office space that it was, with uncomfortable folding chairs lined up tightly around a runway that stood hardly a fifth of a meter above the scuffed linoleum floor. The plywood runway was covered with a thin cheap beige carpet that had actually been worn through in places, and was dangling by threads around the twenty-centimeter high walls. She just *had* to get through to Daddy, because at this point all she wanted to do was cancel.

"Calvet Fashions," a mature woman's voice said clearly over the phone.

"This is Michele. Is my father in?"

"Oh hello Michele. No, as a matter of fact we've been waiting for him. He was supposed to be here at a meeting over two hours ago. We're really wor..."

"Ohh..." Michele moaned interrupting. "It's *extremely* important."

"Yes, but we..."

"*Please* listen," Michele pleaded. "I need to talk to him right away. This is just all *wrong*. I don't know *what* to do."

Josette leaned around again and called – actually sang, "Michele?"

Michele glanced up at Josette with a preoccupied look and pointed her index finger into the air. "Tell him to call me the minute he gets in."

"That's what I'm trying to..."

Michele wasn't listening and snapped the phone shut. She forced a smile at Josette and walked hurriedly to the stage while putting her phone in the white, bulbous purse that swung on her shoulder with every movement.

The back was even worse than the show room. The dressing tables were old and broken, rusting metal racks with bent hangers were scattered haphazardly around the room, and piles of clothing were everywhere. The room was a shambles. Three models were putting on makeup at poorly lit tables with cracked mirrors. None noticed Michele. She felt somewhat better when Martin walked in, carrying his large swaying frame in what could only be identified as a flowing white robe. At least she had someone she could talk to. Josette was busy giving instructions to some models and helpers who were just arriving through a back door, which gave Michele a chance to take Martin off to the side.

"Did you see the show room?" Michele asked in a whispered panic. Martin nodded.

"It's just *awful*," she said. "I'm thinking of canceling."

"Well it *is* just awful," he echoed. "But I think you should go on."

"I tried calling Daddy to ask him, but he wasn't there. I really need to talk to him." She reached for her sat phone again and stepped aside toward a corner of the room. "Let me just try again. Wait here."

Martin stood watching like a helpless orphan while Michele dialed.

"Hi Kathy," she said to the woman on the other end. "It's Michele again. Did he show up?"

"That's what I was trying to tell you," Kathy said. "It really isn't like him to be late for a meeting, let alone miss it altogether."

"Yes, I *know*," Michele said urgently. "Did you try his cell phone?"

"We did, but Daniele says he left it on his dresser in the bedroom. And he didn't even charge it."

Michele was distracted by Josette and didn't hear what Kathy'd said about Leo's cell. Josette had been assigning Michele's outfits to the various models, and was bringing one over. "Michele!" she sang. "This is missing the belt. I know it had a belt from your picture you sent to me. Where is the belt?"

Michele was looking at Josette. "Belt?"

"Belt?" Kathy said.

"No, not you," Michele said to the phone.

"Yes, the belt, where is it?" Josette asked impatiently.

"It should have been packed with the dress. Check again. It should be there." Michele lightly scratched her forehead. "Or…just use a scarf instead." She focused back on the phone. "Anyway, pleeease have him call me the minute he gets in." She hung up.

Martin was sauntering behind Josette now. "I think I know where it is," he said supportively.

Michele stood helpless for a moment, the despair of the underwhelming conditions becoming a general depression. She felt like leaving it to Martin and Josette and going down to the street for a glass of wine at one of the sidewalk cafés.

Two more models had come in, and Michele stood helplessly watching the increasing activity. She stopped herself and gathered her senses, filling her lungs and shoving the air out gradually between her clenched teeth. Finally, she resolved that this was indeed going to happen. And as displeased as she was at the surroundings, she could only hope that there wouldn't be too many photographers to spread this false start around. She wanted to just get it over with and hoped that the next show, the real show, would be better. She was thinking that of course it would be. She'd been to the Gustave Eiffel Room, and it was night and day compared to this.

Her phone started playing "Girls Just Wanna Have Fun" and she pulled it from her purse. "Hello?"

"Michele."

"Oh! Hi Rick!" Michele said, and without any pleasantries went on swiftly. "I really need to find Daddy. Know where he is?"

"Listen to me," Rick said, "and don't hang up."

"Why would I hang up?"

"Kathy says you hung up on her."

"Well," Michele said, "I wasn't trying to be rude. I'm just looking for Daddy." She lowered her voice. "And you should see this place. It's just…"

"I know, I *know*," Rick said emphatically. "But *listen*."

"Okay…" Michele said slowly.

Rick was calm, measured. "You need to come home."

"Now?" she asked, her voice lifting.

"Your dad's missing."

Michele nodded, as though Rick could see her. "That's why I'm calling," she said. "I need to talk to him." She was still focused on the room and wondering, now that she'd given in to the idea that the show must go on, what she needed to do to get involved.

"Did you hear me?" Rick asked. "Your father is missing."

It finally sank in. "What do you mean missing?" Michele asked, her eyes staring straight ahead with her forehead now furrowed.

"We don't know where he is," Rick answered. "I'm standing here next to Kathy, and she doesn't know. No one does. No one in the office knows. Even Daniele doesn't know."

"You've talked to Daniele?" Michele asked.

"Yes," Rick answered. "But she doesn't know where he is. Even the servants at your house haven't seen him since last night. He seems to have disappeared."

Michele's attention was fully on Rick now, while the whirlwind blew around her. She could feel the blood flowing from her face. "Did anyone call the police?"

"Daniele did. She said they usually don't consider an adult missing for twenty-four hours, but that they'd make an exception in this case since it is, ya know, your father. But they don't have any idea where he is either. I think they're checking phone records or something, and Daniele said they're looking at credit cards to see if he's used any, but they said they haven't found anything."

"Where's Daniele?" Michele asked.

"She's at your house. She doesn't know what to do. She says the last time she saw him was last night at the party when he went out the back."

"Me too," Michele remarked blankly, sinking into a hazy light shock. "He was talking to you."

"For a while, then I went over and talked to you," Rick said, and continued. "None of the cars are gone, and not even the drivers know where he is. They all say they didn't drive him anywhere last night. He just went off down the street behind the house and no one's seen him since."

"He was with that girl," Michele said.

"I know," he said. "But no one knows who she is."

"You know, don't you?"

"I'm afraid I don't," Rick said.

Michele stifled a sob. "What should I do?"

Rick didn't answer directly. "I've worked for Leo, for your father, for almost nine years. He's never missed a meeting. Not once." There was a hushed pause. "Ever."

They were both silent for a few moments.

"We're all worried," Rick said. "Very worried."

Michele looked around the room at the fashion show. It all seemed suddenly unimportant.

"Tell Daniele I'm on my way."

3

"Ya know," Rick said, leaning back in his chair with his long-legged jeans extending far under the table, "it really does seem like she's here when I'm sitting across from you."

"Oh please," Daniele said with a smile that belied her irritated tone. "Can we stay focused?"

Rick was well over six feet tall, with thick forearms covered with a thin dark layer of hair and folded across his blue short-sleeved shirt. "Sorry. It's just that even after all this time I don't think I could tell you apart if it wasn't for your hair color."

"We've already established that," Daniele said, now slightly annoyed. He didn't have to go on and on, did he? "What *I'd* like to know is what she said before they left."

"*Daniele*," Rick said exasperated. "*I* thought we'd already established that I don't remember."

"Just humor me. Go over it one more time."

Daniele was sitting forward with her arms on the table, fingers intertwined. She was not so casual as Rick, instead wearing the same attire she would normally wear to work – dark blue slacks and a white blouse. The only casual aspect was that she was missing the matching jacket. Her hair was pinned up the way she usually wore it, with strands hanging down like she'd just come from a hard day at the office.

They were sitting in the vast kitchen just to the right of the patio at a long table made of thick oak, full of cut marks from years of culinary use. The chairs were utility, but comfortable, with rounded backs and thick cushions on the seats. Stainless steel restaurant-grade appliances, including a 48-inch refrigerator, surrounded the kitchen. Next to the 48-inch was a walk-in. The walk-in refrigerator was on the far wall next to a swinging door that led through a wide hallway lined with linen and dish cabinets and through another swinging door to the dining room. A long matching cutting table stood in the center of the room, much taller than the table they were sitting at. Above that table was an elongated oval rack hanging from the ceiling, crammed with various pots and pans and kitchen aids dangling in organized disarray. They'd been sitting there for an hour, ever since Rick had arrived.

"All right," he said, taking a bothered breath and sinking lower in his chair. "I'd just gotten there but I hadn't seen Michele yet. I was in the back of the yard talking to a colleague…"

"Who?" Daniele abruptly interrupted.

Rick scratched his head. "Phil…you know him don't you? What's his name from accounting. Phil somebody. Starts with a 'T' I think."

She released her fingers and raised her palms at him. "Okay, okay, never mind who it was."

Rick raised an eyebrow at her before going on. "So I saw Michele talking to you on the other side of the pool, and I was walking that way to come over. Leo was already standing back there with Ms. Crimson…."

Daniele broke in. "Ms. Crimson?"

"Ms. Crimson. That's how your dad introduced me. I've never met her before. Don't know who she is."

"Sure took you long enough to remember that," Daniele said, folding her hands again and tapping once on the table with her out-stretched index fingers.

Rick shrugged.

"All right, and then what?"

"And then Leo motioned for me to go over there. They were laugh-ing about something when I walked up, but I don't know what it was. Leo said, 'Rick, come on over here,' when I was within earshot, and said he wanted to introduce me to 'his friend.'"

"That's all he said," Daniele asked, "his friend?"

"Yeah, those were his exact words. Actually, 'My friend.' And then he said, 'This is Rick Parker,' told her that I worked for him as his vice president of business development, and then he started to turn to her with his palm out like he was gonna introduce her when Jorge Guerrero walked by. I guess it'd been a while since your dad had seen him, and he was all the sudden distracted - you know, how've you been, whatever happened to your such-and-such deal, how's your third quarter looking. Just catching up. Then he apologized for being so rude and introduced Ms. Crimson to Jorge and me. I know who Jorge is, of course, but I'd never actually spoken to him before."

Rick paused for a moment, got up and ambled across the room. "Then Jorge walked off and Leo started telling me about Jorge's troubles that he'd had the previous year, but that he seemed to be coming through it." Rick opened the 48-inch fridge and took out a bottle of water. He eyed it for a moment before starting back across the room. "Benz water?" he asked.

"What?"

"This bottle of water," Rick said, holding it up, "it says Mercedes-Benz water."

"You get them from the Benz dealer," Daniele said dryly. "So what else did he say?"

Rick studied the bottle as he sat down. "Never seen Mercedes-Benz water. You got a refrigerator full of it."

"Buy a Benz," Daniele said insipidly. "Now could you please stick to the subject?"

Rick cranked the cap off and took a sip. "That was about it. He made some kind of joke about Jorge, but I don't remember what it was. We all laughed and then he said they'd better get going. He waved at you guys…"

"Actually it was a peace sign," Daniele corrected him.

"Whatever," Rick said, taking another gulp.

After several moments Daniele said, "And…?"

Rick swallowed audibly followed by an, "Ah," and looked at her. "And that's it."

She spread her palms open. "That's it?"

"Leo said that they'd better be going, gave you a hippy sign and they took off."

"He never said something like, 'Com'on Barbie let's go?'"

Rick's eyebrows narrowed. "So you *do* know her?"

Daniele's head dipped slightly and her mouth dropped open as she stared.

Rick looked sheepishly back at the bottle. "Oh, so I guess it's not *Barbie* Crimson." He took a much longer drink this time before he changed the subject. "Does Benz actually *own* the water processing plant or do they just buy it from someone and stick their label on them?"

Daniele's stare didn't change, but her head started weaving slowly from side-to-side in a negative gesture. "You really can't stay focused, can you?"

Rick's face was blank.

"You obviously couldn't care less what's happened to my father."

"Of course I care," Rick objected. "But what're we supposed to do? I told you, I've never met her before in my life, and I don't know where they went."

Daniele was silent. She looked as though she might tear up. Her hands re-folded in front of her on the table.

"Look," Rick said soothingly. Leaning forward he set the bottle down and reached across the table to cup her slender hands in his. "I know you're worried. But Leo's a big boy. He's gonna be all right."

"I don't know if something's really happened, or if he's just playing some game," Daniele said desperately. "All those things he said."

"What things?" Rick asked. "What makes you think he's playing a game?"

"Oh, never mind," she said. "He wouldn't do that. I just wish I knew where he was." It was a little too much for Daniele, and as much as she hated it, she choked up to the point that tears were indeed forming. Her eyes were turning red.

Rick went on tenderly. "The police are on it. They have a room full of detectives working it." He let out a small laugh. "He'll probably turn up in Vegas having eloped with what's her name or something." He gently squeezed her hands and their eyes locked. "It really won't help him if you worry, and he wouldn't want you to."

At just that moment, Michele came crashing through the swinging door and screeched to a halt when she saw them, her tennis shoes squeaking on the glossy tiled floor. Her eyes went slightly wide.

Rick and Daniele turned instantly as she yanked her hands from his and slid them into her lap under the table.

Rick's face broke into a genuine smile. "Michele!"

She stood frozen.

Rick slid his chair back and walked briskly to greet her. His intention was to take her in his arms and kiss her, but she held him back.

"Can't *you* tell which one is the blonde?" she said with vinegar.

Rick was taken aback. "Huh?"

"Gimme a break," Daniele interjected. "You think I'd actually let your brainless blonde fiancé touch me?"

"Sandy blonde," Michele corrected her, her eyes like ice. "And what do *you* call it?"

Rick looked at his reflection in a glass cabinet next to the stove and brushed at his hair with the tips of his fingers. "I call it light brown. That's what's on my driver's license."

Daniele leaned back, rolled her eyes and used her fingers surreptitiously to wipe the moisture from them while holding back a laugh.

"Not your hair," Michele said with a snort.

Rick turned to Daniele and then back again. "You mean the hand thing?" Rick asked and chuckled. "Listen. You're jumping to conclusions. Daniele felt a little down and I was just trying to reassure her about your dad. Nothing was going on."

Michele's eyes flashed from Daniele to Rick before the arrows coming from them rested on her sister. "I've heard that one before."

Daniele's face turned stern. "Just drop it, would you? Rick was just trying to be nice. Quit being such a jerk."

"*Me?*" Michele fumed.

Rick tried reaching out again by putting his hand on her bare shoulder. Michele was still wearing the pastel purple tank top she'd had on in Paris. She accepted his touch this time. "I thought you trusted me," he said.

She looked from him to Daniele. "It's not you that I don't trust."

"Would you just give him a kiss so we can get to the business of finding Father?"

They didn't kiss. Instead, the two just walked over to the table and sat down, Michele circling to take the chair next to Daniele, forcing Rick to sit across from her.

Michele seemed somewhat less irate when she saw Daniele's red eyes and asked, "So what's going on? What did the police say?"

Daniele leaned forward, her face changing to a look of concern. She sniffed. "Nothing seems to be going on. The police say they're looking, but they can't find anything. No credit card use…"

"Did he use his cell phone?" Michele asked. "They know if he's using it, don't they?"

"It's on his dresser," Daniele said looking up at her.

Michele gasped. "He always has his cell…"

"I know," Daniele agreed.

"What do you think happened?" Michele asked, hoping she'd hear something encouraging, but fearing the worst.

No one wanted to say it, but Daniele made herself. "Maybe he was kidnapped."

Michele nodded slowly, Leo having explained the hazards of his persona years before – that people of his wealth and stature were sometimes targets for what certain evil people would call easy money. "That's what I was thinking. But why?" She already knew the answer, but wanted to hear it from Daniele.

"Ransom," she said.

"So you don't think he's…" the words came out slowly, painfully from Michele's lips, "you know…dead or anything."

Daniele sighed heavily. "That would be the worst, wouldn't it? But it wouldn't make any sense. Why would someone want to kill Father?"

"I don't think he has any enemies," Michele said. "Everybody loves him."

"The detectives already asked me all those questions," Daniele said. "They think it's probably a kidnapping for ransom too, but no one's heard anything from them."

"No notes? Phone calls?" Michele asked.

"Not so far. But I'd think it would take some time before we heard."

It was still for a moment before Michele asked, "So what do we do?"

Daniele shook her head. "Wait, I guess."

"Should we call the police and see if they found out anything else?" Michele asked.

"I just called them a while ago," Daniele said, rubbing her right shoulder with her left hand.

Rick had been quiet, sipping at his water. "What time is it now?"

Michele looked over Rick's shoulder at the bland clock on the wall behind him with black bold letters and black hands. "It's six ten," she said.

"Well that can't be," Rick said. "I got here at seven."

Daniele flicked her eyes at the clock and back at him. "Eleven after six and fifty-one seconds," she said. "Didn't they teach you that telling time thing in the first grade? Or do you need a digital…" She stopped when she glanced back at the clock.

Rick rotated his head to check it out. "Still six eleven and fifty-one seconds, huh?" He turned back to Daniele with a smug look.

"Oh," Daniele said awkwardly. "I guess it's…um…stopped."

Rick's mouth broke into a sideways smile. "Miss First Grade."

Michele looked at her watch, "It looks like it's two fifteen."

Rick laughed. "Time's goin' backwards…"

"Still on Paris time?" Daniele asked.

"Or forwards…" Rick added.

"Yeah," Michele said dolefully. "I'd set it if I knew what time it was."

"You *could* look at *your* watch and give us a clue," Daniele said to Rick.

He glanced down casually, turning his wrist. "Quarter after eight." He turned around and looked over his shoulder. "Got any batteries?" he asked. "I'll fix it."

"In the pantry," Daniele said.

Rick got up and crossed the room. The pantry was to the right of the swinging door. Opening the door he said, "Wow! This is bigger than my bathroom!"

"Get a bigger house," Daniele said.

"Where are they?"

"Left hand side, third shelf down in the corner," Daniele directed. "See the little white cabinet sitting on the shelf with three drawers?"

"Yep."

"Bottom drawer."

Clattering noises came from the pantry, and then Rick emerged. The girls sat silently watching while Rick took the clock off the wall, removed the old batteries and replaced them. He closed the cover, hooked the clock back on the wall and sat down.

"It still doesn't work," Michele said, twisted sideways with her arm hooked over the back of her chair, her hair falling across her chest.

Rick looked over his shoulder. "Still six eleven fifty-one," he said. He started to get up but Daniele interjected.

"Leave it," she said with a wave of her hand. "We'll fix it later. We have better things to do right now."

"Like what?" Michele asked. "What can we do?"

Daniele contemplated, with Rick and Michele seeming to look to her for guidance. "I don't know," she said after several moments. "I've just been going over and over in my mind what Father said."

"You mean at the party?" Michele asked.

"Yeah, just before he walked out with that red-headed bimbo."

Michele's eyebrows rose. "I didn't think she was a bimbo."

Daniele took a fleeting look at her. "You're so easily distracted," she groaned, but then turned serious again. "What was that thing he said about the Benz?"

Michele looked confused. "What thing?"

Daniele couldn't help herself. "This is going to be hard."

Rick chuckled, looking at Michele to see her reaction.

"At the party," Daniele said slowly, like she was leading a witness, "he said something weird about Benzes? Just before he disappeared?"

"Oh yeah," Michele said. "And something about the Washington Monument."

Rick listened, studying each one in turn but not offering anything.

"He said we needed to go there," Daniele said.

"That's right," Michele agreed, "he did."

"And that stuff about Benzes," Daniele went on. "What was it?" She looked from Michele to Rick.

"Don't look at me," Rick said, "I was over talking to Phil somebody."

Daniele stared off. "Something about the Benz making you see straight."

"No," Michele said, "twenty twenty's what he said."

"That's right," Daniele nodded in agreement. "The Benz gives you twenty twenty."

"Twenty twenty vision."

"Yes," Daniele said remembering, "The Benz gives you twenty twenty vision. No. It was the *late* Benz." She looked through the window in the back of the kitchen toward the garage. "And then something about an upside-down Benz."

"Yeah, the second one," Michele remembered. "What in the world does that mean?" Her hand had wandered to the side of her head and she pushed her hair up haphazardly. "The second one leading you there or something like that."

"Ohhh…," Daniele said in frustration. "Never mind all that. Let's just forget it. That won't get us anywhere. Let's just focus on finding him."

"Well, what do you suggest?" Michele asked.

Neither Rick nor Daniele answered. Both appeared to be deep in thought.

"What about that redhead?" Michele asked. "Maybe we should find out who she is."

"Ms. Crimson," Rick and Daniele said in unison.

Rick added, "Ms. Barbie Crimson."

"Barbie Crimson?" Michele asked.

"Just Ms. Crimson," Daniele said with disgust. "No Barbie."

Michele gazed from one to the other looking glassy eyed.

"Inside joke," Rick said.

"Mm-hmm," Michele said. "Figures."

"Oh stop it," Daniele said sharply. "Are you gonna keep doing the jealousy thing or are we gonna focus on finding Father?"

"Focus and do what?" Michele said harshly. "For all we know he's not even in Washington anymore."

Daniele didn't even hear her. "I have an idea," she said. "Let's check his mail…and his office. Maybe there's a note in his office."

Michele was mocking. "Now how would some kidnapper get into his office and leave a note?"

"Got any better ideas?" Daniele asked.

Michele just sniffed, got up and headed toward the swinging door that led to the dining room. She marched around the eighteen chair rectangular table with three teardrop chandeliers suspended above it, passed a Benz water bottle on the end of the table that one of the servants must have left, and entered the immense marble hall where the ornate stairway led to the second floor. The hall had polished white marble floors, with marble pillars at the far end between the hall and the mansion's entryway. Expansive windows adorned the front of the house, and passing through the hall you could see the lush grounds, scattered with dogwood trees, and the peaceful Potomac River down the hill. Daniele and Rick followed as Michele led them up the wide curved staircase with the mahogany rails, carpeted in lush blue with gold trim. She stopped unexpectedly halfway up and stared at the wall across the room grasping the rail.

Daniele jolted to an abrupt halt two steps behind her. "*What?*" she asked aggravated.

"The grandfather clock," Michele said, staring across the room. "Look at it."

Daniele and Rick both looked across the spacious foyer.

"Eleven after six," she said.

"And fifty-one seconds," Rick added.

"And it's not moving," Michele observed. "Shouldn't that long hanging thing be swinging back and forth?"

"It's definitely stopped," Daniele said.

"Did the power go out?" Rick asked.

Incredulous, Daniele gawked at him. "Batteries in the kitchen clock?"

"Oh yeah," Rick said.

"And this one," Michele explained, "is run by pulling on those two long chains with the pine cones on the ends. The servants do it."

"Sleeping on the job, huh?" Rick quipped.

A chill went up Daniele's spine. "Someone's trying to tell us something about eleven after six."

"And fifty-one seconds," Rick added.

"And fifty-one seconds," Daniele echoed, staring at the unmoving second hand pointing a minute past the elaborately decorated ten.

"Oh, it's just a coincidence," Michele said, and took another step up, her eyes still glued to the clock. The others followed slowly behind.

To Daniele it was suddenly as though their own house had taken on new dimensions. As though someone else was there. "Too much of a coincidence," she mumbled. "Somebody did that."

The three of them were peeking cautiously around as they crossed the railed landing that overlooked the foyer. Beyond that, the hallway stretched past the twins' bedrooms and two additional rooms to Leo's study at the far end. They opened the door to each room on the way and made a cursory inspection without entering. Outside Leo's study, Michele's manicured hand hesitated over the curved brushed nickel handle before she pushed it down to open the solid white wooden door.

Nothing looked out of the ordinary. The curtains were open, illuminating the room with the natural amber hues of a mid-summer twilight, and Leo's large oak desk was sitting as it always did, with his oversized cushioned chair pushed slightly askew as though he'd just gotten up. There were documents in neat piles on the edge of the desk, with a large calendar square in front of where Leo would work. A black computer that was built in to the side of the desk was running, and the screen saver had stars flying out on the matching black nineteen-inch LCD. The bookshelves that lined every wall were stacked neatly with books on a variety of serious subjects. Michele saw nothing strange about the room until she looked at the nautical clock on the wall, encased in a ship's wheel.

She gasped. "Look at that."

"Six eleven and fifty-one seconds," Daniele said following her gaze, and turned to Michele. "Coincidence?"

"I guess not," Michele said, feeling like something was crawling up her back.

"Pretty strange," Rick observed. "What do you s'pose it means?"

Daniele surmised, "Maybe we're going to hear from someone this evening at eleven after six."

"Did you have any messages this morning?" Rick asked and checked his watch. "Can't be this evening. It's already eight thirty."

"Nothing this morning," Daniele answered, studying the room, pacing slowly around the perimeter.

Michele stepped across the room to Leo's desk and strolled around it. She dragged her pink fingernails across the top as she moved to Leo's chair and let herself down by the armrests. She was pondering the clock the whole time, wondering what this six o'clock thing meant. But when she looked down at the desk she gasped again.

"What?" Daniele asked hastily.

Michele was gazing at the calendar. "I don't know," she said breathlessly. "This is too weird."

Daniele and Rick crossed the room and stood looking over from the back of the desk.

"A Benz sign," Daniele almost whispered.

"Looks like an upside-down Benz sign to me," Michele said, and reflected for a moment. "Now why would Daddy draw an upside-down

Benz sign on his desk?"

"What did he say about the upside-down Benz?" Daniele asked urgently.

"The upside-down Benz leads to something," Michele replied.

"No," Daniele said, staring at the sign. "The upside-down Benz sign will lead you *there*." She nodded slowly. "That's what he said."

"If," Michele said as she sat up straight in the chair, put her elbows on the desk and clasped her hands. "If you follow the second one."

"Yes," Daniele agreed. "The second one."

"The second what?" Michele asked perplexed. "Which one's the second Benz?"

"Maybe the second Benz that he bought," Daniele speculated.

Michele leaned back in Leo's chair. "Now what in the world could *that* possibly mean?"

"It means Father knew something was going to happen," Daniele said with certainty.

This was a concept that hadn't occurred to Michele, and she looked up with surprise. "You think he *knew* he was gonna get kidnapped?"

Daniele didn't react. She just stared back at the clock. "Maybe he wasn't kidnapped."

"Oh, and what? Kidnapped himself?" Michele asked sarcastically.

"That's a thought," Daniele said rubbing her eyebrow with the side of her index finger. "Why say such weird things about the Benz? He drew a Benz sign on his desk. He's definitely trying to lead us somewhere." She crossed her arms as she mulled it over. "How would the 'late' Benz give you twenty twenty vision?"

"The lights are on?" Michele asked.

"And no one's home…" Rick finished with a brief chuckle.

"Like we could see in the dark," Daniele said, ignoring Rick and picking up on Michele's logic.

Michele got up and started pacing the room, looking from the clock to the desk. "All right. What could Daddy have been trying to tell us?"

Rick had moved around the desk and taken up Leo's chair. He was leaning back with his hands clutched behind his head, listening.

Michele went on, "What's with all the clocks being stopped at six eleven?" She looked at the calendar on the desk. "And what's this obsession with Benzes?"

"He likes them," Daniele agreed, "or he wouldn't have so many. But drawing Benz signs on his calendar?"

"Upside-down Benz signs," Michele said. She came back around the desk behind Rick and put her hand over the chair onto his shoulder. She seemed to need his touch now. Another sharp breath from Michele made Daniele react.

"What did you find?" she asked quickly.

"Look at this," Michele said, picking up a folded map of the greater Washington D.C. area that was sticking out from under a stack of papers to the left of the calendar.

"A map of Washington?" Daniele asked. "And?"

"Look at what's on it," Michele said, handing it to Daniele.

Daniele took it. "Hmm. A Benz sign," she said, and slowly added, "He drew a Benz sign on it."

"Loves Benzes," Rick said with a smile.

"Not this much," Daniele said, thinking again. "This is just too weird."

"Weird," Michele echoed.

"Maybe he *is* just playing a little game with us."

"A *game?*" Michele asked. "What makes you think…"

Daniele interrupted. "He's certainly trying to tell us something."

"But what?" Michele asked.

"Dunno," Daniele replied and glanced back at the clock. "But I'll bet Ms. Crimson could tell us."

4

They called the police station, but at eight forty on a Sunday night there was no way they were going to get a sketch artist, so they decided to get some rest before they continued their search. By ten the next morning Daniele had called in to her office and told them of her crisis and that she needed to reschedule everything, at least for that week. They'd eaten a quick breakfast around the kitchen table, prepared by one of the two cooks in Leo's employ, and then the three of them were at the station sitting next to a conservative metal desk mesmerized by a screen being manipulated by a police artist.

The wide room was scattered with cheap desks, beat up from years of use, and a constant buzz filled the air from the networked PCs sitting next to each one. A half dozen plain-clothed cops occupied as many workstations, staring at obsolete fat monitors that they were stuck with due to repetitive annual budget cuts that kept the upgrades to flat screens from ever happening. The heavy-set middle-aged computer artist was sitting at a newly acquired state-of-the-art machine with the only large LCD monitor in the room. Her frizzy long gray hair went to split ends that fell chaotically over her shoulders. One chubby hand hovered over the keyboard while the other smothered the mouse. She was asking them questions, machine-gun like, about what Ms. Crimson looked like, and miraculously the image was evolving into the woman they'd seen at the party.

"A little more red in the hair," Michele was saying.

"And her nose was smaller," Daniele said.

"Like one of those French models," Michele added. "She looked very French."

"French?" Daniele said. "I suppose maybe her hair was dyed."

"Maybe not," Michele said.

"Well she could have been Irish," Daniele argued.

Michele was indignant. "Don't French people have red hair too?"

"Well it wasn't necessarily her natural color," Daniele argued further.

"Just because it's red doesn't mean she colors it."

"And it doesn't mean she doesn't."

"Well you never know," Michele huffed, going on the offensive. "You do it."

Rick, amused at the bickering, was unexpectedly curious. "You mean you're not natural brunettes?"

"Like *that* makes some difference," Daniele said, her lips puckering with disdain.

"I just figured Michele was the one who colored her hair," Rick explained. "But are you naturally blondes?"

"Oh, she colors hers too sometimes," Daniele said, before she had a thought that lifted her mouth on one side in delight as she gazed from Rick to Michele and back. "You mean you don't know?"

Rick grinned and shrugged.

"You haven't heard of taking your time?" Michele asked, and then added, "Well, of course *you* wouldn't."

Daniele made a disgusted look. "Would you please just focus on the business at hand?"

"Focus, focus, focus," Michele said. "That's all you ever say."

"Well I wouldn't have to say it if you'd do it."

The computer artist had stopped working on her sketch and was staring at them with amusement when Michele noticed. "Oh," she said, shifting in her chair. "Sorry."

"Is this her?" the artist asked. A humming clattering desk fan, one of those ancient rounded metal ones, was oscillating in front of her, wafting her hair back each time it passed her way.

Rick squinted at the screen. "She was cuter than that."

Michele's mouth dropped slightly as she raised an eyebrow at him.

"Well, she was," Rick said defensively.

"In what way cuter?" the artist asked, brushing a blown strand of tangled hair from her face.

Rick studied the drawing. The woman, who looked to be in her mid-thirties, had long straight red hair, more red now after the artist's last adjustment, with sharp, bright green eyes and dark eyebrows that accented her straight, thin, rounded nose. Her chin was small, with a soft curve at the end.

"Her nose wasn't rounded like that," Rick pointed out.

Daniele leaned forward. "Hm. No, it wasn't, was it?"

The artist clicked and dragged and dropped some magic and the nose sharpened and elongated somewhat.

"That's it," Michele said. "I mean, she was a long ways away, but that looks right."

"Mmm…not so long," Rick added.

After another adjustment the three looked and agreed that she'd captured Ms. Crimson.

"Definitely," Daniele said. "Now who is she?"

The artist spun slowly around and folded her hands across her protruding belly. "That's for Detective Cruse to figure out." She leaned back in the black fabric chair, worrying Rick that the chair might collapse under her, and held her hand out to her art. "If this is Ms. Crimson, my job is done."

"That's her," Michele said, staring hard at the screen. "Cute enough for you?"

Rick was blunt. "That's her."

"Yep," Daniele agreed. "Now get Detective Cruse over here so we can find her."

Two minutes passed while the artist saved the image, sent some bytes to the color printer so they could have a hardcopy, and added the finished product to a database where Detective Cruse could conduct a thorough search. Using the desk as a crutch, the obese woman stood and waddled past them into an adjacent room. Within moments Cruse emerged from the same doorway and briskly rounded the desk.

"Wha'da'we have?" he asked as he sat down in the chair vacated by the artist and swiveled to face the monitor. He rubbed his hands together and cracked his knuckles making Michele cringe.

"Ms. Crimson," Daniele said, still looking hard at the screen.

"No first name?" he asked, scrutinizing the image.

"I'm sure she has one," Daniele said sarcastically.

Rick sat up suddenly and snapped his fingers. "Courtney!" he said.

Daniele blinked. "Courtney?"

"I think so." His eyes were darting, remembering. "Yeah...Courtney."

She crossed her arms, aggravated. "Well why didn't you say so before?"

"I'm not sure if I even heard it right," Rick said. "Leo had already walked off and I was walking toward you when in the distance I think I heard him say, 'Wait up Courtney.'"

Daniele gave him a smirk. "Better late than never, I guess."

"Courtney Crimson," Detective Cruse said, starting to type. "Courtney...Crimson. Well, let's take a look around."

The medium-sized Detective Cruse, with the intense eyes and the brown-mustached face, started right in. He opened up some other application that apparently gave him the ability to access a database that would match Courtney Crimson with other stored photos and sketches. Five minutes went by.

"Hmmm..." Detective Cruse said pensively.

"Yes?" Daniele asked.

"Hmmm..." Cruse repeated.

"What," Daniele asked with impatience, "does 'Hmmm' mean?"

He looked over his shoulder at her. "It means nothing yet."

"As in you don't mean anything, or you have found nothing?"

"I've found nothing," Cruse said, turning back to his work. He closed the application and clicked on something else on the desktop. "Let's try something international."

Daniele fidgeted, playing with a round black paperclip dispenser on the desk. "Meaning you found nothing domestic?"

"Meaning Ms. Courtney Crimson, as far as I can tell, doesn't exist in this country."

"Meaning she could be European."

"Maybe."

Daniele questioned Rick. "Are you sure it's Courtney?"

Rick nodded. "Yep, pretty sure."

"I can check out just Crimson and see what I come up with," Cruse proposed.

"Hmpf," Daniele said. "Meaning you're starting over."

"Not exactly," Cruse said. "But it'll take some time."

"So when do you think you'll know?" Daniele persisted.

Cruse swiveled his chair around to face her and leaned back pulling his arms up behind his head. "Do you want me to find her?"

Daniele's eyebrows lifted. "Of course."

Michele finished for him. "Then leave him alone and let him work." The detective smiled.

Daniele hung her head for a moment, the fan filling the silence with a drone. "Of course. I'm just a little anxious."

"Should we tell him about the Benz signs?" Michele asked, wanting to be helpful.

Cruse's brow furrowed. "The Benz signs?"

Daniele hesitated and swatted the air. "It's nothing really. Just…well…" she chuckled, "…that he drew a Benz sign on his desk calendar."

The detective stared. You could almost see Benz signs in his eyes as he contemplated their significance.

"What about the clocks?" Michele asked.

"The clocks?" Cruse looked from one to the other.

Daniele gave Michele a surreptitious, slightly cross look when Cruse's questioning eyes queried Rick's and were met with an ambiguous gaze. When he turned back to her she said, "We'll let you know if we think there's something to it."

Michele forced a closed-mouth smile that instantly faded, refraining from further comment.

"Anyway," Daniele continued before the detective could ask about clocks and Benzes, "just let me know how long you think it will take to find something, and we'll come back then."

Cruse pinched his chin. "Could be hours," he said, and then shook his head and looked back at the screen. " I don't know, could be days."

The girls were silent.

"Maybe we should let Mr. Cruse work," Rick suggested and stood.

Daniele sighed, letting a paperclip snap back into the magnetized container. "Of course you're right."

"I know," Cruse said sympathetically. "You're anxious to find your dad."

"Very much," Michele agreed.

The detective handed Daniele a business card from a plastic holder on the desk that she glanced at and slipped into her purse. "Call me at that number any time," he said with caring eyes, and then abruptly turned back to his screen. "I'll do what I can."

As the three headed for the door Daniele said, "I guess we should just go home and wait."

"Oh no no no," Michele disagreed. "We need to go to the Washington Monument."

"What in the world for?" Daniele asked with a glare. "Are you nuts? Father's missing and you wanna go *sight-seeing*?"

Michele was pushing the swinging glass door that exited to the parking lot. "Well, he told us to."

"I sure don't see what good it would do." A disgusted frown emerged on Daniele's face as she followed her sister outside, holding the door for Rick. "Do you always have to do what *Daddy* tells you?"

Michele twisted around as she walked. An amused grin spread sideways from her mouth that somehow brightened her eyes while crinkling them, pulling those half-moon dimples down her cheek. "Yep."

5

"So what was *that* look for?" Michele asked when they'd left the building and were walking to the car – one of Leo's Benzes that they'd borrowed from the long garage. They'd taken a good look around at all of the Benzes before they'd left that morning, but couldn't find anything significant, except that the garage clock was also stopped at six eleven and fifty-one seconds. But nothing else in the garage seemed out of the ordinary.

"What look?" Rick asked, smoothing his hair back after a light breeze had pushed it out of place.

Ignoring him, Daniele answered, "It's pretty obvious that Father left us clues, right?"

"Mm-hmm." Michele's long hair was also being tossed behind her.

"Well," Daniele said, taking hurried steps to avoid an approaching patrol car, "it's looking more and more like he wants us to find something."

"Yeah," Michele agreed. "So what's that got to do with the look you gave me in there?"

Rick was following behind them now, listening while he admired the two as they walked side-by-side.

"Do you want Cruse to look for Courtney Crimson or not?"

"Well of *course* I want him to look for her," Michele answered.

"The clock clues, the Benz clues all make me think that Father knew exactly what was happening. I think he wants us to find him."

"Of *course* he wants us to find him," Michele said with slight disbelief.

"Nooo," Daniele said, holding her hand out like she was making a point in a closing argument. "What I mean is there's a possibility that

Father set this up."

Michele opened her palms as they walked. "Now why would he do a thing like that?"

Daniele frowned. "No idea. But if Cruse thinks Father's behind this he's going to call it off. He isn't going to look for Courtney Crimson."

They arrived at the white Benz sedan at the end of the parking lot and Daniele slipped in behind the wheel. Rick slid in the back behind her.

Michele couldn't buy this concept that Leo had actually done all of this, and refused to believe it. "You don't know that Daddy did this. What if somebody *made* him do it?"

"That's why I don't want him to stop searching," Daniele explained, leaning around with her arm over her seat as she backed out. "If he thought that Father was behind his own disappearance then I think he'd put it on a back burner. Maybe he'd tell us he was working on finding her, but he'd probably find things he thought were more important to do. Right now we need his help."

"Yeah, I guess I see what you mean," Michele finally acknowledged, watching the parked cars go by as they left the lot.

It wasn't much of a trip to D.C. from the police station. Only about twelve miles to the Washington Monument. But it was already early afternoon by the time they arrived, since they'd stopped for fast food along the way.

After they'd circled the streets around the monument several times and finally found parking they discovered that you couldn't just get in line, pay your money, and go right on in. The tickets to the monument were free, but there were only so many given out in a day, and that day's quota had been depleted before ten that morning. No amount of Daniele's pleading with the staff would change their minds, even after the shift supervisor had been summoned. They would just have to come back the next day.

On their way home they'd stopped in to see Detective Cruse, who was still at the monitor digging. But he'd come up with nothing yet and urged them to get some rest and come back the next day.

"I'll call you the minute I find something," he assured them.

So there they were again, just where they'd been the night before, sitting in the kitchen staring at the clock that read six eleven and fifty-one seconds. They'd spent the last hour checking around the rest of the house, but all they'd found was that all of the clocks were stopped at eleven minutes after six, and those that had second hands showed fifty-one. Another peculiarity was that there were Benz water bottles sitting on their own nightstands in their rooms, on the dining table, and in the living room on the coffee table. They'd all remarked how they hadn't noticed the one on the dining table, but did recall that the one on Leo's desk had been there the night before. At this point, none of them wanted to change any clocks or move any Benz water bottles. They were intent on going over the clues time and again. The only clue they'd moved was the map from Leo's desk. Daniele had it spread out over the table and was studying the Washington Monument area when Jack walked in through the swinging door.

"The woman who answered the door, um...Martha, told me you were in here," he said. Martha was the night servant on duty. She'd let him in and had directed him to the kitchen.

Michele brightened when she saw him, and thought his light brown hair contrasted nicely with his khaki shirt. Even his hazel brown eyes seemed to match the outfit.

Daniele stared at him for a moment. "What time is it?"

"Good to see you too," Jack said and looked at his watch.

Rick beat him to it. "Ten till six."

Daniele instinctively looked at the clock. If he had something to do with it, then he was twenty minutes early. "So what're you doing here?"

"Hi Jack," Michele said with a good-natured smile, pronouncing the "k" extra hard as she had at the party. "I asked him to come."

Daniele looked at her sister. "Whatever for?"

"Well he was there when Daddy said all that weird Benz stuff. I thought maybe he could help figure it out."

"He gave you his number?"

Michele curled her lip at her. "I do have your office number ya know."

Jack had an uncomfortable grin, and slowed at Daniele's icy reception. He held his arm out to the door starting to make a quick retreat. "Maybe I should go..."

"Sorry Jack," Daniele said. "Please come in. I just thought maybe..." She let the sentence drift off.

"Maybe?" Jack asked as he turned and shoved his hands into his jeans.

"The clock, you know, the time…oh, never mind," Daniele said, and then apologetically, "Really. Please come in. Thanks for coming." She turned to Michele. "What about Martin? Should we call him too? He was there."

"Oh, he's still in Paris," she said, "wrapping up *my* show."

Daniele waved her hand. "He probably wouldn't be much help anyway."

Jack sat down and they told him the story of their day, Ms. Crimson, the sketch artist, Detective Cruse, the trip to the Washington Monument, and all of the clues that they'd found. By the time they'd finished everything Daniele looked up with a start.

"Oh!" she said. "What time is it?"

Jack beat Rick to the punch this time. "Six fifteen."

Daniele, Michele and Rick looked at each other.

"Well," Rick said, "maybe it's tomorrow morning."

"What's tomorrow morning?" Jack asked.

"Com'on," Daniele said mockingly, "get a clue. We just told you about all the clocks being stopped at six eleven and fifty-one seconds. I thought something was going to happen."

Jack looked at the clock on the wall. "Right. I get it."

Michele rolled her eyes at Jack and, looking at him with a teasing smile, asked Daniele, "Why in the world did you pick *him* to go out with?"

Daniele shrugged. "Proximity."

There was eagerness in Jack's tone. "Are we going out?"

"Just the party, Jack," Daniele sighed. "Just the party."

Jack frowned and said, "Hmpf."

They spent the next six hours talking in circles about what the clues might mean, but they'd all drawn a blank. Just before he went home, Jack suggested that he go with them to the monument the next day.

"An extra pair of eyes wouldn't hurt," he'd reasoned.

Daniele had capitalized on his invitation by talking him into being the one to go stand in line at eight o'clock and get the tickets. In the meantime she would go with Rick and Michele to get an update from Detective Cruse and they'd meet him in line.

"Be sure to hold a place for us," she'd instructed as he'd exited through the swinging door.

But he hadn't. After he'd called in sick and made it to the small kiosk by eight, he'd gotten the tickets and had stood in the long line for half an hour until he was at the entrance to the monument, but had stepped out since they hadn't shown up. The security folks had been looking at him with suspicion – talking to each other on their walkie-talkies and circling in on him – as he'd just stood there at the door looking like he was up to something. So he'd wandered back over by the ticket kiosk to make himself less conspicuous.

Daniele promptly chastised him when they arrived, but Jack complained that he couldn't just stand up there looking like a terrorist. He asked why they were so late, and Daniele explained that they'd taken a long time with Detective Cruse, but the look between Rick and Michele made him wonder if they hadn't just gotten a late start. In the mean time, the winding line to the monument had grown to a monumental length. After thirty minutes in line, Daniele was obviously agitated.

"How long is this gonna take?" she grumbled to no one.

Michele, wearing a pink halter-top and dark brown shorts, was tilting her head back with her eyes closed and her sunglasses pushed up onto her head so she could bake in the sun. She looked down, slipped her glasses onto her nose and pointed to a little sign up ahead that read, "One hour from this point." "One hour from there," she said.

Daniele had actually put on a sleeveless green blouse and white shorts, looking very touristy, and felt reasonably comfortable in the bright sunshine. She looked from the sign to the line of overweight tourists and then all the way to the top of the monument. "This is ridiculous."

"It's *not* ridiculous," Michele countered, pushing her glasses up again, closing her eyes and basking. "It's what Daddy told us to do."

"Yeah, and you told us before that he was kidnapped," Daniele argued.

"You're the one who told me he *wasn't* kidnapped," Michele said, shifting the strap of her halter to prevent tan lines.

Rick was standing stoically beside Michele, his arm draped loosely around her waist, almost uncomfortably. "Let's just try to enjoy this," he said. "Maybe Leo just wanted you to come here to relax with each other.

Have some kind of fun together."

Jack was standing next to Daniele, though giving her a wide girth. He gazed up the Mall to the reflecting pool where Abe was sitting upside-down glaring seriously at them. "It *could* be fun, ya know."

"Fun with her isn't possible," was Daniele's knee-jerk reaction. Her hair was down today, and looked identical to Michele's, except for the color of course. She used the back of her hand to push the warm hair off her neck.

"And vice verse," Michele said.

"Vice *vers-sah*," Daniele corrected, lifting her hair again and at least enjoying the coolness of the tiny breeze she'd created on her neck. "Vice versa."

"Whatever. Daddy told us to come here together, so here we are."

It was a beautiful day in Washington. A cloudless sky, seventy-five degrees, and covered with tourists. Washington in July could be muggy misery, or, occasionally, the best day possible. This was one of those perfect Washingtonian days. But shuffling along in the meandering line out in the direct sunlight on the concrete leading up to the monument was mild misery for everyone involved. Only the tourists seemed not to notice, and were busy with their digital cameras capturing the White House to the north, the Lincoln Memorial looking unusually white against the ultra-blue sky to the west, and the domed Congress building in the opposite distance.

To Daniele's consternation, the newlywed couple in front of her – a fact she'd learned early on after joining the line, what with all the nauseating kissing and hugging and darlings being passed – spent the last thirty minutes in a heated argument over whether they had actually seen snipers on top of the White House, or if they were just workmen. The bride had kept insisting that they were Secret Service snipers to the point that, to Daniele's relief, the guy just shut up.

Rick, Jack and Michele, meanwhile, spent the entire foot-dragging wait giggling hushed jokes and off-color comments about what the various people in line were wearing, the authenticity of certain body parts, and their dress and shoe sizes.

Once they'd made it inside the wait was much shorter – and less miserable. When they'd finally taken the ride up, Daniele grumbled nonstop under her breath about being claustrophobic, sardines, and the ridiculousness of this whole adventure.

As they emerged from the elevator into the crowded room, they found a small gathering huddled at each of the four windows overlooking Washington. There were in fact eight windows. Two per side. But one on each side had been commandeered to mount surveillance cameras for security measures, making it even harder to get to a window – even with the uniformed staff occasionally herding people along.

Daniele had muscled herself, gently, but forcefully, to the window facing north toward the White House.

"What can you see?" Michele asked from behind two balding men and their sunburned wives.

"Washington," Daniele said.

It took another minute or so before the four of them had taken over the view from this window.

"So what're we looking for?" Jack asked.

"A clue," Daniele answered. "Anybody have any better questions?"

"See any Benzes?" Rick asked with a chuckle.

"All I see is the White House and a bunch of other buildings," Michele said. After searching for a moment she asked, "What about that circle in front of the White House? That looks kind of like a Benz sign."

"The Ellipse?" Jack asked. "Yeah, it's a circle, but I don't see any Benz signs."

"I doubt the President's holding him for ransom," Daniele remarked, studying the landscape into the distance. The view was magnificent, and as much as she'd resisted this trip, she couldn't help but being taken in by it.

"See if you can see any Benz signs on buildings," Michele said.

Daniele snorted slightly, but didn't make any snide remarks.

"You check north for Benz signs," Jack said, "and I'll go check our six."

"What's our six?" Michele asked, but Jack didn't hear and was already making his way through the people.

"Six is behind us," Rick told her.

Michele looked around behind her.

Rick chuckled while, unseen by Michele, Daniele rolled her eyes.

"It's a military term," Rick explained and pointed north. "It's the hands on a clock. Twelve o'clock is in front of you," he stretched his arm out, "nine o'clock is left, three o'clock is right, and six is behind you."

Michele nodded slowly.

"So from here," Rick pointed over his shoulder with his thumb, "six o'clock is through the south window."

"Huh," Michele said.

Jack had excused his way through the balding-sunburned couple, and had hardly made it another ten feet toward the south window when he heard Daniele exclaim loudly, "That's it!"

"What's it?" Michele asked excitedly, looking farther out the window rather than at Daniele. "Did you find the Benz sign?"

Daniele laughed out loud, a genuine smile on her face. "No! It's the *direction*!"

Rick's eyebrows rose and a slight smile emerged on his face as well.

"Where's the map?" Daniele asked, her enthusiasm brimming over to the rest of them.

Jack had already turned around, but he didn't need to walk over. The three of them were migrating to him through the mob.

"*You* had the map," Michele said.

Daniele turned to Rick. "I thought *you* had it."

"Why would *I* have it?" Rick objected. "Last I saw it you had it on the kitchen table."

Daniele was incredulous. "You mean you didn't bring it?"

"Nobody *asked* me to bring it," Rick complained.

Daniele looked around at each of the windows before she made her way to the south with the others following.

"Would you *please* tell me what you saw?" Michele asked impatiently.

"I haven't seen anything yet," Daniele replied, as she excused herself through huddles of sightseers to the less populated south-facing window and gazed out. "But he's down there somewhere."

"What makes you think so?" Jack asked walking up behind her.

"Because that," Daniele said, pointing with her chin, "is six o'clock."

"Six eleven," Michele said, remembering the clocks.

Daniele's enthusiasm ebbed a little bit. "Six eleven. Right."

She gazed silently at the Reagan International airport beyond the Jefferson Memorial, her fervor waning.

"And fifty-one seconds," Rick added.

"Right," she agreed. "And fifty-one seconds."

"Would someone *please* tell me what you're *talking* about?" Michele whined.

Daniele was confused now. Ignoring Michele she walked over toward the west window and looked between heads and shoulders out slightly to the north. "Or maybe he's over there."

"Look," Rick said, following behind her like a puppy. "Tell us what's on your mind and maybe we can help figure out what you think you know."

Daniele turned to him, and Michele and Jack joined them forming a small circle. "It all makes sense, but it doesn't make sense." Her hands were animated as she spoke. "The Benz signs, the clocks, the map on Father's desk. The upside-down Benz sign points to six o'clock."

Michele listened, trying to understand. "So is he down there or not?"

"The *Benz* sign!" Daniele said impatiently. "Father wanted us to come up here because it would point us in the right *direction*. Remember, the upside-down Benz will lead you there or something like that."

"The upside-down Benz will take you there if you follow the second one," Michele said.

"But what's the second one?" Daniele asked.

Michele added another element, "Yeah, is it the upside-down one or the late one?"

"Right," Daniele said. "I forgot about the late one."

"That's the one that gives you twenty twenty vision," Michele said confidently.

"Twenty twenty vision," Daniele echoed, looking past Jack and across the room out the south window with a blank stare.

They broke their huddle and scattered around the room in different directions, shuffling from window to window, lost in their own machinations about Leo's riddle, until they merged again near the elevator door.

"We're not going to find it here," Daniele said pulling her hair behind her in a temporary ponytail to once again relieve the heat. "We need to get home and take a look at that map."

6

Daniele had her chin in her hand, elbow on the table, staring at the location of the Washington Monument. From time to time she would glance up at the clock, the hands still pointing to six eleven and fifty-one seconds. They hadn't even bothered to stop in and see Detective Cruse. She considered it to be a dead-end anyway, and he'd call if he found anything.

The others were chattering, trying on their own to solve the mystery, but they were really just talking in circles with Jack and Rick both making cracks at whatever amusing thing Michele said next. Michele seemed not to hear them, still lost in visions of Benzes and clocks, her head starting to hurt slightly. This had gone on for hours until early afternoon.

"All right," Daniele said finally. "We need some paper and a pen."

"What for?" Michele asked.

"To write down Father's clues."

"I have a pen," Jack offered, leaning around and producing one from the inside pocket of his beige windbreaker draped over the chair behind him. "Here, I have a notepad too. This good enough?" He pulled a green-covered spiral notepad from the same pocket.

"It'll work," Daniele said, taking the pen and pad and preparing to write. "Okay. Now, what *exactly* did he say?"

Michele looked pensive. "Well, the first thing he said was that the Benz gives you twenty twenty vision."

"The *late* Benz," Daniele said while writing.

"And then he said the upside-down Benz will take us there if we use the second one."

"Wasn't it 'lead' you there?" Daniele asked, trying to remember.

"No," Michele replied. "I'm pretty sure he said take you there if we use the second one."

"Follow," Daniele said. "Follow the second one."

Michele huffed and shook her head. "Well *I* can't remember." She threw her hands up and landed them on her thighs. "How did he expect us to remember all that?"

"Maybe he didn't," Daniele said leaning on her writing arm as she briefly looked up. "Maybe he was just trying to give us enough."

"Well I don't think it is," Michele said in frustration. "Why couldn't he just tell us where he went? What's this all about anyway?"

"He wants us to work together," Daniele said as though it was obvious. "That's what he said, wasn't it?"

Michele's eyes lit up in a moment of revelation. "You mean to say all this is for us to *work* together?"

"Weren't you listening?" Daniele said. "What else would it be?"

"He got kidnapped for instance," Michele said, "and someone's going to ask for a ransom."

"At six eleven and fifty-one seconds, right?" Daniele asked sarcastically.

Michele couldn't help but look at the clock. "Well...you never know."

Daniele stared back at the map. "Nope. This is about us."

Michele got up and started across the room. "Well then *I* don't want to do it!"

Daniele looked up with a mean smile. "What?" she said to Michele's retreating back. "Not do what Daddy wants you to do?"

Michele squeaked to a stop and turned with her hands on her hips. "Well if *I* didn't," she said with disdain, "then *you* wouldn't have gone to the Washington Monument and *we* wouldn't have figured out *this* much."

"*We?*" Daniele said. "What did *you* figure out?"

"As much as *you* did," Michele said. "Do *you* know where he is?"

Jack and Rick smiled as Michele came back and sat down.

"Don't you two *ever* stop arguing?" Rick asked.

Jack chuckled and added, "If that's what this is about, then I'd say Leo's plan's a major bust."

"Look," Daniele said, trying to add some rationality to this outlandishness, "the fact is, even though it looks like he planned it just to get us to work together, which will never happen again, I might add…"

"Amen to that," Michele said with a smirk.

"…we still don't know what happened to him. It could be something serious, although it looks to me right now that it's just a game. But we still need to figure it out so we can be done with it and go back to half of our useful lives." She shoved the notebook roughly aside and glared at the map.

"Half?" Rick asked.

"There's only one of us who does anything useful."

Jack crossed his arms and studied her. "You just can't help it, can you?"

Daniele didn't even look at him. "So…if we're going to get over this, we need to focus…" she scowled at Michele, "focus, focus, focus."

Michele leered at her. "Change the 'o' to a 'u' and that's what you can do with yourself."

Jack chuckled, but Rick just stared blankly at Michele.

Daniele wanted to laugh, but buried it. "Look, can we just fo…stick…to the subject?"

"You can stick it too," Michele said with a proud grin.

Finally Rick caught on and laughed out loud, which made all of them, even Daniele, start a snicker that ended with tension relieving hilarity.

When they'd finally subsided, Daniele eventually got back around to her task at hand.

"All right," she said, "so maybe it's a game. Let's just get on with it." She looked at Michele for some response.

Michele chuckled. "*I* didn't say anything."

"Let's get it on," Jack said, rubbing his hands together, his pun being met by Daniele's bored eyes.

"Just don't get it, do you Jack?" Daniele pronounced the "k" a little hard like Michele did.

Michele let out another little hiccup of a laugh.

Daniele was trying hard now to look at the map. "Late Benzes," she said.

"And the second one will *take* you there," Michele said.

"I still think it was *lead* you there," Daniele said.

"Whatever," Michele said.

"Whatever," Daniele said.

Jack chuckled. "I think you're both wrong. It was *get* you there."

"So how're we supposed to ride in an upside-down Benz?" Michele asked. "How's that gonna get us anywhere?"

"So what do you have?" Jack asked.

Daniele sighed and pulled the notepad back over. "The late Benz gives you twenty twenty vision, and the upside-down Benz will lead, take, get you somewhere if you follow the second one."

Jack nodded reflectively. "That's about what I heard."

Michele agreed. "Me too. Still don't see how an upside-down Benz is gonna take us anywhere."

"Well, let's think." Daniele leaned over and examined the map. "What do Benzes have to do with this map?" They waited for her to continue her monologue. "What's the twenty twenty?"

"Vision," Michele said.

"Twenty twenty *vision*," Daniele said. "Now, what's that got to do with Benzes? The Benz sign *is* the clock."

"I thought we already knew that," Michele said and turned around to point to the clock. "See how it looks like an upside-down Benz sign? You know, look at your six?"

"I know, I *know*," Daniele continued, "but twenty twenty is eight o'clock." Daniele frowned. "So what does it mean?"

"It means," Michele said slowly as though speaking to a child, "that the clock is somehow pointing to where we need to go. I thought you knew that too. But I still can't see how you can ride anywhere in a clock any more than you can ride in an upside-down Benz. How you supposed to follow the second Benz in a clock?"

Daniele continued to stare. "Isn't the upside-down Benz the second one, and the late Benz is the first one?"

Michele brushed her hair over her right shoulder. "Dunno."

Daniele sat up straight and slapped her palms on the table. "I need a computer."

"What for?" Michele asked.

"To do some research," Daniele said as she shoved her chair back and headed off toward Father's study with the others hesitantly in tow. The men exchanged skeptical glances, and Rick took a quick look at his watch before pushing through the swinging door.

By the time they'd caught up with her, Daniele was already at the keyboard. Leo left the machine on all the time, so it was just a matter of her entering his password before she was opening the little clock at the bottom right of the screen.

The clock was analog, sitting in the little window next to a monthly calendar, with the hour, minute, and second hands still running. *At least this one's not stopped on some ridiculous time*, she thought. When she highlighted the hour on the clock and started to change it, the clock seemed to stop and wait for her manipulation. She set the time to eight twenty and stared.

"That's not right," Michele said, pulling an armchair from the side of the room around the desk to sit next to her.

"What's not right?" Daniele asked.

"It's not a Benz sign."

Daniele stared for a moment longer. "Oh yeah," she said, and then moved the second hand straight up to the twelve."

They all stared before Jack, standing behind Michele, spoke over her shoulder. "That's not it either," he said.

"It's not?" Michele asked.

"No, see how the hour hand moved? It's not a *perfect* Benz sign anymore." He looked at Daniele and shrugged. "If that's important."

But Daniele was listening to him now. "So how do you get a perfect Benz sign from eight twenty?"

Michele looked at it. "Switch the minute hand and the second hand," she said.

Daniele did as instructed and smiled at the results. "There's our perfect Benz sign."

"Would you look at that," Rick said with admiration. He'd been standing behind Daniele with his arms folded, watching in silent amusement.

"So when you say twenty twenty, the second twenty isn't talking about the minute hand," Jack observed, "it's talking about the second hand."

"Looks like it," Daniele agreed.

"So now what?" Michele asked.

"Now we put this on the map," Daniele answered.

Michele looked at the screen. "How you gonna do that, lay the monitor on the table?"

Jack's head wobbled briefly.

"Like this," Daniele said. She proceeded to take a screen capture of the clock, opened up a graphic application and pasted it in a new window. She used the graphic tools to draw three straight lines projecting out from the center of the clock straight through the hands. After that she set the image to have a transparent background and saved the file as "twenty twenty.gif."

They were all mesmerized.

"I didn't know you knew how to use a computer," Jack said.

It was enough for Daniele to peek over her shoulder at him. "I use one every day, Jack." Hard "k."

"Not like this you don't," he said in an admiring tone, leaning to one side with his hands on his hips.

Daniele opened up an Internet browser and searched for maps of Washington D.C. It wasn't long before she'd copied a map of Washington into her graphic application and had overlaid the Benz file on top of it and was analyzing. After fifteen minutes of gawking, tracing her finger over each line to the end of the screen, and muttering incomprehensibly, everyone was getting impatient.

"Are you *ever* gonna find what you're looking for?" Michele asked. "This is getting boring."

Jack was hesitant to say anything, not wanting another mocking by Daniele, but he went ahead and spoke his mind anyway. "Um...shouldn't you be looking at six eleven and fifty-one seconds? That's the one on all the clocks."

Daniele stopped and leaned back. "Huh," she said, folding her arms. "Maybe so." She leaned forward and grabbed the mouse again. "Of course. Ah, yes. The upside-down Benz."

"You can be so dense sometimes," Michele said.

Daniele made a frown and turned her head sideways, but not far enough to see Michele. Instead she went right back to work on the clock, setting the hands to six eleven and fifty-one seconds, taking a screen capture, pasting it into a new file, stretching out the hands, making it transparent, and saving this one as "six eleven fifty-one.gif." She put that on top of the map of Washington and studied where the upside-down

Benz lines were pointing.

"And?" Michele asked, lounging in her chair and brushing her fingernails with an emery board.

Daniele leaned back and sighed, flopping her hands in her lap. "I don't know," she said. "The National Airport is off to the south, unless you want to count the Jefferson Memorial; nothing much off to the eleven except for some museums, and George Washington University is where the second hand is pointing."

"Or the road that goes to our house," Michele said blandly, and then blew on her fingers.

Daniele sat up with interest. "It does, doesn't it?"

"So?" Michele said. "That can't be it. Why would he point us back to our house?"

"What'd he say?" Daniele asked no one. "The second one." A growing smile made dimple lines spread in her cheeks like water creasing a window. "Of course! How could I miss it? It's so *simple*. It's the second *hand!*"

"So what's the late Benz?" Michele asked.

"Probably just connecting a regular Benz sign to a clock," Jack reasoned. "Twenty twenty's not just vision, which means if you crack the Benz clue, you'll 'see' where to go, but also the time on the clock of a normal Benz sign. And the late Benz, the twenty twenty, is actually a later time on the clock than the upside-down Benz, which is six eleven and fifty-one seconds. So it's not the late Benz that shows you where to go. It's the upside-down one."

"Oh!" Michele said. "Whatever." She leaned over and whispered to Jack, "So what's Daniele doing?"

Jack whispered back. "I think she's getting a map so she can see where the second hand is pointing to on the upside-down Benz. That's the one pointing off to the northwest."

"Ah," Michele said softly.

Daniele had been searching the Internet for a map of the greater Washington area, but was inundated by the State of Washington. She specified "D.C." but still couldn't get one that covered an area beyond George Washington University, let alone their house.

"I need something bigger," she said anxiously, drumming her fingernails lightly on the keyboard without actually typing anything, making a rhythmic clicking noise. "Something that I can move around on."

"Why don't you try one of those satellite maps?" Jack suggested. "I've tried those before. You can pretty much zoom in on anywhere you want to. I actually saw my house once."

"Where can I find one?" Daniele asked, ready to key the search into her browser.

"Just put in 'satellite maps' and see what comes up," Jack said.

Daniele did, and got a listing of several that looked like they might do it. She zeroed in on one and downloaded it. It was another five minutes before she had it installed, and even had to re-boot to use it, while Michele yawned audibly over and over again.

When she'd finally re-started and opened the program she found that it was exactly what she was looking for. The whole world was there as a globe with the United States facing her. She typed "Washington D.C." into the search field and the application started moving. It was erratic and blurry, but eventually zoomed in on the capital and cleared up with the Washington Monument right there in the center. It must have been late afternoon when the satellite photo was taken, because the shadow of the monument stretched far off onto the Mall to the east. Wherever she clicked on the map the program would move the point where she'd clicked to the center of the screen. She clicked off in the direction of the second hand – northwest; the direction that pointed to their house.

"Let's see our house," Michele said, suddenly interested, leaning forward to watch as Daniele clicked up along the highways that led home.

But it was slow going, and Daniele got lost several times. Frustrated, she stopped and zoomed the image out.

"What're you doing?" Michele asked with a disappointed whine. "I thought you were gonna show us our house."

"What I'm looking for," Daniele said, still clicking, "is where the second hand is pointing."

Michele's tone turned meek. "After you find it can we see our house?"

Daniele zoomed the screen out until the area was large enough that she knew it contained the house that they were in now, right up there on the banks of the Potomac. She could see how the river wound off to the northwest, along the line that Father had pointed them to, if she could just overlay the line. She finally decided to take a snapshot of the map so she could bring it into her graphic program and put the Benz sign on top. When she did she was startled.

"It does!" she said excitedly.

"It does what?" Michele asked.

"It points exactly *here*. I knew it would be close, but not right exactly at our house."

"So if he's pointing us here, let's see it," Michele said urgently, still anxious to see the satellite image of their house.

Daniele obliged, returning to the online map that she could navigate through. She found a tool that would turn on all the names of the streets, so she turned them on and with jerky, faded motions each of the roads on the map had names in red that clarified with each refresh of the screen. She'd zoomed in to where the Washington Monument was, and again started tracing the path home. Within a minute or so they saw it.

"That's it, isn't it?" Michele said eagerly.

"There we are," Daniele said triumphantly. "And there's our street."

Michele was mesmerized. "Wow. It looks so small."

"I'm zooming out now," Daniele said. "Time to see exactly what Father was pointing at."

"Isn't he pointing at our house?"

"We're *assuming* that he's pointing at our house. Maybe it's just the general direction." Daniele was manipulating the map, getting both the Washington Monument and their house with a little more surrounding area into one screen. "Maybe there's something we're missing, because he sure isn't *here*."

Michele looked over her shoulder at the door.

When Daniele had the right altitude she took a screen capture and put the image in her graphic program. Then she overlaid the Benz sign, the one with the elongated lines at six eleven and fifty-one seconds, with the hub of the spokes centered on the monument. Sure enough it pointed right to their house.

"What else is along the second hand line?" Jack asked, intrigued.

Daniele zoomed in on the Washington Monument and followed the line. There was nothing out of the ordinary, really. Once out of D.C.

there was the Potomac, the roads they traveled, their house. Nothing that caught their attention.

"So what's *past* your house?" Rick asked.

Daniele continued along the line until some kind of complex appeared to the left of the line.

"What're those buildings?" Jack asked.

Daniele knew, of course. They were, after all, in the neighborhood. "That's the CIA," she said.

Jack stood up straight. "The CIA?"

"I thought the CIA was in Langley," Rick said.

"That *is* Langley," Daniele told him.

Rick looked confused. "I thought Langley was *southeast* of Washington. You know, on the road down to some place like Pax River."

"That's another Langley," Daniele explained. "This Langley, the one where the CIA is, is really in Mclean, Virginia. Langley is to Mclean like Brooklyn is to New York. Just a part of it."

Rick seemed stunned. "All these years," he said, "I thought the CIA was down there in the *other* Langley."

"*I* knew it was here," Michele remarked smugly.

"I'm surprised they have a satellite photo of it," Jack said.

"Why wouldn't they?" Rick asked. "Nothing secret about the fact that the CIA exists. I just thought it was someplace else. Like in Langley."

Michele laughed. "It *is* in Langley."

"Looks to me like it's in Mclean," Rick argued, leaning over to read the name on the map. "All these years. Somebody should have told me there was more than one Langley."

Daniele snickered. "There's probably a hundred Langleys."

"Huh," Rick said. "In Virginia?"

"Who knows?"

Shoving his hands into his pockets, Rick said awkwardly, "I just never knew you guys were neighbors to the CIA."

Jack had leaned back over, propping himself up on his knees perusing the image. "Zoom in on it."

Daniele complied and soon they were looking at a relatively close up birds-eye view of the CIA and the surrounding area. The whole complex was encircled by a dense green forest, as was typical of the area.

The Potomac was to the east running in a bend around the complex from the west to the south, Leo's house still visible on the banks from this altitude. The buildings were off-white with what looked to be courtyards in several places in the middle of the structures. From the north and along the west and south sides of the complex were vast parking lots about half full of cars, with several cars frozen in the photograph while driving along the road.

"Look at that," Jack said, pointing at a road. "Central Intelligence Agency." The red letters overlaying the satellite photo twisted along the curved road that surrounded the complex.

"What else would you call it?" Daniele asked.

"Look at that one there," Michele said.

"That one what?" Rick asked, now leaning on his knees as Jack was, hovering close enough to Daniele's hair that he could smell the perfume on her neck.

"That street," Michele said.

Daniele asked, "Which one?"

"That one in that neighborhood just below the CIA. It's on the line."

"There's a lot of streets," Daniele commented. "What about it?"

"It sounds familiar," Michele said, "but I've never been over there."

Daniele was a little exasperated. "Which *one?*"

"Crimson Court," Michele said. "See it? Seems like I've heard of it before."

Daniele and Jack spoke simultaneously.

"Where is it?" Daniele asked.

"Point to it," Jack said.

Michele stuck her index finger near the screen. "Right there. See? About halfway between…um…State Route 123 and the CIA. It goes right over your line." Her brow furrowed. "But where have I heard of it before?"

"Courtney Crimson," Daniele told her.

Michele's voice went up a notch. "Oh, right!"

"That's where he is," Daniele said definitively.

"I'd have to agree," Jack said.

Daniele sat back and stared. "So that's why Detective Cruse can't find her."

"I'd have to agree again," Jack agreed. "It's not her real name."

Daniele leaned forward again and zoomed in on Crimson Court. "Now the question is, which house?"

"Which house is the line on?" Jack asked.

"That one there," Daniele pointed. "Right where the road curves."

Jack stood up straight and put his hands on his hips. "I'd say that's our best bet."

Daniele hit the print icon and swung her chair toward the color printer that was on the right side of the desk. Michele made way for her, while Daniele's hands hovered impatiently as the machine seemed to be moving in slow motion, the page creeping out. Finally the printer released the paper and she grabbed it, jumped up, and headed around the desk for the door. "Let's go."

7

It certainly wasn't far. It was mid-afternoon by the time they'd followed the streets on the satellite printout to Crimson Court. It appeared to be just another typical Mclean neighborhood. Slightly upper class, but certainly no higher than upper middle. No Leon Calvets living here. Crimson Court was lined with trees, as were all the streets they'd driven along the way. The neighborhood was relatively new and the houses were in good shape, the yards kept up nicely.

"So this would be where CIA employees live," Jack said pensively.

"Really?" Michele asked. "You know someone in the CIA that lives here?"

Jack smiled. "They *probably* live here."

"Who does?"

"No," Jack laughed. "I mean CIA people probably live here. I don't actually know any."

"Then why did you say they live here?" she asked.

Jack sighed. "It's a few blocks from CIA headquarters," he said, not in the least annoyed at having to explain his remark. "They're just people. They probably don't want to drive a long way to work, so they'd buy or rent houses near their jobs."

Michele chuckled, just slightly self-conscious. "Oh, yeah."

Daniele drove at a crawl as she neared the curve in the road where she believed Leo had directed them. And there, coming up around the bend on the left, was what she believed to be the house. She pulled over to the right hand curb. "That's it," she said.

"You sure?" Michele asked.

"Definitely."

"Well why that one and not one of the others?" Michele asked.

"Look at the address."

Michele read the numbers intricately etched into a large wooden block that was nailed next to the doors. "Oh, yeah. Six eleven."

Jack smiled. "Your dad's pretty clever to get us here with just a Benz and a clock as clues."

"Maybe *we're* the clever ones," Michele said.

"Quite the orchestrater," Rick agreed from the back seat where he was looking across Michele at the house.

The two-story home was white with a quaint blue trim. A red brick veneer around the bottom of the house flowed into a chimney that ran up both floors. A double French front door made the house look warm and inviting. Shrubs surrounded a freshly mowed lawn with a winding sidewalk in the middle that led to a wood porch with pillars on either side of the six steps that led up to the entrance.

"So now what?" Michele asked.

Daniele opened her car door. "So now we go up and ring the doorbell."

The four of them glanced around the neighborhood as they crossed the street and meandered up the walkway and onto the porch. Only one house down the street had any activity, with a middle-aged man mowing his front lawn while two school-aged boys played basketball in the driveway.

Daniele was the first up the steps. She pushed the button to ring the bell.

Thirty seconds passed before she rang the bell again, and then again after fifteen more.

Nothing.

"Looks like nobody's home," Jack said.

Daniele reached up and tried the door. It was one of those ornate gold-colored handles with the lever that you push down with your thumb.

"What're you doing?" Michele asked in slight shock.

The door opened.

"I'm going in," Daniele said simply.

Michele grabbed her arm. "You can't just walk into somebody's house like that. That's like breaking in."

Daniele stopped long enough to look over her shoulder at Michele.

"He led us here," she said. "I'm sure he wants us to go in." She pushed the door open and stepped inside.

Michele looked back at Rick.

He stretched his arm out toward the door. "After you," he said with a grin.

Suddenly the room erupted with a chorus yelling, "Surprise!"

The house was brimming with people in party hats and smiles holding glasses of Champaign and party whistles sounding like a cacophony of kazoos. Purple and blue streamers zigzagged the rooms with balloons tied below them, and a large banner hung across the back wall that read, "Happy 28th Birthday!"

"Oh!" Daniele cried. "So *that's* what this is all about! Where is he?"

Michele was giggling. "I actually forgot all about our birthday. Daddy! I'm gonna get you for this!"

The foyer was larger than it seemed it would be from the outside, and flowed into a spacious living room that was nicely furnished with an oversized light gray sofa and matching loveseat. The partiers were settling back in their seats, now that the surprise was over, with the noise level dropping to a constant chatter. Beyond the living room and up a single step that stretched across the room was a large dining room with a high square dining table surrounded by eight tall chairs nestled snuggly up against it in their places. The table was completely covered with hors d'oeuvres and presents.

Daniele and Michele made their ways into the room accepting best wishes and saying, "Thank you," over and over again. Each was intent on finding Leo.

"Have you seen Daddy?" Michele asked Rick when he'd finally caught up to the sisters.

"He should be here somewhere," Rick said. "He was supposed to come in from Paris this morning."

"You *knew* about this?" Daniele asked.

Rick grinned and held his palms out. "What can I say? Your dad made me do it."

Michele slapped him on the arm.

Turning to Jack, Daniele said with a smirk, "And you knew too, didn't you?"

"Don't look at me," Jack said. "Michele called me, remember? Rick got me too. I thought your dad was really missing."

"So where is he?" Daniele asked Rick.

Rick looked around. "He's supposed to be here," he said. "Hey Bob!" he yelled at a balding, round-bellied man approaching from the kitchen. Rick motioned for him to come over. "Michele, Daniele, I'd like you to meet a friend of mine. Bob Jones."

"Pleasure," Daniele said, shaking his hand, and then he shook Michele's.

"Bob's an old college friend of mine," Rick said. "Used to be one of my professors. He got out of the teaching business and went into advertising and did a bit of work with Leo and me."

"Happy birthday," Bob said with a broad smile. "Gotcha!"

Rick turned to Daniele with a twinkle in his eye. "I've really gotta hand it to you."

"About what?" she asked, an infectious smile coming over her from Rick's look of admiration.

"Well, I was supposed to help you figure out the clues," he said, "but man, I hardly had to do anything."

"What *did* you do?" Daniele asked only half-teasing. "As far as I could tell, you were just uninterested and going along for the ride."

Rick laughed and stroked his hair. "Well, all I can think of was that I suggested you look at your line beyond your house. That was about it."

Daniele reflected back over the events of the day with surprise at his revelation. "You did, didn't you?"

He lifted his shoulders shyly.

"Pretty clever," she said, and then gave him a mock stern look. "Kinda mean, but clever."

Daniele and Michele were cheerful and glowing throughout the afternoon, instantly becoming gracious hosts of the group, primarily made up of people who'd been at Michele's after-show party the other night. But no one knew where Leo was, and Daniele had become more and more concerned as the party had gone on.

Michele had decided to take a look around in the kitchen to see if someone had him cornered in there, but had no success. Leo just didn't seem to be there.

As the afternoon wore on, Daniele and Michele opened their presents and cut the cake. It was a brief party, with people making their

·exits by six thirty. It was, after all, Tuesday, and most everyone had to work the next day. By quarter till seven it was down to just two couples and Bob, still chatting in the dining room. Daniele and Rick had gotten into a long conversation with the couples over the state of Middle Eastern affairs, leaving Jack and Michele to the side talking about Michele's fashions and Jack's cases. They had both decided on another glass of wine. The bottles on the dining table were empty, so they wandered into the kitchen to fetch another.

This was just a normal kitchen, compared to the one in Leo's house, with white appliances and a small tiled island jutting out from one side. A back door led to the yard, and on the other side was a small hallway that led to the master bedroom. Near the back door was yet another door that Jack assumed to be a bathroom.

"I'm just gonna use this real quick," he said, heading for the door.

"Okay," Michele said while struggling with a large corkscrew device versus a bottle of white that she seemed to be strangling by the neck. The cork slipped out with a pop.

Jack went through the door and started to look for a switch, but didn't need to. Instead of a bathroom he found himself at the top of a stairway that led down to what appeared to be a basement, but unlike any basement he'd ever seen.

"Whoa," Jack said, stepping onto the landing. "Take a look at this."

Michele finished pouring the second glass of wine, set the bottle down and walked over to the doorway. "What is it?" As she stepped onto the landing next to Jack, she also let out a soft, "Whoa." She sidled up next to him with her arm rubbing against him. "Now that's a basement."

They started down the steps slowly, Jack in the lead, taking it all in.

The room was massive, for a basement. It appeared to be about three stories tall and was half the size of a basketball court.

"That's weird," Jack said, craning his neck around. "I don't see any lights."

Michele looked around. "But it's so *bright*."

"Like all the walls are lit up or something," Jack observed.

The room was completely empty except for one thing.

"Look down there," Jack said pointing to the far end of the room.

"What is it?" Michele asked, then added, "Looks like an elevator."

They made the bottom of the stairs and started across the vast room, their footsteps echoing off the luminescent white walls.

Jack put his hand in. "Definitely an elevator," he said, leaning in to study it.

Michele felt a shiver. "Maybe we shouldn't be in here."

"Maybe not," Jack agreed, backing out. "Let's go see what Rick knows about this."

The two climbed the stairs and left the room, closing the door behind them in the kitchen. They found Daniele and Rick at the front door saying goodnight to the two couples.

"I'll stick around and help clean up," Bob was saying as they walked up.

"Hey," Jack said. "You gotta see this basement."

Rick and Bob looked at each other. "Basement?" Rick asked.

"Yeah," Jack said. "Never seen anything like it."

"It's got an elevator," Michele said. "And no lights."

"How can you see the elevator?" Daniele asked sarcastically.

Bob looked at his watch. "Ya know, I promised Terry I'd be home by seven, so maybe I'd better take off."

"Yeah," Rick said vaguely. "Probably a good idea. We'll take care of this."

"Sorry to leave you with it," Bob said, already out the door, "but you know how wives can be."

Rick let out a chuckle. "Night Bob."

"Good meeting you, Bob," Daniele said amicably.

Rick didn't close the door. "Maybe we should call it a night too."

"What about the mess?" Daniele asked.

"I'm sure Leo's arranged some kind of clean-up," Rick answered.

Daniele frowned. "Sure wonder why he didn't show up. Especially after all that trouble with his little mystery and putting this whole thing together."

"Probably got grounded in Paris due to weather or something," Rick said hopefully. "At any rate, I'm ready to call it a night."

"Yeah," Jack said with a grin, "but you really oughta see this."

"Oh, I don't know," Rick said. "This *is* somebody else's house. Maybe they don't want us wandering around their basement."

"Don't know if you can really call it that," Jack said.

Michele turned to Daniele, "Com'on," she said, "It'll just take a minute. You should see this. It's *huge*." She started walking off toward the kitchen. "Maybe we should have Daddy put one in our house."

"What would that be for?" Jack asked, following. "Basketball?"

Daniele trailed along, with Rick coming up quickly behind them, one arm outstretched. "Maybe this isn't such a good idea," he said.

Michele had already opened the door, and she and Jack were standing on the landing as they had been before, a strange look on each of their faces.

Daniele came up behind them and stepped through the door. All three were crowded on the landing. "And…" she asked, staring down the stairs at a normal basement, about ten feet tall, with white walls and fluorescent lights hanging from the ceiling. The room was completely empty except for a clock hanging on the opposite wall.

"No way," Jack was mumbling.

"What'm I *dreaming?*" Michele asked, her face going pale. "Where'd the room go?"

Rick came up behind them and looked over everyone's shoulders. "What?"

"I'm telling you it changed," Jack said. "It was this big room. And there weren't any lights, and there was an elevator over there where that clock is, only the clock wasn't there."

"Very funny, you two," Rick said.

Daniele started to turn. "Let's go home," she said. "I'm not really in the mood for any more jokes. Maybe Father will be there when we get there."

Michele started down the steps. "It isn't a joke," she said slowly. "Five minutes ago this was a great big room with no lights." She stopped and turned to look up the stairs at Jack. "How'd that happen?"

"Not a clue," Jack said coming down behind her. "Let's look around."

"Maybe we'd better not go down there," Rick said tensely.

Daniele took another look around from the landing. "Michele," she said, "would you please just…" Something caught her eye and her breath. "What time is it, Rick?"

He looked at his watch. "Look at that," he said, "Seven fifteen. I really need to be going. Early day tomorrow, you know."

"Father loves this game," Daniele said to the clock, then proceeded to check the perimeter of the room.

"What?" Michele asked.

"Look at what time it is," Daniele said, pointing her chin toward the clock on the opposite wall."

"Eight o'clock," Jack said.

Michele piped in. "And twenty seconds."

"Twenty twenty," Daniele said.

Michele finished. "Vision." She stepped down to the bottom of the stairs with Jack just behind her.

Daniele followed slowly, the three of them gazing at the clock.

"Hello!" Daniele called. "Father!" Her voice echoed off the close walls in the empty room.

Michele looked around. "He's not in here."

"Well," Daniele said. "Don't you suppose he's around here somewhere, playing his little game?"

"What makes you say so?" Michele asked.

"The clock," Daniele said. "What else?" She stepped toward the clock. "Father! This is enough!"

Just then the door at the top of the stairs closed.

Daniele bolted around and said angrily, "Rick!" but almost ran into him standing next to her looking up at the door.

The lights went out.

Michele inhaled loudly, the sharp sound making a "Ha!"

"Okay," Daniele's voice shook with a forced calmness, "don't panic."

Jack's hollow voice was next. "Try to make your way to the stairway."

"Ouch!" Michele cried. "Get off my foot!"

"Sorry," Jack's voice resonated in the darkness.

"What's that?" Michele asked as a hissing noise came from the ceiling above her.

"Let's get out of here," Daniele said urgently, trying to find the stairway.

The hissing continued. Within moments, each of them was wheezing.

"Some kind of ga…" Daniele said, but had hardly gotten the words out when she lost consciousness.

8

The basement lights were on when they came to.

Daniele opened her eyes with her head lying on the basement floor, the room horizontal. She sat up and found a glassy-eyed Rick standing over the three of them. Michele was the next to arouse and sit up. She lifted her knees, brushed her hair back over her ears, and wrapped her arms around her legs looking disoriented. Jack was snoring.

Daniele stood and asked, "Are you all right?"

Michele's expression was blank. "I have a headache."

"Me too," Daniele said, massaging her forehead with her palm. "We need to get out of here." She looked up at the basement door. It was open.

"What happened?" Michele asked.

"I think we got gassed," Daniele said. "Didn't you hear the hissing?" She turned to Rick. "Are you okay?"

"I have a headache," Rick responded.

Daniele leaned over to Jack who was curled up on the floor in a fetal position and pushed his arm. "Jack," she said. "Wake up."

Jack, still sawing logs, took a deep snort and let it out.

She pushed him harder. "Jack!" she said loudly.

A startled snort came from Jack's nose as he opened his eyes. "What?"

"You need to wake up," Daniele repeated.

"Oh yeah," Jack said. "What time is it?"

"Eight o'clock," Michele said, actually looking at the clock.

"Don't you remember what happened?" Daniele asked.

Jack sat up and rubbed his eyes, consciousness seeping back in. "Where is this?"

"We're in the basement," Daniele said. "Six eleven Crimson Court, remember? The party?"

"Oh yeah. That noise. Some kind of gas I suppose."

"That's what I was thinking," Daniele said. "We need to get out of here."

Jack struggled to his feet, let out a yawn and stretched his arms, clasping his hands behind his head before he let them down again. He looked up the stairs. "Let's go," he said, reaching down and pulling Michele up brusquely with one hand. He towed her along, leading the others up the steps.

The house looked the same as it had when they'd entered, with no signs of anyone inside. But Daniele knew there must have been someone else besides the partygoers. She looked quickly around downstairs, but no sign. Just the shambles of the party as it had been before they went into the basement. They scurried out the door into the twilight.

"Must not have been out long," Daniele said. "It's still light out."

They were silent during the drive for several minutes. The streets were devoid of traffic.

Michele was sitting in the back with Rick. "Why would Daddy do that to us?" she asked in despair.

Daniele's face was lined with worry. "Father didn't do it."

"Well then who did?" Michele asked.

Daniele was annoyed. "Whoever has Father."

"So now you think he was kidnapped after all?"

"I don't know *what* to think!" Daniele said harshly. "What I need to do right now *is* think!" She made the turn onto their street. "Car feels sluggish," she mumbled absentmindedly, deep in thought. She turned left into their long driveway that wound through the dogwood trees to a semi-circle in front of the house. She swung to the left around a pothole that had needed to be fixed since the last rain, and noticed that someone must have fixed it. She thought she remembered it being there when they'd pulled out only four or five hours ago. However long it was. Fast work. Or had it already been fixed? She chastised herself for letting her thoughts wander to such trivia when she needed to concentrate on what'd just happened to them. She took the side lane that led to the garage behind the house next to the back yard and parked near the access to the kitchen.

Daniele marched straight into the kitchen when she got out of the car, yelling, "Father!" but stopped abruptly at the first thing she saw. The clock, of course. It was frozen on eight o'clock and twenty seconds. She'd stopped so suddenly that Michele ran right into the back of her.

"*What?*" Michele asked impatiently.

"Someone's playing games with us," Daniele said. "I don't think it's Father. He wouldn't do this."

Michele's tone changed. "What is it?"

Daniele moved aside and let Michele in.

"Oh!" she said with a gasp. Her knees seemed to go limp, but she held herself up. She could feel the blood rushing from her face. "I don't wanna do this anymore."

Jack had stopped behind Michele and edged his way in beside her. "Wow. Someone changed the clock."

Daniele felt weak. She walked slowly to the table and sat down.

Jack saw how pale her face looked. "You okay?"

"I'm okay," Daniele said. "I just don't get it."

Jack headed toward the fridge. "I'll get you some water."

Michele moved to the table and plopped down in the chair next to Daniele. "More mysteries," she said disheartened.

Rick came in zombie-like and sat at the end of the table next to Daniele.

"Rick, what time is it, anyway?" Daniele asked.

Rick looked at his watch. "Eight o'clock," he said.

Daniele looked at him with disgust. "Very funny." She turned to Jack as he opened the fridge. Her eyes popped open and she cried, "Wait!"

Jack turned, his hand still grasping the handle. "What?"

Daniele stared at the contents of the fridge. "What's in there?"

Everyone looked at her.

"In the *fridge*," Daniele demanded. "What *kind* of water?"

Jack turned and read one of the labels. "It's Alsatian," he said. "Why?"

Daniele looked at Rick. "I thought Benz water was in the fridge."

Rick just shrugged.

Daniele sat up and looked at him hard. "You said before that it was all Benz water, remember?"

Rick had a blank look, just staring at her.

Daniele raised her voice. "Rick!"

"Yes?" Rick asked.

Daniele spoke slowly. "You said it was all Benz water in there. 'A refrigerator full of it,' you said."

"I have a headache," Rick said without emotion.

"Well there's no Benz water in here," Jack said, leaning down to see all the bottles toward the back. He started to reach in.

"Don't touch it!" Daniele ordered.

Jack turned around with a puzzled look.

"Look," Daniele said, "we've already been gassed, and now someone's changed the water in the fridge. It could be poisoned. It used to be all Benz water." She turned to Rick with a scowl. "Wasn't it, Rick?"

"So what's the Benz water look like?" Jack asked, distracting Daniele from Rick. "Let me see one."

Daniele looked around the room, but there were no bottles of Benz water anywhere. She got up and opened a cabinet door next to the sink and checked the recycle bin and the trashcan. "These are all Alsatian bottles," she said in almost a panicked tone.

"Someone's messin' with us," Jack said flatly, though it was pretty obvious by now.

"That's an understatement," Michele countered. "Someone's messin' with us big time."

Daniele got up unexpectedly and headed out of the kitchen through the swinging door.

Michele, Jack and Rick just watched her go. Michele let out a big yawn, and then the three sat there in silence for at least ten minutes until just as unexpectedly the door swung open and Daniele stormed back in.

"It's gone," she said, a distraught look on her face, leaning on one leg with her hands on her hips.

Michele leaned forward, her eyes drooping from the long day, wine, and too much excitement. Not to mention the effects of getting gassed. "What's gone?"

"The Benz bottles are gone, my printouts are gone, the clocks all say eight o'clock and twenty seconds, the map's gone, and even the Benz sign Father drew on his calendar is gone." She paced the floor. "It's all gone." She was near tears. "What's going on here?"

Michele, seeing her sister in a state that she'd never before seen her in, got up.

Daniele saw the look in her sister's eyes and suddenly felt guilty. *She* was the one who was strong. *She* was the one who always had control, and here she was about to lose it, and her ditzy sister was coming over to comfort her. It was too much for her. She buried her face in her hands and let out a sob that she just couldn't pull back.

"Oh Daniele," Michele said and reached for her.

The two hugged and Daniele put her face onto Michele's shoulder and shuddered with soft sobs. This was something she couldn't have imagined. "Where's Father?"

Michele patted her on the back. "Don't worry, we'll find him," she said. "Daddy's okay. This is just somebody messin' with us. Right Jack?"

Jack stood and walked over, lamely putting his hands on each of their shoulders, but even Daniele accepted it. She took a deep, calming breath. "Oh, happy birthday to us," she said.

After several moments of this Michele looked at Rick. He was stony eyed, staring at the three of them with a vacant look on his face. "Are you *okay*?" she asked.

Rick looked at his watch. "It's twenty seconds after eight," he said. "I have a headache."

Michele broke the embrace and turned Jack around to continue consoling Daniele, then walked toward Rick saying, "You sound like a broken record, you're just repeating yourself."

Daniele let Jack hold her closer, and even leaned her head against his shoulder. But the sobbing had stopped. She felt comfortable there, and was now concerned about Rick from the tone of Michele's voice.

Jack held Daniele tighter – actually enjoying the moment – while the two of them watched Michele transfer her compassion to Rick.

Michele walked around the table and said, "You don't look so good."

Rick stared at her, then looked from Jack to Daniele, his eyes empty.

Michele sat next to him and lifted her arm to his shoulder, but she couldn't touch him. It was as though a barrier had come up between them, like there was a glass wall around him preventing her from touching him.

"Rick?" she asked, and tried harder. "I can't seem to…"

At that moment Rick disappeared, eyes glazed, staring hypnotically into Michele's eyes as he just, simply, vanished.

9

"Rick!" Michele screamed. "Rick!" She pawed at the space where he'd been. She looked around at Daniele and Jack who were only half embracing each other now, each with their mouths slightly open.

Michele blinked. "Rick!" she repeated, and waved her arms again at the space that he'd occupied only moments before. The barrier that she'd run into was gone, just like Rick.

At first Daniele didn't believe it.

"All right," she said, coming to her senses and leaving Jack's embrace. "How'd he do that?"

To say they were shocked was the least of it. This was absolutely impossible. For Daniele, it'd gone from someone "messing" with them, to downright absurd. Her rational thinking had kicked back in. She'd left Jack standing with his mouth open, and had gone around the table and waved her hands in the space where Rick had been, just as Michele had done. Daniele sat at the table, actually in Rick's chair, hoping that whatever had happened to him would happen to her so she could *know* what was going on.

Jack was dumbfounded, staggered to the table, and sat there with a new case of wobbly brain syndrome going on and on with phrases like, "He just up and disappeared! Did you see that? Just up and was *gone!*"

Michele, on the other hand, was beside herself. She'd fallen into the seat next to where Rick had been, occupied by Daniele now, and stared at Rick's chair. She kept saying things like, "Am I still in Paris? This is a dream, right?" And then she cried, "Rick! Rick!"

Michele seemed completely helpless, and now looked to her strong sister, Daniele, the serious, down-to-earth Daniele, to somehow find an answer.

Daniele was thoroughly skeptical at the whole situation. Rick, obviously, just like Father, was somehow in on it. Wasn't he? She looked up at the ceiling. "Okay Rick. This isn't funny anymore." She jumped up and said, "I'm gonna get to the bottom of this."

She marched off, shoving the swinging door aside, and investigated the house, noticing everything now. The Benz bottle on the dining table was gone. Did the servants take it? Where were they, anyway? The house was empty except for the four of them…three rather. How'd he do it?

The grandfather clock said eight o'clock and twenty seconds. *Where's that point to?* she wondered. Up the stairs she ran down the hall to the study. The nautical clock was the same as all the others in the house, the same as in the Crimson Court house…Courtney Crimson…very clever Father…very clever. *Who's doing this?*

The computer was turned off. She knew she'd left it on. It was *always* on. Who'd turned it off? The shadow behind the open door seemed to move, and her heart fluttered. Slowly, apprehensively she skirted a wide circle around to where she could see. No one. Empty. But she felt shadows in the twilight filled room. Darting her eyes it seemed as though someone was watching her. Her skin prickled with bumps. Bumps up her back and down her arms and legs. She took deep breaths and longed for Jack and Michele's company, thinking she should have brought them with her. But to what fate?

She went to the desk but stopped short. The chair obscured the space under the desk, and she leaned to see from a distance. Again, nothing but the cubbyhole where Father would plant his feet. She watched the door as she approached the desk, waiting for whoever was doing this to appear; someone willing to gas them, possibly poison them – certainly willing to take Father. And worse?

The Benz sign drawn in her father's hand was gone. The month was the same – July. *It was July before, wasn't it? It had to be.* It was still July, but the upside-down Benz sign in her father's own hand – *in ink!* – was gone. She tried lifting the calendar page to look at the page under it but couldn't. It was as though the calendar pages were glued together. And then she tried to pick the calendar up and it seemed to be glued to the table. The whole world was beginning to not make sense.

Scouting her way back downstairs she saw nothing else, except for shadows. Shadows and the feeling of eyes on her. Shadows and the absence of a servant. There was always a servant. She called out, but no servant came to ask what she required. Servants had always come when she'd called. Always, in her father's house. Was she even *in* her father's house? *Who's here besides us?* She strode back into the kitchen, gaining strength the closer she got, trotting through the dining room and the claustrophobic hallway in between, until the sight of Jack and Michele gave her comfort, and a new strength. A new resolve to know.

"This is just too bizarre," she said.

Michele looked a mess. Her makeup had run down her face leaving black streaks under her faded blue eyes. *Why does blue makeup leave black streaks?* Daniele wondered for a moment, before her rapid-fire thoughts rambled on.

"What time is it?" Daniele asked.

Jack looked up at the clock and back to Daniele.

Michele looked at her watch. "Six o'clock," she said.

"Six o'clock?" Daniele asked. "Paris time, right? You didn't change it did you?"

"Paris time," Michele replied in a whiney voice. "I can't seem to find out what time it really is anymore."

"Midnight," Daniele said. "That means it's midnight." She looked at Jack, no longer trusting him. "Come with me," she demanded.

"Now what?" Michele said as she stood up obediently. "I don't want any more…"

But Daniele's resolve made them follow. Jack first, followed by a groggy Michele.

Daniele went out the back and walked along the side of the house with Michele and Jack just behind her. She walked down the driveway to the street and stood, staring at the sun that hung low in the hazy sky. The orange ball just sat there, apparently in the same place it had been when she'd driven home almost an hour before. Just sitting there in the sky like it had nothing better to do.

"See that?" Daniele asked.

"What?" Michele asked looking around and then to the sky following Daniele's gaze.

"Remember?" Daniele asked. "When we left the Crimson house the sun was right about there in the sky."

"It was?" Michele asked.

"Yep," Daniele said with certainty. "And when we got home it was there too."

Jack was staring, mouth agape, right at the orange sun. "It was, wasn't it?"

"And we've been here for an hour, and Rick's disappeared, and it's midnight." She looked at Michele. "Or six o'clock, Paris time."

Michele looked at her watch again and back at the sun. "Ya know," she said, "I admire Daddy. He's done a lot of amazing stuff in his life..." She looked around at the constantly fading sunlight, "but even *he* can't stop the sun from going down. Can he?"

"Of course not," Daniele said. "I don't know what's going on, but this just isn't real. Maybe I've been drugged or something. Maybe I'm still unconscious from that gas."

"Me too," Michele agreed. "Are we all going nuts? Or what?"

They stared at the sun hovering stiff in the sky.

"There's an explanation to this," Daniele said, believing something that her eyes weren't telling her. "Father and Rick are somehow..."

Just then, Rick appeared around the corner, down the slight hill that led to their house, walking briskly toward them.

"Rick!" Michele exclaimed when she saw him. He had a firm, worried look on his face as he trudged up the hill.

Michele ran to him and jumped to embrace him, her hands aiming for his neck. Daniele stood watching with crossed arms. And then as strangely as Rick had vanished, an equally strange thing happened. Michele flew right through him, her body passing through his, and she landed hard on her hands and knees. "Ah!" she shrieked as she fell.

Rick, or whatever he was, turned to her. "Please be careful," he said. "Things are not as they seem."

"No kidding," Daniele said, her eyes stern and her hands moving defiantly to her hips.

Jack's head was wobbling. "What in the world..." he said dumb-founded.

Michele stayed there on all fours for a moment, and then looked around at him, her eyes filling with tears.

"I'll explain everything," Rick said. "I wish I could help you up, but I can't."

Michele was pale.

"Are you all right?" Rick asked.

"Well, that's a stupid question," Michele whined. She got to her feet and looked at her hands and knees expecting to see them scraped up the way they'd been when she went down on concrete as a kid. But her hands were fine. Her knees were fine, except for being a little sore. But it wasn't as bad as she'd expected. "I'm okay," she said, taking a wide girth around him to return to Daniele. She looked at Daniele with suspicious eyes for a moment and touched her shoulder when she approached, as though checking to see if she was solid.

"I'm not the fake one," Daniele assured her.

Rick walked up, and Michele edged her way behind Jack a bit. Rick spoke directly to Daniele. "Leo's missing," he said.

Daniele looked at him like he was some kind of idiot and snorted. "Well duh."

"No," Rick said intensely. "You don't understand. I mean he's really missing."

"And before this he was…what? Hiding?" Daniele's icy voice somehow reassured Michele, and even Jack. "Setting up a birthday party?" And then she had a revelation. "This is still part of the party, right?" She almost smiled, but then glanced at the sun. "But how could he…" She turned back angrily and demanded, "What's going on here!"

Daniele couldn't help herself. She seemed to have no fear, and even surprised herself at that fact. This was still Rick, or some facsimile of him, and somehow Father was behind this, and now Rick was in on it. She reached her hand out and it passed right through Rick's arm, through his chest, and out as though he was a ghost.

"What *are* you?" Michele asked.

"I'm about to show you," Rick said. And then his voice suddenly changed. The next time he spoke it didn't come from him, from the facsimile of him, but from the sky itself, as though he was God talking to the three of them.

"I'm going to do something now…"

Jack hunched down instinctively, looking at the sky.

Michele's mouth dropped open in dreadful anticipation, but Daniele continued to stare into Rick's eyes.

"I don't want you to be alarmed."

"It's a little late for that, don't you think?" Daniele asked.

Rick's voice echoed from the sky. "You're not really where you think you are."

A disgusted frown came over Daniele's face. "Would you just get on with it?"

"Right," Rick's voice said. "Sorry. Eve, end program."

The sky turned white, the sun disappeared, the street, the trees, the house, the image of Rick all disappeared. They were in an immense room with white walls.

"Wow…" Michele whispered.

Jack said, "If this won't make you pee in your pants, I don't know what will."

Rick's voice boomed. "Do you know where you are?"

Michele shook her head. "Uh uh."

"The Twilight Zone?" Jack asked.

Rick's voice chuckled off the walls.

Daniele sighed. "Six eleven Crimson Court."

10

"So what is this?" Daniele asked. "The Holodeck?"

"Good guess," Rick's voice said, reverberating throughout the room. "Kind of like that."

Daniele crossed her arms. "I can't *wait* to hear how you did this."

"Where *are* we?" Michele asked.

"Michele," Rick said earnestly, "I'm so sorry about all this, but it had to be done."

"So where'd the stairs go?" Daniele asked.

"Virtual," Rick said.

"Even *I* know you can't walk down virtual stairs," Daniele said. "Virtual clocks, sure. Virtual stairs…"

"Sort of virtual," Rick's voice said.

Jack was looking around. "Any way out of here?"

The room was a perfectly empty cube. There was no glare, but there was also no obvious source of light. The rows of hanging lights in the basement were gone. The walls just seemed to glow.

Daniele started strolling through the space. "So are we prisoners here Rick, or what?"

"Oh, no, of course not," his voice said. "Sorry."

A rectangular area of the far wall seemed to melt away, or more like decompose, and the clock that still had eight o'clock and twenty seconds melted away with it. It was as though the wall dissolved, revealing what appeared to be an elevator.

"See!" Jack said excitedly. "I *told* you there was an elevator."

Michele nodded. "This is it," she said. "This is the basement." She turned around. "'Cept no stairs."

The three moved cautiously toward the opening. Jack went in first, followed by Michele. Daniele paused before entering the elevator and pressed her hand against the wall next to the opening and found that it was solid. She stepped in.

The elevator, from all appearances, was just that. It had a panel with several buttons labeled with floor numbers from four to one. Daniele thought it odd that they were on the fourth floor. *Aren't we in the basement?*

Once inside, a normal metal door slid across and they instantly began to slowly drop to the third floor, apparently one story beneath the basement of the Crimson Court house. Daniele again tested the reality of the door and learned that it was cool metal, just as it seemed to be.

Rick was standing there smiling when the door opened. "Michele," he said, and held his arms out to embrace her.

Michele forced a smile, but stayed put in the elevator looking at him with distrust. "Hello Rick," she said, saying the "k" extra hard.

Rick let one arm fall, but kept the other extended in a gesture of helping her out of the elevator.

Daniele, instead, took his hand and stepped out into a long hallway. "Thank you, Rick," she said, also with special emphasis to the "k."

Jack craned his neck to peer out the elevator before he ventured out. To the left was a wall, and to the right, a long hallway with a white tiled floor and white walls trimmed with chrome or aluminum. Some kind of shiny metal. At least the ceiling had lights that he recognized as the fluorescent tube type. An element of familiarity. "Pristine," he said absentmindedly.

Daniele was also looking around. "Sterile," she said.

Michele crossed her arms and stepped out away from Rick, her face regaining color and her brow furrowing. "You better have a pretty good explanation for all this," she said.

Rick smiled. "I do." He extended his arm pointing down the hallway to the left of the elevator. "Follow me."

From the elevator you couldn't see the doors that were recessed in the walls, but they passed several. Each door was labeled with a plate that described the contents of the room. Daniele took note of each one as they walked. Doors were seemingly only on the left side of the hallway. They passed one called "Data Center," then the next was "Virtual Environment Generator," and a third labeled "Silicon Supply Chamber"

– which seemed odd to her. Each door also had a red sign that said "Restricted Access."

"Government operation, isn't it?" Daniele asked in more of a statement than a question.

Rick turned with amused surprise, "Yes, but what made you think so?"

"The Restricted Access signs," she said. "How many average Joe's are gonna be wandering this hall? Only the Government would waste money on signs that serve no purpose."

Rick chuckled as he reached for the only door on the right side of the hallway with a plastic plate that read "Operations Center." Below it was another red "Restricted Access" sign. He opened it and led them inside.

The room was darkened, with red glowing lights that made it look like the bridge on a ship at night. The perimeter of the large room was lined with equipment, and several technicians, or operators, were busy at small workstations with focused white lights on their desks. One semicircular workstation stretched across the far wall with two black padded swivel chairs that looked very similar to the one that Leo had in his office at home. One of the chairs was occupied by a balding man in his mid-forties who had just enough long hair on one side to drag it over the top, giving the flawed illusion that he actually had hair up there. The man was leaning forward with his right hand clicking a wireless mouse next to a keyboard. His eyes were darting around one very large, wide monitor that had room for half a dozen windows that were open without overlapping each other. Another monitor, currently blank, was in front of the chair beside him. A microphone attached to an earpiece, also wireless, was strapped over his left ear.

Daniele approached. "Bob," she said, crossing her arms again.

"You work here?" Michele asked.

Bob turned. "Good to see you again so soon." He nodded to each in turn. "Daniele, Michele, Jack."

Michele forced a barely noticeable toothless grin that disappeared faster than she'd produced it, and stood her ground with her arms crossed.

Jack grinned and looked at both Bob and Rick with his head tilted sideways.

"Well," Daniele said. "Now that we're all here, how 'bout filling us in?"

Rick stretched both arms out. "Welcome to Eve."

"Eve?" Daniele asked.

"The Enhanced Virtual Environment," Rick explained. "We call her Eve for short."

"The government loves its acronyms," Daniele said. "I suppose you call the room across the hall, 'Veg.'"

"You don't miss much," Rick said with some admiration. "We actually call it 'The Veggie.'"

Michele looked confused. "The Veggie?"

"Virtual Environment Generator," Rick explained.

Bob cleared his throat and looked nervously at each one. "Um, uh…how much should we be telling them?"

"Who knows?" Rick said. "But it's definitely something we'll have to explain to Leo."

"Daddy?" Michele asked with alarm. "What would Daddy know about a place like this?"

Daniele's eyes closed a little. "So you're not the only one who's not what he appears to be."

"No," Rick said somewhat sheepishly, "I'm not." He looked at Bob. "I'm not exactly comfortable with this either. How much *should* we tell them?"

"Cats out o' the bag now, buddy," Jack said with a chuckle.

"Just spill it," Daniele agreed.

Bob shrugged. "Hey, you brought them here. I wasn't comfortable with it either, at first. But after all, Leo led them to the house. He must have wanted them to know."

"I don't think so," Rick disagreed with a negative nod. "This wasn't part of his plan, and this isn't exactly the way you go about getting a clearance. This isn't gonna go over well with the CSA."

"The CSA?" Jack asked.

"Cognizant Security Agency," Rick replied offhandedly.

"Well, I suppose we should have thought of this sooner," Bob said. "But we'll worry about that later. Right now I'm just concerned about finding Leo, and maybe these guys can help. After all, he had you bring them here."

Rick turned with exasperation in his voice. "That was a *birthday* party."

"So he really is missing?" Daniele asked.

Bob nodded.

"And he's some kind of agent or something?" Daniele looked from Rick to Bob and back. "What is this? The CIA?"

"Another good guess," Rick said.

"Well they're right over there," Daniele said, pointing with her thumb. "What else would it be?"

Rick looked them all in the eyes one by one. "You realize that everything you're seeing is secret, and everything we're telling you is secret."

Michele and Jack just stared, but Daniele nodded affirmatively.

Bob spoke to Rick again. "His daughters I can half go for, but who's Jack?" It was as though Jack wasn't even there.

Rick ran his hand through his hair. "He came over and went with us to find Leo. *I* didn't know you were gonna show them Eve. But for now, under the circumstances, I guess he's in."

"Not *my* decision," Bob said and threw up his hands. "You should have just taken them home and let them sleep it off."

He glanced at the girls. "You think they'd actually let that go?" He grunted. "They'd have been back here snooping around tomorrow morning."

"Got that right," Daniele said.

"This is both our necks, ya know." Bob stated. "And maybe even Leo's."

"In what?" Daniele asked.

"In what?" Rick asked, confused by her question.

"You said Jack's in. In what?"

Rick paused. "Maybe we should go someplace where we can sit down and talk about the situation."

"What situation?" Daniele demanded.

"About how we're going to find your dad."

The four of them left Bob behind with one hand on his ample waist and the other scratching his chin. Rick led them out of the room and farther down the hall to another room labeled "Cafeteria." No "Restricted Access" sign. This room was far larger than the Operations

Center, with perhaps forty round tables and four times as many chairs, indicating to Daniele that this was a fairly large operation, with perhaps four or five hundred people involved, if you took it as a twenty four seven complex. About a dozen groups of three or four people were scattered throughout the room eating meals from trays. At the far end was a buffet of food with a server wearing a white mesh cap over her hair and a bored cashier at the end of the line.

"Hungry?" Rick asked.

It occurred to each of them that, other than a piece of cake, they hadn't eaten since the fast food on the way to the Washington Monument. So they decided to have a bite, and filled their trays with government food at Rick's expense and settled into a table in the far corner of the room, out of earshot of everyone else. The low murmur of voices throughout the room further obscured their conversation. Once settled, Daniele was the first to speak.

"So why don't you start at the beginning?"

Rick took a sip of his coke and began. "Well, Leo and I work under cover."

"No kidding," Daniele said twisting her mouth to the side.

"You mean Daddy's a *spy?*" Michele asked.

"Well," Rick said, "he's an agent of the CIA. I wouldn't exactly call him a spy."

"A *what* then?" Daniele asked.

"He's an administrator. He oversees Eve."

Daniele's eyebrows rose. "This is *Father's* operation?"

"Yes," Rick said.

"Wow," Michele said, looking directly at Rick. "I don't know *anyone* anymore."

"Just give it time to sink in," Rick said.

"So being Father's VP for Business Development is just a ruse," Daniele said.

"No, not really," Rick said. "Your dad's business is legitimate."

"So why is he doing this?" Daniele asked.

"He was an agent before he went into the fashion business. The business was…"

"How *long?*" Daniele interrupted.

"Um…" Rick shifted uncomfortably, "about twenty years, I think."

"Since I was *eight?*" Michele asked in mild shock.

"Well…um…that'd be about right," Rick said. "um…like I was saying…his business was just going to be a cover, but it was *his* cover that he came up with on his own. He had a real interest in the fashion business, and figured he didn't have anything to lose if he set that up as a front. He'd gotten authorization, of course, but it was still *his* business. No one here thought it was going to be so successful. Not even Leo."

Jack looked amazed. "So all this time he's been doin' spy work?"

"Intelligence gathering," Rick replied. "At first. But as of about eight years ago he's been working Project Eve. His business was a perfect cover. Allowed him to travel, made him high profile, and gave him the fiscal means to work in the background. Gave him great exposure to certain circles."

"What about you?" Michele asked. "Are you a businessman or a spy?"

"*Agent*," he said, and chuckled. "Okay, spy, if that's what you want to call it. I was recruited before I met your dad. He knew about me, but I didn't know about him." A slight smile flashed over Rick's face before he concealed it, then he looked down at his plate of food and added, "He hand picked me for Project Eve."

"But you've been working for Daddy at Calvet for eight years," Michele said.

"That's how long it took to build Eve."

Michele seemed stunned. "So you don't actually *do* business development? What about my *show?*"

"Oh I do," Rick said. "And I did set up the show after your dad closed the deal with Benz. I really went to Paris on that last trip. Even set up a couple of new players that paid really well to get in." He was hoping that this would help get him out of the doghouse. "Calvet is a great cover for me just like it is for your dad. Allows me to travel and mix in circles that the Company is interested in."

"What makes you think Calvet is interested in *anything* like this?" Michele asked.

"He means the CIA, deary," Daniele interjected. "They call it the Company."

Rick continued, "But for the most part, I have to confess that when I told you I was on travel I was actually here working on the project."

"You're both a couple of *liars*," Michele said with dismay.

Rick hung his head a little and looked up past his eyebrows. "Goes with the territory," he said. "I hope you don't hold it against me."

"So far you're not scoring extra points," she said icily.

"Don't know why that's such a shock," Daniele said, then sadly, "I thought Father was different than other men, but just goes to show you."

"What?" Michele asked.

"They're all alike. Even Leo Calvet."

Michele sneered. "Well you're not gonna hate him like you hate all the other men, are you?"

"Oh I don't hate them," Daniele said agitated. "It just doesn't surprise me."

"Well you shouldn't hold it against him," Michele said.

Rick was incensed. "Then don't hold it against *me*."

Michele twisted her mouth and zipped her eyes away.

Rick leaned back in his chair and pushed both hands through his thick hair, inhaling loudly and exhaling just as strongly through a circle in his lips. "Do you have any idea," he started, thankful that at last he could let the dragons out, "what it's like to not only be responsible for maintaining and operating a ten billion dollar system, but to try to pose as the vice president of business development for a fashion business with tens of millions of dollars in revenue per year?" He looked away. "I made an oath," he said. "*An oath!* To the United States of America, to not disclose what I do. And all the while I have to keep it a secret from my fiancé." He shook his head with a smirk. "Look at this," he said, lifting his arms in the air and slapping his hands on his thighs. "You're not even supposed to be here."

Michele's eyes were cast down at her plate.

"And you don't think that distracts me somewhat? Makes me feel guilty?"

Michele didn't look up. "Well, you could have told me," she said uneasily.

Rick just took a deep breath, an elongated sigh, and wordlessly let it out.

Silence followed. Awkward, with Rick and Michele both trying to come to grips with the circumstances, not having anything else to say between them.

Daniele did a "tsk" with her tongue, as much in an effort to diffuse the moment as to let Rick off the hook. "Just get back to Father. What's going on?"

"This was all *his* idea," Rick said with frustration. "He wanted to get you two to bury the hatchet, so he set up this elaborate Benz/clock thing so that you'd have to work together."

"Who's Courtney Crimson?" Daniele asked.

"That's something *I'd* like to know," Rick said. "She's as much a mystery to me as she is to you. Your dad just told me to tell you her name was Courtney Crimson. I knew why, but I'd never met her before. I thought maybe she was a new girlfriend or something, and they'd cooked this up together. I told him it wasn't a good idea to lead you here, but he said you'd just go in the living room and he'd be there, and we'd have this big surprise party, and you'd never know the significance of the house. And then to actually have you go into Eve like that, I just didn't know what to do. I mean it was nuts. We had a house full of people, most of whom don't know anything about the project, and Bob forgot – can you believe it, *forgot* – to lock the chamber access door." He moaned. "Leo's gonna kill me when he finds out. Bob too. Both of us."

"What about the gas?" Daniele asked. "What'd you have, a gas mask or something?"

"Nope," Rick said. "Bob gassed me too. He came and got me before you guys woke up. That's when I learned that Leo was really missing. Bob ran off to the control room so he could make the chamber a basement before you guys went back down there. But it was already too late. Jack and Michele saw what they saw, so how could we cover it? So then there you were and Bob kind of panicked. There wasn't any way to explain it, so he decided he'd just put us all out, get me, then go figure out what to do next." He snickered. "Pretty stupid, really."

"Nice guy," Daniele sneered.

"So the stairs really don't exist?" Jack asked.

"Not really," Rick said. "Sort of. Of course they existed, but they were virtual. Virtual, but enhanced."

"So what's that mean?" Daniele asked. "How does all this work?"

"Well it's all classified," Rick answered, "but I suppose if you're going to be using it you should know…"

"*Using* it?" Michele asked with alarm. "*Using* it? *I'm* not *ever* going in there again!"

Daniele stuck to business and ignored Michele's outburst. "Using it for what?"

"To find your dad. When Bob came over to the Operations Center, everyone that had gone to the party…"

"The people that work here were at the party?" Daniele asked.

"Some of them," Rick replied. He looked at Michele. "You'd know some of them from Calvet."

"You mean the people I work with are *spies*?" Michele asked with incredulity.

"Yeah," Rick said. "Some of them. It's been a cover for a lot of us. Anyway, when Bob got here they were all scrambling around trying to find out where Leo was. He didn't answer his cell, his plane had never taken off from Paris, and no one there at Calvet…"

"They're spies too?" Michele asked.

"Not there, no," Rick said. "But they might know where he is. He'd been missing meetings and now, still, no one in Paris knows where he is. Bob figured maybe you guys could help because of the clocks. The clock in the basement showing twenty twenty is a mystery to us. We didn't put it there. And we didn't manipulate any of the clocks in your virtual house when you were there. Someone's not only messin' with you, they're messin' with Eve. Everyone's going a little nuts around here about that."

"So who do you s'pose is messin' with Eve?" Jack asked.

"That's the problem. We don't know," Rick said. "We think maybe Leo, which is why Bob and I decided we should bring you in and get your help."

"So how would this thing…how would Eve…help us find him?" Daniele asked.

"Well," Rick replied, "because we can use it for research. Might lead us to where he is. Since you did such a stellar job of solving Leo's riddle, and you're his daughters so you might recognize something that we missed, we thought you might be able to figure out what the clocks are pointing to." He paused. "We sure can't."

"So what is this?" Jack asked. "What is Eve, anyway?"

"It's a virtual reality chamber," Rick explained. "We use a DNA computer to manipulate silicon to provide the appearance of real objects…"

Jack broke in, "You mean DNA computers exist?"

Rick nodded, "A few. I'm sure this is the most advanced."

Michele was leaning back in her chair tapping her plate with the side of her fork. "What in the world is a DNA computer?"

"Well…like it sounds. It's a computer that uses DNA to perform operations and store data," Rick explained, which meant absolutely nothing to Michele.

Daniele was intrigued. "How would that work?"

Rick shifted to professional, and went into it like he was giving a briefing to some senator, a function he was occasionally required to carry out. "Well, you use DNA to perform input output operations. We use it to manipulate silicon molecules by structuring them into objects. Think of enzymes as hardware and DNA molecules as software. The enzymes work to perform operations on the DNA. The amazing thing is the parallelism. That's how we create the objects. We call them Enhanced Virtual Objects, or EVOs. For information retrieval and processing we mostly use biochips, but we're also using DNA logic gates to manipulate the silicon that creates and colors the EVOs. The database that sculpts the objects in Eve is in about ten pounds of DNA material in the Data Center." He had a proud slight smile when he added, "We've put pretty much everything we could get off of every accessible computer in the world into that database."

"Accessible computers?" Daniele asked.

"Anything connected to the Internet," Rick answered.

Jack looked shocked. "You mean like from my PC at work?"

"You get on the Internet?"

"Well yeah, but it's all behind a firewall and encrypted."

Rick chuckled. "Firewalls and encryption ain't what they used to be when you've got DNA cracking codes."

Jack was suddenly embarrassed about some of the places he'd surfed, but dropped the subject while Rick went on.

"We have fifty tons of silicon in the Silicon Supply Chamber."

"Let me guess, the SSC?" Daniele asked.

Rick chuckled again. "We call it the SPP."

Daniele struggled with that one for a moment, but couldn't decipher it.

Rick was still smiling. "The Silly Putty Pot."

"Oh good grief," Michele said.

"Some of us call it the Silly Putty Potty." He looked for a reaction but was met with blank stares. He screwed up his face and said half-embarrassed, "Or the Silly Sucker."

"Silly Sucker?" Michele asked.

"You know," Rick said fidgeting, "because the Veggie sucks the silicon into Eve and…" Michele seemed to be looking at him like he was some kind of freak, "…well…um…never mind that."

"These are CIA technicians?" Daniele asked with amazement.

"Hey," he said defensively. "Even spies get playful."

They just stared so he went on.

"So when the Virtual World Processor creates an environment in Eve, it retrieves it from the DNA database and 'builds' it using the silicon in the Silly Sucker…I mean, the um…SPP. Eve is really like a honeycomb, with microscopic holes throughout the entire structure. The silicon is more or less piped through the holes using genetic gates that we call "And gates" that link two DNA outputs by chemically binding them. It's kind of like Legos. You just keep locking and inter-locking them until you've built a structure. Then we use an outer layer of silicon that we can apply color to."

"And all that happens just like that?" Jack snapped his fingers.

"To us it seems so. To fill Eve and move the environment dynamically, like when you thought you were leaving the Crimson Court house, driving home, going into your kitchen…"

"You saw all that?" Michele asked.

"Um…yeah."

She curled her lip. "Creep."

Rick looked at her sadly for a moment.

"Go on," Daniele said, completely enthralled.

"Um…oh yeah…all that movement, like you're moving through an environment, takes several trillion calculations per second, not to mention the DNA chains that have to be built and linked, and then, of course, unlinked. All that's done by another jar of DNA in the Veggie, which, oddly enough, is enhanced by silicon chips."

"And the Veggie is…." Jack led him.

"The Virtual Environment Generator. That's the real computing power of the place. But Eve is always a couple of steps ahead of the human brain, reconstructing the silicon when you move, or making…" he searched for a case in point, "a doorknob, for example, when you want to go open a door. It's really a complex mixture of holograms and silicon."

"Unreal," Daniele said. "No pun intended."

"It's real enough," Rick said, "but it still has its limitations."

Daniele asked, "Like what?"

"Like virtual people," he said.

"But you can manipulate the environment?" Daniele asked.

"Quite a bit, but not completely. There are limitations to everything."

"So why couldn't I hug the virtual you?" Michele asked.

"Well, when it comes to computer-generated people, we're not all that advanced. That was a holographic image of me, so to keep you from passing your hand through it, I had to encase the image in a transparent silicon bubble. Then I just figured that was probably pretty weird to you, so I deleted the image, which, I guess, was just as freaky."

"Pretty freaky," Michele agreed.

Rick went on, leaning on the table and talking with his hands. "It's easy to simulate things like cars, tables, chairs, even streets and skies. But for animals or insects or people, the movements are too complex and unpredictable for Eve to manipulate all of them at once, even with the system's computing power, so we had to settle for holograms. They work just fine, and as long as you don't try to touch them, you really can't tell they're not real."

Michele nodded. "I'll say."

"So the 'Enhanced' part is the silicon," Daniele remarked.

"And the holograms," Rick added. "There are other enhancements."

"But what about movements?" Daniele asked. "It sure felt like I was driving the car."

"It's still just silicon adjustments. For instance, to give you the sense that you're moving forward, the Veggie just tilts you back slightly. You feel a slight 'G' force, so you have the sense that you're moving forward, even though in Eve you're pretty much stationary. One problem might be if you all went off in different directions. Then Eve has to put you into silicon bubbles and manipulate each one separately. So even though all of you are in the same room, which is Eve, you know, the chamber, you would each have the sensations that you're really somewhere else."

"Pretty impressive," Daniele said with true admiration. "What's *your* function here?"

"I head up the Operations Directorate. Basically oversee the maintenance and real-time operation of the systems."

Daniele saw Rick in a whole new light. "And you pass yourself off as V.P. of B.D.?"

Rick's look changed to one of seriousness. "And I still will, with your help. None of this can be divulged, you know."

Daniele nodded, somewhat deferentially, and said softly, "I understand."

He looked at Michele.

"I have no idea what any of what you just said means anyway," she said. "You don't have to worry about me."

"Jack?"

"Lips are sealed," Jack said, drawing a zipper across his mouth.

Rick wasn't reassured.

But Daniele was mesmerized. "So what about the sun? Why can't you make the sun go down?"

"Oh, we can. It was just an oversight. When I saw that you'd figured it out I didn't see the point anymore. What was I gonna do, have the sun suddenly drop out of the sky? That's why I decided it was time to bring you in."

"Why didn't you just 'bring us in,'" Daniele said making quotation marks with her fingers, "from the beginning?"

"I hadn't planned on bringing you in at *all*. Leo was supposed to be in the living room. It was really Bob that brought you in." Rick shrugged. "Like I said, he panicked. He just wanted to take you all home, but I knew that wasn't gonna work." He leaned back in his chair and exhaled. He waved slightly with his hand. "This's all Top Secret, ya know, but even after that most of what goes on in here is compartmented."

"Compartmented?" Jack asked.

"Eyes only," Rick tried to explain, but how do you explain the security classifications of the United States in a single sentence? "Beyond top secret. You know, there are different levels from the most mundane, which would be Confidential, to the very top, which would be compartmented, and even beyond that. In our case, this is mostly compartmented, which means I don't even know everything that goes on here. I can tell you generally about the system, but the real details of Eve are locked in Bob's and his people's minds."

"What's Bob do?" Daniele asked.

"Research and Development. He's the R and D guy. I'm the operator."

"So you guys don't talk?" Daniele inquired further.

Rick laughed. "Of course we do, but there are limits. I don't tell him, he doesn't tell me. That's why he's so worried about you guys." Rick took a deep breath and looked at Jack. "And, frankly, so am I. You were never supposed to know about this."

Michele slumped a little. "So you would have married me and spent the rest of your whole life in a lie?"

Rick had a pained look, but what else could he say? "I guess if I had too. I always thought it would come out somehow. I'm a little surprised you didn't suspect anything this far."

Michele's eyes pierced his. "Well, you pulled it off. I never suspected *anything*." She turned her gaze from him. "I don't even know who you are."

Rick's head sank a little.

"Good job," she continued, sticking the knife in deeper.

Rick rolled his lips together, but then went on. "The main reason I decided to bring you in…well, Bob actually …was that I…we…like I said…we believe Leo is somehow communicating to us through Eve."

"With the clocks," Daniele stated.

Rick nodded.

Daniele shook her head, and said, "So Father's leading us on *another* wild goose chase."

"We can only hope so," Rick said. "You never know with Leo."

"What's that supposed to mean?" Michele asked.

Rick looked at her seriously. "Sometimes in our business you just don't have a clue what's going on."

"Hmpf," Daniele snorted. "Well *I* have a clue. And when he finally leads us to him, I'm gonna kill 'im."

Michele sneered at her. "Oh stop it. He's doing this for a reason, and I'm sure it's a good one."

"The birthday party I can understand," Daniele said. "But what now?"

Rick was silent, puckering his mouth and shaking his head.

"Well then let's just get on with it," Daniele said.

Michele yawned. It appeared that she wasn't so worried about Daddy anymore. "Not me," she said. "I'm going home and go to sleep."

"No time for that," Rick said. "We need to find your dad."

"Now's not the time for sleep," Daniele agreed. "We need to do this and find him."

"Well, you go on without me," Michele said. "Gimme the keys to the car."

Daniele hesitated while Rick turned from one to the other, stopping on Daniele. "Maybe she's right."

"Of course I'm right," Michele said, trying unsuccessfully to stifle a yawn. "It's…um…" she looked at her watch, "seven thirty. In the *morning!*"

"And it's one thirty here," Rick said, glancing at his watch. "Maybe we should call it a day and start up early tomorrow."

Daniele looked at Jack. "You tired?"

"I'm totally into this," he said. "I'll go with whatever flow you say."

Michele's eyes were drooping.

"All right," Rick said, standing up. "I'll go set Michele up in Eve…"

Michele woke slightly, "What'd'ya mean?"

Rick took her hand, which she accepted this time, and said, "I'm just gonna go create your bedroom, with your bed, so you can get some sleep while Daniele and Jack and I sit here and talk things over for a bit."

Michele's eyes brightened. "My room?"

"Yes," Rick said. "Your room."

"And I can sleep as long as I want?"

Rick looked from Daniele to Jack, then back at Michele. "Of course."

Daniele popped in, "We'll come and get you when it's time to go."

Michele yawned. "Okay. Just give me a little sleep time and I'll be all right."

Rick stood and Michele followed. None of their food had been touched except for Jack's. He'd eaten all of his and had been bumming food off the other three, "Since it's just sittin' there gettin' cold."

Michele let Rick put his arm around her shoulder and laid her head there as they walked to the exit. Within a few minutes, true to his word, Rick had taken Michele to the Operations Center to set it up, then up the elevator and into Eve, where she found herself in her own room, with yet another clock frozen on eight o'clock and twenty seconds.

As all rooms in Leo's house, Michele's was spacious, with the semi-circular outer wall that faced the outside garden filled entirely with large framed windows, with a door to an expansive redwood balcony set in the middle. There were two sets of curtains; the inner was sheer off-white, and the outer the thick tapestry-type, with green and brown earthy tones, and cream-colored decorative tassels that cinched the outer curtains to the sides of the room during the day. Under the windows was a curved credenza, and in the middle of the circular part of the room, two comfortable chairs sat beside a coffee table covered with fashion magazines where Michele would often read. She had her father's taste for mahogany, with crown moldings and wall panels that filled the bottom third of the walls made of the wood. The ceiling and the walls were painted in a tea-stained, light beige that the painters had to redo four times to get right. Of course Michele's initial description of the color as "mud" didn't help, but they'd finally found it, calling it "dark sand," with lightly painted plum trees, white columns and arches with vines climbing around them that blended the room into the outside garden.

Rick hovered for a moment while Michele got in bed, staring at the clock. "Bob, you do that?"

"If you mean the clock," Bob said through the walls, "nope."

A concerned look came over Rick, but then he turned his attention back to Michele, brushing his hand over her hair as she lay down.

The queen size mahogany canopy bed looked like her own, lined with satin cream sheets and topped with a goose-down comforter, and though it was uncharacteristically stiff, she lay on the somewhat soft pillow and pulled the surprisingly warm silicon comforter over her. She snuggled, enjoying Rick's hand through her hair, feeling secure at his touch, and settled onto her side with the curve of her hip pushing the silicon up in a graceful round line that Rick couldn't help but admire, and within a moment was fast asleep.

11

It couldn't have been ten minutes, Michele thought in a deep fog. Her name was echoing in her brain and she had a brief dream that she was in an earthquake.

"Michele," a familiar voice said in the distance.

She rolled over onto her side with her back to the voice.

"Michele," the voice insisted.

"What?" she mumbled, visions of shaking becoming real.

"It's time to go," the voice said.

"Go where?"

"We need to find Father."

"Daddy?" she murmured. "Is he here?"

"No. We don't know where he is. That's why you need to wake up – so we can find him."

Michele stirred again. "Oh yeah. Just give me a minute." She snuggled under the replicated blanket.

"Michele!" the voice demanded.

Her eyes opened with a start. "What?"

"Get up!" Daniele said. "It's time to do this."

"Do what?" Michele pushed herself up in bed, her face with a drowsy, cross expression.

"We have to go into the virtual world…well, we're already there…but we have to go explore and look for clues to find Father."

"Do we have to do it right now?" Michele asked with a whimper.

"Right now," Daniele said firmly.

Michele yawned, then submissively said, "Okay," as she turned and put her feet on the floor, her eyes still closed.

"She gonna make it?" Rick asked from behind Daniele.

"She'll be fine," Daniele said.

"I'm fine," Michele said. "Just give me a minute to take a shower and change clothes."

"Um…" Rick said apologetically, "you, uh, can't do that."

Michele glared at him through slits in her eyes like he was some kind of mean ogre. "Why not?"

"Well, you're still in Eve. You can't actually do things like take a shower in Eve, unless you want everyone in the CIA watching. And you can't change clothes."

This was like ice water in Michele's face, and she suddenly felt self-conscious. "Everyone was watching me sleep, weren't they?"

Rick tried to reassure her, "No they weren't, of course not."

Michele looked around the room. "Bob?" she said.

"Yes?" The voice emerged from the ceiling.

She looked at Rick. "See?"

Rick sneered at the virtual bedroom wall.

"Can I at least get something to eat?" Michele asked. "Don't you people ever need food or sleep?"

"Well, um," Rick said, scratching the back of his head. "We actually did sleep. I took Daniele home after about an hour, and Jack slept on my couch."

Michele gave Daniele's clothes the once over. "So you showered and changed?"

Daniele looked at her clean fingernails a little guiltily, but said nothing.

Michele pushed herself up and put her hand out wiggling her fingers. "Gimme the keys."

Daniele obliged, and she and Jack waited in the cafeteria while Michele, with Rick along with her, went home and cleaned up. Michele came bouncing through the cafeteria door about two hours later wearing clean jeans, a blue-flowered tee shirt and comfortable shoes.

"That sure took long enough," Daniele said.

Michele slapped the table when she sat down, and had an inexplicable smile that was just frozen there.

"Been busy?" Jack asked with a twinkle. "You sure seem to be in good spirits."

"Nothing like a hot shower," she said beaming, without further explanation. "Get me some coffee?"

Jack winked at Rick as he stood to venture off to the coffee maker, but Rick either didn't notice or decidedly ignored him.

"'Bout ready to get started?" Rick asked, always the serious one.

"Oh no no no," Michele objected. "Food first."

Rick took Michele's order and headed for the serving line, returning minutes later with a brimming plate.

So for the next half hour, Michele stuffed herself with powdered eggs, greasy bacon, and under-cooked pancakes. The conversation between Rick and Daniele was non-stop, with Daniele asking more and more penetrating questions about Eve. Rick, abandoning all pretensions of trying to keep anything secret, was animatedly explaining in great detail Eve's inner-workings.

"I don't mean to interrupt," Michele said touching a paper napkin to her lips, "but what are we supposed to do now?"

Rick leaned back. "Now we go back into Eve. We'll be looking for Leo, but mostly this session is about training you guys how it works, and getting your bodies oriented to Eve's sensations."

"Eve's sensations?" Daniele asked.

"If you're in Eve too long you start getting the feeling of vertigo because your eyes seem to realize that things you're seeing in the distance aren't really distant at all. We call it the 'fish bowl effect,' though we haven't figured out what causes it. Kind of like motion sickness. You don't really know it's happening until you start feeling slightly nauseas."

"Oh great," Jack said rubbing his stomach. "I have to take a pill to ride a boat. Am I gonna throw up or something?"

Rick smiled. "No, it's usually not severe at all, and you may not even feel it. I felt it the first few times I was in Eve, but I haven't felt the fish bowl effect since then."

Michele suddenly pushed her chair back and energetically slapped her hands on her thighs. "What are we waiting for? Let's go."

Rick raised his eyebrows. "I thought we wouldn't be able to get you back in there unless we pulled you kicking and screaming."

Michele shrugged and a smile came over her face. "Nothing like a little rest and food."

Rick turned to Jack. "Jack?"

"Got any Dramamine?" Jack asked, eliciting a giggle from Michele. "Just kidding. I'm ready."

Rick got up and held his hand out to Michele. She took it this time and let Rick lead her to the elevator.

"So where we going?" Daniele asked, standing in the antiseptic hallway facing the elevator door. She was expecting to see the Crimson basement, but then realized that the last time she was here it was Michele's room.

Rick didn't have time to answer. The elevator door opened to Leo's office in Calvet's headquarters.

Daniele stepped in. "Good thinking. This is a great place to start."

"Wow," Jack said. "Nice office. Look at that view of the Mall. Great shot of the Washington Monument."

Michele hardly noticed. Instead, she crossed the expansive room to Leo's peanut shaped desk. She rounded the desk in time to see the opening they'd come through dissolve from an elevator to the wall in Leo's office. Even the Rembrandt knock-off appeared where it always was. She pressed the intercom button on Leo's desk.

"Kathy," she said leaning over.

Kathy's synthetic voice came through the little black speaker. "Yes?"

"Can you come in here please?"

A moment later the door opened and Kathy emerged with a notepad and pencil. "Hi Michele. Hi Daniele. How did you get in here?"

Daniele was surprised, and, not wanting to be rude, almost didn't say what was on her mind, but she decided she couldn't possibly hurt Kathy's feelings. "She can see us?"

"Depends on what you mean by 'see us,'" Rick said. "She'll appear and act exactly according to everything Eve knows about her. And you'd be surprised at how much Eve knows about everybody."

Jack turned. "Everybody as in everybody in the world?"

"Pretty much everybody in the world."

A thin grin cracked Jack's lips. "Then why don't you go tell somebody where Bin Laden is?"

Rick chuckled. "It's not quite *that* simple. If someone isn't in computers, then we can't locate them. Someone like Bin Laden is cut off from the modern world, at least hands on. I'm sure he's got people coming and going, but no one ever mentions him electronically, so we have no idea where he is."

Daniele was still scrutinizing Kathy, dressed in a light brown business suit, her hair pinned up precisely, standing at her usual rigid attention, ready to serve. Daniele was unnerved by the resemblance to the real secretary. "Where's my father?" she asked.

"He's away on business," Kathy answered promptly.

"Where?"

Kathy had a blank expression. "I don't know."

"Well you're his administrative assistant," Daniele pointed out, "why don't you know?"

"He didn't tell me."

Rick stepped in. "She only knows what Eve knows. Eve doesn't know where Leo is, which means his whereabouts aren't known in any system that Eve has access to, so Kathy doesn't know where he is."

"Too weird," Michele said.

Jack sat down in an overstuffed chair next to Leo's desk half expecting it to be hard. "Comfy chair," he said pleasantly surprised.

"Can I get something for you?" Kathy asked.

"Only if you know where Father is."

"I'm very sorry, Daniele, but I'm afraid I don't know."

Daniele turned to Rick. "How is it that you have her exact voice? And the intonation is just like Kathy."

"Digitized voice," Rick said. "Everybody makes phone calls. 'Cept for Bin Laden maybe. You'd be amazed at what the CIA and other agencies have in their systems."

A chill went up Jack's spine. "Big brother really is watching," he said.

Rick nodded, almost with guilt. "Sort of."

Daniele left Kathy standing and started looking around the room. It was in perfect condition. The papers that were always on Leo's desk weren't there. Every book was stacked neatly in the bookshelves behind his chair – the same chair, she realized, as those in the Operations Center and in his home office. "I guess Father likes those chairs," she said.

Rick smiled. "Got them all together in a discount deal. Comfortable chairs, though."

Michele seemed to worry that Kathy was just standing there holding her notepad. "You can go now Kathy."

"Thank you," Kathy said, and as she pulled the door closed behind her added, "Just buzz me if you need anything."

"Look at the clock," Daniele said.

They all looked. It was not stopped on any particular time, but, strangely, it wasn't local time either. At least she didn't think so. "What time is it Rick?"

Rick looked at his watch. "Eight thirty."

"So why is this clock six hours ahead?" Daniele asked. "Shouldn't it be local time? Or is this just another one of your glitches?"

"Bob?" Rick said to the ceiling.

"Yeah?" the ceiling said.

"Any ideas?"

"I didn't set it," Bob said. "Eve set it when you went in."

"Is it always like that?" Daniele asked. "Eve just sets the time to anything she wants?"

"It's usually set to local time," Rick replied. "Don't know why this one is set forward, unless the real one in your dad's office is set to that time."

"How would Eve know that?" Jack asked.

"Good point," Rick said. "Another mystery, I guess."

"Well, I'm not seeing any other clues," Daniele said. "Maybe we should go somewhere else." She started walking toward the wall where the Rembrandt was.

"Where do you want to go?" Rick asked.

"Let's go check out Detective Cruse," she said.

"Eve," Rick said to the air, "modify environment to Detective Cruse's office."

Instantly, everything in the room started to deform, looking like transparent molasses, and morphed from Leo's office to the police station and Detective Cruse's desk. Within a second or two they were standing in front of Cruse, who just happened to be sitting at the computer with the sketch of Courtney Crimson up on the screen.

"Wow," Jack said, his hands on the arms of the chair about to stand up. After a moment he settled back down, his chair having morphed into one of the station's less comfortable metal chairs. "That's a little overwhelming."

"You get used to it," Rick reassured him.

Jack was intrigued. "Yeah, but there's gotta be a hundred Detective Cruse's in the world. How would Eve know which one you were talking about?"

"Proximity of information," Rick said. "Eve takes the most recent association and connects the dots. In your case, Eve knew that you'd gone to see Detective Cruse."

"How'd she know that?" Daniele asked.

"Cruse must have put your names in a report or something," Rick explained. "I'm certain that Leo's name is in there. Eve just puts two and two together."

"What a brain," Jack said with awe.

"You'd be amazed at what Eve can do," Rick said proudly.

"I already am," Jack said. "So you just say the magic words like that and you can be anywhere?"

Rick smiled. "Yeah. It is kind of like 'open sesame.'"

Jack went on. "What if you want to go somewhere like the moon or something, where the environment would just suck?"

"Eve maintains an atmosphere wherever you decide to go. She won't kill you, or let you be killed."

"That's reassuring," Michele said, listening intently, now standing behind Cruse.

"So how do you do it?" Jack asked.

Daniele interrupted. "Shouldn't we be asking Detective Cruse here if he's found Father? Maybe he found out who this Courtney Crimson is."

"Don't get too far ahead of yourself," Rick said. "Jack's on the right track here. This is supposed to be an orientation and training session. Besides, Bob already talked to Detective Cruse in here before we started our mission."

"So?" Jack asked again. "How do you do it? What were those magic words?"

"You have to address Eve so that the system knows that you're talking to it. You can also just tell Bob to do it. But once you have Eve's attention, you just tell the system what you want."

"No special word sequence?" Jack asked.

"No, just as long as the system understands."

A timid grin broke over Jack's face. "Can I try it?"

"Sure," Rick said. "That's what we're here for."

Jack stood up and looked at the ceiling. "Eve?"

He waited for something to happen.

Rick nodded to him, "Go on. Tell the system what you want."

"She doesn't answer? Or let you know that you got her attention?"

Rick smiled. "No. The system knows you're talking to it."

"Eve," Jack commanded, "take us to Yoda."

Daniele's eyebrows shot up. "*Yoda?* What in the world for?"

But as she was talking the room was morphing, oozing into the darkened Jedi council chamber with Yoda sitting in a chair across from Jack, looking just like the movie character, but in real life. Or virtual life, as it were.

Michele was delighted, and let out a small laugh while clapping her hands once.

Jack crossed the chamber to Yoda and said, "Why everything backwards you say?"

Yoda looked at him with wise eyes. "Screenwriter created am I." He folded his arms and shook his head. "Choice have I not."

Michele let out another laugh, and Daniele couldn't help but smirk a little.

Jack turned to the others. "I always wanted to ask him that." Back to Yoda he said, "Where's Leo Calvet?"

Yoda closed his eyes contemplatively, and then half-opened them. "Difficult to see, it is. About Leo Calvet, current information have I not," Yoda said. "Uncertain, the future of Leo Calvet is."

"He doesn't know anything more than Kathy," Rick explained.

Daniele tried to wipe the smile off her face, but couldn't. "Doesn't bother you that he's…abusing…your system like that?"

Rick smiled. "Well," he said looking sheepish, "I've actually met Yoda a couple of times myself."

"Eve?" Jack said.

Daniele frowned. "Oh now what?"

"Take us to Alan Shepherd's golf ball on the moon."

"Jack!" Daniele objected.

But it was too late. The morphing had already started. The room suddenly went black except for a moonscape of rocks, and the half-earth hanging white and blue in the lunar sky.

Michele gasped. "Oh my," She said. "It's *beautiful*."

In the lunar dust at Jack's feet was a golf ball, glaring brilliantly white like a giant pitted pearl in the dull surroundings.

Michele's mouth was in a little circle as she loudly filled her lungs. She blew it out at Daniele's hair, lifting it in the back. "I didn't know there was air on the moon."

Daniele swatted at her and smoothed out her hair. "Don't you *ever* listen?"

"Eve won't let you go without air," Rick said. "Don't worry."

"Airhead," Daniele cracked.

Jack was craning his neck. "So where's the lunar module?"

Rick scanned the horizon. "Who knows? Probably several miles from here in one direction or another."

A furrow came over Jack's brow. "So how does Eve know where the ball is? She couldn't have actually seen it land."

"Yeah," Rick said remembering, "but didn't they have a video of it? Eve would have the video. The system's probably taken the visible strength of the swing and the trajectory of the ball and the gravity of the moon and projected an approximate position. Weight of the ball, you know. The ground we're standing on is Eve's estimation of what it would look like based upon the information in the system. And…the moon pretty much looks like this wherever you go. At least everywhere we've landed."

Despite her previous objections, Daniele had become enamored by the vision of the earth, and was staring in awe at the universe. "This is absolutely amazing," she said, more impressed by Rick's knowledge than the surroundings. This was a far cry from the clueless Vice President of Business Development she thought she knew.

"Eve," Jack demanded, "take us to the Apollo 11 module."

"Shepherd was on Apollo 14," Rick pointed out.

"I know," Jack said, "but I want to see where Armstrong walked."

Daniele didn't object this time. The morphing started happening, but it was as though the lunar module materialized on the soil where they were standing. An American flag lay on the ground next to the bottom half of the module, the top half having blasted off with the astronauts to join the service module.

"How come the flag's layin' on the ground?" Michele asked.

"The rocket blast knocked it over when they took off," Rick explained, hanging onto the module's ladder with one hand and kicking dust absentmindedly into Armstrong's first footprint. "According to Buzz Aldrin, anyway. I'd think he would know." Seeing his careless destruction of history, he took a quick sudden breath as guilt flushed red down his face. He ceased his foot play and stood up seriously straight. "We all like to think it's still standing, but it's not."

Jack broke into a mischievous smile at Rick's footwork. "There goes one small step."

"Well it's standing up in all the movies," Michele said, looking at the flag.

They all just looked at her.

"Eve." It was Daniele this time, still shaking her head at her sister. "Take us to Oliver Wendell Holmes, Junior."

The chamber morphed and there, before them, was the famous Supreme Court Justice, standing behind a large wooden desk in his black robe, his gray, thick handlebar mustache obscuring his mouth. The walls behind him in the darkly hued room were completely encased in bookshelves crammed with thick volumes of the law.

An awestruck look came over Daniele's face as she extended her hand. "I'm honored."

"The honor is mine," Holmes said genteelly with a slight bow at the waist and his arm reaching out.

Daniele's hand passed through his as she tried to grasp it. "Oh, that's right," she said. "Look, but can't touch." She continued to stare into his eyes with wonder as though she had met the real man.

"Who's he?" Michele asked.

"Only one of the most important figures in American legal history," Jack replied. "I've read all of your decisions," he said with admiration.

Daniele glanced at Jack with new approval.

Oliver Wendell Holmes' bushy gray eyebrows rose. "That, I believe, would take considerable time. I'm flattered."

"Well," Jack said modestly, "most of them, anyway. I know it's not really you, but I'd like you to know that I have great respect for you."

"My sincerest gratitude," Holmes said with a refined nod.

"Let's go see *Sherlock* Holmes," Michele said gleefully.

"Just a moment," Daniele said. "Mr. Holmes, where's my father?"

Oliver Wendell Holmes, Jr., looked solemn. "I am truly sorry at your plight, and I do hope sincerely that you find him. But I do not know."

Rick said, "He's just like Kathy. It won't matter who in the virtual world you ask, they will never know until Eve knows something."

Michele lifted herself on the balls of her feet, her hands clasped behind her back. "Can we go see Sherlock now?"

"Certainly," Rick said. "Just tell Eve."

Michele had a giddy smile as she looked at the ceiling of Oliver Wendell Holmes' office. "Eve?" she asked tentatively. "Can we go see Sherlock Holmes?"

The morphing was instantaneous, and the form of Sherlock in his pinstriped suit replaced Oliver.

"Top o' the mornin'," Holmes said, touching the brim of his bowler.

Michele let out a gleeful little shriek. "I did it! He's really here. How'd I do that?"

"Elementary my dear…" Holmes had a puzzled look on his face, "…anyone here named Watson?"

"Sherlock," Michele said, "…can I call you Sherlock?"

"At your pleasure," Holmes said with a slight bow.

"Do *you* know where Daddy is?"

"You have a hearing problem?" Daniele asked.

"I'm afraid I don't have a clue," Holmes said.

Michele's eyes wandered off and then back to Holmes. "Well then what about the clock in Daddy's office?"

"Would that be Leo Calvet's office?" Holmes asked.

"Yes," Michele said, "that one."

Holmes's face turned to serious deliberation. He crossed his arms and rubbed his chin. "The time zone is actually wrong for Washington D.C."

"Yes," Michele said. "We know."

"I don't believe I can help much, except that it isn't London. That would be an hour earlier."

"What cities are in that time zone?" Daniele asked, following Michele's line of questioning.

"Define a 'city,'" Holmes said.

"You know, a place with a name where people live," Michele said.

"North *and* south of the equator?" Holmes asked.

"Just north," Jack said.

"Do you want to know all of them?" Holmes asked. "There are eight thousand seven hundred and forty two. It will take me six days, one hour and forty seven minutes to list them all at this rate of speech."

They were all stunned.

Jack picked up the inquiry and continued. "How about four *major* cites," he said touching his forehead, "um…just in Europe."

Holmes didn't hesitate. "Brussels, Copenhagen, Madrid, and Paris."

"Paris!" Michele said excitedly. "Maybe Daddy's in Paris!" She turned to Holmes. "Is Daddy in Paris?"

"I'm afraid I don't know," Holmes said. "I am lacking sufficient information to draw any concrete conclusions."

"Well let's go there," Michele said. "I can go see what's happening with my show."

"The show's over," Daniele said.

Michele's face dropped, but brightened in an instant as a new idea occurred to her. "What happened at the show yesterday at the Galeries Rouquet?"

"It was a great success," Holmes said.

"And the source of the information?" Jack asked, becoming more and more savvy about Eve.

Rick nodded approvingly.

"Newspapers," Holmes said. "Would you like to know which ones?"

"*No!*" Michele said emphatically. "I just want to know what they said."

"Martin Jackson c'est magnifique…" Holmes began.

"Hey!" Jack said. "In English."

Holmes didn't skip a beat. "Martin Jackson was magnificent, standing in for the strangely absent Michele Calvet, the show's lead designer." Holmes looked at her with blank eyes. "Would you like more?"

"Yes," Michele said in earnest, "of course!"

"Jackson was masterful, and may be pursued by such industry giants as Vogue, Channel, and Christian Dior, all of whom are looking for new talent to organize their fall shows."

"Vogue came?" Michele asked with her mouth open.

"Yes," Holmes replied.

"Eve," Michele said, "take us to the Galeries Rouquet in Paris."

"No!" Daniele said harshly, but the room was already morphing.

Michele ignored her and gave Eve more specifics. "Right at the end of the fashion show. *My* fashion show," she said to make sure Eve understood. "And make sure Martin Jackson is there."

The next thing they knew they were standing against the wall opposite the double metal doors of the room's entrance watching the last model of the evening parading on stage. Cameras clicked as the slim beauty with a wispy smile twirled one last time at the end of the runway and sashayed to center stage, wearing a Michele Calvet creation. One more turn, her hand on her hip, and she pranced off-stage behind the right curtain. Within moments, the whole cast emerged with plastic frozen smiles on their faces and took a bow. The audience, most of them with shopping bags at their feet, gave a standing ovation with enthusiastic applause.

Michele was standing tiptoed trying in vain to see over the heads. Rick and Jack were on either side of her, so she grabbed a shoulder each and used them to pull herself up as she started hopping up and down trying to see, her hair flopping with each bounce. "Where's…Martin?" she asked, "Can…you…see…him?"

"Wait!" Daniele shouted.

Michele landed and turned in irritation. "Com'on. We need to go back stage." She grabbed Rick's hand and pulled. "We're going with or without you!"

Daniele didn't even look Michele's way, but pointed at the double doors on the other side of the room that had just been opened to provide an exit. The whole crowd was gravitating toward them like water in a funnel. "It's her!" she cried in earnest.

"*Who?*" Michele asked, still annoyed.

Jack and Rick both followed Daniele's stare and saw her at the same time.

"Crimson Courtney!" Daniele said, shuffling toward her. "Uh…Courtney Crimson."

Courtney Crimson looked their way and winked before disappearing through the doorway like she was adrift in the slow moving crowd.

Michele was divided, looking at the stage and saying, "Ooo," in frustration before she followed after Daniele – Rick and Jack both prompting her decision by each grabbing an arm and tugging.

All four struggled to push their way through the crowd. Daniele was ordering every one to move aside and get out of the way. At long last they reached the doorway. Immediately to the right was the escalator, packed with people, moving slowly down. Daniele and the others jammed their way along the side of the escalator riders, slipping slowly past one and then another. Halfway down Daniele could see Courtney Crimson's red hair near the bottom of the next floor. At the bottom, she hobbled with the crowd around the landing to the next escalator down.

As much as they tried they couldn't seem to catch up to Courtney, even after Daniele realized that she didn't need to excuse herself around people. She just needed to walk through them. They passed the appliance floor, the furniture floor, the children's, the men's, and the women's – where Jack was fleetingly sidetracked by the lingerie section. It seemed to take ages to make it to the first floor, the one with all the perfumes imaginable. Once off the escalator Daniele took a frenzied look around. "There she is!" she said, pointing frantically.

Courtney Crimson, wearing a dark green dress with a summer cut, her long, straight red hair trimmed neatly across the middle of her back, disappeared out the double glass doors on the far side of the vast perfume section.

"*Man*, she walks fast," Jack said.

"Or maybe she's being pushed by someone," Rick observed. As they ran across the room after her, making a beeline right through the mass of shoppers, he further explained, "She's computer generated, you know. Bob, what's she doing here?"

Bob's voice emerged, sounding like an announcer over the intercom in the busy store. "No idea."

"You didn't put her here?" Rick asked, trotting along behind Daniele, weaving back and forth through the shoppers.

"Nope."

"Then how'd she get here?"

Bob's voice echoed. "That's what I'd like to know."

Daniele had finally reached the doorway before the others and had swung one open wide with a thrust of her arms and jolted to a stop on the sidewalk. She was surveying the street in both directions by the time they caught up.

"Do you see her?" Jack asked, panting.

Daniele looked dejected. "No," she said, and flopped her hands to her side in frustration.

"Which way did she go?" Michele asked, emerging through the swinging glass door.

"I couldn't see," Daniele said. "I lost her."

The street was a busy Parisian scene, completely familiar to Michele. Drivers from the chateau frequently dropped her off on this very spot in one of Daddy's Benzes. Even now the street was lined with Benzes, Lexuses, and BMWs driven by obviously well to do people. Delivery trucks were double parked at the opposite corner, being unloaded by workmen with hand trucks, and a police van was parked across the street. A lone policeman was occupied chasing drivers away who, apparently, didn't belong.

"Now what?" Jack asked.

"I'm gonna sit down," Michele said, heading straight for the sidewalk café across the narrow street.

Jack was right behind her. "What about Martin?"

"Screw him," Michele said, plopping down in an empty chair at the end of the line of tables. Most of them were occupied, as they normally were, with shoppers, tourists, and workers taking breaks before continuing on with the day. The air was heavy with diesel exhaust.

The others followed her and seated themselves in a semi-circle around the small round table. Daniele and Rick continued scanning the street from their chairs.

"More games," Daniele mumbled, craning her neck back and forth.

Rick sighed. "Does seem like someone's just giving us the run around."

"Well why don't they just let us catch up to her so we can talk to her?" Daniele asked. "Doesn't make any sense."

Michele waved her hand at the nearby waiter. "I'd like a glass of red wine," she said. "A Bordeaux please."

Rick smiled. "You can't drink the wine here."

Michele looked at him with a long blank stare. "I'm beginning to hate your little world."

He reached his hand to her but she withdrew hers.

"Where's Sherlock?" she asked. "Eve, bring Sherlock Holmes to the table."

A moment later, Sherlock Holmes emerged around the corner at the end of the street. He was wearing his famous hat and overcoat, looking extremely uncomfortable in the July heat, with a streaming billow trailing behind him from his curved, ornate pipe. He walked up briskly and sat down beside Michele.

"Where'd Courtney Crimson go?" Michele asked.

Holmes waved to the waiter. "Watson! Red wine, please. Make it a Bordeaux."

The waiter turned smartly with a nod and entered the bar.

"I'm afraid I don't know," Holmes said with a puff on his pipe. "Bloody odd."

"How'd she get in the program?" Rick asked.

Holmes furrowed his brow. "Well, most of the people you see are randomly generated. Perhaps she was random."

Daniele, who had still been scouring the street, suddenly turned. "*Random?* Gimme a break."

"It does seem quite improbable," Holmes said.

"No shit, Sherlock," Daniele agreed. Turning to a passing waiter she added, "Excuse my French."

Sherlock's left eye rose as "Watson" the waiter returned and placed a glass of Bordeaux in front of Holmes, who proceeded to take a long drink.

Michele stared with disdain. "Get me outta here."

Bob's voice emerged from the sky. "Good idea," echoed off the tall buildings that lined the street. The busy people seemed not to notice and hurried on their ways. "I've got a nine thirty meeting."

Rick puffed his cheeks and exhaled loudly through them. "Maybe that's enough for one session." He stood. "Besides, Bob and I need time to figure out how Courtney Crimson can be here without us knowing." He looked at the blue Parisian sky. "Eve, end program."

The street dissolved to white and became the immense basement chamber with Daniele, Michele and Jack all sinking backwards onto the floor as their chairs seemed to deflate under them.

"Thanks a lot, Rick," Daniele said, rolling over and pushing herself up.

Jack was laughing. "Give us a little heads up next time, okay?"

"Sorry," Rick said. "Forgot that would happen."

"I think you did it on purpose," Michele said chuckling.

The elevator door first appeared and then opened. Needlessly brushing themselves off, the four of them strolled to the end of the room and left Eve behind.

When the elevator door clanked shut, without looking at her sister, Michele said, "I remember when mom washed your mouth out with soap for using that word."

Daniele sighed. "Couldn't pass it up."

12

"What's that?" Rick asked.

"Back pack," Michele said, slinging it off her arm and around to Rick.

"What's in it?"

"Supplies," she said.

While Bob was in meetings with Rick and Bob's staff, Michele, Daniele, and Jack had gone to see the real Detective Cruse, who'd informed them that there wasn't any Courtney Crimson in Europe either – that fit the description at any rate. He'd found several in the U.K., but they all had dark hair and were twenty years older than the woman they'd described. After that they'd gone home and had the cook make a lunch that they ate in the kitchen where the clock still read six eleven and fifty-one seconds. At least the water in the fridge was reassuringly in Benz bottles, just as it should have been.

It was mid-afternoon by the time they'd gone back to the Eve Project. Bob and Rick had left the opening and the stairway into the basement of the Crimson Court house, and had opened the elevator door for them when they walked across the chamber. Rick was in the elevator to greet them.

"What kind of supplies?" Rick asked. "Oh man!" he said taking the bag. "What's in here?"

"Oh, don't be such a wimp," she said, ignoring his question.

Rick complied as they entered the Operations Center and discussed the "mission" with Bob. Every expedition into Eve was called a mission, and no one used the system without a purpose.

"It's pretty simple," Michele said when they began discussing where they should go next. "We go back to the Galeries Rouquet and see what happens."

"What in the world for?" Daniele asked, believing that Michele's only intent was to go find Martin.

"To see if Courtney Crimson comes around."

"Makes sense," Rick said. "She was there last time."

"She wasn't on the moon," Jack noted. "I'd say there's a good chance she'll show up at the Galeries again."

"Well how can you come to that conclusion?" Daniele asked. "It's a *computer*. She could show up anywhere."

Rick interceded. "No, his logic's right. Bob and I didn't program Courtney into the scene, so someone else did. Or, as Sherlock suggested, she was just random, which we all agree isn't very likely. If we go back to where we were, and someone unknown to us really is planting personas into the system, though I have no idea how they could, then there's a good probability we'll see her again."

Daniele couldn't think of a reason not to, and lacking any other recommendations about where Eve should take them, she agreed without comment and followed Rick to the elevator.

The door opened to the exact place they'd stepped out of a few hours before.

The Galeries Rouquet was to the left, and the sidewalk café, a Brasserie, was to the right. As before, the street scene was busy with people walking here and there, and the police van was parked where it had been – but with a different policeman casually chasing cars away that tried to double-park in front of the department store on the one-way street. The café was still packed on both the inside and outside, with the row of small round tables lining the front, and just a step above, beyond the windows that disappeared somewhere during the summer months, another cluster of tables inside the Brasserie that were in two rows behind the low wall that separated the inside tables from the outside. Inside, a bar lined the right wall, with several patrons sitting with bottled water and newspapers. A decorative clock was on the wall beyond the inside tables, right next to the his-and-her toilette.

"Now what?" Daniele asked.

A virtual car passed through them, making both girls gasp.

"Get out of the street?" Jack recommended.

"I guess that was a hologram," Michele said with some amazement.

"Yep," Rick said. "Eve won't materialize an object that would run into you. Most of the things you see *are* holographic images."

Regaining her composure Michele pointed and said, "Right there."

Jack sniffed the air as they walked. "Smells like diesel."

Michele looked at Jack. "I noticed that the last time we were here."

Walking beside Rick, Jack pointed out, "I can smell some kind of food too. Smells like fresh bread." He stopped and looked around. "Eve makes smells too?"

"We have an atmospheric generator that injects appropriate particles to stimulate the body's olfactory system," Rick explained, seeming not to notice as another car passed through him. "We need it for the total experience. Your body would sense that something was missing if you didn't smell anything."

"Smellivision," Jack said jokingly.

Rick chuckled. "Yeah, it's kind of like that."

"What's smellivision?" Michele asked.

Jack explained, "I think it was in the early eighties when someone had the idea of sticking a box onto your TV that would put out smells to go along with whatever program was on." He shrugged. "Didn't work."

"Hmm," Michele said.

Jack inhaled deeply through his nose. "I guess you could call this smellaneve," he said, which made Michele laugh, covering her mouth with her palm.

"It seems to go away fairly rapidly when scenes change," Daniele observed, which brought more explanation from Rick.

"It's vented out of Eve the same way that it's vented in. So even if a smell lingers, your brain doesn't sense it because smells linger anyway. By the time a new scent has been introduced, your brain has already filtered out the old one. It's also localized, which means we can project the smell of a particular food directly from the source."

"You just can't eat it," Michele said insipidly.

Rick laughed. "No. You can't eat it." He looked reflective for a moment. "Took eighteen months to come up with that subsystem...three more years to make it work."

"Well com'on," Michele said, getting them moving again. "Let's go sit down."

The same table they'd sat at earlier was conveniently empty. They each took a wicker-backed chair around the cramped table and sat.

"Well, this should be fun," Daniele remarked sarcastically.

"It will be," Michele said with a gleam. "Hand me that."

Rick had already taken the hefty backpack off his shoulder and set it on the sidewalk. He lifted it with a grunt and swung it over next to Michele. Opening it, she took out a bottle of wine.

Daniele was flabbergasted. "Are you *nuts?*"

"Wine!" Jack said enthusiastically. "Good idea! Count me in."

Michele was busy cutting the cap off the top of the cork. "I just thought if we're gonna be sitting here waiting for Courtney to show up we'd need something to do."

Rick had a slight look of alarm. "I'm not sure if bringing foreign organic matter into Eve is a good idea. Bob?"

"Don't see how it could hurt anything," Bob's voice echoed down the street.

"See?" Michele was downright bubbly. "Now all we need is glasses," she said, turning to flag down a waiter. Switching to French she said, "May we have four wine glasses, si vous plait? And an ashtray."

"Cendier?" Daniele asked, understanding at least one of the French words that Michele had said. "Why an ashtray?"

"An *ashtray?*" Rick's forehead wrinkled. "I didn't know you smoked."

"Only in Europe," Michele replied with a playful grin.

"Well we're *not* in Europe," Daniele said.

The waiter asked in English, "What kind of wine would you like?"

"Oh, none," Michele said. "We have our own."

The waiter looked disturbed. "I am very sorry, but you cannot drink your own wine at this table."

Michele looked around. "At which table *can* we drink our wine?"

Jack chuckled. "I think he means in this restaurant."

"Oh!" Michele smiled. "Of *course* we can."

The waiter looked bewildered. "No, I am afraid you will have to leave."

Michele was unshaken. "Bob, tell Jacque here…" saying the "que" hard like she did with Jack's name, "that we have our own wine to drink and for him to bring glasses."

Bob's voice came down from the sky and rang through the street.

"Can't do that. It's Eve. The system is just following French customs."

Now Michele was getting irritated. "Forget it then," she told the waiter as she reached into the backpack. "I thought something like this might happen so I came prepared." With a triumphant smile she produced four plastic cups and set them on the table.

"I am sorry Mademoiselle," the waiter said. "You will all have to leave."

"How do I get it through his digital head that we're going to sit here drinking wine while we wait for Courtney to show up?"

Daniele gave her a harsh look. "It was a stupid idea bringing it in here in the first place. Why don't you just go leave it in the elevator?"

"What?" Jack said in her defense, but looked at Rick rather than Daniele. "You can't drink a little wine in Eve?"

"Well," Rick said, tapping is forefinger to his lips, "I suppose you can. But we'll have to use your cups. You can't pick up objects in Eve. They're all just projected silicon, so everything you see is connected to the Silly Sucker...I mean the Silicon Supply Chamber."

Jack laughed. "Silly Sucker works for me."

"Well that doesn't make any sense," Daniele said. "How can the waiter walk around if he's connected?"

Rick looked around. "Well remember, he's a hologram. But even when Eve needs him to be solid enough to perform some task that calls for silicon manipulation, he'll still be connected to the source. In those cases, like with this waiter, Eve produces a combination of holographic images enhanced by a silicon channel, like a pipe passing through the hologram that allows a silicon structure to be constructed. Every object in Eve is always connected to the source..."

"The Silly Sucker," Michele said smiling.

Rick grinned, "Yeah, the Silly Sucker."

"You must leave now," the waiter said more firmly, "or I shall summon the police."

Michele made a smirk and turned to Jack, "Can you believe this guy? Lot of gall for a pile of silicon."

"Downright surrounded by Gauls," Jack quipped, leaving Michele with a blank look.

"Just order something from him," Daniele said, "and let him bring it. Then we'll drink your silly wine."

Jack's eyes opened wider and he grinned. "I sure hope it isn't *silly* wine."

"Silly Sucker wine," Michele added with her own grin at Jack. "The only Silly Sucker here is Daniele."

"Who you calling Silly?" Jack bantered with a wicked twinkle in his eyes.

Michele laughed and looked in mock surprise at her sister. "*Daniele!*" she said. "I'm *shocked!*"

"In your dreams," Daniele said to Jack without looking at him.

"Well, then," Michele said turning to the waiter. She ordered in English, "Give us a bottle of your most expensive red wine."

Satisfied, the waiter turned and walked into the Brasserie.

"Who'll do the honors?" Michele asked, folding the small knife back into the corkscrew.

"Allow me," Jack said, taking the corkscrew and bottle and getting to work.

Slipping the cork out, Jack poured a half-cup each around the table. As he set the bottle down the waiter returned. He poured the red contents of the silicon bottle into each of the four silicon glasses, ignoring the four real glasses on the table.

"Now that's not connected, is it?" Jack asked. "How can he pour?"

Rick was swollen with pride at their creation. "It's simple," he said with a grin. "Eve constructs a silicon channel through the hologram, probably up through his right leg and through his right arm to the bottle. The silicon wine pours out of the bottle, then when it hits the bottom of the cup – see," he said pointing, "now it's connected again, and Eve transfers the silicon source from the bottle to the glass. Then the system removes the silicon channel from the holographic waiter."

Even Daniele was impressed and looked at Rick with admiration. "Ingenious."

The waiter left the bottle in the middle of the table, set an ashtray in front of Michele, and then set a small silver dish with the bill in front of her.

Michele looked at him. "Thank you," she said politely, and brushed the air with the back of her hand. "Now go away."

Jack chuckled.

Daniele was slightly alarmed. "You're certainly being rude."

"He's a Silly Sucker Server," Michele said. "You really think I'm gonna hurt his feelings?"

"I am sorry, Mademoiselle," the waiter said. "You must pay now."

Michele eyed him. "And why, exactly, do I have to pay now?"

"It is our policy," the waiter replied.

"It was never your policy when I sat here when you were real," she said. "Come to think of it, I don't think you even work here, *Jacque*." Emphasis on the "que." "I've never even seen you before."

The waiter's hand emerged palm up in front of her. "I am terribly sorry, but that is our policy."

"Bob," Michele said to the air. "Change their policy."

Rick smiled again. "He can't, Michele. The system is just operating on what it believes would happen in this situation. He's reacting like a real French waiter."

"Who'd of thought I'd have such a hard time drinking my own wine in some concocted sidewalk café?" Michele asked. She looked at Rick. "You need to fix your system."

"Well this was a silly…stupid idea to begin with," Daniele said crossly. "It sure isn't helping us do our…" she made quotes in the air, "mission."

"Oh mission smission," Michele said. "We're just looking for some computer image of someone we don't even know, who may or may not have anything to do with Daddy, and we can't even have a little wine while we're sitting here?"

Jack snapped his fingers. "I'll take care of it," he said.

Everyone looked at him, including the waiter, who turned his hand toward Jack.

"Eve," Jack said, "send Bill Gates to the table with a wad of euros."

Around the corner came Bill Gates. In his hand, indeed, was a "wad" of euros, all crumpled up.

"Pay the man," Jack demanded when Gates approached.

The waiter turned to Bill and said in French, "Seventy-five euros si vous plait."

Gates looked at the silicon wine on the table. "Seventy-five euros for a bottle of Baron Sauvadet Gaillac Rouge? Outrageous."

Michele was admiring Jack with an amused look of appreciation of his solution. "Oh shut up Bill and pay the man."

As Gates pulled several bills from his hand and laid them one by one in the waiter's hand, Jack asked, "Hey Bill, still think 640k ought to be enough for anybody?"

Bill looked at him with dull eyes.

"Goodbye Bill," Daniele said in a singsong after Bill had passed the bills.

Daniele's tone pleasantly surprised Michele. The problem having been resolved, Michele lifted her cup. "To finding Courtney."

Rick and Daniele hesitantly lifted theirs also, as Bill rounded the corner at the end of the street muttering about the price. They each took a sip, but Jack and Michele slammed theirs back. Jack reached for the bottle and poured another for Michele and him.

Daniele watched them, and then surrendered. "Oh, why not?" She tossed the wine down her throat and held her cup out for Jack to fill it.

"Good wine," Rick said absentmindedly after he'd followed Daniele's lead.

Michele hunched her shoulders a bit, dipped her head and with a sly grin that made her eyes squint said, "Stole it from Daddy's cellar."

"Michele!" Daniele took a sharp breath and grabbed the bottle, turning the label so she could read it. "Not his seventy-one Cameron Valley!"

Michele giggled.

"He's gonna kill you when we find him," Daniele said with a growing smile of slight admiration for her sister's nerve.

Michele's grin got wider and she sunk her head to a sneaky position reaching for the backpack. "There's more where that came from."

"Now you're talkin'," Jack said, raising his cup and downing another.

"How many more?" Rick asked, the lines between his eyebrows deepening.

Michele leaned over and in a conspiratorial whisper squeaked, "Four."

Rick fidgeted. "I'm not sure it's such a good idea to drink a lot of wine while we're on a mission."

"This isn't a party," Daniele added, trying to regain Rick's seriousness. "We're supposed to be trying to find Father."

"So who says we can't have a little fun while we're doing it?"

Michele asked while reaching into the backpack and bringing out a pack of cigarettes and a lighter. "Wouldn't you agree that Daddy led us here?"

"Just to the house," Rick said.

"But here we are," Michele argued, opening the pack and slipping a cigarette between her lips. "He must have wanted us to be here," she said clenching the smoke.

Daniele wasn't convinced. "So we're just supposed to act like he isn't missing and wait for Courtney Crimson to show up like she's the answer to this whole thing?"

Jack slipped the lighter from Michele's hand. "Allow me."

"Got any better ideas?" Michele asked, cupping her hands around Jack's and lighting up. "Thank you."

Rick was even more concerned. "I'm not sure it's such a good idea to be smoking in here either."

"Why not?" Michele asked, flicking an ash into the tray on the table. "Silicon's not flammable is it?"

Jack smiled again and reached for the pack. "May I?"

Michele pointed at the pack with her lit cigarette.

"Bob?" Rick asked.

"Gonna be a mess on the floor when they're done," Bob's voice said, "but I don't think it'll hurt anything."

"See?" Michele smiled disarmingly.

Jack hacked when he took his first puff.

"Don't smoke?" Michele asked.

"Not since college," Jack said. "But this is certainly one of those rare occasions that calls for it."

"Really?" Daniele asked. "Whatever for?"

Jack leaned back, took another drink and said, "I've never been on a sidewalk café in Paris." He too pointed with his cigarette. "Look around."

The scene was controlled chaos. Dozens of Parisians were walking in short, quick steps, eyes forward, serious, determined and busy. And *everyone*, apparently, smoked.

"When in Rome," Jack said with his palms turned up.

By the end of the first bottle they were all smoking, and laughing, including Daniele and even Rick, who had never actually smoked before, except for that one behind the gym in high school. Halfway into the second bottle they seemed to lose all pretense of looking for Courtney Crimson, and were hysterically engaged in commenting on everyone that passed by.

"They all seem to walk with really short, quick steps," Rick observed, dragging comfortably, and in his mind, with sophistication, on his second cigarette.

"Yeah," Jack said, "they're like salmon swimming upstream, bobbing and weaving around each other."

"Excellent posture, though," Michele said and sighed. "Everyone here dresses so *well*."

"Especially the younger women," Rick agreed.

Michele started to give him a glare but then they all laughed when she just said, "Pig," instead.

"And they strut," Rick added.

"Look at that one," Daniele said pointing rudely to a young woman emerging from the Galeries Rouquet. "Her strut is so pronounced that her feet seem to be two steps ahead."

"Looks like she's moon-walking forwards," Jack said, which elicited another round of snickering.

They were all having quite a good time with their banter until the conversation abruptly turned sour – just after they'd uncorked the third – when Rick inadvertently brought up the past, the alcohol becoming a truth serum to the sisters.

Rick was stretched out with one hand in his pocket and brushing his hair back with the other. He was trying to get them back to the mission, since they were, after all, in the system. "Daniele and I were thinking we need to go to the Eiffel Tower."

"Daniele and I?" Michele said, turning to him with a slight smile.

"Well, uh, yeah," Rick said. "We were talking about it earlier."

"Earlier?" Michele asked, turning to Daniele.

"Oh stop it," Daniele said. "Why don't you just leave him alone?"

"I don't think I'm the one who needs to leave him alone."

Jack butted in. "Okay. What's going on here?"

"Why don't you tell him?" Michele asked.

"Can't you ever forget?" Daniele asked sincerely. "It was a long time ago."

The silence was thick.

"Uh oh," Jack said, slinking down in his chair a little like he was trying to get himself out of the line of fire.

"What was a long time ago?" Rick asked.

"Oh," Daniele said with a tired voice. "She thinks I stole the love of her life."

Rick looked at Michele and sipped his wine, swallowing hard. "The love of your life?"

Michele's eyes darted self-consciously when she saw Rick's look. "Well…" she struggled, "it *was* a long time ago."

Rick crossed his arms as best he could, the wine cup dangling precariously next to his elbow. "*Who* was the love of your life?"

Michele forced a smile, trying to make it look sincere. "*You* are, of course."

Rick didn't look convinced.

Michele's noisy sigh almost whistled when she let it out. "It's about a boyfriend from our college days." She looked back at Daniele and decided to just be out with it. "*She* dyed her hair to make herself look like me so she could sleep with him."

"That's not exactly true," Daniele said.

"Oh?" Michele asked. "So what's the truth?"

Daniele looked from Jack to Rick and back to Michele. "Do we really want to do this right now?"

"Why not now?" Michele asked, lighting another cigarette. "When are you *ever* gonna admit what you did?"

"Admit it?" Daniele said, as incensed as was possible under her current condition. "I didn't *do* it. The so-called love of your life did it! *I* can't help it if he preferred someone with a head on her shoulders."

"A deceitful, lying head," Michele said with disdain.

"He's the one who came after *me!*" Daniele argued.

Michele raised her voice. "So why didn't you just tell him who you were and that would have been the end of it!"

Her words seemed to echo off the Galeries Rouquet long after the sound had dissipated, being absorbed somehow by the rumble of a passing car.

"Good audio work too," Jack said to Rick in a futile attempt to change the subject.

"You don't have to yell," Daniele said, resting her chin in her hands, propped up on the table by her elbows. "It wasn't that simple."

"So what was it?" Michele toned her voice down, starting to feel a little ridiculous about the whole thing – especially with Rick and Jack listening in. After all, it *was* ancient history.

"All right," Daniele said finally. "I *liked* him. He was handsome and strong and could talk circles around the other guys. *I* can't help it if he found out he was with the wrong sister."

"You and your high-mindedness," Michele said with a smirk. "You think you're so much better than me."

Daniele fell to the back of her chair, her voice a weary calm. "No I don't," she said. "We were both young and foolish. I'm sorry about what happened. There, good enough? Did we really have to let it ruin our lives?"

Michele was taken aback by her sister's final admission of guilt. And what she'd just said sounded like half a plea to become friends – sisters – again; or at least remorse that they'd lost it so long ago. She sounded as though she actually regretted what she'd done. And it wasn't in her to keep pushing when Daniele had just done what she'd been begging her to do for nearly eight years: admit it. She herself became hesitant. "I just wish you hadn't done it."

"Me too," Daniele said. "He wasn't worth it."

Michele's eyebrows rose at that statement. "He wasn't?"

Daniele shook her head. "He was a jerk." She wasn't sure if she should add the next, but did it anyway. "I actually did you a favor."

Michele didn't know what to say, so she just listened.

Daniele looked at Rick, then back to Michele. "Are you sure you want to talk about this right now?"

"Yes," was all she said.

"Okay," Daniele said, as though it was inevitable. But it wasn't anything that Michele expected. "I never slept with him, if you want to put it that way."

"What do you mean you never slept with him?" Michele asked.

"Could I help it if you listened to him? You listened to everyone, but never once, never, asked me what happened. You just assumed." Daniele had an agonized, distant look. Her eyes were clouding over and the end of her nose was going red. "But what did happen was…horrible."

"Horrible?" Michele echoed, wondering what could possibly have been so bad. "If you didn't sleep with him, then what happened?"

She nodded dismally, all the pressures of the past to keep it hidden seeming irrelevant now. "I might as well tell you."

"Tell me what?"

She took a deep breath, actually glad that she could finally be out with this disgusting weight. "I went out with him. That's true enough. And it was a wonderful evening, and he was quite the gentleman."

"I know," Michele said. "He was really nice."

"Really?" Daniele asked. "You never wanted to know the truth because you assumed I would do what you would probably do."

"I would not!" Michele said angrily. "You're the one who did it."

"Want to know the truth now, or not?"

Michele sat back. "Okay, so tell me."

"So the next day I told him we shouldn't have gone out like we did. That it wasn't fair to you." She rubbed her forehead. "Oh, I was willing, but I told him he'd have to break it off with you first. We were parked on Yorkshire Hill overlooking the lights of the city, where everybody used to go."

"Yeah," Michele said, listening with a stare off into the tall buildings beyond the end of the street.

"But there was no one else parked up there that night. Just us. He kissed me, and I liked it at first, but then felt guilty about you and told him I didn't want to kiss anymore. Not until he'd broken it off with you. He got angry when I drew the line. I guess he thought that since I was there in the first place I was open game. I told him it wasn't right, that I shouldn't have done that to you, and had just wanted to go up there so I could call it off. He kept after me, getting more and more aggressive to the point that he actually ripped my blouse off. I tried pushing him away but he slapped me. He was all over me. He tore the front of my bra apart. I was struggling with him, trying to get him off." She looked down at her hands cupped in her lap now, and a tear streamed from her left eye that hung on her chin. "He was strong. I fought him for a long time – all that I could – but he finally had my arms pinned. He'd pulled my jeans open and shoved his hand…" her throat constricted to the point that she couldn't finish.

"Go ahead," Michele said gently. "I need to know. Did he…"

Daniele swallowed and cleared her throat. "I was lucky, I guess.

When I thought he was gonna, you know…well, just then a car pulled up. It made him stop. He settled down and drove me home."

Michele sat in shock. "Jim did that?"

"Jim did that," Daniele said.

"Why didn't you jump out and get help from the people in the car that drove up?"

Daniele's mouth dropped in disbelief and she looked up at her sister with red-streaked eyes, her mascara running. "Can't you ever see *anything*? If I did that, then word would get out and *everyone* would know, including you, that I was up there with him. It's not like I could tell you, so I just let it go."

"But," Rick intruded gently, "if you didn't tell anyone, then how did Michele find out? I mean, you've been fighting over this ever since I met you, but neither of you would tell me what it was about."

Now Rick was the target of Daniele's icy stare. "The limits I have to go to to spell out the obvious. *He* told everyone he could find that he'd slept with both of us."

"That's not true!" Michele said. "*I* never slept with him."

"I should hope not," Rick said, and then stupidly, "I'd be feeling a little left out if you had." He regretted it as soon as he said it.

Jack's face broke into a half grin. "You mean to say you've never done it?"

Rick looked at the string of people that lined the bar inside the Brasserie.

Jack looked puzzled. "But I thought you guys took so long this morning because…"

"Of course not," Michele said, and then somewhat indignantly, "We're not married yet."

Jack let out a little laugh that he stifled, but curiosity made him inquire further. "You mean to say you're a twenty-eight year old virgin?"

This time Michele looked over her shoulder at the patrons at the bar.

Daniele sniffed a little and wiped the tear off her face. "Virtue was something she seemed to acquire after she met Rick."

"I never slept with him," Michele said sheepishly.

"But you slept with other guys," Rick observed.

Michele was silent.

"What really happened is not what Jim told all your friends,"

Daniele said sadly. "They just didn't tell you the whole story that Jim told them."

Michele sat with her mouth hung slightly open. "So you never slept with him?"

Daniele shook her head. "How many times do I have to say it? That was something you assumed." She looked up at her sister with eyes that cut Michele deeply. "The first thing you did was accuse me, when I didn't even do it. All I did was go to dinner with him."

Michele was stunned.

Rick grunted, then shifted uncomfortably in his chair, taking gulps of wine now, and grabbing for Michele's pack.

Daniele, as young and beautiful as she still was, somehow looked haggard, lines seeming to form on her face instantly.

"I'm so sorry," Michele said slowly, realizing now that she was in fact the one who'd changed her sister. She'd piled guilt upon guilt for all those years for nothing. And that bastard Jim had ruined her for any man that would be worthy of her. It had all become clear. "I didn't know..."

Daniele's hand was pressed against her cheek. "No, you didn't..."

"Why didn't you tell me?" Michele asked.

Daniele looked at her with eyes filled with eight years of hurt. "I thought you knew me. We're twins for crying out loud. How could you not even ask me for the truth? This is the first time you ever did."

Michele thought back over time and realized that she hadn't. She'd just come to conclusions that she'd wrongly tormented her sister with for years.

Daniele looked back at her hands after wiping another tear. "I swore to myself eight years ago that I'd never tell you. At first I waited for you to find out on your own. And then I waited for you to ask. And the longer I waited, the more incensed I got until I just wrote you off. I wrote us off. And Jim...it was just as well," she said. "Jim made me realize what men are."

"Please don't think that all men are like that," Jack said compassionately.

Rick had a sorrowful look, worsened by the effects of the wine. "I'm very sorry that something so terrible happened to you Daniele. But you shouldn't have let it ruin your life. There are people that care about you, ya know. And there are men who would love you and not want to just use you."

Michele was looking down now. "I'm the one who did it," she said forlornly. "I'm so sorry…"

Trying to lighten the moment, Jack looked from Michele to Daniele and said softly, "Hey, c'est la vie. You should forgive each other and go on. And Daniele should forgive all the men who wouldn't do anything like that to her, and try to trust somebody again."

Daniele looked up at him.

"Ya know," Jack said. "I know a little something about being falsely accused. It's a terrible thing. But I was accused by someone who knew what they were doing."

Michele was sniffling now, dabbing at her eyes with the back of her hand.

"But Michele didn't really know," Jack continued. "You know she wouldn't really mean to hurt you. This thing between you was just a terrible misunderstanding, and actions that were bent all out of proportion."

Daniele and Michele had that mirrored look again, both slouched back in their chairs, faces shiny from tears, the tips of their noses the same shade of pink, and both picking at their fingernails.

"And it's not fair to men who would love you," Jack went on, "for you to imply that they did it to you, any more than Michele should have assumed that you did it." He turned to Michele. "And don't you start beating yourself up either over a mistake you made." He huffed angrily. "Jim's the jerk who did this to the both of you, and he's probably married by now to some poor woman who's trying to escape. I'd cut his nuts off if he was sitting here right now." He chuckled as he glared off down the street where Michele's gaze had taken her. "I'd cut my ex's nuts off if she had any."

Michele looked meekly up into her sister's eyes. "Can you ever forgive me?"

Daniele just nodded, "Yes, but it'll take a while." Leaning forward she looked closely at Michele. "I hope you never tell Father any of this."

Michele was using her palm against the moisture on her face. "I won't," she promised. "Never."

Daniele looked at Rick.

"Why would I ever do something like that?" he asked.

And then she looked at Jack.

"Don't look at me," he said. "I don't even know your dad."

She continued to stare.

He shrugged. "Lips are sealed," he said and did the zipper thing just as he'd done about national security. He felt like it wasn't enough. "I'm really sorry that happened to you. But you know, not all men are like that."

"They're not," Michele said sympathetically. "It may be a lot to ask, but I've missed you all these years. Can we just let it go and be friends again?"

"I'd say, let bygones be bygones," Jack said hopefully.

"Well…" Daniele started, but didn't finish.

They all fell to silence, each with their own thoughts. The honking of a passing car seemed to break their spell, and they all looked around again.

Rick took another quick gulp of wine and broke the ice. He set his cup on the table and crossed his arms. "Let's change the subject."

Michele looked up at him. "Shouldn't *we* talk about this?"

Rick scanned each of their faces, returning to Michele's. "That's a conversation I think we should have alone."

Things got lighter as they polished off the third bottle. Daniele had dried her eyes, and was actually feeling giddy after getting the horrid episode off her chest. And there was a certain satisfaction in finally telling her sister what she'd done, along with a regret that she herself had taken it so far. It was all so stupid, and she was embarrassed about it. But now, for the moment, the world, or the virtual world – though she had temporarily forgotten where they were – was definitely lighter. She was actually smiling, and back to making sarcastic cracks at the world around them.

When the fourth bottle was empty and they'd started on the fifth, they were all sitting sloppily on their chairs, the silicon ashtray over-flowing with butts. The discussion had melted back into humorous observations of the French, and eventually, finally, back to their mission. But not before they were all drunker than a bar full of sailors on their first liberty after four months at sea.

The waiter approached them. "Can I bring you anything else?" he asked politely.

"Only if you can fill this," Michele said, swinging her cup sharply around to him, splashing some that went right through him. "Oops!"

"Pretty porous people," Jack said, and chuckled. "Pretty porous putty people."

Michele started laughing, though Daniele looked confused.

"Pretty porous Parisian putty people," Jack went on, amusing himself.

All of it was lost on Daniele, who was the first to bring their attention back to the "mission." "Wait jus'a minute," she said with a heavy slur. "What about Crimney Courtson?"

Michele's face fell forward. "You mean Crimson Courtney, don't you?"

Rick had a serious look on his face. "Isn't it six eleven Crimson Courtney?"

Jack pointed at the air with his cigarette. "That's her!"

They all looked around and said nearly in unison, "Where?"

Jack's chest heaved a guffaw. "Ha! No! I mean what Rick said. I just think 'six eleven' is her middle name."

"Her middle name," Michele laughed and covered her mouth with one hand while slapping him on the leg with the other.

"You didn't shee her?" Daniele asked, taking the pins from her hair and shaking it out.

"Nope," Jack said, then mocked her, "I didn't shee Crimson sith eleven Courtney."

"Well lesh finder," Daniele said standing up, knocking her chair over backwards to the ground.

"How'd you do that?" Jack said with amazement as he stared at the chair. "That Shilly Shucker sure makeshit look real."

"The Shilly Shucker sure," Michele said wheezing through the smoke she'd just inhaled. She let out a hoarse cough.

"Makes…it," Jack enunciated clearly, correcting himself, but then folded over at his own words. "Makeshit look real!" he said with a raspy laugh.

"Eve!" Daniele demanded. "Take us to Crimson siseleven Courtney."

The scene suddenly changed to nighttime on the street outside the Crimson Court house, where they were all sitting on the front porch in the same chairs, except for Daniele. Her chair had vanished and she was swinging her torso and head around looking for it, her long hair flailing. The empty bottles fell to the floor along with the cups, spilling whatever wine was left in them, and the ashtray disappeared with all of the butts and ashes falling to the silicon porch.

"Hey!" Michele said. "You spilt the wine!"

"Pretty porous pompous Parisian putty people," Jack muttered and chuckled again.

Daniele looked around, confused. "What're we doing here?"

"Don't look at me," Rick said, his hands raised up at the elbows like he was being robbed. "You're the one who told Eve to take us here." He took another sophisticated drag on his cig, the end of it glowing red in the darkness.

"Nooo," Daniele said with a wave of her hand. "I wanted Eve to take us to Courtson Crimney."

"Crisney Courtson," Jack corrected her, his index finger pointing into the air.

Rick's eyes were wandering, gazing on the scene around him. A concerned look came over him. "I too have a confession to make."

Michele was trying to focus.

He leaned back in his chair and threw both arms wide in the air. "I'm in *love* with Eve!"

"Oooo!" Michele said. "A knife in my heart." She giggled. "A dull knife." Her brow furrowed. "Who's Eve?"

"This," Rick said, feeling the wine, "is a great project. I *love* this project." He clapped his hands once, crushing his cigarette and dodging the falling ashes by spreading his legs apart.

Michele slapped his arm with a wheezy laugh. "Another woman! You didn't even tell me!"

"Couldn't," Rick said and put his index finger to his lips looking at Daniele. "Top Shecret."

"Well," Michele said magnanimously, throwing her arms wide as Rick had, "you can love us all!"

"Crazy cute Crisney Courtson comes calling," Jack was saying to himself.

Rick looked up and down the street. There was no movement. Just the shadows of a sleepy suburban neighborhood in the middle of the night. "Where are we?"

"Thas right. We shouldn't be here at all!" Michele said. "Eve! Back to Par-eeee!"

The scene changed again and they were back at the table in front of the Brasserie, with the exception that the bottles were now covered with butts and ashes and heaped on the sidewalk under the table like the makings of a bonfire.

"This isn't where we need to be," Daniele said angrily. "Eve! Take us to see Delective Croos."

The Detective morphed to his desk, looking at the sketch of Courtney Crimson on his screen. "Just can't find her," he said, shaking his head seriously.

"Stop it!" Michele said, slapping her hand on Cruse's desk with an out of breath laugh. "If we're going anywhere we're gonna find Martin. That's who I need to talk to."

Michele gave the command and they were suddenly in the Galeries Rouquet fashion show.

"Would you *shtop* it!" Daniele said, shabbily angry now. "Eve! Detetive Crooz." She changed her mind. "No! Take us to Oviler Wenell Homes."

Cruse flashed by all misty before Oliver solidified, twisting his handlebar mustache.

Michele threw the empty pack of cigarettes at Daniele. "Eve! Martin!"

The scene changed again, but not to the Galeries Rouquet. Instead they were in deep snow, the landscape barren and white for as far as the eye could see. The wind was blowing fiercely, and the sun was low on the horizon. Jack, Rick and Michele were still sitting in their chairs, the bottles and cups at their feet, while Daniele was standing, a crushed empty cigarette pack in the snow in front of her.

"Where *are* we?" Daniele demanded with a shiver in her voice.

Michele wrapped her hands over her arms. "Rick! Whasappening?"

"Bob?" Rick asked without emotion.

"North Pole," Bob's voice echoed from the crystal blue sky. "And if you don't *shtop* it I'll put you on the South Pole where it's nighttime all the time."

13

Daniele was in the kitchen the next morning, sitting and staring at the clock, nursing some kind of hangover concoction that Martha had cooked up. Michele, who had promptly passed out on the North Pole creating an unintentional snow angel, was still asleep, having been carried there from six eleven Crimson Court by Jack. Rick had remained behind cleaning up the mess they'd made all over Eve – especially the little problem created when Daniele had thrown up on the empty cigarette case. Jack had remarked at the time how interesting it was that it didn't soak into the snow, which had prompted a brief, but serious conversation with Rick about the properties of enhanced silicon when brought into contact with organic matter, which had been abruptly ended by an angry outburst from Daniele about no one noticing her condition, right before Michele fell off her chair. That's when Rick, sobered up enough by Daniele's fury, had finally commanded, "Eve, end program." Bob sure hadn't been inclined to do it.

Jack, having laid Michele fully clothed in her bed, had said goodnight to Daniele, who at the time had been retrieving a seltzer from the kitchen. Daniele had subsequently directed Jack to the guest room to sleep it off.

Daniele was trying to will the frozen hands on the clock to stop moving when Rick walked in.

"Well," Rick said as he walked over and took a seat across from her, "I guess we can safely say that the mission was a failure."

"Bob?" she asked.

"He says he'll monitor another mission as long as we don't bring any 'props,' I think he called them."

"No more props," Daniele said earnestly, burying her head in her hands, her palms pressed against her swollen eyes. "I must look a mess."

Rick agreed with a smile. "You've looked better."

Daniele didn't hold it against him. "The little airhead," she said. "What was she thinking?"

"Seems to me," Rick said in Michele's defense, "that we all kind of had a hand in it."

"Several," Daniele agreed.

They sat in silence for a moment.

"Now what?" Daniele asked forlornly. "We haven't gone a step forward in finding Father."

"Coffee would be a good move right now."

"Oh, I'm sorry." Daniele started to get up.

Rick put his hand on her arm. "Don't bother. Just tell me where everything is and I'll make it."

She gave him directions as they talked.

"I was thinking," Rick said as he measured out the coffee and poured it into the filter. "Maybe we need to go back to that little sidewalk café one more time."

Daniele's hand was pressed against her head. "What ever for?" she whined.

"We weren't paying attention."

"That's an understatement."

"Did you happen to notice any clocks?"

Daniele tried to remember as best she could. "Nope. I missed that one completely."

"Me too," Rick said.

"Well that was pretty dumb," Daniele rebuked herself, "...all of Father's clock clues and everything."

"Sorry," Rick said apologetically. "I should have been looking."

Daniele looked up. "I wasn't taking about *you*," she said, "*I'm* the one who should have thought of it."

"Oh," Rick said kindheartedly over his shoulder. "You can't think of everything. You put too much pressure on yourself."

Daniele saw the kindness in his eyes. "If *I* don't, who *will*?"

"You don't need to do it at *all*," Rick said.

"Like you don't." She rested her chin in her hand. "If it was only that simple. But somebody's got to find Father, game or no game."

"Don't worry," Rick reassured her. "We will."

They were silent while Rick walked back to the table and sat down.

"Do you love her?" she asked out of the blue.

Rick was taken aback. "Of *course*. Yes." And then his eyes were pondering as he stared at her. He pulled himself out of his trance. "Yes, of course," he repeated. "We'll be married one of these days."

Daniele had an unexplained sadness come over her.

Rick was still staring at her, himself deep in thought.

"You don't touch each other much," she said.

"We don't?"

She pressed her lips together and gave him a negative nod.

"Well," he said awkwardly, "we're not...uh...we're...we'll have to work on that." He quickly redirected the inquiry toward her. "So why aren't you in a relationship? I would hope it's not just because of Jim. Is it true that you hate men?"

"Oh, of course not," she swatted the air. "There's just not enough time. Being a prosecutor just takes it all up."

"If you want it to," he said. "But wouldn't you rather have a man around? Someone to take care of you?"

She laughed unhappily. "Men like that don't exist. They usually just want to take advantage of you, or use you."

"Not all men."

"Show me one."

After several moments of the two looking into each other's eyes, Daniele's breathing growing heavier by the second, Rick broke the silence. "We need to go back one more time and check out the clocks."

He walked to the cupboard, retrieving two cups.

Daniele nodded. "Seems reasonable to me."

The swinging door opened and Jack walked in, looking refreshed and cheerful. "Mornin'!" he said enthusiastically.

Daniele moaned, once again burying her head in her hands. "I hate morning people."

"Sorry," Jack said, his expression fading.

"Coffee?" Rick asked.

"Coffee sounds great," Jack said, sitting down next to Daniele. "Feelin' okay?"

She looked at him with half-crossed eyes. "Do I look okay?"

Rick smiled as he pulled another cup from the cabinet.

The door opened slowly and Michele walked in wearing her crumpled clothes from the day before, her face painted in grogginess and her blonde hair matted in dark tangles. Her cell phone was in her hand, as was her usual habit when she wasn't carrying a purse. She was rarely out of touch with the outside world.

Daniele looked at her then turned away. "There's the culprit now."

"Ungh," Michele groaned, shuffled to the table and sat heavily in the chair.

"Mornin' sunshine," Jack said softly.

Michele gave him a wispy smile. "About as sunny as the South Pole on a hard night out."

Jack chuckled.

Rick had taken yet another cup from the cupboard and poured them all. He balanced three and brought them to the table, handing one to Michele first, and then to Daniele and Jack.

Michele grinned. "Thanks."

"A scholar and a gentleman," Jack said, taking the cup in both hands to warm them.

Michele looked at Rick. "Thanks for tucking me in last night," she said. "I don't even remember how I got home."

"Oh," Rick said, a little embarrassed. He headed to retrieve his own cup. "That was Jack."

Michele looked at Jack. "*You* tucked me in?"

A slight smile rippled over Jack's face. "I wouldn't exactly call it 'tucked in,'" he said. "More like poured you under the covers."

Michele let out a little chuckle. "Well, thanks Jack." No emphasis on the "k."

"Any time," Jack said. He looked at his coffee in his hands. "Any time."

It was silent again until Jack broke it. "So is it back to Paris?"

Just then Michele's cell phone played her song. She picked it up and unfolded it. "Hello?"

They all stared at her.

"Oh hi!" she exclaimed with a bright smile. "We were all…"

Whoever was on the other end had apparently interrupted her.

"Okay," she said slowly, glancing with darting eyes at the others.

"Right now?"

They waited.

"All right," she said. "Give me a half hour."

She clicked her phone shut.

"And?" Daniele asked.

Michele got up. "Gotta go to the office. Meeting about the Eiffel Tower show, and they need me." She sighed with a grin. "Just can't seem to get along without me."

"Need me to go?" Rick asked.

"Nope," she said crossing the room. "Just laying out the line up."

Daniele frowned as Michele pushed the swinging door. "Well make it quick," she said after her, "we really need to get back to Eve."

"Just be a few," Michele said lightly as the door swung behind her.

But of course it wasn't. It was, in fact, three hours of discussion about court cases, business development, and Benz clues – all the while nurturing their hangovers with Martha's remedy – before she burst back through the door with a cheerful smile.

"Finally," Daniele said impatiently. "What took you so long?"

"Oh," Michele said lightly. "Lots of details. You know, which gown first, this one or that one. You know how those meetings can get."

"Can't say that I do," Daniele remarked. "Now can we please get back to finding Father? You'd think he wasn't even missing the way you're acting."

"How'm I acting?" Michele asked with a disturbed look.

"Well you don't seem to be too concerned about finding Father."

Michele scowled. "Of course I am."

"Seems to me like your show's more important," Daniele said getting up. "We should have just gone on without you."

"Well I'm here now," Michele said crossly, "so stop going on and on about it and let's go."

They all agreed, and headed, without conversation, back to the Crimson Court house, after Rick had phoned Bob and given him a heads up to man the control room.

When they arrived, Bob acted unhappy about the situation. He did, after all, have work to do. "How'm I supposed to figure out who's putting clocks in my system if I'm holding you guys' hands all the time?"

Daniele and Rick were acquiescent, and worried about abusing

Bob's friendship, while Michele and Jack sensed that Bob was actually intrigued by the whole situation, and seemed to be in high spirits when, with a slight grin, he complained that he, "Had to cancel a meeting with my staff."

Within minutes of their brief conversation about Bob's self-sacrifices they were back in Paris, standing in the middle of the street with the elevator closing behind them like a hole being filled up.

"Michele?" Bob's voice echoed lightheartedly off the virtual buildings.

"Yes?" she replied as they settled back into their empty seats at the end table, rushing out of the busy street, virtual cars passing right through them.

"No supplies?"

"Nooo," Michele said.

Daniele touched her head. "Thank goodness."

"Eight o'clock and twenty seconds," Rick said, which turned everyone's attention to him.

The clock inside the café on the wall in front of the toilet was stopped at eight o'clock and twenty seconds.

"Look down there," Daniele said, pointing down the street.

Michele craned her neck. "What?"

"Oh yeah," Jack said. "There does seem to be a pattern."

A clock stood on what looked like a lamppost, showing the time to all the people walking up and down the street. It was eight o'clock and twenty seconds.

Jack studied the clock and the people walking by, and then looked up into the virtual sky. "Eight o'clock in the morning?"

"No, silly!" Michele snickered. "Eight o'clock at night."

Jack studied the sky again. "Shouldn't it be getting dark right about now?"

Michele let out a real laugh this time. "Paris in July?" she asked. "No way."

Jack was astounded. "Well what time *does* it get dark?"

Michele looked to Daniele for support. "Nine thirty? Ten?"

"There's still a little glow at quarter after," Daniele remarked.

Jack took a hard look around. "Why didn't I ever come to Paris in July before?"

Michele looked at him with mischievous eyes. "Wait till midnight," she said. "That's when the fun starts."

Jack grew a playful smile. "I'd be happy to take lessons." A statement that made Michele giggle and turned Rick's head.

Daniele smirked at Jack with disbelief. "You were *never* like this in front of a judge," she said, then added, "or in the office."

Jack waved his hand expansively, "*This*," he said, "is *not* the office."

"Ah Parie," Michele said, waving her hand in a mimicking motion.

"Ah Parie," Rick said, with a scornful look toward Jack. "Can we *focus* on the clocks?"

"Love that word focus," Michele said with a naughty glance toward Daniele.

Daniele grimaced. "Oh, just keep it up."

Michele sat up excitedly in her chair, her eyes bright. "I have an idea!"

"What?" Jack asked with a grin of anticipation.

"How 'bout showing me our new sponsors?" Michele asked. "I haven't met them yet."

"What for?" Daniele asked.

"Just so I'll know what they look like when I get to Paris for my show."

"What's that got to do with the mission?" Rick asked. "Shouldn't we be looking for Courtney?"

"Com'on," she pleaded. "It'll just take a minute. I'm sure Martin's already met them, hasn't he?"

Rick shrugged. "I don't know."

"Well I don't want to look like I'm completely *out* of it. What if everyone knows them but me? I'll look like an idiot."

"Why change now?" Daniele asked.

Michele curled her lip at her.

Rick looked at Daniele who made a consenting smirk.

"Just don't take too long," Daniele said.

"Eve," Rick said. "Bring us Gunter Hartmann and Marlene Ramsauer."

They waited, and within moments a man and a woman emerged from around the corner. They were ashen faced, their skin almost black. Their eyes were sunken in and their skin dried up like dehydrated prunes.

Jack laughed. "Dead couple walkin'."

The others would have laughed too if the sight wasn't so ghoulish. Michele grimaced. "Eeww…"

Daniele turned around to see them. "'Bout right for your show."

"Hey Bob," Rick called, his forehead wrinkled. "What's this?"

Bob boomed down the lane. "No idea."

"Huh," Rick said. "Not funny, Eve." He looked up at the sky. "Fix your system, Bob! Eve," he commanded. "Take Gunter and Marlene away."

Instantly the two walking corpses disappeared.

"Someone loves their jokes," Rick said with a snort. He leaned back in his chair. "Sorry. System glitch, I guess."

"Sorry I asked," Michele said, her face still contorted. "I guess, um, maybe I *don't* want to meet them."

Jack was still chuckling. "Probably don't have to worry about competition from them."

"I'll have someone check it out," Bob's voice said.

"Okay. Let's recap," Rick said, bringing everyone's attention back to the mission. "You got six eleven and fifty-one seconds from the clock in the kitchen."

"And everywhere else in the house," Daniele added.

Michele sniffed. "Not to mention the fact that you knew about it all along."

"That led you to the Eve Project," Rick continued, ignoring her comment. "I brought you in, which led to more clocks that we can't explain reading eight o'clock and twenty seconds, or twenty hundred and twenty seconds. Because of the time difference, we asked Sherlock which cities in Europe were six hours ahead of local Washington time, to which Eve responded with four cities, the last of which was Paris. Then we came here because Michele wanted to see the Galeries Rouquet."

"I wanted to see *Martin*," she corrected him. "And I still want to." She shuddered. "Just don't bring me the new sponsors again."

Daniele looked at her sternly. "Don't even think of it."

Rick went on. "Then Daniele saw Courtney Crimson, we followed her but lost her, and we were distracted from looking at the clocks, or even thinking about the clocks. So we came back…"

"And got distracted again…" Jack inserted with a sly grin to

Michele.

Rick smiled, "…again…and now we're back *again*, and have learned that the clocks indeed read eight and twenty or twenty and twenty."

"They also form a perfect Benz sign," Daniele observed, "whereas the six eleven and fifty-one seconds was upside-down."

"Right," Rick said. "And if we use the same logic, then the hands on the clock are pointing somewhere."

"Which means," Michele said decidedly, "we need to go back to the Washington Monument."

Daniele swung her eyes at her sister. "What kind of logic is that?"

"Why there?" Jack asked.

Michele looked at him as though it was obvious. "Because that's where Daddy *told* us to go."

"Hmm. It worked last time," Daniele agreed.

"Maybe," Jack said, "we should just go back to your house and use your dad's computer to put twenty twenty on it and see what it points at."

"Well we're here already," Michele pointed out, "in Eve I mean. It'd take two seconds to at least take a look from the monument and see what we can see."

"Sounds reasonable to me," Daniele said.

Rick gave the command and within moments the four of them were looking out the north window of the Washington Monument. They scanned the horizon to the north, the southwest, and the southeast. It was much easier this time after Rick ordered Eve to clear the room of the virtual people milling about.

"So what's out there?" Michele asked.

"The white house to the north," Jack replied.

"Not exactly," Daniele pointed out. "It's off to the left of due north."

"The USDA's to the southeast," Rick said.

"As in USDA choice?" Jack asked flippantly.

Rick turned. "Actually, yes."

"Seems like the Pentagon's over in that direction," Michele said pointing to the southwest.

"But which direction are we supposed to be looking?" Rick asked. "If you're sticking with the second hand, then it's pointing to the

USDA."

Jack asked, "So Leo might be in there?"

"You never know," Rick replied.

"Let's give it a try," Daniele said.

Rick once again gave the command, the others somewhat timid, since the North Pole experience, about telling Eve where to take them.

They were instantly outside the USDA building, gazing at the governmental gray structure. Daniele turned to look up at the Washington Monument but her eyes didn't get that far. "There she is!" she nearly yelled.

They didn't have to ask who. They all turned to see Courtney Crimson, not a hundred feet away, slipping her slender frame into a blue Benz sedan just up the street from them, tossing her crimson hair behind her with a flip of her head as she started the car. They started walking toward her, then running, but before they'd gotten anywhere near close to her, Courtney had whisked past them.

"Eve," Rick demanded, "put us in a car."

"Make it a Benz," Michele added.

A white Benz S500 oozed out of the street, enveloping each of them until they were all in seated positions with the top of the car closing over their heads. The car was pointing in the direction opposite Courtney.

"What?" Michele asked with her hands in the air when she found herself behind the wheel. Jack was sitting next to her in the front seat, with Rick behind Michele next to Daniele. "I don't want to drive!"

"Just put it in gear and go!" Daniele ordered. "She's getting away!"

Courtney's Benz had turned left onto 15th Street Southwest and disappeared out of sight around the USDA building.

Michele did as she was told. Pulling hard on the steering wheel with her foot to the floor she made a screeching U-turn in front of three oncoming cars that barely missed her. One of them veered hard right to avoid Michele's car and ruined someone's implicit day with a fender bender that left horns blaring while Michele pulled a hit and run.

Her foot didn't let up at the corner and the car seemed to lift onto two wheels. She ended the left turn a little too late and was rocketing head-on into another car coming north on 15th before she overcompensated and clipped a parked car to the right, jostling all of them in their seats.

"There she is!" Jack said, pointing ahead.

"I see her!" Michele cried excitedly, panting hard, her heart pounding.

Jack clapped his hands. "Woo hoo! Drive girl!"

Daniele's face was going white. "Maybe you should slow down a little."

An energized smile had grown on Michele's face at Jack's "Woo hoo," and her eyes were getting wide with glee. "I think I can catch her," she said with determination.

Daniele's hand grabbed Rick's instinctively and clutched it hard. "We're in Eve, right?"

Rick's eyes were almost as wide as Daniele's, but he took control of his emotions and answered, "Yes," as calmly as he could.

Michele followed Courtney on another wild left turn that became a gradual, high speed right rounding of the Jefferson Memorial.

"We can't be killed in Eve, can we?" Daniele asked apprehensively.

"I don't think so," Rick said, sounding very much to Daniele like he wasn't sure.

She looked at him, her hand still grasping his. "You don't *think* so?"

He reached his other hand over and held her forearm to give her comfort. "No," he said more evenly. "Of course not."

"She's getting on 395," Jack said, pointing through the windshield.

"I'm on her," Michele said without hesitation, hopping joyfully in her seat.

She gunned it onto the interstate and followed Courtney's Benz onto the bridge that crossed the Potomac. Michele was racing now, weaving in and out of the slower moving traffic and gaining considerably on Courtney. She was hardly six car lengths ahead when Michele screwed up.

A tight bunch of cars separated her from Courtney, so she weaved right around one in the left lane, then left around one in the right lane, but the gap between that car and another on the left lane was too close, forcing her to whip the car hard right to avoid the left lane car. But she hadn't cleared the car she was passing in the right lane before swerving. Her right rear fender clipped the car on the right sending the S500 into a horizontal slide that aimed them straight at the rail. In a flash, with the grinding and screeching of metal as the car's undercarriage skidded over the steel railing, they'd gone airborne and were plunging for the Potomac, the water below rising fast to meet them head-on.

"Aaahhh!" Michele screamed.

No sound came from Jack, but he grabbed onto the door handle on his right, pulled his knees into a crash position, and used his left arm to reach out and hold Michele's chest just under her throat as though he could use his strength to keep her from impacting against the steering wheel.

Daniele's eyes looked like cue balls, and her mouth was wide with a scream that didn't come out. As she saw the water rushing toward her she turned away and grabbed Rick around the neck.

Rick tossed an arm over Daniele's shoulder and calmly said, "Bob?"

The car seemed to make a turn on its own, like an airplane pulling out of a dive, and gained altitude, banking to the left, and then back up over the rail and onto the highway, gliding down and hovering momentarily behind Courtney's car before the wheels touched, even screeching like an airplane landing as they made contact with the concrete. The landing was smooth, without so much as a bounce. And there they were, following just behind Courtney, as though none of the events had even happened.

"Oh my, oh my," Daniele said breathlessly, her head suddenly going limp on Rick's shoulder.

Jack loosened his grip on the handle, brought his left arm down and patted Michele on the thigh while he let his legs down to the floor. "Good driving."

Michele was still in shock, her hands pushing against the steering wheel with her arms almost locked straight in the position she'd gravitated to anticipating the impact. The car started drifting to the left again.

"Michele dear," Jack said quietly, patting her thigh once again.

"Yes?" she managed to respond.

"I think you should start driving again."

Michele abruptly became aware of what she was supposed to be doing and moved the wheel slightly to the right, centering the car in the left lane. The first thing she did was press the brakes a little to keep from hitting Courtney from behind. Then she just stayed there, about a car length behind the blue Benz, following at a reasonable, normal driving pace.

Soon, thankfully, they were over the river. Daniele loosened her grip on Rick and pushed away a little, but not before she looked at his eyes, her face close to his, and whispered, "Thank you." But in her mind was, *Oh...It's been so long...* She nestled up next to him feeling secure.

Rick pulled his arm back from her shoulder and said, "Thank Bob."

Daniele smiled with relief. "Thanks Bob!" she said. Though she eased her grip a little as she settled back into her seat, her left hand still held Rick's left, stretched across his lap. He pulled his right over and held hers with both hands.

Bob's voice seemed to come through the car stereo. "Don't mention it."

"Cars aren't holographic, Bob," Rick stated.

"Noticed that," Bob said.

Rick didn't pull his hand away, but rather turned his palm up and clasped Daniele's lightly, his heart pounding more now than it had been during the near-fatal, or virtually fatal, accident.

The Pentagon glided by lazily on the right as they followed Courtney west on 395.

"She's taking the 27," Jack said.

"Signs give it away?" Michele asked playfully, having regained her composure, with a sign reading "27" on the right.

They followed closely for several miles until Jack said, "Now she's taking 66."

Michele slapped him on his left thigh with a teasing smile. "You do state the obvious, don't you?"

"Just doin' my part," Jack said with an easy smile in return.

They followed up 66 for a while before Jack said, "Should I tell you where I think she's headed?"

"Um...let me guess," Michele said. "The airport?"

"What was your first clue?" Jack asked as they passed a sign saying the Dulles International was so many miles away.

Courtney was indeed headed to the airport, and entered the frontage road that skirted all of the terminals. Weaving through the chaotic traffic, she pulled to the curb in front of Air France.

Courtney didn't bother to get any baggage from the trunk, or even to take the keys. As soon as she'd put it in park she opened the door, got out, and was headed straight into the terminal.

"You think she's meeting someone?" Michele asked as she pulled up behind her and put it in park.

"Um...departures," Jack said, sticking his chin out toward a large sign directly in front of them.

"Ah," Michele said, opening her door. She exited as fast as Courtney had and ran across the sidewalk to the automatic sliding double doors. The others were right behind her.

"There she is," Daniele said pointing. Somehow she had already passed through security and was on the other side of the massive line waiting to be scanned.

"Get us through," Rick said to the room.

A moment later they were also beyond security and walking briskly about fifty feet behind Courtney, her red hair swinging from side to side on her bare white back.

Jack looked over his shoulder. "Getting through security should always be like that."

They followed her onto a crowded custom-made bus used for transporting people to the terminals where the aircraft were parked. The bus was oversized, with doors in front and back rather than on the sides. Courtney was standing at the opposite end with her back to them, staring through the windows in the double doors. Arriving at the terminal they flowed through the other passengers, disembarked the bus, and followed close behind.

Courtney turned right at a gate that was boarding. She ignored the line, somehow seemed to have a ticket appear in her hand, and handed the ticket to the attendant who fed it through the machine and then handed it back.

The four of them followed close behind her and went to the head of the line.

"Tickets?" the attendant asked.

"Get us through," Rick said.

To everyone's surprise Bob replied through the airport's public address system, "I can't."

"What do you mean you can't?" Rick asked, staring at the attendant's empty hand.

"I'm trying," Bob said, but there's some kind of override.

"So someone else *is* in the system," Rick exclaimed with an alarm that went beyond car crashes.

"Seems so," Bob said. "You're just going to have to go with it."

"I'm sorry sir," the attendant said, "you can't board without a ticket."

"Bob, can you get us tickets?" Rick asked.

"I'm trying to put them in the attendant's hand, but it just isn't happening," Bob said. They could actually hear Bob's keyboard clicking through the PA system. As soon as he'd said it the system continued in Bob's voice, "The white zone is for loading and unloading of passengers only. No parking."

"Quit joking around!" Rick said sternly.

"Didn't do that either," Bob's voice came over the PA along with his insistent clicking.

A second attendant behind the counter lifted a microphone and said in her own French-accented voice over the PA, "Last call for Air France Flight 27 non-stop to Paris."

"Then we'll go without tickets," Rick said as he started to walk toward the gate. He immediately ran into an invisible silicon wall. He stepped to the side and tried again but was met with the same barrier. He put his hands up against it looking like a mime in an imaginary glass cubicle.

"Please sir," the attendant taking tickets said. "You're holding up the line."

Rick opened his mouth to argue, but saw the futility of it and stepped away, watching as Courtney Crimson rounded the corner at the end of the jet way. "Eve just isn't going to cooperate," he said. "Someone's infiltrated the system." He stroked his fingers through his hair and stepped away. "At least we know where she's going."

Jack smiled and waved his arm expansively. "Back to Parie!" he said with delight.

14

"Whoa!" Daniele said. "I think I'm ready to sit down for a minute before we go."

They all agreed that a little rest before their next session in Eve would be appropriate. Daniele's nerves were still somewhat frayed from her near death experience. And the others were getting hungry anyway.

"Bob," Rick said, "get us outta here."

The scene morphed away and they took the elevator and spent about an hour in the cafeteria discussing Courtney Crimson and the mystery of twenty twenty over two-day old vending machine croissants and ultra-strong coffee.

They agreed that Leo was obviously leading them to Paris – or someone who had kidnapped Leo. And it was also agreed by all that eight o'clock and twenty seconds was pointing to some physical location there, just as six eleven and fifty-one seconds had directed them to the Crimson Court house. A considerable amount of discussion went into the Eiffel Tower. After all, it was the tallest structure in the heart of Paris, and with Michele's fashion show being on the first floor, it was only logical to all of them that they needed to go to the top and look in the Benz directions on the clock. For eight o'clock and twenty seconds, it would be a true Benz sign pointing due north, southwest, and southeast. But before they went there, it was also agreed that they should go meet Courtney Crimson's flight in Eve.

"She's in here for some reason," Rick observed, stating the obvious.

They dropped Bob off at the controls while Rick led the way to the elevator and out into the busy Air France terminal where Flight 27 was to arrive at the Charles de Gaul airport. They stood in the crowded room outside security watching the arrival monitors, along with dozens of virtual husbands, wives, grandparents, and boyfriends waiting for their virtual loved ones. The monitor showed that Flight 27 had arrived two minutes ago. A minute later a stream of passengers dragging carry-on luggage began to exit the terminal area beyond security where the gates were. Courtney Crimson, empty handed, was in the lead group.

"Must have flown first class," Jack remarked.

"Who wouldn't?" Michele asked.

Jack just smiled and teased, "Spoiled rich girl," which earned him a slap on the arm.

Daniele started toward Courtney, but stopped when she felt Rick's hand on her shoulder.

"Let's just follow her," he said. "She's virtual anyway, and unless someone's programmed her with answers, she won't know where Leo is, or where we need to go to find him."

Daniele acquiesced, taking a step back, her gaze glued on Courtney's green eyes.

Courtney led them out of the terminal and immediately hailed a taxi. The four of them hopped into the next available cab. Several seconds were lost while the white-haired driver explained that there was a surcharge for four people, but Michele jumped in the front passenger seat and told him in French to just drive and don't worry about the surcharge. Daniele was sandwiched between Jack and Rick in the back, with Jack having to slide all the way across behind the elderly Frenchman.

"Follow that taxi," she commanded.

The driver pulled out and kept a safe distance, following Courtney's car onto the A1 motorway toward the heart of Paris. They passed the Parc des Princes stadium with its towering modern arches on the left of the highway as they neared the center of the city. Soon they'd left the highway and followed the cab onto a busy boulevard with the Arc de Triomphe just ahead. They entered the chaotic traffic circle around the monument and emerged on the Avenue Des Champs Elysees heading for the Place de la Concorde.

The Champs Elysees was wider than Jack had imagined. "Look at all the sidewalk cafés," he said, and astounded by the number of people walking the streets, commented, "There must be fifty thousand people here."

"Wouldn't be surprised," Daniele said. "A little too crowded for me."

"She's turning!" Rick said, pulling himself forward by the back of Michele's seat.

Courtney's taxi turned right onto Avenue Montaigne where the elite fashion houses of Paris occupied the historic buildings up and down both sides.

"She's turning on to our street," Michele said impatiently. "Do you suppose she works for some fashion house?"

"She's virtual," Daniele said with a chuckle.

"Someone's leading us there somewhere," Rick said.

"Look at where she's getting out!" Michele said excitedly. "It's *our* store!"

Avenue Montaigne was a fairly wide street, divided into sections. A two-way lane ran down the middle, with tree-lined islands and narrow access roads on either side next to the tall, side-by-side buildings that housed the stores. Courtney's taxi had not used the access road, but rather had stopped right in the lane long enough for Courtney to exit, then sped away.

Courtney walked briskly across the island and the access road, slipped between two cars parked at the curb, and then took the ten steps up to the double wood doors that led into the store. The shiny but modest gold sign next to the door had "Calvet" etched into it in obsidian letters.

"Stop here!" Michele told the driver.

Directly in front of the building, Michele jumped out and started across the island to the driver's heated objections.

Michele turned and called over her shoulder, "Pay the man, Jack."

"How'm I s'possed…" she heard him say, but a car horn, blaring at the double-parked taxi, obscured his words as she hopped hurriedly up the steps.

Michele was already at the door by the time Rick and Daniele were crossing the access road, and had slipped inside with a look behind her to see Jack outside of the car with his palms up arguing with the irate cabbie. "Just keep him occupied," she heard Daniele say, and Jack in the distance saying, "Bob, can't you make him go away?"

The inside of the store seemed to be solid white marble, with marble floors, a marble fountain in the middle of the room, and marble walls surrounded by glass display cases that stretched from the floor to the ceiling. There were remarkably few items on display, as is the case for all stores where one should not go if price is a consideration.

Daniele and Rick entered just in time to hear Michele speaking rapidly in French.

"What's she saying?" Rick asked.

"She's asking where the woman who just came in went," Daniele explained.

Michele was talking to a strikingly beautiful young woman who Michele seemed to think should know her, but apparently didn't. She did, however, disappear through a door into a back room saying she would go get Courtney.

Within moments, Courtney Crimson emerged smiling and in English asking, "How may I help you?"

"You work here?" Michele asked.

"Yes," Courtney replied, her green eyes sparkling. "What might you be looking for today?"

"How come I don't know you?" Michele asked. "I know *everyone* who works here."

Courtney had a slightly dumbfounded look, but kept her professional deportment.

"Someone planted her here," Daniele said. "This isn't Father's *real* store. Try to remember."

Michele didn't respond, but continued with her inquiry. "Who are you?"

"Courtney Crimson," Courtney said, and extended her hand with a smile. "It is a pleasure to meet you."

Michele tried to take her hand out of instinct but it passed through.

"I would be happy to show you our latest collection," Courtney said, extending her arm elegantly to the displays. "What were you looking for today?"

Michele perused the room. "I'd like to see what you have in back."

Courtney's smile broadened. "Are you with a distributor?"

"Um…yes," Michele said. "I'm, um, looking for the fall fashions. Not something you have on display."

"Ah yes," Courtney said. "Please, follow me."

She led them through a door and into a room lined with outfits.

"Oh," Michele said as she examined a rack of clothes. "Are we...I mean you...still selling those? They're so last season."

Courtney looked impressed. "Some clients ask for them," she said, "so we will accommodate them as long as we have stock."

Looking across the room Michele recognized many of the designs as her own that she'd created for the Benz product line. "I'm interested in the Benz line."

Courtney looked surprised. "You know the Benz line?"

"Yes," Michele answered. "I'm familiar with it."

"Did you attend the show at the Galeries Rouquet?" Courtney asked, her green eyes looking completely real to Michele. "I believe the line was very secret until that point. Even the Benz people did not reveal it."

"I'm afraid I missed it," Michele replied with a sigh. "I did catch the end of it though...sort of."

"A marvelous production," Courtney said, and then leaned over conspiratorially. "They say Martin Jackson will be the new Dominique Lamour."

Michele snickered at Martin being compared to the famous fashion show organizer. "So I've heard."

"Will you be attending the Eiffel Tower show?" Courtney asked as she led them to the Benz collection and began pointing them out. "These are some of the designs that will be featured."

"I certainly hope I'll be there," Michele said ardently. "I'm very anxious to see how the models look in these designs." Michele had obviously fallen back into her passion, and was explaining to Courtney the genesis of the ideas for each of the garments, with Courtney expressing her amazement at how Michele knew so much about fashion and the inspiration behind it.

"Where are we going with this?" Daniele asked after Michele had begun explaining another dress. "Courtney?" she asked, interrupting the two women.

"Mademoiselle?" Courtney asked politely.

"Where's Leo Calvet?"

"Oh, I do not know," Courtney replied.

"You know who he is, don't you?"

"Oh yes yes," Courtney said smiling. "He is the owner of Calvet Fashions." She opened her arms wide. "He owns this store." Daniele was taken aback at how her emotion seemed so real when Courtney's eyes lit up as she added, "He is a very great man."

"He sure is," Michele agreed.

"We're looking for him," Daniele went on. "And we followed you here because you were across the street from the Washington Monument. We also saw you in the Galeries Rouquet. What were you doing there?"

Courtney looked pleasantly at her. "A little of this, a little of that."

Daniele grimaced. "Like pulling teeth."

"But she's here for a reason," Rick said.

"What is it?" Michele asked, as though Rick knew.

"I have no idea," Rick answered. "But we were led here."

Daniele turned back to Courtney who'd been listening patiently with a lovely smile. "Do you know who we are?"

"You are shoppers," Courtney answered, "looking for the fall fashions. And as you see Calvet has some beautiful…"

"We're Leo Calvet's daughters," Daniele interrupted. "And we need to find him."

Courtney's eyes lit up. "You are Michele?" she asked.

"Daniele," Daniele said.

"I'm Michele," Michele said with a smile.

"Ah yes, the twins," Courtney said. "Though we only know Michele. Some of my co-workers have actually met you."

"Yes, I know," Michele said affably.

"You might try his downtown office," Courtney suggested, "but I would think that he is in New York or Washington. The Eiffel Tower show is not for another two days, not until Saturday, and I believe he only comes to the shows, not to visit the stores."

Just then a side door opened from an adjoining room and the young woman who Michele had spoken to earlier appeared and said in English, "Paris Hilton is here for your eight o'clock."

Rick instinctively looked at the clock on the wall. Eight o'clock and twenty seconds. The second hand wasn't moving. He nudged Daniele who looked and nodded.

"I am sorry," Courtney said graciously, "but I will have to leave you now."

Rick had an idea. "I'd like to meet Paris Hilton," he said, and turning to Daniele added, "Wouldn't you?"

"I certainly *would*," Daniele said pleasantly, straying toward Courtney.

"Oh, I am sorry," Courtney said, making her way to the door, "but Ms. Hilton always wants to meet in private."

Courtney was halfway through the doorway when she stopped abruptly and turned. "Remember what your father said?"

Daniele lurched to a stop. "Yes? What about what Father said?"

"Follow the big hand this time," Courtney said, and turning to Michele added, "and keep doing what he told you to do."

Michele's eyebrows went up. "What did he tell me to do?"

But Courtney had disappeared through the door.

Daniele and Rick rushed to follow, Michele still standing and pondering. Daniele reached the door first and opened it.

"Oh!" she exclaimed, as she almost collided with the marble wall that had filled the opening beyond the door.

15

They were so abruptly dead-ended, what with the doorway that Courtney Crimson had just gone through turning into a marble wall, that they wandered aimlessly and wordlessly through the store and out to Avenue Montaigne where they found Jack, surrounded by two police cars with red lights flashing, four French policemen all seeming to be talking at once, and the agitated driver vehemently demanding his payment. The pockets of Jack's jeans were turned inside out, and his palms were still up in the position they'd been in when the others had left him. The policemen were trying to grab him, but Jack was amusing himself by jumping through them, all the while with a playful grin on his face calling, "Bob!"

When a policeman looked in the direction of the Calvet front door, Jack followed his gaze and saw his compatriots.

"Hey!" he yelled with a laugh. "Would someone *please* get me out of this?"

"Eve," Rick said calmly, stopping on the steps, "take us to the third floor of the Eiffel Tower."

The policemen and cars morphed away, along with Avenue Montaigne and the elite shopping district. The last of the scene to fade was the voice of the angry old driver still shouting in Jack's ear. A moment later they were standing on the top floor of the Eiffel, outside on the platform that skirts the re-creation of the Gustave Eiffel office, with Paris spread magnificently below them in all directions.

Jack took a deep breath. "Whew," he said. "I gotta get me one of these. Would've kept me out of that night in jail."

Daniele's eyebrows shot up. "You were in *jail?*"

"DUI," Jack said. "Years ago. Don't tell okay?"

Daniele mocked Jack's lip zipper. "Lips are sealed."

"How come you just didn't tell Eve to take you somewhere else?" Michele asked.

"Thought of it," Jack replied, "but it seemed to me like it'd take you with me, and I knew you were talking to Courtney Crimson." He paused. "You *did* talk to her, didn't you?"

"Yeah," Michele answered. "She didn't say much."

"No clues?" Jack asked.

"Nothing new, really," Michele replied. "Just the same sort of thing Daddy told us at the party before he left." She looked perplexed. "But I wonder what she meant about listening to Daddy."

The small historical office was behind Jack, scattered with late nineteenth century antiques, plans for the tower laid out on a table, and a wax display of Gustave Eiffel. Jack turned around and looked through the window. "Hey, cool!" he said excitedly. "Look at this! Isn't that Thomas Edison? Who's he talking to?"

"Gustave," Daniele said, walking past him. She patted his shoulder. "Take it easy Jack, they're not real."

Daniele rounded the platform to the southwest and was scanning the city below. Rick followed and came up behind her. She sensed him over her shoulder. "He's out there somewhere," she said, staring off over the rooftops into the distance.

"Somewhere," Rick echoed. He had an impulse to put his hands on her shoulders, but resisted.

"So how do we know where?" she asked.

Jack and Michele were completely preoccupied with the wrong direction, leaning on the rail opposite Rick and Daniele and pointing out the various landmarks. The Arc de Triomphe, the Champs Elysees, the Louvre. Jack became enthralled when Michele turned dreamy and described in glorious detail the beauty of the city at night from a boat on the Seine. In a wispy voice, her hair wafting feather-like in the breeze, she said, "Maybe I should hang out here more often."

"I've never even been here in reality," Jack said taking quick glances at Michele while acting like he was exploring the city. "I think I know where my next vacation will be. I *love* the virtual Paris."

"Oh, you'll love the real one even more," Michele said. "I'd love to show you some time." She realized what she'd said and awkwardly added, "Maybe you and Daniele can take a trip with me and Rick." She pondered further, brushing her hair behind her ear, flashing her ring at him. "After the wedding of course."

"Of course," Jack said with forced seriousness.

Daniele and Rick came up behind them. "We've decided we need to come here."

"*We've* decided?" Michele asked, turning sharply to look at Rick.

"Not again…" Jack said.

Daniele was aggravated. "I thought we were over that. Anyway, we have the clues." She pointed to the southwest. "He's somewhere over there, but not in Eve. If we're really going to find him we need to go to Paris and search there."

"That's where all the clues are leading," Rick said agreeably. "Leo's definitely not *in* Eve."

"What do you think?" Daniele asked Jack.

Jack beamed, nodding with each phrase. "I think you're right. Absolutely. Definitely. Count me in."

"Should we take that as a yes?" Michele giggled. "Guess you'll get that Paris trip sooner than you thought."

Rick looked up at a cotton-ball cloud drifting lazily in the virtual Parisian sky. "Show us the exit, Bob."

Bob was more than happy to, remarking that maybe he could salvage some much needed work out of the rest of the day. The fact that someone was in *his* system seemed to be gnawing at him.

Once out of the chamber, they all decided that they should wait until about five o'clock to fly, since the seven hour flight would get them there at about six the next morning with the time difference, and they could get a whole day in.

They went to their various homes to pack and met back at Leo's house. Michele ordered the flight, and had them driven in Leo's stretch black Benz limo to Dulles International where one of Leo's, or rather Calvet's, jets was parked. The company actually had a fleet of four, but this was the other large one, the same type as the one Leo had flown in to Paris. It was in fact the same Gulfstream that Michele had used for her quick trip to the Galeries Rouquet fashion show.

Jack was enthralled with the experience. The sleek, ivory white aircraft – looking like a winged missile with six oval windows in perfect symmetry along the side, twin engines mounted above the fuselage just under the tail wing, and vertical wingtips that helped stabilize the aircraft in flight – somehow gave him the impression that it was moving while sitting stationary on the tarmac. The gray-capped chauffer with a matching gray uniform proceeded in measured rigid movements to open the door for them, holding a hand to each of the girls as they exited the vehicle. Jack was amused that neither of the girls gave the driver even a passing glance in appreciation for his efforts, completely comfortable with his role – and theirs. Jack was not so snobbish, thanking the man profusely for his courtesy.

They hopped on board and were soon relaxed in mid-cabin, settling in to four dark gray leather seats at a small round drink table. Farther back were four more identical chairs at a rectangular club table made of a high-gloss Australian mahogany veneer where they would assemble for the in-flight meal. They each accepted the first glass of Champaign offered to them by the lone attractive young flight attendant, dressed in a playful orange and white short-skirted outfit designed by Michele, complete with the round cupped hat of the classic airline days. A mahogany credenza that converted into four bunks was built-in along the curved skin of the aircraft. Michele instructed the flight attendant to remove the cushions and prepare the cots so they could get some sleep after they'd dined on chicken, steak and lobster.

"I could definitely get into this," Jack said, taking the window seat facing forward next to Daniele and sinking back into the comfortable cushioned seat with padded armrests, checking out the surroundings. The cabin had all the amenities, including thirteen-inch DVD players mounted at each chair, and a ten speaker stereo system on the bulkhead next to the lavatory with a remote that was somewhere astray in the cabin.

When they were a quarter of the way across the Atlantic, while the flight attendant was in the galley preparing their meals, Rick, Michele and Daniele got up at the same time to use the lavatory, chuckling about the coincidence. Rick insisted that Michele go first, which left him standing there with Daniele, the constant muffled roar of the engines dampening their voices.

"What a wild ride, huh?" Daniele said.

Rick, leaning on a bulkhead with his arms crossed, was taken aback.

"Seems pretty smooth so far."

Daniele laughed. "Not the flight," she said. "All this looking for Father, and Eve…" she pointed her thumb at him, "and you."

"Me?"

An amused look came over her. "You're not exactly who I thought you were."

"I'm not?"

Daniele actually giggled, something uncharacteristic for her. "I just took you for another airhead that my father hired." She looked away a little. "I'm not exactly into the fashion business, you know."

"Not everyone in the fashion business is an airhead."

Daniele pointed with her chin at the lavatory door. "Some are." She instantly felt remorse. "I'm sorry, I know you must love her…for whatever reason. I just don't get that world."

Rick shrugged. "It's like any other."

"Like the CIA?" she asked.

Rick took an uneasy look around, but they were out of earshot of the flight attendant.

Daniele noticed and made a quick apology. "I'm sorry," she said, peering around as Rick had. "Should I keep my mouth shut about that?"

"It's all right," he said. "The flight attendant can't hear us here." He looked to be pondering before going on. "It actually *is* like the CIA. You find when you work in two completely different worlds like I do that people are pretty much the same no matter what they do."

"I'm sure the CIA's more serious," she said. "At least you're doing something meaningful there."

"Fashion is meaningful," Rick said defensively. "After all, someone has to make the clothes."

"Yeah," she agreed, "but they don't have to be so expensive. *Everyone* can't buy those kinds of clothes."

"But everyone *does*," Rick argued. "High fashion determines how your jeans are gonna look next year."

Daniele nodded. "I suppose you're right," she said, and then looked back into his eyes. She hesitated for a moment and almost didn't say it, but went ahead. "And I can certainly see why Michele is attracted to you."

Rick lowered his head bashfully and grinned. "I would hope there's more than fashion."

"Oh, there's so much more," she said without thinking, wrapping a strand of her hair around her index finger, playing with it as it hung loosely across her shoulders lacking the pins that usually kept it wrapped tightly to her head.

Rick smiled.

"But how is Michele attractive to you?" Daniele asked. "You two are so different."

"Oh," he said, "that's easy. I love her eyes, and she has such an infectious smile. Lights up a room, ya know? And she loves her work. It's really great that we get to work together. Really good cover too." He thought it sounded like he was using her and tried to correct it. "But…uh…you know…that's just a little side benefit. She's just a lovely woman."

Daniele was nodding. "But everything you just said was about what she *looks* like and what she *does*. I'm curious about what attracts you to *her*, you know, to her personality."

"Well," Rick said, thinking, "she's got a great personality. She's wonderful. Bubbly and light. Sometimes she's a little too frivolous, but you get used to it."

"Do you?" she asked.

"Oh yeah," he said. "That's not a problem. We just get along great." He was nodding his head briskly. "Really great. She's the most beautiful woman I know."

Daniele was smiling, though Rick didn't know why. "I would have thought you'd like a more serious woman."

Rick nodded in agreement. "I like serious women. Take you for instance. You're very down to earth, logical, good head on your shoulders. Sometimes it's like it's easier to talk to you than to Michele, but that's just because you and I think so much more alike."

"You think so?"

"Yeah," he said. "You'd be a lot of fun, I think."

"Fun in what way?"

"We're both serious about what we do," Rick explained. "And you're easy to talk to. I think we understand each other. Sometimes Michele just doesn't take anything seriously, so it's a little aggravating."

"Sometimes?"

Rick chuckled. "Well, almost never, I guess," but was quick to add, "She certainly takes her fashion seriously."

"She does that," she agreed.

"Sometimes I wish that she could be a little more serious. I've tried to become lighter, you know, like she is, but I guess I am who I am."

"I know what you mean," Daniele said.

"Kind of hard to picture her with kids," Rick added. "She's definitely not there yet."

"You want them?"

"Absolutely," Rick said with a smile.

"I guess I do too," Daniele said sadly, "but I'd want to settle down with a pretty good guy first, and as far as I can tell, they don't exist."

"You mentioned that," Rick said.

"I did?"

"In Eve, remember?"

"Oh, right…"

He laughed. "If we can remember any of that episode."

She sighed. "I don't think I'll forget it any time soon."

Wrinkles appeared on Rick's forehead. "Not all guys are rotten, you know."

"Oh!" she put her fingers to her mouth and smiled, touching his forearm with her other hand. "I didn't mean *you*, of course. I think you're a *great* guy."

"Really?" the lines faded from his face, replaced by a shy grin.

Just then the lavatory door opened, and Michele emerged, giving them a "gotcha" look. "Can't keep your hands off 'im, huh?"

Daniele smirked, slipped by her and latched the door while Michele went back and sat across from Jack, leaving Rick standing there without a word.

"This is a great jet," Jack said as she sat down.

"I like traveling in Eve better," Michele said, taking a sip of Champaign.

"It's definitely faster," Jack noted. "But I like the hassle of a plane ride."

"You do?" she asked with a smile that made her nose and eyes crinkle.

"Yeah, always have. It's a break from the ordinary." He smiled. "The airport, the people, getting off in a new place. Of course I'm not a rich jet setter like you, so I don't travel all that often. You're probably tired of it."

"It does take a lot of time," she agreed. "And these seats are so uncomfortable."

Jack couldn't help but chuckle. "You've never ridden in coach in your life, have you?"

"No," Michele said, and asked naively, "Is it different?"

Jack burst into a flabbergasted laugh, leaning forward onto the cushioned arms.

"What?" Michele asked innocently, a broad grin coming across her face. "Is that funny?"

Jack nodded. "Yeah, it's funny. Let's see. How do I describe coach? It's like sitting in a cardboard box. A lot like when you're sitting in front of a judge at the defense table and it's the prosecutor's turn. It's definitely different." He leaned back in his chair and spread his arms. "This feels free."

Michele considered that for a moment, and then changed the subject. "You know, you don't seem the type to be one of those lawyer kind of guys."

"No?"

"I know lawyers," Michele said, "and they don't act like you. You actually have a sense of humor."

"You think?"

"Yeah. Most of the lawyers I know are like, you know, totally boring. Always business business business."

"Pretty much," Jack reflected. "Most of the time it really is just serious business."

"I hate that," Michele said.

"Me too," Jack agreed.

She smiled. "So why are you a lawyer?"

Jack contemplated the question. "Just got into it," he said. "Seemed like a good thing to do in college. And then once you get there, there's bills to pay and cases to try. Kind of hard to change horses in the middle of the stream."

Michele looked pensive. "That's so sad," she said. "I'd hate to be stuck like that."

"You learn to get by," he said. "It's not so bad. I get to work with Daniele, so that's a good thing."

"You really like her?"

Jack nodded. "Yeah. It'd be nice if she was more like you, though."

Michele's face lit up. "Really? Why?" She stretched her left thumb under her middle finger and started playing unconsciously with her ring.

Jack studied the back of his hand. "She's really beautiful, ya know, but she's so solemn all the time. Never really lets up."

"I know," Michele said, sad again.

"And you're so lively," Jack said with a grin. "If I could just get your personality into her, that'd be fun."

"It would?" Michele beamed, and without her knowing it, she cupped her left hand under her right, leaning forward with her elbows on the armrests.

"Absolutely," Jack said. "Of course she doesn't give me the time of day anyway. I was actually shocked that she agreed to go out with me, if you can call it that."

"Yeah, what happened there?" she asked. "Seems like she was the one who asked *you* to the party."

"Sort of, I guess…yeah," he admitted. "As far as I can tell, no one can get close to her. I guess she just hates men."

"Oh, I don't think she hates them," she said. "I think she's just mad at them. Avoiding them. I guess I know why now." Feeling guilty, her gaze drifted out the window to the Atlantic far below. "She's afraid. Cautious." She shook her head.

"Good ol' Jim," Jack growled. "Sounds like he nearly raped her."

"I guess so." Her mouth opened a little as she stared down at the ocean. She almost looked as though she would tear up. "Come to think of it, she hasn't had a long term relationship since then."

"Well I've been asking her out for two years now, and every time I do she always says no. Kind of an office joke lately. So when I asked her out this last time and she said okay I was really floored. But then it turned out she just wanted me to go with her to your party."

"I wonder why?" she leaned farther, bending down at the waist toward Jack with her elbows on her knees looking genuinely puzzled. With a grin she looked up at him and said, "You're goin' wobbly on me, Jack."

"Wobbly?" Jack asked.

"Yeah, that wobbly brain thing."

"You know about that?"

"Daniele told me. Sorry about your ex." She made a sympathetic grimace. "So why'd you get all wobbly?"

"Oh," Jack waved his hand, "'Cause of what you said."

Michele looked perplexed. "About the wobbly thing?"

Jack chuckled. "Nope. 'Cause you wondered why Daniele brought me to the party. Seems pretty obvious to me."

"Oh right. Why?"

"I think she just didn't want to go empty handed."

"Empty handed?"

"You know, like she was alone."

"Oh, of course," Michele said like a light coming on, understanding completely.

"I was just an easy way for her to not go alone. Has to do with the competition between the two of you, I would suspect."

"There's no competition, silly," she said, and slapped his knee.

He smiled at her touch. "Of course there is! But I'm still surprised she did it. Seems like her reputation will suffer after this. I'm sure everyone's going to give her a hard time, and they'll all want to know if we slept together."

"Did you Jack?"

He chuckled. "I think I've gotta get the time of day first."

Michele laughed. "I sure like the way you say things. Makes me laugh."

"Can't help it," he said. "It's just the way I am."

"Well," Michele said with another pat on Jack's knee that lingered for a moment. "I like the way you are."

Daniele came up just then and stood hovering, looking from Michele's hand to Jack's face. "Getting better acquainted?"

Michele pulled her hand away and turned around. "Always the snide remarks."

"You always give me good reason," Daniele retorted.

She took her seat next to Jack and the three sipped Champaign wordlessly until Rick returned and they settled into an amicable planning conference about what to do in Paris. It began getting dark after dinner was served, so they slipped to the bunks for some sleep. No telling when they'd have an opportunity to rest once they landed.

16

The sun had come up somewhere over the UK an hour or so before pulling up to the terminal at Charles de Gaul. By seven thirty a Calvet limo had picked them up and driven them to Leo's chateau on the outskirts of Paris. The servants had hustled their bags to their rooms and set Rick and Jack up in two guest rooms. They all had a chance to shower and change before setting off in Michele's car, which was really Leo's car – a white Benz E350.

One thing Jack had made sure of before they'd left the airport was that everyone's pockets were well-lined with euros. Virtual cops were bad enough. He didn't want to get stuck holding a real bill without any cash. The odds of Bill Gates showing up here to bail him out were pretty slim. Daniele's main pre-occupation had been to make sure to bring a map of the city. Leo had half a dozen in his office at the chateau, one of which she'd wedged into her purse.

They took the winding roads into Paris to the riverfront road that led past Notre Dame and the Louvre, making a beeline for the Eiffel Tower. They agreed that it was a good thing they'd gotten here before noon, since the lines would be long, and the only way to the top of the Eiffel was the elevator – or taking the steps, which Jack actually suggested to a chorus of objections.

"There's too many of them," Michele said with a pained expression. "Besides, you can't go to the top up the stairs anyway. Gotta use an elevator from the second floor."

"Ah," Jack said.

Just after they'd passed the Louvre, Jack unwittingly changed their plans.

"Hey!" he said excitedly. "There's the Eiffel Tower!"

"Right where they left it," Daniele remarked.

Jack ignored her. "Look at that," he said, pointing off to the right. "Looks like a little Washington Monument."

Michele saw it instantly, let out a gasp, slammed on the brakes, and pulled over to the side with the horn in the car behind her blaring, the driver cursing at her in colorful French.

"That's it!" Daniele cried out jubilantly.

"What's it?" Rick asked, craning his neck to see.

"Do what Daddy told me," Michele said, finally understanding. She pulled sharply on the wheel to round the corner into a crowded parking lot, and took a spot that had just opened up.

Rick looked bewildered. "What did Daddy…your dad…tell you to do?"

"He told both of us," Daniele answered.

"He told us to go to the Washington Monument," Michele said.

"That's not the Washington Monument," Rick observed.

Jack almost laughed but held it. "Pretty good reproduction. Small, but identical. 'Cept for all the calligraphy."

Michele and Daniele were getting out.

"It's not a reproduction," Daniele said, speaking to Jack across the car door as she slammed it. "In fact it pre-dates the Washington Monument by several thousand years."

"It's been here for several thousand years?" Jack asked astounded.

Daniele would have been amused except that her attention was completely focused on the obelisk. "No," she replied. "It was a gift from Egypt."

"That would explain the hieroglyphics," Jack said, swinging the door with the solid thump of a Benz closing, and stepping lively.

"Well what is it?" Rick asked walking briskly to keep up with her.

"It's called the Obélisque de Luxor," Daniele replied. "This's the Place de la Concorde."

Rick gawked at it. "I'm assuming there's something special about it."

They were crossing the wide boulevard now, heading toward the obelisk. The open-air square, the largest public square in Paris, was in the shape of an octagon and covered with blacktop and cement. Statues sat at each corner of the octagon, with the obelisk standing directly in the center of the square.

"Well it's a fascinating place," Daniele went on, slightly breathless from her brisk pace. "They put the obelisk right on the spot where they had the guillotine."

That got Jack's attention and he took a harder look at the monument. "Maric Antoinette?"

"Among a thousand or two others," Daniele replied.

"Does look like the Washington Monument," Jack agreed, and then added with a grin, "Love those phallic symbols."

"What's a phallic symbol?" Michele asked, also taking short trotting steps across the wide boulevard, looking repeatedly from the obelisk to her left watching for reckless cars rounding the square.

Daniele snickered. "How is it you just don't seem to know anything?"

Rick was serious. "It's a large symbol of a penis."

"Oh!" Michele said and giggled.

"I'm sure you know what those are," Daniele remarked stepping up the curb.

"Well," Michele said slyly, "I've never actually seen one, but..."

"I could help you out in that department," Jack offered with a mischievous grin.

Daniele was not amused and turned briefly to Jack, freezing momentarily on the square. "Never met a man whose mind was so obviously hanging between his thighs."

This elicited a shocked, "Hah!" from Michele, who looked at Jack and giggled again.

Jack shrugged.

Reaching the base of the monument, Daniele took the map from her purse and laid it down on the cement. Unfolding it, she motioned for Rick and Jack to kneel down with her and hold the edges. Studying the map briefly she found the obelisk, and then scanned the map for the legend. "Yeah," she said, and pointed at the obelisk, adjusting the paper. "That's definitely north." She looked over her shoulder to the southwest. "Now I need a watch or something that looks like a Benz sign." She looked around. "Um," she said, drumming her fingertips on her thigh. "Michele, give me your keys."

They were still in Michele's hand. "What for?" She asked, handing over the jingling mass.

Daniele took them and fumbled. "There should be...here it is."

On the chain was a small metal Benz medallion that had come with the key chain. She unhooked it from the chain and laid it on the map over the obelisk. Adjusting it so that the twelve o'clock Benz leg was pointing due north, she traced the southwest line with her finger, mumbling, "Follow the big hand."

"Follow the big hand?" Jack asked.

"Oh yeah," Michele said, "You didn't talk to Courtney. She told Daniele to follow the big hand this time."

Jack nodded with understanding. "And she told you to do what Daddy told you."

"Right," Michele said. "So here we are at the Washington Monument of Paris."

"Got it," Jack said.

Rick scratched his head. "Someone's certainly leading us somewhere."

"We need something straight," Daniele said, "and a pen or a pencil."

Michele dug around in her purse and found a pen, but no one could find anything straight that she could stretch out over the map. Daniele looked around and zeroed in on something.

"Take your belt off, Rick," she said.

He complied, looking around the square self-consciously as he unbuckled it, pulled it out, and handed it to her. She stretched one edge through the middle of the Benz sign and off the map. "Help me hold it," she said, adjusting it to go directly through eight o'clock as best she could, making sure the map was lined up due north.

"Huh," Jack said. "So it doesn't point to the Eiffel Tower."

Michele leaned over. "Pretty close."

"But not exactly," Daniele remarked, then slowly traced along the edge of the belt with the pen. "Remember, the line went right through the Crimson Court house. If it's the same way here, we should be looking on this line."

"But looking for what?" Rick asked.

"We'll know it when we see it," Daniele said looking over her shoulder in the direction of the line.

Daniele struggled to her feet and folded the map in such a way that they could follow segments of the line through town. Rick put his belt on while Michele clipped her Benz medallion back on the key chain and stuffed her keys and pen in her purse.

"So?" Jack asked, looking in the southwest direction toward the Eiffel Tower. "Walk or drive?"

Daniele followed Jack's gaze across the Seine to the Eiffel. "Let's drive it first," she answered, "and if we don't find anything we'll try walking it."

That sounded reasonable to all of them, so they hurried across the traffic circle and hopped back in the car. Michele drove them off, circling the square and making her way across the nearest bridge over the Seine. The bridge wasn't on the line, so once across she immediately back-tracked along the river and turned right onto a small Parisian lane lined with picturesque shops and cafés.

"So what do we look for?" Jack asked, perusing the street.

"How 'bout something with a clock stopped at eight o'clock and twenty seconds?" Daniele suggested.

"Or a Benz sign," Michele added helpfully.

They zigzagged through the area, keeping to the line as best they could. Nothing seemed to catch their attention. After fifteen minutes of driving slowly, often with horn-honking irritated drivers behind her, she was nearing the end of Rue de General Camou, skirting Daniele's line just to the north.

"We're going to run into the Champs de Mars," Daniele noted.

"Yep," Michele agreed. "There it is."

"What's the Champs de Mars?" Jack asked.

"Big Eiffel Tower park," Daniele said without further explanation.

"It's *huge!*" Jack said amazed, leaning over to gaze out his window up at the tower. "I didn't know it was that tall."

"Three hundred meters," Rick observed.

"Pretty tall," Daniele said as though to a child who kept interrupting. "Just don't say, 'Are we there yet?'"

"Hey, it's my first time," Jack said lamely, sinking back into his seat. He tried to shut up, keeping his astonishments to himself.

Looking at the map she gave directions. "Let's take the Avenue de la Bourdonnais around the Eiffel and come back to the line on Avenue de Suffren."

Michele drove to the next intersection. "This it?"

"Yep," Daniele said.

"Just tell me which way to go."

"Go right here," Daniele said, directing her to the busy street between the tower and the Seine, and then left toward the intersection directly in front of the tower.

Jack just couldn't help himself. "Look at those crowds!"

"It *is* the Eiffel Tower, Jack," Daniele said.

"You know they built it for the 1889 World's Fair?" Rick asked.

Daniele looked over her shoulder at him. "Got any more useful information?"

Rick didn't realize she was being sarcastic. "Well, like I said, it's three hundred meters high, and I've heard they get more than two million visitors a year."

"Rick!" Daniele laughed.

He finally understood and chuckled. Just to spite her he added, "Weighs ten thousand tons."

She just looked at him and curled her lip.

"Five hundred employees…their own police station…"

Jack had his head half-hanging out the window like a dog as they passed through the intersection in front of the tower. The Seine was on his right, with a broad stairway that led down to the river. A kiosk jammed with tourists was next to the stairway, with dozens of people milling about, checking out relatively cheap Parisian souvenirs. The intersection itself was packed with cars and trucks and motorcycles driven by business people and sightseers, stopped at the light waiting their turns while one string of traffic flowed through. At the end of the intersection was a bridge that led to Trocadero, a large amphitheatre-like museum that caught Jack's eye in the distance, with small groups of pedestrians traipsing up and down the wide graded walkway that led to the museum or the tower, depending upon the direction they were traveling. To his left was the tower, set back a hundred meters or so from the road, swarming with tourists carrying bags and backpacks, and scattered French soldiers in berets toting automatic firearms. Craning his head from side-to-side, he just couldn't capture it all.

Once beyond the crowds and the tower, with Jack turning to look through the rear window, Daniele told Michele to make a left onto

Avenue de Suffren.

"Okay," Michele said, "how far are we from the line?"

Daniele looked briefly at the map. "Just up ahead."

"There's the Paris Hilton," Jack said, turning forward again and watching through the front windshield, just as Michele and Daniele saw it.

Daniele's heart fluttered. "We're here."

"Gotta be," Michele said.

"Huh?" Jack said. "Didn't even know that was a clue."

Rick was confused again. "What was a clue?"

Daniele looked at him with an amused grin and turned to Jack. "Courtney Crimson got called away because she had an eight o'clock appointment with Paris Hilton."

"Ah," Jack said. "I guess I pretty much missed everything."

"A few things happened when we were talking to Courtney," Daniele conceded.

Jack took a stiff, excited drag of air and blew it out. "So *this* is where we're being led."

Daniele surveyed the building. "Looks like it."

"So what do we do now?" Michele asked.

"Find a place to park and we'll go in. I have an idea."

The Hilton Paris stood ten stories above the narrow street, with rows of balconies from which, if you looked to the right, you could see the Eiffel Tower. The architecture was modern, making the hotel stand out even more among the much older provincial seventeenth century Parisian architecture – reminiscent of the Louis the Fourteenth era – of the six and seven story buildings that lined the streets around it. Michele found a spot right in front and backed the Benz in. They all piled out and stepped across the narrow street to the sidewalk in front of the hotel.

"So what's the plan?" Rick asked as they stepped past the doormen in their pressed uniforms, up the wide steps to the entrance, and into the massive glass gold-trimmed revolving door.

"Go see Father," Daniele said, as though she knew he was inside.

Jack stuck his hand out to push the door, but it spun slowly away in front of him, finding that the door was in perpetual motion. There was plenty of room for two people pulling suitcases behind them, but Jack's hesitation at the door made them cram in.

"Hurry, hurry," Michele said frantically taking short shuffling steps as the door came up behind her.

Jack emerged first into the large foyer with the black marble topped reception desk to the right, and craned his neck to look around the expansive elegant lobby.

Daniele didn't hesitate and walked past him to the desk, Michele and Rick right behind her.

"I'm looking for Leo Calvet's room," Daniele told the young dark-haired girl at the desk looking prim and professional in her pressed blue uniform with the knee-high skirt and matching jacket over a white blouse.

"Leo Calvet?" the girl asked and started clicking with her mouse while studying the monitor in front of her.

"Yes," Daniele said. "He should be here."

The girl's shoulder-length hair swung as she nodded. "Yes, I have a Leo Calvet. Would you like me to call him?"

"Please do," Daniele said, "tell him his daughters are here."

The girl picked up a phone and dialed. She waited through several rings. "I'm sorry, but he is not answering. Would you like to leave him a message?"

"Can you tell me what room he's in?" Daniele asked. "Perhaps we can just wait for him there."

The woman looked troubled. "No, I am sorry. It is against hotel policy."

Michele piped in. "He said he'd leave us a key. Can you check his mailbox? It should say Michele and Daniele Calvet on it, or something like that."

"One moment please," the girl said, and walked smartly across the room to a bank of boxes on the far wall. When she returned she had an envelope in her hand. "Yes," she said. "He did leave something for you."

Michele held out her hand.

The woman looked embarrassed. "I am sorry, do you have identification?"

"Yes, of course," Michele said.

She and Daniele both took out their passports and laid them open on the counter with their photos showing.

"Ah, yes, thank you," the girl said, and held out the envelope.

Daniele grabbed it and ripped it open as she marched across the lobby to a bank of three elevators.

"Well?" Jack asked.

"It's a key," Daniele said, holding out the electronic card key for them to see.

"Which room?" Rick asked.

"It doesn't say," Daniele said, but pressed the "Up" button on the wall between the elevators nevertheless.

"Twenty twenty?" Michele asked hopefully.

"I don't think there's that many floors," Jack said.

"Eight twenty," Daniele said with certainty.

The elevator bell rang and they all stepped inside.

"Fancy hotel," Jack said admiring the stylish elevator, also trimmed in gold.

They took the ride up and walked the hall to room 820, all the way at the end on the side facing the Eiffel Tower.

Daniele hesitated at the door.

"Well *open* it," Michele said impatiently.

"Just seems too easy after all this," Daniele said, and then slipped the key in and out.

A green light on the door handle lit up and Daniele pulled the handle down and pressed the door open with her palm. Hesitantly, they went inside.

The radio was playing, "When a Man Loves a Woman," through a black Phillips TV sitting inside a cabinet with the doors swung open.

"Cool room," Jack said stepping in.

The room was large, with striped wallpaper and crown moldings. A large mirror was hung over an oak-veneered tall desk, the kind for dressing, not working. The French attention to detail was demonstrated by a long light above a painting on the wall opposite the mirror, as though they were in a museum. The three meter high ceiling made the room even larger, and allowed for a step down from the foyer into the living room. Outside was a small balcony laid in small red tiles with a rusting metal rail above a clear plastic screen surrounding the catwalk-like structure.

"It's so clean," Michele said inspecting the room.

"But no one's here," Daniele observed.

"No bags, nothing on the tables," Rick said. "Looks like the room's just for us."

"With two king-sized beds?" Daniele asked and looked at Jack. "Don't think so."

Jack went out onto the balcony. "Look at this view of the Eiffel!"

"Wow!" Michele said following him. "I've never seen it from this angle. I bet it looks good at night when they turn the twinkling lights on."

"It has twinkling lights?" Jack asked.

"Oh, there must be thousands of them," Michele said. "It's very beautiful."

"Like Christmas lights?"

"Um-hm. All white."

"Gotta see that," Jack said as they re-entered the room.

The four of them searched for signs of…something. They looked in the closet, under the bed, in all the drawers and even in the small refrigerator.

"Hey look at this," Jack said excitedly.

Daniele quickly turned. "Did you find something?"

"It even has a little safe," Jack said, "where you can lock things up when you go out."

"Good idea," Rick said.

Daniele was perturbed. "Try to tell us about things that matter, okay Jack?"

Michele had wandered past Jack and into the bathroom. "What's this?" she asked, pointing to a small, weird looking button on the wall next to the shower curtain.

Daniele was checking out a closet next to the bathroom and leaned her head so she could see through the door. "That's a clothes line." She pointed to the other side of the shower where a receptacle was mounted to hold it tight. "You hook it on that thing over there. Haven't you ever stayed in a hotel before?"

"Yep," Michele replied. "Just haven't ever noticed one of these."

She pulled on it, and sure enough a line stretched out.

Suddenly the shower started moving.

"Oh!" Michele said lurching back, her hand jumping to her mouth.

A quiet whirr of motors could be heard as the floor of the shower started rising. Michele backtracked and leaned with one hand on the sink as the shower floor moved clear up to the ceiling. In its place emerged what looked like an elevator.

"What's going on?" Jack asked coming in with Rick crowding in behind him. Daniele had already abandoned her closet search and was in the bathroom next to Michele.

"I found something," Michele said.

Daniele studied it. "I think it's an elevator."

Jack stretched around Daniele to check it out.

"Looks like it'll fit four," he said.

"*I'm* not getting in there," Michele said.

Daniele disagreed. "Seems like we have to."

"No *way!*" Michele argued.

Daniele wasn't harsh when she turned to Michele, but spoke deliberately. "Father led us here, I don't think he's going to let anything happen to us now."

Michele looked doubtful. "You *think* he led us here. What if it was somebody else? Somebody who kidnapped him?"

"One way to find out," Jack said stepping in. "Look, there's buttons like an elevator."

Rick, not to be outdone, stepped in next to Jack, followed by a cautious Daniele.

"Coming?" Daniele asked smugly, crossing her arms.

"Ohh…." Michele moaned as she stepped lightly into the rectangular box, grabbing Jack's arm as she did so.

Jack stared at the panel that had only two buttons. Up and down.

"What'd'ya think?" Jack asked. "Up or down?"

"Down!" Michele said, and Jack pressed the down button.

Metal doors came out of the walls on either side and clapped shut. There was a slight jolt as the elevator started down.

"Do you s'pose Daddy's gonna be here?" Michele asked, just before the elevator bumped to a stop.

"We'll find out," Daniele said as another set of doors opened behind them.

"Oh!" Michele said, looking over her shoulder. They all did an about face and gazed for a moment before venturing out.

Instead of Leo, before them was just an empty courtyard. They stepped out and looked around. A tall fence surrounded the yard, with shrubs and small trees aside a winding pathway through the middle.

Jack craned his neck to look up at the hotel above them. A few steps further out and he could see the balcony of room 820. The others followed, looking warily around the courtyard. When they were all well away from the elevator, the doors closed and an outside door closed over it blending in perfectly with the side wall of the hotel. They could hear the faint whirr of a motor and then silence.

Jack checked out the wall looking for buttons. "No controls from here," he said.

Michele looked around one more time. "Now what?"

"This is just too much!" Daniele said, her hands on her hips and her eyebrows flashing anger. "I'm not playing his stupid little game anymore! I'm going home!"

17

Daniele quickly examined the courtyard, spotted a door that led into the hotel and headed straight for it.

"Daniele!" Michele called after her. "We just got here!"

"I don't care," Daniele said over her shoulder. "I'm outta here."

"But we still haven't found *Daddy*," Michele complained.

Daniele stopped and turned, her hands once again with a firm grip on her hips. "As far as *I* can tell we aren't *going* to, either. I've had enough of chasing around all over Washington and Paris looking for him."

"But what if he's in trouble?"

"Oh, he's in trouble all right," Daniele fumed. "Why don't we leave him a trail of breadcrumbs that lead right back to Washington?" She turned and made for the door.

Michele held her car keys out and dangled them with a jingle and a mischievous grin. "How're you gonna get there?"

Daniele stopped and turned again, reaching into her purse and taking out a fist full of euros. "Taxi," she said, shaking it at her, and then disappeared through the doorway with Michele running behind her yelling, "Wait!"

Rick and Jack looked at each other.

"Here we go," Jack said, as they both started off after them.

Daniele was already through the swinging glass door with Michele quickly coming up behind her at a prancing trot, Jack and Rick more leisurely pulling up the rear. They passed through a restaurant, up some stairs, through a broad hallway with small shops on either side, past the manager's desk, an information booth manned by nonchalantly curious dark suited men, and out the revolving glass door next to reception. The young receptionist was standing at her monitor and looked up to see the four of them chasing each other outside. "Americans," she murmured to herself with a shake of her head.

Outside and down the steps Daniele headed for the first taxi in line.

"Wait!" Michele called after her, almost stumbling down the steps, but Daniele was already getting in. It wasn't until Michele had decided to follow her in the Benz that she noticed the car wasn't there.

"Hey!" she said to no one – to everyone. "Somebody took my Benz!"

Daniele was in the cab giving directions to the driver when she saw the look on her sister's face. "Wait," she told the driver. She opened the window and yelled at Michele, "What now?"

Michele's bare arm was outstretched with her index finger shivering. "Someone stole my car!"

Daniele looked over. Michele could get a cab just as well as she could. "Go ahead," she told the driver. But before she'd even gotten to the end of the street she felt guilty. "Oh, stop the car," she said irritated.

She was even more annoyed that the driver insisted she pay the minimum fare for the five-second drive, but handed him the euros anyway and stepped out to return to the evolving scene.

The doormen had become engaged in the situation, and the senior man had already sent the younger in to have the desk call the police. Michele was asking them if they'd seen who took it, but the older man was shrugging saying he hadn't seen anything, and then questioned the younger man when he came back out. The younger hadn't seen anything either, in fact, could not remember that there had even been a white Benz parked there. He insisted that the truck that was there had been there all day.

Michele, of course, scoffed at them for being so blind and was busy arguing with the doormen, along with Daniele now, insisting that the car had been there, when two policemen arrived in a single car, siren and lights blaring.

The policemen listened to their story, took notes, took down license numbers, took down the plate number, took absolutely useless statements from the doormen, and then drove off half an hour later chattering with each other.

"So now what?" Daniele asked.

"Maybe we should wait for Daddy in his room," Michele suggested.

"We could call room service," Jack said, "maybe have a little lunch."

"I'll go along with that," Rick said. "I'd say he definitely led us there, so it probably wouldn't be a bad idea to wait."

Daniele followed unenthusiastically, muttering unintelligible complaints, but at least for the moment giving up her idea of jetting home.

They took the elevator up and tried the key to room 820, but it didn't work. Daniele gave up after two tries and Michele took her place and tried four times with the same result.

"Must've demagnetized," Jack said, standing behind Michele with his arms crossed.

Michele said she'd get another, but the others said they didn't want to stand there in the hall so they all crowded back into the elevator and went down to reception. The same young lady was there to help them.

"This key doesn't work," Michele told her, holding it over the counter with her hand on her hip. "Can you get me another one?"

"Yes, of course," the young girl said. "Which room?"

"Eight twenty," Michele answered.

"And the name?"

"It's registered to Leo Calvet," Michele replied. "We're his daughters, remember?"

The girl looked at her like she was missing something, but clicked on her mouse without comment. A puzzled look came over her face. "You say the name is Leo Calvet?"

"That's right," Michele said.

"I am sorry, but a Mr. Leo Calvet is not registered in the hotel."

Michele grinned. "Of course he is. He's in room eight twenty. You just gave us this key about an hour ago."

The girl smiled awkwardly. "I am very sorry, but I did not give you that key."

"What're you talking about?" Daniele asked, stepping up next to Michele. "You don't remember the four of us standing right here?"

"No," she answered. "Perhaps it was another employee?"

"It was you!" Daniele said irritated. "Just give us another key to eight twenty."

The girl looked flustered. "But you are not registered."

"No," Daniele said patiently, slowly. "Leo *Calvet* is registered. C-A-L-V-E-T. He's in room eight twenty, and you gave us this key just a little while ago. Has everyone in the hotel lost their minds?"

The girl didn't know what to do now. "I am sorry," she said flustered, "but we have no Leo Calvet registered in the hotel, and I did not give you that key."

"This is ridiculous," Michele said, and stormed to the revolving door and outside.

The others followed a moment later. They took the steps down and stood on the sidewalk in a circle.

"More games," Daniele said with disgust. "Now he's got the whole hotel playing it."

"Well," Jack said, "I suppose we could stand out *here* and wait for him."

"According to Ms. Hilton in there," Daniele said, "Father's not even checked in. What good's it gonna do to wait? I say we all just get on the airplane and go home. He can find us there."

"Maybe she's right," Rick said. "I sure don't know what else to do."

"We could follow your line further out," Michele proposed.

"What good would that do?" Daniele said annoyed. "You *know* this is the place. Com'on, the Paris Hilton clue, the 'Follow the big hand' clue, your 'Do what Daddy tells you' clue…"

"You said it was *our* clue," Michele said defensively.

Daniele crossed her arms. "…eight twenty, Father's here, Father's not here, your car's not here, nobody recalls *us* even being here. They're all in on it."

"Yeah, but what's the point?" Jack asked.

"Who knows?" Daniele said throwing her arms up and dropping them to her sides. "Who *cares?*"

"Well *I* care," Michele said, her exasperation aimed at Daniele's face. "We still can't be *certain* that he's not in trouble."

"Well *I'm* getting pretty certain," Daniele said harshly. "I say we just get out of here."

Michele raised her voice, "And *I* say we look around!"

Jack put his arms out, palms down and said, "All right, all right. Let's just cool down." He looked around. "Sidewalk café." He pointed across the street. "Can't get enough of 'em. Let's just go sit down, relax,

have something to drink, maybe eat a little snack, and we'll decide what
to do next."

"Sounds good to me," Michele said and started off briskly.

"I'm leaving," Daniele said, and turned toward the cabs.

"Daniele," Rick said tenderly. "Why don't we just stick together?
We've come this far. I'm sure your dad has a good reason for all of this,
if he's the one doing it."

Daniele hesitated, her heart pounding from the argument and Rick's
eyes.

He put his palm under her elbow and urged her gently. "Come with
us," he said persuasively. "We'll talk it over and if we decide to go home,
we'll go home. But, like Jack said, let's cool off a little bit and think this
through rationally."

"There's nothing rational about it that I can see," Daniele said, but
had given in and let Rick lead her by the arm all the way to the café.

Jack had been looking up at the Eiffel, towering before them down
the street and across the park, and had just crossed the street and stepped
up the curb onto the sidewalk when he said, "Whoa…" and put his hand
to his head.

"What's the matter?" Michele asked.

"Just felt dizzy a little bit," Jack replied. He moved his hand over his
stomach. "Feel kind of queasy."

Michele took his arm and led him to an empty table. The café was
like so many others, with small tables lined up outside on the sidewalk
and more tables inside. The table was in mid-span of the café on the
sidewalk.

"You don't suppose it was something you ate on the plane, do you?"
Rick asked, holding a chair out while Daniele set herself huffily down
and crossed her arms.

"I hope not," Jack said, "but something's making me sick."

Daniele looked at Michele. "Give me a cigarette," she demanded.

"What makes you think I have any?"

Daniele sneered. "We're in Europe, aren't we?"

"Thought you didn't smoke," Michele sneered back, taking her
cigarettes from her purse along with some matches.

While Daniele lit up, Michele called a waiter. "A seltzer water
please."

The waiter marched smartly to the bar.

Jack was leaning his elbows on his knees.

"Still feeling bad?" Michele asked, tenderly rubbing Jack's back.

Within those few moments the waiter returned and set a bubbling glass on the table.

"Maybe getting worse," Jack said and rubbed his eyes.

"Try this," Michele said reaching for the water. She intended to hand it to Jack, but knocked it over instead. The water spilled on the table toward Jack and splashed over his knee and onto the sidewalk.

Michele looked for a napkin but there weren't any, so she was going to brush it off his pants leg with her hand, but the water had apparently missed him.

The waiter heard the glass fall, and had already turned, retrieved the glass that had been knocked over, and was rushing to the bar to get another. When he returned he set it once again in front of Michele, and she promptly knocked that one over as well.

"Oh!" Michele said with a chuckle, covering her mouth with her hand. "I know I'm clumsy, but I didn't think I was *that* clumsy." She looked shamefaced at the waiter. "Sorry. Could you please get us another one?"

Once again it looked like the water had spilled on Jack's knee, but when she went to wipe it off it was dry.

"Too much excitement," Michele explained lamely, touching her hand to her forehead.

"Feels like I'm gonna throw up," Jack said.

Just then Michele noticed that Rick looked pale as well. "Rick, are you okay?" She asked.

The question caught Daniele's attention. She'd been perusing the boulevard and gazing up at the room 820 balcony.

"Feeling a bit queasy myself," Rick complained.

"What'd you have on the plane?" Daniele asked.

"Chicken," he answered.

"So did I," Daniele said. "Must be something else. I feel fine."

"It's a lot like the fish bowl effect," Rick said, and then his eyes got wide and he looked around as though seeing the world for the first time. He looked at Jack, at Jack's dry knee, and then around the whole street as though looking for some out of the ordinary manifestation. The waiter returned with a third glass of seltzer water, but before he could take it off the tray Rick half-stood and grabbed it. He pulled but the glass didn't budge.

"This place is virtual," he said in a hushed voice, sinking back into his seat.

A tingle went up Daniele's spine.

Michele shivered.

Jack threw up.

"Where are we Bob?" Rick asked.

"You mean the plane ride was virtual?" Daniele asked.

"Bob?" Rick repeated. He waited a moment. "Eve, end the program."

Nothing happened. A car drove by, the people in the café continued talking and laughing, and there were sounds of construction down the street.

"Rick," Daniele said sternly. "Was the plane ride virtual?"

Rick didn't look at her, but continued to look around with a serious, confused, and definitely concerned look. "Couldn't have been. We all ate."

"So where are we?" Michele asked with a quiver in her voice.

"In a virtual environment," Rick replied, and then tried again. "Bob! Take us to the Crimson Court house."

Still nothing.

Jack was bent over with Michele massaging his back, hacking and spitting vehemently into the puddle between his legs.

"You okay?" Michele asked gingerly.

Jack sat up straight. "Yeah, I think it's passed." The color was returning to his face as he looked across at Rick. "So this isn't real?" he asked.

"Can't be," Rick said. "At least I don't think so."

"Well what else can we do to be certain?" Daniele asked. She reached out and touched the waiter's arm as he walked by. The waiter glanced back at her but kept going. "He seems real."

"Not a hologram," Rick said brooding. "But a silicon object." He looked dismayed. "This is more advanced than Eve."

"More advanced?" Daniele asked.

"Yes. The people are silicon objects rather than holograms."

Daniele became more urgent. "Then are you certain we're in a virtual environment? The waiter sure seemed real to me."

"A silicon object *would*," Rick said, then got up abruptly and walked to the curb. Just as a car passed he put his hand out. It passed right through it. Rick came back and sat down. "Holographic," he said. "So that answers that."

"Bob?" Michele called.

"This isn't Eve," Rick said.

"You know that for sure?" Michele asked. "Maybe Bob's gone to the bathroom. Give him a couple minutes and try again."

"Eve!" Rick said louder. "Show us the exit."

No change in the environment.

Jack looked suspiciously at Rick. "So what's going on, Rick?"

Rick leaned back. "I wish I knew."

"Well maybe you *do* know, Rick," Jack said, saying the "k" a little hard.

"How would *I* know what this is?"

"You got us into this," Jack said flatly, "now get us out."

"I *didn't* get us into this," Rick complained. "I don't even know when we entered this environment."

"Maybe it was on the airplane," Michele said eagerly.

Daniele looked at her. "En route?"

Michele shrugged. "Could've been."

"Dye your hair a different color."

Jack was still staring at Rick. "Seems like you've been leading us all along," he said. "How do we know this is even you?"

Michele looked at Rick skeptically. "It *is* you, isn't it?"

Rick was exasperated. "Of *course* it's me."

"Well then *do* something," Michele pleaded.

"If I *could* do something, I *would*," Rick said defensively.

"Bob?" Michele said with a little more desperation.

Jack carried on in his inquisition of Rick. "So what now, Rick? Can't get out, can't eat, can't drink. What're we gonna do, just stay in here until we starve?"

"I'm hungry," Michele said with a whimper. "I don't like this."

"Are we your prisoners, Rick?" Jack asked.

Rick raised his voice. "Of course not!"

Michele was staring at Rick. "But you must know there's another virtual world that you don't know about, don't you?"

Daniele would have laughed if she too wasn't frightened. "Listen to yourself," she said. "You sound ridiculous. And see what you did to Jack?"

Michele glanced.

"He's gone all wobbly brained. And give Rick a break. He already told you he doesn't know what's going on. Why can't you believe him? He's *your* fiancé for crying out loud."

Rick's eyes were sorrowful. "How can you not believe me?"

Michele looked down. "I'm sorry Rick, this is just freaking me out. I'd get up and run but I wouldn't know where."

"All right," Jack said, easing up. "Let's think of something else."

Rick took a relaxing breath. "Sounds good to me."

"Can we break it somehow?" Jack asked.

"Not that I know of," Rick replied, "but this isn't Eve, so maybe it has weaknesses."

A thought occurred to Michele that made her ask in alarm, "Remember how you said we couldn't get hurt in Eve?"

Rick nodded.

"If this isn't Eve, then you don't know if that's true or not."

"No, I don't," Rick said gloomily.

"Not sounding good to me," Jack said. "But let's think it through. If this is another virtual world just like Eve, then that means somebody's watching us right now just like Bob did."

Rick's face changed as he thought about it. "That's right."

"This is getting creepy," Michele whined.

Jack went on, "So maybe you should try talking to that person."

Rick looked up at the sky. Ominous storm clouds were moving in the distance across the city, though the sun was still shining where they sat. "Whoever you are, please let us know your intentions."

The world around was noisy, but the lack of response made it feel threateningly silent.

"So you think there's a French Bob?" Michele asked.

"Has to be," Rick replied.

"Robespierre?" Michele called to the street.

"Robespierre?" Jack asked.

"Sounds like Bob, doesn't it?" Michele asked. "Robert,

Robespierre?"

"Good a guess as any," Rick agreed.

"Who could do this?" Daniele asked. "Who else besides the CIA?"

Rick pondered that as well. "No one that *I* know of. Could be a foreign government."

"The French?" Michele asked.

Daniele shook her head at her. "Ya think?"

Rick nodded affirmatively. "Could be. I suppose since we actually did come to Paris, I think, in the real world, then we are still in Paris in a virtual world, which means they have one. But who has it, I don't know."

"Well who could have it besides the government?" Jack asked.

"I suppose anyone with a lot of money," Rick said, "but we're talking the kind of money that only someone like Bill Gates would have. Tens of billions."

"Bill!" Michele called.

"So they're listening to us," Jack said, "but they won't reveal themselves to us."

Rick looked up. "What's the mission?"

Silence.

"Are we on a mission?"

Daniele slapped the table. "It's obvious!"

Rick raised an eyebrow and turned to her. "So what's the mission?"

"No," she said. "I mean it's obvious when we got into this virtual environment."

"The elevator," Jack said.

"Oh yeah," Michele said glancing at Jack.

"The elevator," Daniele repeated.

"So let's go," Jack said.

Michele sat back. "Back over there?"

Jack got up. "Maybe we missed something. Could be we can get into the elevator. At least we know where it is. I'll push the 'Up' button this time."

"What do you think, Rick?" Daniele asked deferentially.

"Makes sense to me," he said, "and unless someone's willing to talk to us, I don't know what else we can do."

"What about *that*," Michele asked, pointing to the reeking puddle of Jack's lost airplane food.

"Leave it to whoever's virtual world this is to clean it up," Rick said. "It sure won't be Bob."

"Robespierre can do it," Jack said, clearing his throat.

Daniele looked at it. "If I'm understanding how these virtual environments work, won't it kind of, um, follow us around?"

Rick hadn't thought of that. He looked down at it, and then set off toward the Hilton, saying, "Better hold your noses."

"And watch where you step," Jack added, stepping over it.

They strode as a flock across the street, walking with determination toward the hotel.

As they passed the doormen going in, Daniele said snidely, "Remember us this time?"

The doormen just smiled, their hands folded in front of them.

They marched through the lobby, up the steps and past the manager, through the hallway with the shops and out the back through the restaurant. In the courtyard they went straight to the wall where the elevator had been. But now it just looked like a wall. No indication of an opening, or any kind of controls.

"Think we can break through it?" Jack asked.

Rick brushed his hair back. "With what?"

Jack tried to pick up a chair but it wouldn't budge. Frustrated, he went back over and kicked the wall. Not a dent.

"Let's try the room again," Daniele said, marching off toward rear entrance.

They all trudged back in, past all the virtual employees staring at them and took the elevator to the eighth floor. At room 820 Michele tried the key they'd used to get into the real room 820 one more time. Didn't work.

Jack lifted his leg and kicked the door, which seemed to give a little just like a real door would. He tried it again.

"Stop!" a maid yelled in French from down the hall. "You cannot do that!"

Jack kicked again.

"Give me a hand, Rick," he said. "Seems like I'm making progress."

They stood shoulder to shoulder and kicked simultaneously. The door seemed to be breaking.

"Maybe their system accommodates actions that give the silicon an effect that the real world would have. You could certainly do it with silicon," he said, grunting as they tried another kick, "but Eve isn't this advanced yet."

The hotel manager, a round well dressed older woman summoned by the maid, emerged from the elevator a minute later as the guys kept kicking and came trotting down the hallway toward them. "You must stop!" she yelled. "We will call the police!"

"One more time," Jack said. "One two three…"

They both kicked hard and at last the door broke open. The manager stopped a distance down the hall and spoke into her cell phone before proceeding briskly toward them. Michele and Daniele stood shoulder-to-shoulder, arms crossed in defiance, to intercept the manager while Rick and Jack entered the room.

"Remember us?" Daniele asked, and then she noticed something at the manager's feet and laughed.

"What?" Michele asked.

"Look where she's standing."

"You cannot break into the room," the manager said in a stern voice, her feet firmly planted in the remains of Jack's dinner.

"Why cannot we break into the room?" Daniele said, mimicking her French accent.

Michele was polite. "It's just a silly-con door, anyway. What's the big deal?" She looked at the ceiling and yelled. "Tell her it's silly-con!"

The manager was irate. "I have called the police. We will wait for them." She waved her arm toward them. "You are all in big trouble. Big trouble."

"Oh," Daniele said. "Get a life."

Michele laughed. "That's good. Get a life," and then she sneered at the manager. "Silly Sucker."

"You will not think les Silly Sucker is funny when you are all in jail," the manager said, pointing a manicured stubby finger at them.

Daniele held a palm out to Michele. "Cigarette."

Michele took the pack out and handed one to Daniele, gazing all the while at the manager.

"There is no smoking in the hallway!" the manager scolded.

Michele lit Daniele's cigarette then took one for herself.

"You are all in big trouble. *Big* trouble."

Daniele blew smoke in her face then flicked an ash at her.

The manager gasped and marched away.

Michele watched her retreat and then yelled after her, "And tell all your other Silly Suckers they can kiss my virtual patootie!"

Four policemen emerged from the elevator at the end of the hall just in time for the manager, her neck craned around shouting French obscenities at Daniele and Michele, to run into the lead cop.

She began pointing and speaking in rapid fire French. The policemen strolled to the end of the hall, the manager waddling behind them, just as Jack and Rick emerged from the room.

"Nothing there," Jack said disappointed. "It's just a clothes line."

"I'm out of ideas," Rick added.

Daniele was watching the policemen approach. "So we're stuck here with the Keystones? This should be interesting."

The four cops came up rattling off stern French decrees. Only Michele had an inkling of what they were saying, Daniele's French not being so proficient.

"No, no," Michele was saying in English as the lead cop grabbed her arms, pinned them behind her back and ushered her off toward the elevator. "You don't understand. You're *virtual*."

Another cop grabbed Daniele's arm and started pulling her down the hall. "I don't think they're aware of that," she said, jerking against him to no avail.

"Hey!" Jack said as the third cop grabbed him. He struggled, but the cop seemed to have super strength with an iron grip around Jack's wrist. "These guys are tough," he commented.

Rick had taken up a defensive posture and tried some of his CIA training on the last officer, a much smaller man than he, but flipped himself over when the silicon didn't react to his martial arts move. He was flat on his back. The cop lifted him with one hand under an armpit and lugged him off, feet dragging by the heels behind him, down the hall toward the others with Rick mumbling, "Impressive system…"

18

The virtual ride in a virtual French paddy wagon to the virtual police station didn't give them any comfort. In fact, the knowledge that this was all a silicon based environment made them that much more demoralized.

"How're we gonna fight sand?" Jack asked in the back of the police van on the way to the station.

"Well, they do use it to make steel," Rick responded, nursing his sore armpit.

"Steel?" Daniele said. "I thought it was gooey, you know like in breast implants."

"Well, that too," Rick said. "But it's in all kinds of stuff."

Michele was stunned. "They make *breasts* out of this?"

"Used to," Rick said.

"Breashts of shteel," Jack said, cupping his hands in front of his chest.

"They use it in glass and semiconductors too," Rick added.

"You're not a computer girl, are you?" Jack asked Michele, glancing down at her breasts.

Michele sat up straighter. "No silicon here," she said proudly, and then looked down. "I don't think…"

Daniele was upset and cried out, "Will you all please *focus?*"

They stared at her.

"What do you think? This is a game? Someone's kidnapped us, and for all we know we're in for the same fate as Father!"

"Same *fate?*" Michele said with dismay. "You said Daddy made all this happen!"

"Do you really think he'd put us through all this?"

There wasn't time to answer, or even think. The van had stopped and

the door had burst open at that moment. They were herded out into the
station, uncannily similar to Detective Cruse's, processed in by a pencil
nosed mustached plain-clothesman, escorted into the back, and shoved
into two adjoining cells separated by bars. The cells were sparse, each
furnished with two cots – a single blanket and pillow on each – and a
stainless steel sink and toilet. The cops had secured the barred doors and
disappeared back into the office.

They'd each commandeered a cot and sat lamenting the situation.

"You're the one who got us into this," Michele said to Daniele.

"*Me*? How'd *I* get us into this?"

"Well…you just…you just did."

Daniele snorted. "More false accusations…"

"She didn't do it," Rick said through the bars. "Someone that we
don't know did it."

"Leo did it," Jack said. "He's the one that used you to get us into
that stupid…" he made quotes in the air, "…CIA world."

Rick was offended. "He didn't *use* me," he said. "We're *both* CIA."

"Oh really?" Jack asked. "Then how do you explain this?" He
spread his arms out displaying the cells.

"Oh, leave him alone, Jack," Daniele said, hard on the "k." "He
doesn't know what's going on any more than you do."

"Well of anyone here," Jack asked exasperated, "who should
know?"

Michele glared at Daniele. "Why're *you* defending him?"

"The real question is, why aren't *you*?" Daniele countered.

Michele was taken aback by that, but recovered with, "I'm not even
sure that *is* Rick."

Rick's forehead creased in anger. "Well then who *am* I, anyway? You
think I'm *behind* this? Gimme one good reason."

"You said it yourself," Michele yelled at him. "To get Daniele and
me back together."

"Well that was a great success," Jack said sarcastically, then looked
at the two of them sitting on their separate cots behind bars. "Then again,
they are together. Poetic justice."

"If that's all this is," Daniele said, slumping onto the thin mattress
of her cot, "then I'm really gonna kill 'im."

"Daddy isn't going to go to all this trouble just to make you make up with me," Michele said.

"*Me* make up with *you*? Are you *nuts*? *I* didn't do anything."

Michele rolled her eyes. "Oh, except for trying to steal my boyfriend."

Daniele sat up. "Haven't we already settled that? Bygones, remember?"

"You and your bygones," Michele said. "I can see the way you look at Rick."

Rick leaned over and propped himself up on one elbow with a foot on the cot and his knee in the air. "How does she look at me?"

"Oh, gimme a break," Michele said.

"Goin' for it again, huh?" Jack shot at Daniele.

"No, I am *not!*" She shrieked. "I can't help it if no-brain over here never pays any attention to her."

"Would you stop with the 'no-brain' stuff?" Rick asked like a wounded animal.

Daniele looked at him. "I didn't mean that," she said hastily, truly sorrowful. "It's just that sometimes…"

"See?" Michele said. "I think there's something going on here."

Daniele started. "There's nothing…"

"Like what?" Rick asked. "Like she listens to me? Like we can have a conversation? You're the one who doesn't even think I'm real." He leaned back against the wall and crossed his arms.

"So who knows if you *are* real?" Jack asked. "Michele's not the one dumb enough to lead us into some booby trap."

"I didn't see *you* objecting to any of the missions," Rick said defensively. He brushed the air with his hand. "And no one pushed you onto the plane." He huffed. "What do you know anyway?"

"I could try to kill you," Jack said, "and if you're silicon, nothing would happen. And if you're real, knowing you, you wouldn't notice."

Rick was silent. Trying to figure out what he meant by that.

"The only thing stopping me is homophobia," Jack added. He too leaned against the wall and crossed his arms.

"The only thing stopping you is *jail*," Michele retorted.

"That's what I said."

"Well, in case you haven't noticed, we're in jail already," Rick said, and then took a sideways glance at Jack.

Jack shuffled a little farther away from Rick. "What're *you* lookin' at?"

Michele couldn't help but chuckle. "*See*. At least *he* knows how to make me laugh," she said, and then regretted it.

"Is that all you care about?" Rick asked. "Do you know how hard it is for someone like *me* to make you laugh?"

"The world is her playground," Daniele said, "and everyone in it a playmate."

"Oh, and that's so bad?" Michele said. "It's better than running around with a frown all the time, acting so important but not ever really doing anything."

"Who really does anything important anyway?" Jack asked. "It certainly isn't Rick."

"And you do?" Rick said. "I suppose getting criminals out of jail is important."

"See?" Jack said. "Typical CIA. Trounce on everyone's rights. Well those criminals have a right to a good lawyer."

"Then they should look for one," Rick said.

"Oh that's cute, Rick," Michele said. "Jack's probably a great lawyer, aren't you Jack?"

"Okay great lawyer," Rick growled, "get us out of here!"

Daniele sniffed. "Oh, I've seen him in action."

"Meaning?" Jack asked.

She sniffed again. "Meaning I'd rather have Jack the Ripper for counsel."

"Well, that'd fit you just fine," he said indignantly. "You're not the only one who's been watching."

"Watching what?"

"That Gonzales case for example."

"He was *guilty!*" Daniele argued.

"Huh," Jack said. "Like my mother."

Daniele countered. "Oh, and I suppose you didn't get Stevens off." Jack was silent.

Daniele knew she had the upper hand. "You know as well as I do that he did it."

"It's my job," Jack said. "Can I help it if I'm good at it?"

"You lawyers are all alike," Rick scoffed. "Defend the guilty.

Convict the innocent." He glanced and saw in Daniele's eyes that she was hurt and immediately felt remorse. "Some of you, anyway," he said in a pitiful attempt to undo his slight.

"So what's so great about the CIA?" Michele asked, firing once again at Rick. "A bunch of spies. Liars. Look at how you've lied to *me!*"

"Well, so did *Daddy*," Rick said, making a childish voice.

"Oh!" Michele buried her head in her silicon pillow and burst out crying.

"Now look what you've done," Jack said.

"*Me?* You're the one who's been attacking me all morning!"

Michele lifted her head off the pillow. "And why do we have to sit here with *that!*" she said, pointing to Jack's leftovers in the corner of her cell. Looking at Rick she cried, "Why couldn't they put it in *your* cell? If it wasn't for you we wouldn't even be here."

Jack couldn't help it, and started chuckling.

Michele glared at him. "You think this is *funny?*"

Jack glanced at the glob in the corner and back with a gleam in his eye. "Well, it is, sort of."

Michele looked at Jack's mess and tittered through her tears. "It'd be better if we weren't trapped in here."

"Seems like we're really trapped," Daniele agreed dismally.

"As far as I can tell," Rick said. "I wish I could do something, but I'm as trapped as you are."

Jack looked at Rick's eyes, thinking maybe he'd gone overboard. "So you really don't know what's going on here?"

"Not a clue," Rick said miserably.

Michele started sniffling and buried her head in her pillow again, making Daniele's heart go out to her. She got up and moved to Michele's cot, sat beside her sister and put her hand on her back with Rick and Jack watching silently.

"It's okay, honey," Daniele said soothingly.

Michele's sobs became spasmodic, as though they were forced. "I just…wish…" she said, her breathing erratic, "that I could be like you."

Daniele was stunned.

"You're so calm and nothing ever seems to bother you," Michele sniffed. "You would think that since we're twins I'd be as smart as you, but I'm not."

"Of course you are," Daniele said, knowing that it was the truth.

"Oh, no I'm not," Michele said pathetically. "You know so much more than I do."

Daniele's hand stopped and she lay back against the brick wall, flabbergasted. "If you only knew."

"Knew what?" Michele asked, sitting up at the release of Daniele's hand.

Their eyes met.

Daniele looked over at the guys, and then spoke softly to Michele. "I am so *jealous* of you."

Rick and Jack both sat up on their cots, but still couldn't hear.

"You are?" Michele said with surprise. "*Why?*"

Daniele sighed. "Because *you're* the one who never lets anything get to her. *You're* the popular one. Everyone *loves* you." She leaned her head against the wall. "But I'm just the serious stick in the mud."

"No you're not," Michele said sympathetically, sitting up and turning toward her, bringing one knee up onto the cot. "I have so much admiration for what you do. You actually do something worthwhile. You put criminals in jail." She shrugged dejectedly. "I just design clothes."

"Well that's a meaningful thing to do," Daniele said, sitting up. "*Everyone* has to buy clothes."

"Nobody buys our clothes," Michele said, "except for rich people."

"True," Daniele agreed, and found herself using Rick's argument. "But your designs are what determine what everyone else's jeans will look like next year."

"I suppose," Michele said, "but I wouldn't even be doing that if it wasn't for Daddy. I wouldn't be anybody if it wasn't for Daddy."

"Well neither of us would be," Daniele agreed. "Where do you think I get the serious side?"

"Hm," Michele said, and then smiled. "Where do you think I get the playful side?"

"He is an amazing man," Daniele said, but then added, "But I'm still gonna kill 'im."

Michele snorted. "Me too."

"Hey!" Jack said from the other cell. "Can you speak up?"

"Oh, quit being so nosey," Daniele said loudly. She settled back and held her sister's hand. She looked over and back at Michele, and then in a conspiratorial, cautious tone, asked, "Why are you with Rick?"

Michele turned to look in her eyes. "I don't know anymore, really. He's a great guy and all that, but I don't know if it's right."

"How come?"

Rick and Jack had both left their cots and moved over next to the girls' cell.

Michele glanced over at Jack. "He doesn't make me laugh." Turning back to Daniele she said, "I've seen how you look at Rick."

Daniele looked at her hands, let go of Michele's, and starting picking at her nails.

"It's *okay*," Michele said in a comforting tone. "You really like him don't you?"

Daniele didn't look up, and just nodded yes.

"Guess what?" Michele said.

"Hmm?"

"I really like Jack." She giggled.

The tension in Daniele's face lifted and she looked into Michele's eyes. "Really?"

Michele nodded vigorously.

"What're you two talking about?" Rick asked, leaning with one shoulder against the bars.

"Oh, nothing," Michele replied in a singsong voice. Turning back to Daniele, she asked, "So what is it you like about him?"

"I don't know," Daniele said and settled back. "Gimme a cigarette." Michele did, and lit one for herself. "He is kind of oblivious, I guess."

Michele chuckled. "That part *is* charming, isn't it?"

"Absolutely," Daniele said. "But he has such a good heart."

Michele turned and looked at him. "Does he?"

"Of *course*," Daniele said. "You're lucky to have him."

"Probably," Michele said dispassionately. "But you know me. I want the fun ones."

"I do too," Daniele said, "I guess. But I can make him fun." She glanced over at him. "He *is* fun for me. I like that serious side."

"I sure couldn't make him fun," Michele said. And then her tone turned to a saddened guilt. "I do love him, but I don't know that I want to marry him."

Daniele looked at her seriously. "Really? You're having second thoughts?"

"Oh, for a long time now."

"Then why haven't you broken it off?"

"Um…I…uh, you know, don't want to hurt him. He *is* a great guy."

"I know what you mean," Daniele said. "But that's no reason to go ahead and get married."

"I guess I never really thought about it that way," Michele said. "It's all been so busy."

"I know what you mean," Daniele repeated herself, and then wistfully said, "Funny how life's decisions are sometimes made because you're too busy to really think about the ramifications."

"See?" Michele said. "I can't talk like that. You know so much." She took a sorrowful breath. "I am *such* a blonde jerk."

"Oh, no you're not," Daniele said, "and you know it."

Michele laughed. "I suppose I do."

"I just wish I could be light and breezy like you. You have so much fun, and all I do is work."

"Too much fun," Michele said. "Makes me feel useless sometimes."

Rick and Jack both had their heads turned and pressed up against the bars to hear, but they couldn't.

"Wanna clue us in?" Jack asked.

Daniele leaned forward. "Nope," she said, and then she and Michele both giggled. They tossed their burnt butts across the room and into the guys' cell and lit up another one each.

"So what's the deal with Jack?" Michele asked. "He says you were just using him so you wouldn't have to go to the party alone."

Daniele looked down. "Um…yeah," she said hesitantly. "He's right." She looked at Michele with pitiful eyes. "I was just using him. Pretty bad, huh?"

"He's a wonderful man ya know," Michele said. "He actually *is* very responsible. But he still wants to play. I like that."

"You're right about that," Daniele said. "But what to do? He's more your type than mine."

Michele sighed. "I wasn't gonna tell you this. It's been so awkward."

"What has?"

"Well, we had that big engagement party and everything. It was such a big deal."

Daniele eyed her sister. "Yeah, and…"

"Well, we actually," she looked over at Rick and fiddled with her ring, "um…we decided about three months ago that we didn't want to go through with it."

"You *what?*" Daniele said, her eyes popping.

"'You what' what?" Jack asked.

Daniele lowered her voice. "You mean to say you're not really engaged?"

Michele had a sneaky smile and shook her head. "We just don't know how to tell everyone. It was such a big deal and everything. And then we decided to just go along with it and see if we really wanted to or not. So far nothing's really changed."

"That's the most ridiculous thing I ever heard," Daniele said, her mouth still agape. "Why don't you just call if off and tell everyone. There's no crime in that."

"I know," Michele said embarrassed. "It's silly." She looked at her hand. "I like the ring though."

"So what's with all the acting jealous of Rick and me? And he's acted like he was all bent out of shape about you and Jim."

"Well, you're right," she said lamely. "It was an act. We've been doing it for months so it's kind of become natural."

Daniele snickered. "I take it back. You are a blonde numbskull. The both of you."

Michele looked down with a sad face.

"What?" Daniele asked.

"I just," she said slowly, "think, you know, that I was the one who made you hate men."

"You didn't do it," Daniele said. "Jim did."

"Yeah, but I've been making you feel guilty about it for all these years."

"Doin' a pretty good job of it," Daniele agreed.

"I just didn't know," she said and looked her in the eyes. "I'm so sorry."

"I'm over it," Daniele said. "Don't worry about it anymore, okay?"

Michele briskly shook her head. "Yeah, but I'm trying to make it right." And then she looked as though she'd had an idea, an open-mouthed childish grin washing over her. She glanced surreptitiously at the two men, giggled, and whispered in Daniele's ear. "Wanna switch?"

Daniele gasped and stole a peek at the guys, a slow smile turning to half-moons in her cheeks below her nose. She nodded rapidly without a word.

"Bygones?" Michele asked.

"Bygones," Daniele agreed.

Michele took Daniele's hands in her own. "Let's never let anything keep us apart again."

Daniele was beaming. "Never."

"So how're we gonna tell them?" Michele asked with her eyes crinkled up conspiratorially.

"I guess we'll just tell them," Daniele said, equally as excited. She looked over at the guys and then turned back to Michele's ear and added, "But we need to get out of here and find Father first."

Michele looked around, her face fearful again. "What if we *can't* get out of here?"

"You mean like, we're stuck here forever?"

"I mean like, if I don't get out of here soon," she looked at the corner, "there's gonna be another little something following us around wherever we go."

Daniele chuckled. "Me too."

Michele sat up and yelled at the ceiling, "Robespierre! I gotta go!" her voice echoing off the cell walls.

"What'd'ya mean you gotta go?" Jack asked with alarm. "As in, you want out?"

"As in, I gotta *go*," Michele said emphatically.

Jack looked around the room. "Hey Rick. I don't suppose we can use these toilets, can we?"

"Never know," Rick said.

"Don't see how that'd make a difference," Daniele said. "It'd just regurgitate it anyway. Stupid Silly Sucker seats." She tossed another butt into the guys' cell, and Michele followed suit.

"Hey! Which number we talkin' here?" Jack asked, a rapid spell of wobbly brain syndrome setting in.

"Robespierre!" Michele said. Then looked at the guys. "Well I'm not leaving it over here." She got up and started for the bars next to their cell, unbuttoning her jeans.

"Oh no you don't," Jack said with his palms raised toward her, a grin emerging.

Michele laughed. "Just watch me."

"Well as much as the prospect amuses me," Jack said, stepping back from the bars, "I'm not sure I want to live with the consequences."

Michele continued over. "Well if ol' Robespierre here doesn't get us out of here in the next minute or two, you're gonna have to."

Daniele was laughing with jerky motions, her hand limp and sideways to her lips. "Michele, are you sure you want to just drop your pants in front of the caged animals?"

"No choice," Michele said, her buttons coming off. "Bring that blanket over here so I can have some privacy, would you?"

Daniele tried to oblige, but the blanket wouldn't budge from the cot. "Stupid Silly Sucker sheet," she said, pulling one side over onto the floor and dragging it to Michele. She mumbled to herself, "Just gotta make sure it keeps in touch with the source."

Michele turned and grabbed a corner of the blanket and draped it over her shoulder.

"Now wait just a minute," Rick said. "Why not just collect it all in the same place over there with Jack's stuff?"

"Not a chance," Michele said as Daniele helped hold the blanket. She started to squat, pulling at her jeans from one side to the other. "I think it's only fair…"

At that moment, the bars disappeared, the cots disappeared and the police station disappeared. Michele wrenched upright as quickly as she could, Daniele's hands hanging empty in the air above her shoulders, the blanket oozing away into the floor.

"Oh!" Michele cried yanking frantically at her jeans, a momentary glimpse of her bare behind etched in the minds of the two smiling men. They were standing in the middle of a white chamber, vacant, except for Jack's dinner and an elevator door across the room.

"Been spending some time by the pool, have we?" Jack remarked.

19

The doors opened automatically, and they approached with trepidation while Michele struggled to stretch the top button of her extra-tight jeans into place. But where else would they go? Time to meet their captors. Stepping inside, again the door closed automatically, and to their astonishment went down rather than up.

"Deeper into the bowels…" Jack commented.

Michele had just finished buckling her wide white belt when the elevator stopped. She held her breath. Rick had edged his way to the front of the girls and had taken a defensive posture that would allow him to spring into action if necessary. Jack had noticed and slipped around Daniele to provide a level of protection. Though what good it would do if they were met by more silicon, he didn't know.

The doors opened to find Courtney Crimson standing before them in a hallway that looked almost exactly like the one at Project Eve.

"Hello," Courtney said lightly. She extended her hand and in a charming French accent introduced herself. "I'm Valerie Vachet."

Rick relaxed his stance, stepped out and took her hand. "Good to finally meet you…uh…again."

Jack exhaled and let his muscles loosen up. He followed Rick out but stepped off to the side.

Valerie's smile was lovely, creating the slightest little dimples on both cheeks along with thin crow's-feet next to her eyes. "Oui. Yes. I am not Courtney Crimson. As you have discovered, Courtney Crimson does not exist." She looked beyond Jack. "Ah! Michele and Daniele!" She stepped closer with her hand reaching out again. "So happy to finally meet you."

"Daniele," Daniele said, slapping her hand once before taking it.

"You *are* real, aren't you?"

Valerie's laugh was disarming. "Oui, I am real. I am so sorry for the...um...deception, but it was necessary."

Michele was next.

"Your father has told me much about you," Valerie said as they shook. Her face turned solemn. "But I must tell you, you're father is missing."

"So what's new?" Jack muttered.

Michele's face dropped, "Not again..."

"I'm gonna kill 'im when I see 'im," Daniele snarled, fed up with the whole mystery.

"I think the fact that Leo's missing is pretty well established," Rick added.

Valerie's expression flushed from cordial to serious. "I'm so sorry. But he is really missing. We are all so worried."

"Valerie," Rick said. "I'm afraid I have a lot of questions."

"I knew you would," Valerie said, but then turned with her charming smile to Jack. "Ah. Mr. Crenshaw."

"So it's Valerie, not Courtney," Jack said, leaning over to shake hands.

"You should not be here," Valerie said.

Jack grinned. "I wouldn't have taken you for making understatements."

Valerie grinned. "Well, we'll have to talk."

"At your leisure," Jack said, and added, "I suppose you being here means we're not actually prisoners."

Valerie smiled at that, and fading to a mischievous grin said, "Only you."

"Ah," Jack said with an awkward smirk.

"So where are we?" Rick asked. "And who are you?"

"You did all this, didn't you?" Daniele asked.

Valerie nodded.

"What for?" Michele asked.

"Several reasons," Valerie replied, "at least one of which you know. But we have a lot to discuss and I'd prefer not to do it here. Why don't we go to Leo's office?" She stretched her arm to point down the hallway.

"Leo has an office *here?*" Rick asked with bewilderment.

"Follow me," Valerie said, and led them past recessed doors with French labeling in a lay out nearly identical to Eve, and finally through yet another recessed door with Leo's name on it.

Leo's office was similar to the one he kept in the Project Eve facility. Windowless, lined with bookshelves full of books. His desk was against the far wall facing the door, with dual flat screen monitors set squarely in the middle that he would have to look around to see whoever came in. But he rarely had meetings from behind his desk. Across the spacious room in the corner was a large carpeted area, where a comfortable corner sofa and matching overstuffed chairs – enough to seat eight – were placed around a rectangular oak coffee table centered in thick glass.

"Coffee?" Valerie offered, pointing to a coffee service set into the bookshelf next to the sofa. A few feet from that was the door to a private washroom.

"I need to go there," Michele said pointing from her chest with her hand hooked at the wrist and her index finger jabbing repeatedly toward the washroom. "Desperately."

Valerie laughed. "Ah, yes, forgive me, I forgot."

"So you were watching and listening," Daniele stated.

Valerie touched her forehead as if to tip a non-existent hat. "Robespierre, at your service."

Daniele rubbed her eye in pained disgust, especially recalling their last antics. She avoided eye contact while she asked the next couple of questions, busying herself with the coffee making process. "So I suppose you saw Michele's little escapade there at the end?"

"Why do you think I closed the program?" Valerie asked. And then in a hushed tone, "Do you think she was actually going to go through with it?"

"Probably," Daniele said.

Valerie nodded. "So she was, wasn't she," she said flatly. "Americans are very interesting people."

"And I would have too," Daniele admitted. "What else were we going to do?"

"Yes, I suppose so," Valerie said, settling into the chair at the head of the coffee table.

Daniele turned to Rick and Jack who were taking seats on the sofa. "*I* was just afraid the boys here would return the favor."

"Didn't think of it," Rick said.

Jack mused, "Wish I *had* thought of it."

Daniele turned around and poured creamer in her cup, her back to Valerie. "So you could hear everything?"

"Everything," Valerie said, her crossed leg swinging slightly.

She turned to her. "So what if someone said something they wouldn't want other people to know?"

Valerie had a gleam. "Everything in this facility is classified," she said reassuringly, "you know that."

"I'm sure there are recordings."

"Some particularly sensitive information has already been deleted," Valerie remarked offhandedly.

"Like what?" Rick asked. "I don't remember hearing anything sensitive while we were in there." He scratched his temple and mumbled. "Couldn't have been something *I* said."

Jack spoke to Daniele's back. "Like female secrets."

She smiled to herself.

"Sure would be nice to know what was said," Jack commented when he got no reaction. "What with all that giggling going on."

Michele emerged from the washroom with a breezy, "Whew!" She sat across from Rick next to Valerie.

"Michele and I were just mending fences," Daniele said, picking up her coffee and joining the others. "Isn't that right?"

"When?" Michele asked.

Daniele switched her gaze to Valerie. "When we were in the hoosegow."

Michele was perplexed. "What's a hoosegow?"

"You know," Jack said. "The pokey, the big house."

Michele laughed. "What *are* you talking about?"

"Jail," Rick said.

"Ah. So what happened in jail?" Michele asked.

"*Secrets*," Jack said emphatically. "Lots of 'em."

"Oh that," Michele said. "Daniele and I were just making up. You know, 'Sorry I did this, sorry I did that.'"

Daniele was impressed at how well Michele covered.

Rick ignored the girls. "How much can we talk freely here?"

"Anything you want," Valerie responded. "No secrets here. At least not on any of the current subjects. You realize, of course, that the discussion should be limited to information that these three have already gained over the last several days."

Rick looked at Valerie. "I don't mean to be rude," he said, "but who are you, and why are you here? And where are we, by the way?"

"All good questions," Valerie said. "I am the head of the Operations Directorate for Project Eva."

Rick lurched forward. "Director of Operations?"

"Your counterpart," she said affably.

"And Project Eva is…I'm assuming we're really in Paris…a French version of Eve?"

.   "It is almost the same, no?" Valerie said. "But it is Environnement Virtuel Amélioré. So we call her Eva."

"Should have called it Adam," Jack mumbled, massaging his sore wrist. "It's the macho one…"

"Where are we, anyway?" Daniele asked. "Seems like the complex would have to be *under* the Eiffel Tower, considering the entrance from the Hilton and the size."

"It actually is a vast underground maze that stretches from under the Hilton courtyard to the large area under the Eiffel Tower," Valerie explained. "The primary control room is ten stories below the southern leg of the tower, held up by ten meters of reinforced concrete. The Eva chamber ends under the Hilton courtyard, but there are several additional access points under the government and apartment buildings across the street, between the Hilton and the tower."

"Huh," Rick grunted. "More access points than Eve too."

Valerie nodded at the comment and went on. "Our governments have been working in parallel on the virtual environments for the past four years."

Rick's eyebrows shot up. "This only took four years?"

"Yes," she answered. "But remember, Leo's team had the ben…"

"Leo's team?" Rick interrupted.

"Yes, Leo is in charge of the Eva project."

Rick shook his head in amazement.

"Father is in charge of Eva too?" Daniele asked in disbelief.

Michele had a blank stare. "Just don't know *anyone* anymore."

Valerie continued. "Leo's team here had the benefit of Project Eve's research. Leo still intends to upgrade Eve, but we needed to test some systems first."

"So you've solved the problem of creating realistic silicon people," Rick observed.

"Yes," Valerie said. "With the advantage of building on Bob's research, we've made rapid advances that you've yet to achieve. Leo intends to transfer the technology to Eve soon."

"But how could I not know of Eva?" Rick asked. "Wouldn't it have gone faster had I been here to contribute?"

"Perhaps," Valerie said, "but it was compartmented."

"Well I never thought of *me* as being compartmented out of something like this," Rick complained.

"Oh, you know it happens all the time," Valerie said. "Leo, of course, doesn't know everything the President knows."

"But why the French?" Jack asked, momentarily forgetting that Valerie was herself French. He was more worried that his questioning her was impertinent. After all, he wasn't even supposed to be here. "Aren't they almost an enemy nowadays?"

Valerie chuckled enchantingly, and didn't seem to mind the question in the least, explaining it away. "You watch too many news shows. The American public is being fed propaganda, just like the French public. But that will all change. In reality, the French and American intelligence services have been working extremely well together for decades. The cooperation seems to only have gotten deeper since nine eleven. Some time after the events of that terrible day, Leo was directed by the President to transfer the Project Eve technology here. We'll be using both systems, in tandem, in support of the Global War on Terror. But the American National Security Advisor wanted extremely limited exposure, for obvious reasons. We're still trying to establish if it's an effective counter terrorism tool."

"By 'in tandem' you mean that the two systems will be networked?" Rick asked.

Valerie smiled. "They already *are*, Rick."

Rick nodded. "I guess they would have to be, wouldn't they."

"Why would they have to be?" Michele asked.

"Courtney Crimson," Jack answered. "And the clocks."

Valerie looked at Jack with a raised eyebrow of respect. "So you understand?"

Jack grinned. "Just the surface, I'm sure. But I *would* like to pick Robespierre's mind sometime about a given conversation."

"Watch out for him," Valerie said half-jokingly to Daniele. "He's a lot more perceptive than he lets on."

"Why now?" Daniele asked in earnest.

Valerie was puzzled.

"My father has kept this secret life from us all these years," Daniele went on, "so why tell us now?" She looked at her coffee. "I'm not sure what to think of him anymore."

"It was me," Valerie said softly. "Or Bob Jones, actually."

"You've been watching?" Rick asked.

Valerie nodded.

"And it was you setting clocks in Eve."

"Yes," Valerie acknowledged.

"But why the ruse?" Rick asked. "Why not just tell me about Eva?"

"As I said, everything was compartmented. You were just supposed to get Daniele and Michele to a birthday party." Valerie smiled. "Leo knew it would take something like his disappearance to get his daughters working together. The little Benz mystery was just enough cloak and dagger to keep them chasing after him long enough to get them to the party. Your job, as I believe you were briefed, Rick, was to make sure they got the clues right to get them there. What happened after that it seems, was a mistake."

Rick's forehead wrinkled. "Screwed up, huh?"

"Perhaps," Valerie said with a brief smile. "Bob doesn't know about Eva any more than you did, and he still doesn't. At this point Bob still doesn't have a need to know, but he will soon when his team will be directed to collaborate with the French team. Eva has a lot of upgrades that need to be applied to Eve."

Rick sat back. "And you and I will collaborate?"

"Yes," Valerie said. She hesitated for a moment and looked at each of them around the coffee table. There were no comments or questions so she went on. "I would like you to help us find your father, and we will need to use Eva to do it. Part of it would be learning to manipulate the system, which is basically learning a few French words and commands, then just doing whatever you would like to do so you can become accustomed to the system. After that, we will start the reconnaissance mission."

"Same drill as with Eve," Jack observed.

"What will we be looking for?" Rick asked.

"Clues," Valerie answered cagily. "Will you help me?"

"Sure," Michele said with a little shrug.

Daniele had no reason why not, still wary of whether her father had actually disappeared, or if this was yet another deception. "If you want us to."

"Will *I* be part of it?" Rick asked.

"Certainly," Valerie said, then looked at Jack.

Jack looked playfully askance at Valerie. "I sure hope I'm not the one who has to be shot for knowing too much."

Valerie laughed and turned to Daniele. "Good wit too." Back to Jack she said, "No, not right now, anyway." She winked. "We'd like for you to join the team, since you've already been such an integral part of the team so far, albeit unwittingly for all of us."

Jack nodded.

"Sounds good to me," Michele said amicably. "How long do you think it'll take?"

"As long as you want," Valerie said, "but no less than a two hour mission, if you don't mind."

"I'm game," Jack said.

"So when will we do this mission?" Daniele asked.

Valerie looked at the clock on the wall. "Shall we start now?"

Rick nodded. "Probably a good idea. I'm anxious to introduce the technology into Eve," Rick said, and turning to Valerie, "That's something I'd really like to discuss with you."

"All in good time," Valerie said. "Let's get down to the mission."

"So," Daniele asked, "where we going?"

"Well," Valerie said, "I thought I'd leave that up to you. What we're interested in is getting you oriented. I will be along to teach you the proper commands, and I'll have someone in the control room overseeing the operation."

"Robespierre?" Jack asked with a grin.

"Someone like that," Valerie smiled back. "Eva will accept commands essentially in the same manner that Eve does, but they're obviously in French. This will be similar to your second exposure to Eve," she looked at Jack with a sideways glance, "though I would prefer that you stay off the moon and stick to a Parisian experience."

Jack lifted his cup in a sign of agreement.

"Perhaps your fashion show?" Valerie asked.

Michele spoke right up. "Oh, yes! I wanna see my fashion show."

"That'd be good," Valerie said, nodding approvingly. "The Galeries or the Eiffel?"

"Really," Michele said, "I want to go to the office so I can meet some people that I haven't seen for a while. I'd especially like to talk to Martin."

"Ah yes," Valerie said understandingly. "Perhaps you can meet your new sponsors." She took a quick glance at Rick.

"Good idea," Rick said. "We tried in the café but Eve couldn't produce them."

Jack's cheek was leaning on his hand. "Produced stiffs," he said.

Rick went on, "Maybe you'll have better luck."

Valerie looked at Daniele. "What do you think?"

"Sure," she said. "Whatever."

"Then it's decided," Valerie said and stood up. "Shall we?"

Within a few minutes they were in the Calvet Fashions office located in La Grande Arche de La Défense, the ultra-modern white archway of an office building built by the socialist Francois Mitterand. Sitting at the end of the axis that stretches from the Place de la Concorde down the Champs Elysees and through the Arc de Triomphe, Mitterand ostensibly built it to symbolize France's role in politics, art, and the world economy. Leo Calvet decidedly considered it a wonderful tribute to capitalism, and stuck his offices there.

As magnificent as the outside of the building, Leo's office was elegantly subdued inside. The simple sofas and peanut-shaped desk, identical to his office in the States, were typical of Leo's understatement.

"So how do we get the new sponsors here?" Michele asked.

"Oh, we just ask," Valerie said. "Go ahead and try."

Michele said to the ceiling, "Eva?"

"No no," Valerie said. "The system is called Eva. You are saying Ava. It is like the 'E' in...um...bed. You know, bed, bed...E...vah."

"I see," Michele said. "Eva?" she called, pronouncing it correctly.

"Bring us the new sponsors for the Calvet show."

"You know French, yes?" Valerie asked.

"Ah, yes," Michele said, "a little."

"Please," Valerie said, gesturing with her hand. "In French."

"Right," Michele said. "Eva?" She looked at the ceiling.

Valerie laughed playfully and asked, "Why does everyone believe they need to speak to Eva at the ceiling?"

Rick's eyes shifted a bit.

Michele smiled. "Yes, of course. Eva?" she said to the wall, and then in French, "Bring us the new sponsors for the Calvet show."

They waited a moment. Then they all looked at the door to Leo's office. Then they looked at each other.

"Eva?" Valerie asked, and in non-accented French said, "Bring us the new sponsors for the Calvet show."

Still nothing.

Daniele remembered something from Leo's office in Eve. "Does my father have an administrative assistant?"

"Yes," Valerie replied with a curious look.

"Her name?" Daniele asked.

"Marie," Valerie answered.

"Oh right," Michele said, picking up on Daniele's train of thought. "Gotcha." She walked to the desk and pressed Leo's intercom button. "Marie, please come in here."

A moment later a middle-aged French woman with reading glasses lowered onto her nose walked in looking over the rims. "Oui?"

"Are there any gentlemen waiting for us in the office?" Daniele asked in English.

"No," Marie said.

"Who are the new sponsors?" Daniele asked.

Marie shrugged, and in English said, "I do not know."

Valerie, guarded, intervened and asked in French, "Marie, you must know who the new sponsors are."

"I am sorry," she said. "I do not know who they are."

Valerie turned to Rick. "Did you not make a contract with the new sponsors?"

"Yes, of course," Rick answered.

"Who are they?" Valerie asked.

"Why they're from Rossman Fashions. From Hamburg, Germany."

"Eva," Valerie said, not taking her eyes off of Rick. "Bring us the representatives from Rossman Fashions, located in Hamburg, Germany."

Still no response from Eva.

"Couldn't get them into Eve, either," Rick said.

"No, you couldn't," Valerie stated.

"Well since we're striking out here," Michele said, "why don't you just bring in Martin Jackson?" There were no objections, so she looked up at the ceiling. "Eva," she said, "bring us Martin Jackson."

There was a tentative knock on the door before Martin stuck his head in.

"Martin!" Michele said excitedly, and rushed to give the silicon-Martin a hug, her blonde hair swinging freely across her back. "How are you?"

"Silicon," Jack said.

Martin smiled and reacted the way Martin would, giving her a hug that enveloped her.

"Couldn't do that in Eve," Rick said with admiration in his voice.

Valerie stifled a proud look. "We'll compare notes. This is one of the major upgrades for Eve."

"Can't wait," Rick said.

"So how was the show?" Michele asked.

"Ah! Wonderful!" Martin said passionately. He was wearing one of those cover-everything robes like he had on at the party. "It was *such* a success."

"I'm very proud of you," Michele said in a giggly voice.

"Oh, thank you Michele," Martin said. "It's *sooo* good to *see* you!"

"So," Daniele said, "you were in all the newspapers."

Martin bowed his head in an "aw shucks" gesture as he quickly turned the spotlight to Michele. "They just *loved* your designs. I was so *proud* of you!" He gave her another bear hug.

"He's so *real*!" Michele said openly, turning to Valerie with appreciation. "Like, he's really *here*."

"I would say thank you," Valerie said, "but it was really the research team, building on Bob's work on Eve."

Just then a voice came through the walls. "We have a slight problem with the system."

"A problem?" Valerie asked making a puzzled look.

"Yes, a technical problem," the voice said. "I'm shutting down."

Instantly the scene disappeared, along with Martin and poor Marie who was still standing there as though waiting for another command, and the white walls of Eva materialized.

20

Like Eve, the Eva facility had a bare white hallway from the elevator to the Operations Center, with doors to the databases, environment generating DNA computer and silicon supply chamber across the way. "Let's go in here and see what the problem is," Valerie said as the group approached the Operations Center.

"Oh, not me," Michele said, "I'd just as soon get some coffee in Daddy's office."

Jack wandered along behind Michele. "I think I'll head over to Leo's office myself and use his washroom."

"I'd like to hang around," Daniele said expectantly.

Valerie held the door as Rick entered, and then turned to Daniele and whispered, "You might not like this, but it has to be done."

Daniele followed her in without question or comment.

"Listen Rick," Valerie said, stepping through the door and closing it. The operations room was empty except for the three of them and a mid-thirties dark haired man at the console, his chair turned facing them. "What do you know about your new sponsors?"

Rick glanced at the man.

Valerie looked over. "Oh, sorry. This is Jean-Claude, AKA Robespierre."

Rick and Jean-Claude nodded to each other.

"Ah, Robespierre," Daniele said with a grin.

Valerie took a breath. "The real purpose of this mission was to see if Eva could produce your new sponsors."

"Hmm," Rick said.

"When you tried in the café in Eve, the system brought out dead people."

"Very strange," Rick said.

"Not our typical system response either," Valerie said. "I tasked Jean-Claude to interrupt us due to a technical difficulty if we couldn't produce them in Eva. We added an override so that the system wouldn't produce walking corpses."

"Ah," Rick said slowly, though not understanding where this was going.

Valerie pulled an armchair over and indicated for Rick to sit. "We already know, Rick, that your new sponsors, or who you think are your new sponsors, are dead."

Rick had started to sit but stood back up. "*Dead?*"

Daniele took in a brief gasp, but didn't say anything.

"Please," Valerie said, motioning to the chair. She pulled another chair around for herself, leaving Daniele standing a few feet away with her arms crossed. "They were killed in a car crash in Hamburg last week. A single car accident that ended in a fireball. Both bodies were burned beyond recognition."

"So Marlene Ramsauer and Gunter Hartmann are dead?" Rick asked.

"Yes," Valerie said. "The day before you signed your contract with them."

Rick slumped back in his chair.

"I must confess," Valerie said, "that I suspected you at first."

Rick's eyes squinted. "*Me?*"

Daniele shifted nervously from one leg to the other, a look of concern on her face as she stared at Rick.

"You brought them in," Valerie said. "You signed the contract, and four days later Leo disappeared."

"So you know when he disappeared?" Rick asked.

"I know the day," Valerie said. "I was with him the day before. He was going to Charles de Gaul to fly back to Dulles for the birthday party and that's the last anyone saw of him. He'd driven one of his Benzes from his house to the airport, but never arrived. The police and Secret Service have been looking ever since, but we haven't found either him or the car."

"Why didn't you tell me?" Rick asked.

"Like I said," Valerie explained, "I suspected you."

"Of what?"

"Of somehow being involved with the substituted sponsors. With Leo's disappearance. That's why I lured you here with Benz signs. When you produced the dead sponsors at the café in Eve, I thought it possible that you were simply unaware, but I needed to be certain. I needed you in Eva to see where you would take us. We thought you might separate yourself from the group and lead us to your sponsors' murderers, but you discovered too quickly that you were in a virtual environment. And your reaction, going back to the hotel and crashing through that door, made us think that you really were unaware. You're either a very good actor, or oblivious to what's going on. Our last thought was that we'd arrange for you to be let out of the jail cell, but knowing you were in a virtual environment, even if you were in on it, you wouldn't have led us any-where. I heard some things from Daniele and Michele that made me believe you weren't a part of it anyway."

"Like what?"

"Just things they said about you."

Rick looked at Daniele who made a tight-lipped grin.

"Anyway, Michele put an end to our use of Eva."

Rick wrung his hands and looked across the room, avoiding Daniele's eyes. "I guess I should have run backgrounds on them."

"Don't you usually?" Valerie asked.

Rick sighed miserably. "Not for the Calvet business."

"Sloppy," Valerie said offhandedly, making Rick wince.

"So why're you telling me all this now?"

"Because we need to find your sponsors," Valerie said, as though it was obvious.

"Well we already know the systems can't identify them," Rick said. "Produced stiffs in Eve, as Jack put it, and Eva doesn't seem to know who they are. Doesn't even know about Rossman Fashions. A technical oddity that I really don't understand."

"Eva *does* know about Rossman," Valerie corrected him. "Eve probably does too. But our requests in both systems were for specific people who were practically unknown to the systems, so they couldn't produce them."

"Hmm." Rick nodded. "Pretty strange that you'd even have to program a 'non-dead people' override. We produce historical figures all the time and they don't appear dead."

"It's the timeliness of the information," Valerie said, "and the volume. There's not much in Eve about Gunter and Marlene, so the system produced the most current portrait that it could. But we'll review all of that later. Right now I think we need to concentrate on the problem at hand."

Rick sat there looking like a chastised schoolboy. "So, what's the next move?"

Valerie looked somewhat stunned that she had to lead him this way. "Well," she said, "you could *call* them."

Rick instinctively felt for his cell phone in his side pocket. "Call them."

"Quickest route from A to B," Valerie observed. "We'd have done it ourselves, but they don't know us. You need to get them on the phone."

"And ask them what?" Rick asked. "What did you do with Leo?"

Valerie smiled a pained smile. "Just see if you can reach them. See if they're still in character. Ask them to dinner."

Rick chuckled. "*Dinner?*"

"We don't know what they're doing. We have no idea why they kidnapped Leo, but I have a theory."

"Which is?"

"Something to do with the fashion show," Valerie said.

Rick rubbed his chin. "Why would someone want to kidnap Leo because of the fashion show?"

"I don't know," Valerie said. "But before he disappeared, Leo told me he was going to do a quick background on your new sponsors. I guess he's been doing it all along."

Rick's eyebrows rose. "He's been following up on my contacts?"

"Somebody needed to do it."

"But why?" Rick asked. "It's just a *fashion* business."

"Run by the head of a secret CIA project and an even more secret French Secret Service project."

"But Calvet's just a cover," Rick said. "How would anyone trace that back to Eve and Eva?"

"I don't believe his abductors know," she replied. "I think this is all about the fashion show."

Rick was silent while he took all this in.

"Could be something about the Eiffel Tower," Valerie went on. "If your new sponsors were planning some terrorist act…"

"*Terrorist* act?" Rick asked with immediate shock.

It was Valerie's turn to sit back. "Look at the major countries that have been hit hard. The U.S., Spain, Britain. We French are asking ourselves if we're next. My theory is that your new sponsors are planning just that, and Leo got onto them. He made a call or something that was monitored and so they kidnapped him," her head lowered and her eyes dropped, "or worse."

"So if all that was true," Rick said, "why would they just come to dinner with us? They're probably out of the country by now."

"Not if they need to *be* at the fashion show for some reason," Valerie said. "Then they might have to meet with us to keep up the pretense. They might not know that we suspect them, whoever they are."

"So dinner would do what?" Rick asked.

"Give us prints," Valerie said. "Maybe we can identify them."

"And what should I tell them is the purpose of the dinner?" Rick asked. "I mean so that they believe it's legitimate."

"Tell them Michele wants to meet them before the show," she answered simply.

He nodded in reflection. "Mm-hmm."

"If we can ID them, then we'll find them," Valerie said with certainty.

Rick sat forward and leaned his elbows on his knees clasping his hands in front of him. "Guess I pretty well screwed up."

Daniele was embarrassed for Rick, and felt like he needed someone right then. If she only could.

Valerie was silent.

"Can I call from here?" he asked, reaching in his pocket for his cell.

Valerie chuckled. "We're in Eva, remember? You'll have to go up to room 820, or somewhere outside. RF won't penetrate the walls here."

"Oh yeah, of course. Same as Eve," Rick said standing. "I'll see if I can get them. When and where?"

"Eight o'clock at Le Fontaine Bleau on the Champs Elysees," Valerie said.

While Rick made his way to room 820, Valerie, with Daniele following, headed back to Leo's office with another agenda. Daniele went to the coffee table and sat next to Michele who was slouched in her chair.

"Where's Jack?" Valerie asked.

Michele twitched her head toward Leo's washroom.

Valerie smiled. "Good," she said, sitting down in Leo's chair. "I need to talk to the two of you alone."

This got their attention and they both sat up straighter.

"What about Rick?" Michele asked, turning to look at the door.

"Rick's making a call," she said. It took her several minutes to explain the situation. Michele shuddered at the news that her new sponsors were dead and possibly replaced by terrorists. Daniele had a terrible foreboding about their father's fate while Valerie went on to explain to Michele who Rick was calling and why.

"Which brings me to what I'm going to ask you to do," Valerie said.

"Anything," Daniele offered.

Michele nodded agreement.

"I need you to switch identities for this dinner."

The girls sat in stunned silence for a moment before Daniele asked, "What in the world for?"

"I don't mean to offend anyone," Valerie said, looking at Michele, "but I need Daniele to question them."

"About what?" Daniele asked. "If you already know they're terrorists, why not just arrest them?"

"We need to find your father first," Valerie answered. "If we pick them up, it'll blow their operation and they might not need Leo anymore."

"Right," Daniele said softly. "They might kill him."

"And that's what I want you to find out," Valerie said. As gently as possible, she went on. "We need to find out if your father is still alive."

"So they might have killed him?" Michele asked.

"I don't mean to alarm you," Valerie said. "But if we just pick them up it could have a worse effect. If we believed that your father had been killed, then we would arrest them at dinner if Rick gets them to come. So I need a professional there. Someone who knows how to phrase questions that lead a suspect without letting them know their intentions." She turned to Daniele. "Someone like a prosecuting attorney."

Daniele nodded understandingly. "Yes."

"Well, *I* can ask them questions," Michele said.

Valerie looked at her seriously. "Sister rivalry aside, do you really think you're as good at it as Daniele?"

Michele had an abashed smile. "No, of course not."

"So why can't I just ask them questions as myself?" Daniele asked. "I'll be there."

Valerie opened her palm while she explained. "Because their focus will be on Michele. She's the designer. It's her show. They're her sponsors. You asking them questions of any depth would bring suspicion."

Daniele nodded silently while Valerie turned again to Michele, expecting perhaps an argument, but Michele just nodded as well.

"This could help find your father." Back to Daniele she said, "I don't know if you'll gain any useful information, but it's worth a try."

"I'll do it," Michele said, and then asked Daniele, "But can you really act like me?"

Daniele grinned. "It'll be a challenge."

"I suppose I'll have to act all serious," Michele lamented.

"And it'll probably be best if we don't tell Rick and Jack," Valerie said.

"Why not?" Michele asked.

"It'll be hard enough for the two of you to pull off a switch like this without anyone noticing," she explained, "but to have five of us in the same situation, trying not to call you by your real names, I just think the odds that your covers will be blown will be much higher."

Daniele began, "So when will we…"

The door opened and Jack emerged from the washroom. He strode wordlessly back to his chair and plopped into it, hardly settling before the office door opened and Rick walked in.

"Back to the mission?" Rick asked as he crossed the room.

"What did they say?" Valerie asked.

Rick flashed his eyes at Michele and Jack and then back to Valerie.

"I've told Michele," Valerie said. "I haven't had a chance to tell Jack yet, but I will."

"Tell me what?" Jack asked.

"About dinner tonight," Valerie said still looking at Rick. "So what's happening?"

"They'll be there," Rick answered, but had a quizzical look. "It was funny though…"

"Funny?" Valerie asked.

"Seemed kind of resistant to the idea," Rick said. "Maybe they suspect something. I had to kind of insist. Michele is, after all, the daughter of the president of the company and the lead designer on the Benz project. They put in two million euros. If they were real sponsors, you'd think they'd be anxious to meet her."

"Well, we already know they're not," Valerie said. "So maybe they suspect something by just the invitation."

"Not sure," Rick said.

"But just the fact that they're willing to meet tells us that their part of the mission isn't over," Valerie surmised.

"They're staying at the Intercontinental," Rick said. "I told them we'd have a limo come around and pick them up at seven thirty."

"I'll get some people on it," Valerie said.

"So should we go back into Eva?" Rick asked. "See what we can find out?"

Jack was slouched deep in his chair and pushed himself up by his elbows. "Back to the salt mines."

"Not right now," Valerie said. "I've got some things to prepare." Valerie turned to the twins with a sly grin. "Besides, Daniele and Michele would probably like some time to do their nails or something before dinner, wouldn't you?"

"Our *nails*," Michele said. "While Daddy's still missing?"

"Yes, I know that you are worried. I am too. But we're doing everything we can, and I really need time with Rick to discuss the situation." She looked at Rick and then turned back to the girls and gave them a wink. "If we work together, we might find him sooner."

Daniele caught Valerie's wink, and realized what she meant. "Yes, I suppose doing our nails would be a good idea," she said, and then turned to Michele. "Besides, your show's tomorrow." She waved her hands vivaciously. "The show must go on."

Jack looked up suspiciously.

Michele sat up. "Right. It's been a pretty long couple of days for me anyway." She forced a smile. "Big show tomorrow night."

"So where're we going?" Jack asked. "Beauty salon?"

"Daniele and I are going to get our nails done," Michele said. "You can go do whatever."

Jack was thrown. "*Whatever?* What would *that* entail?"

"Oh com'on Jack," Daniele said, emphasis on the "k." "You're a big boy. Can't you think of anything you'd like to do in Paris?"

"We'll help you decide," Valerie said. "But first we need to talk."

"Ah yes, the talk," Jack said.

"You realize the national and international security aspects of everything you've seen, and the ramifications of divulging such information?" Valerie asked.

"Hey," Jack assured her, "I'm as patriotic as the next guy. You don't have to worry about me jeopardizing the Eve and Eva operations in any way."

"Well," Valerie said with a sigh, looking at her watch, "I guess we can talk about that in detail another time." She turned to Rick. "I suppose first I should give you a tour of Eva."

"That'd be great," Rick said. "I'm pretty anxious to see the advancements your team has made."

So while Rick was busy with Valerie, Daniele and Michele left Eva and dropped Jack at a randomly selected sidewalk café on the Champs Elysees. From there they headed straight to Michele's favorite Parisian beauty salon a few blocks across the Champs Elysees from the Calvet store.

The shop was on an obscure side lane, frequented by models and the well to do. Michele had discovered it through her contacts at Calvet. The façade was all glass, with chrome frames around the windowpanes and door that was three concrete steps up from the busy narrow sidewalk. The white-walled interior was nearly covered in mirrors, accented by willowy hanging plants and a blonde wood and chrome trim. Deep and narrow as were many of the shops on the lane, only six stations lined one side of the room, three of which were already occupied by reclining women.

For the next two hours they were pampered, polished, and dyed, making their switch, all the while giving each other instructions about how to act.

"Oh, twins!" the beautician said, upon Michele's direction to dye their hair the exact color of the other's. "You are switching, yes?"

As the beautician was setting them up in side-by-side chairs, going from one to the other with their heads inclined into sinks designed with a notch to hold your neck, they told her the whole story, at least the whole story about Rick and Jack.

"Ah!" The beautician said breathlessly. Her voice turned wistful, practically singing, "L'amoure!"

The more they explored the details of the swap, the more they realized it would be a good way to see what Rick and Jack felt about the two of them.

"Why don't we just stay switched for a couple of days?" Daniele asked.

"I suppose we could," Michele initially agreed. "Especially if we find Daddy."

"Remember in the jail cell?" Daniele asked. "We were gonna switch anyway. Maybe not like this, but I suppose this could be my chance to see how Rick really feels about me."

"And I could find out about Jack," Michele said with anticipation. But then she realized something else. "Wait a minute! That'd mean *you'd* be doing the fashion show!"

"Hmm. I suppose it does," Daniele agreed, worried that Michele's attachment to her show could bring her whole plan to a screeching halt.

"No way," Michele said with a brush of her hand.

This stimulated a thirty-minute conversation during which Daniele had to urge Michele not to change her mind and back out of the switch as soon as the dinner was over.

"I've worked so long and hard on this," Michele pleaded. "Can't we switch again *after* the show?"

"*After* the show, we all go back home," Daniele reasoned with her. "Assuming we find Father. If we want to find out what they really think and want, we need to do this now, here, in Paris." Thoughts of Michele trying to pass herself off as a Beltway lawyer blazed through Daniele's mind from amusing to downright catastrophic.

In the end, Michele agreed. "I guess I'll be there anyway," she said, "only acting like you. But you think Jack is even gonna believe it? Normally, you wouldn't even stay for my show."

"Well I'm not going anywhere until we find Father," Daniele assured her. "That's reason enough for me to be around. Besides, a cursory look at the fashion world won't hurt me."

"Will I have to use words like 'cursory?'" Michele asked with a chuckle.

This, of course, made Daniele laugh. "It's not like you don't know them."

"Yeah, but it'd ruin my image to start talking that way…um…conversing that way."

Daniele frowned. "And I suppose I'll have to dumb-down my own vocabulary."

Michele smiled. "No," she said. "You'll have to talk less smartly and not use big words."

"There's a whole grammatical thing going on there that I haven't practiced since high school," Daniele remarked.

"Yep," Michele said. "Looks like you need a quick lesson in DBS."

"DBS?"

"Dumb Blonde Speak," Michele said. "You have to use words like 'like' and 'ya know' and 'totally' and 'awesome.' Like totally awesome, ya know? It's really just Val speak, but a little different on the East Coast."

"I've always wanted to know what a 'Val' was," Daniele said idly.

"Talking like a Val," Michele said. "You know, like totally awe-some."

"I know what you're talking about, but do you know where it came from? What *is* a Val?"

Michele smiled like her sister was so oblivious. "They're from the San Fernando Valley in L.A. It started, probably, back in the early seventies. Maybe even the sixties. Dunno."

"Huh," Daniele said. "Like I totally never even knew that, ya know?"

Michele laughed. "That's it!"

"I won't have to say 'gag me with a spoon' or 'as if' will I?"

Michele chuckled again. "No, that's old school. Maybe 'as if.' I don't think the Vals do that anymore, if they even exist now'days with that vocabulary. It was a passing phase."

"So what else do I need to know?" Daniele asked.

"Well, you can't really *know* anything," Michele said. "It means you just have to acquiesce to the demands of men that they know more than you." She giggled. "Acquiesce. Like that? Sounds like you."

"You would do that?" Daniele asked, the idea making her cringe.

"Do it all the time!" Michele said with a playful laugh. "Can't help it. I just *love* men. Especially Jack. I'd do it for him any time. But it's best if you just make it a practice to do that to all the men. Makes them feel good."

Daniele was flabbergasted. "Isn't it kind of like, ya know, prostitution?"

"*As if*," Michele said. Her eyes darted to the side. "Huh. I guess you can use 'as if' after all. Anyway," she waved from her wrist, "that's just sex. I'd put this in the category of 'getting along.' What's wrong with stroking a man's ego?"

It was still a bit repugnant to Daniele, but she didn't say so. "Seems like you're belittling yourself and him at the same time," she said. "Doesn't it seem just a bit dishonest?"

"I suppose so," Michele conceded. "I guess that's the way it was with Rick. No real honesty there."

"Funny you should say that," Daniele said. "I think he's the most honest man I ever knew."

Michele had a distant stare. "Yeah, maybe you're right," she said, and confessed further, "I think I'd have eventually felt guilty about it, because he doesn't really know the real me."

"If you act like that, does anybody?" Daniele asked.

Michele didn't hesitate. "I think Jack does."

"We'll see after he finds out that we played this little joke on them. If it goes that far."

"Yeah, I guess we'll have to tell them some time," Michele said. "But this isn't about them right now anyway."

"What if," Daniele said hesitantly, "what if we pull this off, and, you know, we go ahead with the dinner, and then we keep going, and then Rick tells me he's really in love with you?"

"He might," Michele said. "Both of them might tell us that they love the wrong one. What if Jack is really in love with you?"

They were silent for a while, both starting to feel guilt and anxiety about the outcome.

"Let's play it out anyway," Daniele said and sighed. "They'll get over it if they really love us."

Michele smiled. "They always do." She stuffed a loose strand of hair up under the towel. "It'd probably be a lot of fun if it wasn't for Daddy being missing."

"Sure hope we find him," Daniele said longingly.

"Oh, we'll find him," Michele said with certainty.

"You think?"

"Don't worry."

Daniele glanced over at her sister. Michele's eyes were closed and she seemed to be completely relaxed and relishing the indulgence. She leaned back, wishing she could be more like her sister. So carefree, even in the face of Leo's disappearance. "I sure hope you're right."

The beautician further accommodated them by letting them change clothes in the back room, where they also swapped purses, lipsticks, and perfumes, dabbing a little here and there. And Michele grimaced, struggled slowly saying, "Ungr…ungh," and reluctantly gave up her engagement ring.

21

They saw Rick when they got back to Leo's chateau. Rick, overwhelmed and deep in thought, had hardly noticed them coming in. He'd already showered and dressed for dinner, and was sitting in the large living room furnished like a French palace with ceiling-to-floor tapestries on the walls and flowery stuffed sofas and chairs trimmed in natural woods painted a deep gold. Rick stood as they passed through, heading upstairs toward their individual suites, and there was an awkward, though rewarding, moment for Daniele when Rick gave her a quick kiss on the lips while she fondled the ring on her finger. She was a little saddened by the fact that that would forever be their first kiss, assuming there would be more, and Rick didn't even know it. Their first mistake was that they each went to their own rooms, and then met frantically in the hall while correcting their slip-up, admonishing each other to be careful.

Jack had not come to the chateau all afternoon, and they worried that maybe he'd gotten lost. They were apprehensive when they came around the Arc de Triomphe at seven thirty and found the café where they'd dropped him, wondering how in the world they would find him if he'd wandered off. He indeed wasn't there, so they went on to Le Fontaine Bleau. To their relief, he was there, sitting at one of the tables outside with two other men, singing a French cabaret song. Four empty bottles of wine were on the table, one on its side with a large wet spot below the mouth.

"Oh Jack!" Michele said, jumping out of the car at the curb and sounding like a mother scolding a child. "Don't you know we have work to do? We're supposed to have dinner!"

"Daniele, my dear," Jack said rising and flowing to her side. "I'm not as think as you drunk I am."

Michele leaned against him to help hold him up, but he seemed to be able to stand on his own power, her hand under his arm.

He looked at her, trying to adjust his vision. "Why Daniele," he said, "I didn't know you cared."

Michele let go of him suddenly. "I...uh...I don't," she said. "You're just...um...you're making a spectacle of yourself!"

Jack stood up straight. "You're right, of course." He steadied himself on the back of his chair. "Just kidding with the think and drunk thing," he said. "I am just slightly inebriated, but I think those two," he pointed at his new friends with his thumb, "drank most of the wine." Jack leaned over conspiratorially and cupped his hand to his mouth. "Can't even speak English," he said. "Been trying to talk to them all afternoon." He shook his head. "Nothin'."

Michele looked at them.

The men waved with dull grins, their eyes drooping.

Jack looked and waved back. "Sing pretty good, though." He turned back to Michele with a serious look. "Jus' couldn't get in sync with the words, ya know?"

Michele made as low a growl as her vocal chords would allow, and yanked Jack along by his elbow.

Jack staggered his first two steps. "Hey Michele," he said waving like an imbecile at Daniele who was handing a valet parking attendant the keys to the Benz.

Daniele made a gun out of her thumb and forefinger. "Hi Jack!" she said. She'd always wanted to do that, but now it seemed so lame.

"Lame," Michele said, pushing a strand of her brunette hair back into place.

It was ten till eight by the time they'd found Jack at the restaurant. Le Fontaine Bleau was close to the end of the Champs Elysees down there near the Arc de Triomphe where the drug store is on the corner. Valerie had arranged a long table in the back of the restaurant on a terrace above the main dining room. The restaurant was deep and narrow, with off-white tablecloths and matching napkins embossed with images of the Arc.

Jack was softly humming the cabaret song while Valerie showed him his seat to the right of Rick. Taking Daniele off to the side, she asked, "Daniele?"

"Um-hmm," Daniele said with a grin.

"Good," Valerie said, then rapidly, "I came here earlier and arranged for one of my agents to be the waiter. The restaurant manager believes I'm an undercover police officer and that this is some kind of sting operation."

Daniele nodded.

"All we need," Valerie continued, "is their fingerprints. I intend to get them from the wine glasses. I don't want the Germans to leave before I've verified that we've gotten good prints. Okay?"

Daniele shook her head.

"When I go to the ladies room," Valerie went on, "and come back, if I say, 'I think I'm ready to call it a night,' that means the prints are good. Understand?"

Daniele nodded again.

"Very good," Valerie said, and somewhat desperately, "Try to find out what you can about your father."

She placed Daniele on one end while Rick took the other. Valerie sat to Rick's left, and Michele to Daniele's right. Normally Rick would have complained that he should be sitting down by Michele, but knew his role at this dinner as the senior Calvet representative.

Rick had ordered several bottles of wine, already open and on the table.

Valerie took a long careful look at each of the girls when they sat down, satisfied that their true identities were outwardly indistinguishable, but wanted to test Michele's competence in her role as Daniele before the subjects arrived. "So Daniele," she asked, taking a sip of wine. "What do you think of the tactile characteristics of the silicon-based humanoid projections?"

Rick looked up at the question.

Michele didn't falter. "An amazingly true-to-life rendering," she said. "Admirable work."

Daniele's mouth almost dropped, but she was able to stifle any reaction.

Valerie nodded approvingly, and settled back with a sip of wine and a quick humorous look at the befuddled Rick.

Daniele went through great Michele-like ecstatic pleasantries when Martin came in, praising him excessively for his work on the Galeries show.

Valerie looked uneasy when Daniele introduced her. "Martin," she said amiably, glancing hard at Daniele. "What a pleasant surprise. I didn't know you were coming."

"Oh," Michele said, "Michele invited him." She was sitting up stiff-backed in her chair, looking all sophisticated like she thought Daniele would look, her hair pinned in an updo. She turned her head left to look at Daniele. "Didn't you?"

Daniele giggled. "Yes, I thought Martin might want to meet the new sponsors since he'll be seeing them at the show tomorrow night."

"How marvelous," Valerie said with a forced smile.

"I was thinking," Daniele said as Martin came around the table – actually dressed in a normal, albeit extra large, blue suit, white shirt and red tie – and sat between Michele and Valerie, "that since you did such a great job on the Galeries show, you might like to go ahead," she hunched her shoulders and said gleefully, letting out a little Michele-like squeak, "and take charge of the Eiffel Tower show."

Martin slowly broke out into a genuine smile. "Are you sure you wouldn't mind?"

Michele, with a pleasant smile on her face, kicked Daniele under the table, which Daniele ignored.

"Oh, of *course* not," Daniele said enthusiastically. "Besides, I need to escort Daniele and Jack and Rick around, so I'll probably be too busy to get much involved. I'd really appreciate it if you took care of it for me."

"*Oh!*" Martin said. "It would *absolutely* be my *pleasure*." He clapped his hands rapidly in front of him like a small child, and almost squealed when he said. "I can't *wait!*"

He suddenly became even more animated, a feat which Daniele didn't think possible.

"I'll get right on it tomorrow," he said, eyes fluttering, and his hands suddenly fiddling with every item on the table in front of him. "I've got to get to the office and then go meet with Arlette – you remember Arlette don't you?" he asked Daniele. "From the Eiffel staff? She's got the cutest little pin nose," he said flapping his hand down at the wrist.

Martin went on and on until the new sponsors arrived about ten minutes late. They shook hands all around and introduced themselves as

Gunter Hartmann and Marlene Ramsauer.

"Gunter," Rick pumped his hand harshly and bowed slightly before switching to Marlene. "Marlene. Good to see you both again." Rick went around the table introducing everyone, starting with Daniele, who he of course introduced as Michele. Valerie was introduced as the manager of the Avenue Montaigne store, Jack as a friend of Daniele, Martin as Michele's assistant, and Michele as Michele's twin sister Daniele.

"Remarkable resemblance," Gunter said, shaking Michele's hand.

Gunter was dressed in a very fine suit, while Marlene was wearing an elegant, obviously high-fashioned, knee-length glittery dress. Gunter and Marlene both had black hair and dark eyes, and each appeared to have an even tan, or unusually dark skin for Germans.

"Lovely dress," Michele said to Marlene. "Monica Soisson, isn't it?"

"Yes, yes, it is," Marlene said nervously. "Thank you."

The entire conversation became easier when they learned that the Germans could speak English, although heavily accented. This was an extremely great relief to Daniele, who'd been worried all evening that they would want to converse in French.

The Germans explained how they had just established their new fashion house in Hamburg, and were very excited about being a part of Michele's show. They asked Daniele to give them a hint about what her new line would look like, which made both Daniele and Michele freeze up for a moment.

"Oh, why don't *you* tell them Martin?" Daniele said touching his forearm lightly with her pink freshly manicured fingernails with little flowers painted on them. "After all, you're in charge of the show now."

Martin spent the next twenty minutes dominating the conversation, animatedly describing one of Michele's *wonderful* creations after another, until even Michele had become bored with it. In the meantime they'd all ordered, gone through appetizers, and were now being served their entrees. Martin finally took a break when his lamb arrived, and Daniele capitalized on the moment having thought of an angle.

"So Gunter," Daniele began, "my father says he met you a few weeks back."

Gunter reached for his wine and took a sip. "Yes, um, I did meet him."

"He said you were very excited about my new line," she said with a delighted, broad smile.

"Yes, yes," Gunter said, stroking his wine glass. "We are very interested in seeing it."

Daniele's look turned to one of concern. "And how's your wife?"

"My wife?" Gunter tried to look nonchalant.

"Yes, her medical condition," Daniele said, her eyebrows narrowing.

Marlene tried to intervene. "Oh…um…she is much better now."

"Still in hospital?" Daniele asked.

"Oh, no," Gunter said. "Um…she came home last week."

"Really?" Daniele said, touching her cheek with her fingertips. "I'm surprised. The chemo must be working."

Gunter took another hasty sip of wine. "Um…yes…it is working."

"You know," Daniele said as though she had a new thought. "You probably saw my F…Da…dy since I saw him last," she said. "When was it again?"

"Oh, um, last week," Gunter said, "I believe. Yes. It was…um…in his office."

"Probably where he is now," Daniele said with a soft smirk. She had her elbow on the table and swatted the air without moving her wrist. "I haven't even seen him since I arrived. You can just imagine how busy we both are."

"And you have not tried to call him?" Gunter asked with too much apprehension.

Daniele chuckled. "Whatever for? I'll see him tomorrow night."

"Ah yes," Gunter said, "at the show."

"Yes," she said, and then hesitated. "Well, of course I *do* have to talk to him before then."

"You do?" Gunter asked, his eyes squinting uneasily.

"Absolutely," Daniele said, hunching her head down with a little more urgency. "Well, I probably shouldn't be telling you this, but we have a real problem."

"A problem?" Marlene asked, looking disturbed. "You cannot find your father?"

Daniele almost looked at her, but forced herself into a smile. "Oh, he's around somewhere. He's just so busy all the time. I keep trying his cell but just get his answering machine."

"You said you did not try to call him," Marlene said, her forehead wrinkled.

"Oh," Daniele said, thinking quickly of a way to cover her error. "I…um…I meant his office. I haven't tried there."

"I am certain you will see him at the show," Gunter said.

"Gotta talk to him before that," Daniele said lightly. "I'm mean, like, I need to know."

"Need to know what?" Marlene asked.

Everyone around the table was glued to her conversation. Valerie had a deer in the headlights look.

"About the other line," she whined. "If he thinks he's gonna go have Monica Soisson showing *her* fall line at *my* show, then he's got another thing coming." She leaned back in her chair and waved her arm. "I'll cancel before I ever let that happen."

"Cancel?" Gunter asked with an alarm that he didn't hide very well.

"Cancel," Daniele said. She smiled. "Oh, don't worry about it. You'll get your money back." She sniffed. "He's got plenty of it."

"Oh, I am sure he will call you before then," Gunter assured her.

"Well he'd better," she said. "He'd better call tonight, or first thing in the morning I'm calling the whole thing off." She made an indignant face. "Monica Soisson. Hmpf."

No one could see Gunter tap Marlene's leg under the table.

"Ah, excuse me," Marlene said, touching her napkin to her lips before she rose. "I need to use the toilet."

Daniele went on and on about Monica Soisson while Marlene was gone, and even after she'd returned. She even kept it up about canceling and the lousy thing "Daddy" had done to her to the point that Michele was becoming incensed at her characterization of her. She went on right up to the time Michele's cell phone rang. It was a detail that they hadn't anticipated, but fortunately the phone had migrated to Daniele along with the rest of the contents of Michele's purse, and was thankfully out of Michele's reach when she forgot her role and extended her hand toward it when it started playing, "Girls Just Wanna Have Fun."

Daniele groped around in the purse for several measures of the song before she found it and flipped it open. "Hello?"

Her heart almost stopped when she heard his voice, and it took all her concentration to act like nothing was wrong. "Daddy!" she said anxiously.

Leo said something that only Daniele could hear.

"Good to hear your voice too," she said. She didn't know if it was wise, but she asked anyway, thinking that it was only normal that she would. "Where are you?"

Another pause while she listened.

Gunter and Marlene exchanged glances, their brows furrowed. Gunter's right hand slipped off the table to his stomach, hovering over his tie and inching toward the inside of his coat.

Jack had shifted up in his chair and was staring intently.

A lot of kicking was going on under the table, and Valerie joined in, kicking Jack softly on the leg. When he looked she made a slight negative nod. He winked with his left eye, the one away from Gunter and Marlene, hidden, he thought, by his nose.

"Oh, that's good," Daniele was saying. "Well, I just need to know if you're really going to let Monica Soisson show her line at my show tomorrow night."

Gunter and Marlene were fidgeting, a bead of sweat forming on Gunter's brow and the tips of his fingers disappearing slightly under his lapel.

"Oh, good," she said with obvious relief, the lines in her face relaxing. "Well, don't worry about a thing." She looked at Michele. "Daniele's here with me, and so is Rick. We'll all be at the show tomorrow night."

Martin smiled wide. "Tell him I said hi!"

"And Martin says hi," Daniele said with a quick grin at Martin.

Valerie stared at Daniele intensely while Leo was obviously saying something else.

"Okay Daddy," she said. "See you tomorrow night. Oh! And Daddy?"

She listened.

"Eve says hi too."

She snapped the phone shut and giggled. "Looks like we won't have to cancel after all," she said.

"Anything else?" Rick asked.

"Just that he's at a friend's house," Daniele said, "though he didn't say who."

"Well that's great," Rick said energetically. "Great. It would have been a nightmare if you'd gone through with canceling."

"How 'bout that Gunter?" Daniele asked, smiling and looking intently at him. "Good timing, huh?"

"Very good," Gunter agreed, and brought his trembling hand back to his wine glass and took a gulp.

"Funny how we were just talking about how he'd better call," Daniele went on and laughed playfully. "Must've heard us."

Marlene shifted uncomfortably in her chair, and Valerie leaned around and gave Daniele a look as though it was time to drop it already.

Daniele saw her and obeyed. She gave a wide smile to Gunter and Marlene. "Well, I guess we're on for tomorrow night after all."

Valerie was silent through all of this, listening with controlled breathing. The whole table seemed to come to life with the knowledge that he was somewhere near, and alive.

Daniele had an impulse to just grab Gunter and Marlene on the spot, but suppressed it. She knew their time would come.

After the dinner plates had been cleared, Valerie ordered a different wine, which prompted the waiters to clear the wine glasses. But the Germans had not finished theirs and kept their glasses, politely refusing the new wine. So she waited for a while, and then ordered a digestif for everyone. This time she was successful. The Germans drank the liqueur and the waiter cleared the small glasses.

About five minutes later Valerie excused herself to the ladies room and went instead through a different door to the kitchen. It was Rick's job during her absence to prevent anyone else, especially Marlene, from leaving the table. This turned out to be no problem, as no one started to get up until Valerie had returned.

She sat down and waited five more minutes before she yawned, covering her mouth elegantly. She turned to Rick and said loudly enough for Daniele to hear, "I think I'm ready to call it a night."

Rick objected lightly, as was the plan, but Valerie insisted. Rick agreed and everyone followed suit when he stood, including the German guests, who sprung up at an almost absolute attention. Hands were shaken and pleasantries passed. Daniele and Martin both reiterated how they hoped to see them at the Eiffel Tower show, and the two Germans said they'd be there.

"Absolutely brilliant," Valerie said as she stood next to Daniele and Michele watching the black limo weaving into the thick Champs Elysees traffic. "Brilliant."

"You were really, really great," Jack said to Daniele.

"So he *is* alive!" Michele said with glee, clapping her hands together rapidly.

Jack looked at her with red blurry eyes as his eyebrows went up. "Daniele," he said, breaking into a grin, "never seen you quite so, um, enthusiastic."

"Well," Michele said, "Father's never been missing before, and now we know he's alive."

"True enough," Jack said, but still looked askance at her.

"They were sooo three years ago," Michele said, shaking her head as the limo was consumed by the mass of vehicles. "And what was with that make up? She's definitively *not* a winter." She looked around with shifty eyes to see if anyone noticed that she hadn't exactly spoken like Daniele. "How do they think they're going to pull off being in the fashion industry?"

Jack looked and winked at her, causing Michele's eyes to open wide.

Daniele tried to cover. "Like, they were totally awesome, ya know?"

Jack let out a little chuckle, which made both girls squirm.

"Awesome?" Rick asked.

"I think…um…sh…she means," Michele stammered, "that they were so in three *years* ago. They were definitely awesome at that time." She tried to cover her own blunder further by adding more sophistication, her palms turned up in an explanatory gesture. "They were definitely cutting-edge at that time, but you know fashion. Every year is new, and designers have to collaborate and push the edge of the envelope to find that new frontier." She stood in horrid silence while they all took this in, the noise of the traffic covering her excited panting as she felt she was sinking into a hole.

Jack chuckled again while Daniele was going pale.

Rick looked over at Jack's chuckle, saw him looking at Daniele and asked, "Michele, are you all right?"

Daniele smiled and wrung her hands. "Just nerves from actually talking to FDad…dy." She almost even rolled her eyes at herself for her continual missing of something so simple as "Daddy" vice "Father."

"I didn't know you knew so much about fashion, Daniele," Valerie said with a twinkle in her eye, noting that they were still keeping up the deception now that the mission was over.

"Well, I *am* a woman, after all," Michele said. "I may not show it, but I follow fashion like any other woman. What's her name, Marlene, did you see that dress? That was one of Monica Soisson's designs three or four years ago. Where'd she get it? Some seventy-five percent off sale in the low rent district? I was just surprised that she was still wearing something that old." She turned to Daniele. "Michele, don't you think she'll really look out of place at your show if she actually does show up and dresses in something old like that? Might have a negative impact on the overall impression that the press will have."

"Totally," Daniele said.

"And the guy's suit," Michele went on, "was at least five years old. It was a Gérard Boisserie."

Everyone was staring at her.

"Wasn't it Michele?"

"Absolutely," Daniele said. "They were so totally out of date." She cleared her throat. "Awesome though."

Michele just couldn't help herself. "I'm just surprised they didn't wear something from their own house...um...establishment."

"Probably not likely since they don't actually work there," Rick said.

"Oh yeah," Michele said. "Right."

Daniele, amazed that their cover wasn't blown already, said, "Can't we just like, go home or something?"

22

Rick and Valerie concluded that they needed to go back to Eva to flush out the information they'd gathered, while Jack decided to just hang around on the Champs Elysees. He tried desperately to talk Michele and Daniele into staying around for a while, but Michele insisted she needed to rest up for the next day, which elicited an awkward moment when Michele added, "you know, for Michele's show."

Daniele was adamant that she didn't want to drink any more since they might find Leo at any moment, and wanted to tag along with Rick and Valerie to look for "Daddy." They had another uncomfortable instance when Jack pointed out that "Michele" had wanted to go home, but now she wanted to go with Rick and Valerie.

"You two just aren't making any sense," Jack said, doing the wobbly with a sly grin.

"Hey," Daniele said earnestly, "shouldn't I go along with my fiancé?"

So Daniele went with Rick and Valerie, anxious to follow their leads, while Michele had "Michele's" Benz brought around. She waved to Jack, standing alone in the middle of the stream of people passing on the extraordinarily wide sidewalk, as she drove off to Leo's chateau.

The control room was darkened, as usual, when Rick, Valerie, and Daniele walked in. Jean-Claude was at the console.

"Any location on the trace?" Valerie asked without a hello.

"We have a general area," Jean-Claude said, "but no address yet."

"This the cell call?" Rick asked.

"Yes," Valerie said. "And what about the prints?"

"Identified," Jean-Claude affirmed. "Marlene Ramsauer is really Atisheh Larijani. And Gunter Hartmann is Ghadir Mirsalim. Both originally from Tehran, living in Hamburg for the past fifteen years."

"Associations?" Valerie asked.

"Eva ties them to an emergent group called Hesam, which means 'a sharp sword.' The system doesn't know much about them yet, but the information is accumulating fairly rapidly."

Valerie turned to Rick, "Let's go."

She marched out of the room, down the hall and into the elevator to Eva – Rick and Daniele right behind her.

"Eva, take us to Gunter Hartmann and Marlene Ramsauer's room in the Intercontinental Hotel in Paris."

The room morphed from the white cube to the chic room in the hotel. The walls were papered in white-striped peach, slightly contrasted by the tan floor with blue circular designs.

Valerie paced around the room, looked out the window and back in at the phone on a small dark desk. "We need to trace the calls from this room," she said.

Rick smiled. "Have the system bring Sherlock Holmes."

"Oh, not him again," Daniele said with her nose crinkled up. She almost corrected herself, realizing that Michele would have reacted with glee to the conjuring of Holmes, but let it go when Rick didn't seem to notice.

A grin broke on Valerie's face. "Sherlock Holmes?"

"A little joke," Rick said.

"Ah yes," Valerie said. "The episode in Eve." She looked toward the phone. "Eva, bring us Sherlock Holmes."

They heard the toilet flush, and moments later Holmes walked into the room from the bathroom, trailing smoke from his pipe and pulling his overcoat around his waist. "Good to see you again, Rick." He nodded. "Michele."

"Mr. Holmes," Rick said. "We need to know the destination of all of the phone calls made from this room by the current registered guests."

"Would you like them in alphabetical order?" Holmes asked between his teeth clamped onto his pipe.

Rick scratched his cheek and modified the request. "Just calls made to locations here in Paris."

"Five eighty-five Rue Gabrielle," Holmes said without hesitation in his heavy British accent.

They waited.

"That's all?" Valerie asked.

"Yes," Holmes said. "Only one local destination."

"How many calls?" Valerie asked.

"Twenty-six," Holmes replied.

Valerie looked at Rick. "That's it," she said. "Eva, take us to five eighty-five Rue Gabrielle."

The room morphed away along with Holmes.

"Bring Sherlock with us," she said.

Holmes materialized on a narrow, dirty street. The houses were small and run-down, the street lined with mostly old, worn cars. The sidewalks were slim and cracked, with the doors to the houses barely a meter from the road, virtual dust from the traffic covering the windows – a touch that made Daniele even more impressed with Eva, now that she was understanding the differences between the systems. As with the rest of the houses on the street, it was constricted, and three stories high.

"So what now?" Rick asked.

"We go inside," Valerie said, turning the dented brass knob and pushing the door open.

The inside was as dismal as the street. A torn brown sofa sat against one wall, with a marred coffee table in the center of a green threadbare throw rug. A stairway hugged the wall just inside the door, which Valerie started up slowly, Rick, Daniele, and Sherlock Holmes coming up behind her.

The second floor had several rooms down a hall that stretched along the stairs with a loose wood railing that ran continuously to the next set of stairs up. She opened each door as she looked through the second floor, finding two bedrooms and a bathroom. The same arrangement was up the next set of stairs, and she tried each of the doors, stopping in the last bedroom.

"Sherlock," she said, "is this where Leo Calvet's phone call came from?"

"I'm sorry, I have insufficient data to confirm the location," Holmes said. "However, there is some probability."

"What's the probability that this is the room where Leo made the call?" Valerie asked.

Holmes puffed on his pipe. "Sixty-two percent."

"Not bad," Rick said.

"We'd better check it out," Valerie said.

"But that room," Holmes added, pointing to the other end of the hall with the end of his pipe, "has a probability of ninety-two percent."

Valerie looked at him with a blank stare. "What's the probability that the phone call came from this house?"

"Would that be Leo Calvet's phone call?" Holmes asked politely.

"What other phone call are we talking about?" Daniele asked impatiently.

"Could be..." Holmes began.

"Yes!" Daniele said in exasperation, and then calmed herself. "Yes, yes, the Leo Calvet phone call."

Holmes puffed on his pipe pensively. "Ninety-eight point six two percent."

Valerie turned to Rick. "Let's go." But she didn't actually "go" anywhere. Instead, she started barking commands in French. "Eva, terminate programme. Eva print two copies of the floor plan for five eighty-five Rue Gabrielle. Eva, print out two copies of a map highlighting the fastest route from this location to five eighty-five Rue Gabrielle. Eva, print out a listing of the destinations of all phone calls made from Gunter Hartmann's room in the Intercontinental, and every phone call made from five eighty-five Rue Gabrielle in the last year. Jean-Claude?"

"Yes?" Jean-Claude's voice echoed as the room turned white and the elevator appeared.

Valerie, in total control, continued as she, Rick, and Daniele stepped in. "Call Richard and tell him to assemble a team."

"Size?" Jean-Claude asked.

"Eight," she said without faltering. "Fully armed. And get him the floor plan and route."

She was tapping her foot impatiently as the elevator rose. "And have Paulette begin analyses of the phone lists."

They emerged in room 820 and took the elevator back down and out the revolving door of the Hilton to a waiting black car. Rick almost had to trot to keep up.

"What about her?" Valerie asked Rick, grasping the handle on the car door, referring to Daniele.

"I'm going," Daniele said. "This is my father we're talking about."

Valerie acquiesced without a word and jumped in the front passenger seat, while Daniele slipped in the back with Rick behind her.

The car was moving before Rick was even able to close his door. Around the corner they met two other cars, one containing three men and the other four.

The ride across town was fast paced, with tires screeching. But the roads were fairly void of traffic at two o'clock in the morning, busy mostly with taxis. The driver seemed to be in constant radio contact with someone, wearing an earpiece with a boom microphone glued to his lips. Valerie, meanwhile, had somehow produced two handguns and was busy checking the magazines in the dim glow of the back seat light. She slipped one in with a snap and held it around her seat to Rick.

"I have one of these," Rick said, taking the gun and admiring it.

"Good," Valerie said. "Then you know how to use it?"

Rick smiled. "They do train us, you know."

Valerie smiled briefly, and then watched out the window as Paris flew by, her eyes sharp and attentive.

Daniele looked at the gun and shivered. She said softly to Rick, "Be careful with that thing."

Rick placed his free hand on her leg and squeezed with a grin. "Don't worry, Michele."

Daniele felt remorse at her deception, but was warmed by his hand. The passing Parisian glow silhouetted her face as she watched the surrounding lights flicker over his eyes.

They rounded the Arc de Triomphe, with the Champs Elysees as busy as if it were early evening. Rick had a fleeting glimpse of someone who looked very much like Jack and craned his neck around. Sure enough, Jack was sitting with two other men in front of Le Fontaine Bleau, bottles of wine and glasses scattered on the table. They seemed to be engaged in singing something, mouths open and arms flung wide.

Fifteen minutes later they came to the narrow street. The other two cars had turned right at the previous intersection with Rick wondering why, but he soon knew the reason. His driver stopped without a screech, the car blocking the intersection into the lane. Before they'd gotten out, the other two cars had emerged at the far end of the street blocking the opposite intersection. Within moments the team of eight had noiselessly gathered outside the house on the poorly lit lane. A dim glow of light came through the upstairs windows, but the downstairs was ominously dark.

Each team member was dressed in black clothing with bulging body armor underneath, wearing black hoods pulled over their faces to eliminate any reflection. Each man had an Uzi strapped around his forearm.

The lead man tried the doorknob, but it was locked. He reached back and kicked with his boot, splintering the wood and swinging the door back hard against the wall. One by one they scrambled in with methodical patience, apparently knowing their order of insertion. The leader moved up the stairs followed by his team, while the trailing two men branched out into the downstairs rooms.

They did the same pattern on the second floor. The leader moved rapidly to the stairs, three men behind him, while two men started kicking in doors.

Shouting could be heard from the third floor now. Rick started to run upstairs, but Valerie held him back, reaching and pulling on his black shirt so hard that he almost fell backwards as he climbed the first two steps.

"Not our job," Valerie said.

"This is *my* fight," Rick argued, regaining his balance at the bottom of the stairs and pointed with his gun. "That's Leo Calvet up there."

"You know how these things go," Valerie said.

Rick looked up the stairs but held his place.

Daniele's eyes were wide as she stood behind Rick, her breathing erratic.

A sudden popping came from upstairs, followed by much louder bursts. Men were shouting orders and warnings as Daniele heard a thud on the floor. Hopefully it wasn't one of their team. The two men who had searched downstairs rushed to the foot of the stairway, guns at the ready, and gazed up. Rick, Daniele and Valerie made way for them and shuffled aside into the cramped living room. Rick prodded Daniele behind him with the back of his arm putting himself between danger and her, his pistol held at the ready, safety off. The men held their posts, looking up as the gunfire continued with intermittent bursts followed by an occasional groan. Thirty tense seconds later the shooting ceased.

The men at the foot of the stairs shouted up, and a voice replied from the third floor.

"Let's go," Valerie said, as she slipped past the two agents.

But before she'd taken two steps up, the wall behind her exploded in splintering circles as a burst of gunfire came from the kitchen. The shots were spraying in a line that puffed across the agents' vests, knocking both back against the stairway wall, each slumping unconscious. The second commando fell onto Valerie, inadvertently protecting her from the fire.

"Rick!" Daniele shrieked and swung herself around to shield his body, clutching him around the neck with her back to the gunman, willing to take the bullets, her back muscles contracting in fearful anticipation of the piercing lead.

Rick grabbed her around her waist and spun her, lifting her feet off the floor and putting his back, this time, in harm's way. Debris from the wall was flying into their hair like confetti, the sound of the machine gun ringing in their ears. Twisting around he stretched his gun hand, aimed deliberately, and squeezed off round after round at the lone man's head. The man was half-crouched in the kitchen doorway, his eyes frenzied, screaming words that were incomprehensible to them. Rick's third round met its mark, creating an instant red dot on the man's forehead that whipped his head back. The automatic continued to spray its deadly globs of lead across the ceiling as his legs collapsed beneath him and he fell backwards. Halfway to the floor the firing stopped as the gun drifted from his hand and clattered on the green linoleum.

The two agents on the floor above them were halfway down the stairs, their guns in the firing position, by the time the assailant had fallen. They stepped over Valerie and their fallen comrades and worked past Rick and Daniele to the kitchen, the first man kicking the gun away from the reach of the dead man.

Valerie struggled to free herself from beneath her protectors, and then checked the pulse of each.

"Val?" Rick asked.

"They'll be all right," Valerie said. "Body armor shots." Even as she said it the two men were stirring.

Daniele still had Rick by the neck.

"You saved my life," he said, and kissed her quickly on the lips. "Thank you."

Daniele shook her head. "I think it was you who saved mine."

"Let's go," Valerie said, stepping carefully over the men, their eyes open and groggy. Both were struggling to their feet now, their hands grasping at their chests as they each let out soft moans.

Rick followed behind her, with Daniele behind him clutching his shirt. The second floor was empty, and even the stairway going to the third. But the first casualty was there, sprawled on his back on the top three steps, his legs spread eagle on the landing, an AK-47 propped across his bloody torso, his hand limp over the trigger, eyes still open and glazed.

One of the team was standing guard at the top of the stairs.

Valerie asked him something in French, and the man answered.

"No casualties," Valerie said with relief. "Just two more like him."

"Leo?" Rick asked, stepping over the body.

"He's here," she said.

"Where?" Daniele asked anxiously.

Valerie pointed down the hall.

Rick passed one of the rooms to see Gunter Hartmann with his arms raised high, terror in his eyes. "Hey Gunter!" he said as he passed, then mumbled, "Good, you can feel a little terror."

"What's that?" Valerie asked.

"Nothing," Rick said. "Nothing."

Approaching the last room at the end of the hall, Rick and Daniele saw their first glimpses of Leo. He was sitting upright against the frame of a twin bed, his legs stretched out straight and his torso tied with a thin rope wrapped repeatedly around his chest and the bars in the metal headboard. His hands were taped in front of him, and one of the soldiers was cutting at the tape and the rope with a long knife.

Valerie ran to him. "Leo!" she cried as the soldier cleared the last of the tape and made way for her. She sat on the bed beside him. "Oh Leo!"

To Daniele's surprise, she kissed him repeatedly on his forehead and cheek, even on his lips. She cradled his head on her shoulder and stroked his hair.

"Leo, darling," she said. "I was so worried."

Leo managed a smile. "I knew you'd come."

Daniele came up behind her. "Father!" she said, forgetting her role as Michele, and knelt on the floor next to Valerie.

"Michele!" Leo said in a half-groan, his eyes lighting up. He seemed to just see her blonde hair and had missed her slip-up calling him "Father."

"Oh Dad," she said, Valerie scooting aside so that she could hug him.

"Thank you," he said, "for the message from Eve. It really gave me hope. I knew you were coming."

Daniele smiled and lightly kissed his cheek.

"Don't worry," Valerie said, "we'll have an ambulance here soon."

"No ambulance," he said, chopping his hand to the side.

"You must," Valerie said. "You need a doctor."

"What for?" Leo asked. "I'm all right. What about Daniele?"

"She's fine, sir," Rick said.

Leo saw him for the first time. "Rick," he said with a welcome smile.

"You really need to see a doctor, Leo," Rick said.

"What I need," Leo said, grunting and shuffling past Valerie to swing his feet energetically to the floor as Rick rushed to help lift him under his arm, "is to get to Eva."

"No," Valerie said. "I insist that you see a doctor."

"*Please*, Father," Daniele said, her forehead lined with worry.

"It's not over," he explained. "I've overhead them. It's the Eiffel – tonight."

"The fashion show?" Rick asked.

"I'm fairly certain," Leo said. "But I don't know for sure. I couldn't understand them completely." He shook his head regretfully. "Always knew I should learn Arabic."

"They're Iranian," Rick said.

Leo had a surprised look. "Huh. Persian too. Whatever they speak over there."

"Leo please…" Valerie began.

Leo leaned to her and kissed her passionately on the mouth.

"There something here I don't know about?" Daniele asked.

Leo looked at her and back to Valerie. "You didn't tell them?"

She shook her head.

A sly smile stretched across Leo's face. "Michele, I'd like you to meet Valerie Vachet. My fiancé."

23

Leo, Valerie, Rick, and Daniele reached the chateau at four in the morning. Valerie at least convinced him to go see "Daniele" and clean up before he went to Eva. She wanted him to sleep, but he argued that, "All I've been doing is laying around for the last couple days."

They immediately went to Daniele's suite to wake her and tell her the news.

"Daniele," he said tenderly, sitting on the bed beside Michele and stroking her hair. Daniele and Rick were standing near the door.

"Mmm…" Michele moaned, turning over to one side.

He stroked her hair. "Daniele."

Her eyes opened. "Oh!"

"Hey, sleepy head," Leo said.

"Oh Daddy!" she said, throwing her arms up around his neck, while Daniele rolled her eyes and took a quick glance at Rick. "Wow! You look so *real!*"

"Of course I'm real," he said, and then leaned back a little with a confused look. "Daniele?"

Michele winked at him. "Yes…um…Father."

Leo's eyebrows rose.

She studied his face. "You look terrible."

"Not too much sleep lately," he explained.

"Careful," Valerie said standing in the doorway. "Everyone please don't hurt the patient any more than he's already hurt."

"Oh! Sorry Daddy," Michele said, leaning back and dropping her arms to her side.

He looked her in the eye. "That's all right…*Daniele.*"

"Hah!" she gasped and glanced fleetingly at Rick. "Oh yeah, I uh, guess you already talked to…um…Michele a bit."

"Besides," he said, helping to gloss over her blunders. "I'm not hurt, other than a sore behind from sitting like a stuffed doll for days."

"Maybe now's a good time to tell her about Valerie," Rick said, every "Daddy" having passed him by.

"What about Valerie?" Michele asked.

"Your father and I," Valerie said, sitting on the bed next to Leo and wrapping her arm around him, "are engaged."

"Engaged!" Michele said with a gleeful smile. "That's *wonderful!*"

Valerie beamed. "I didn't want to tell you without Leo being here."

"Well everyone," Leo said, pushing himself up slowly from the bed. "I don't want to break this up, but we still have work to do."

"Sure you won't stay here and rest?" Valerie asked, even though it was futile. Leo's decision had obviously been made.

"Not until the Eiffel is secure," he said. "And we have a guest, I believe, at Eva, who I'd just *love* to talk to."

Valerie stayed behind to get Leo cleaned up before driving him over to Eva, while Rick, Daniele and Michele found Jack at Le Fontaine Bleau on the Champs Elysees where Rick had seen him earlier, still singing songs with the Frenchmen.

The rest of that morning passed uneventfully, with the four of them hanging around Leo's office, Jack mostly passed out on the sofa with his arms and legs flailing every which way. By evening, a sobered up Jack was wearing a black tuxedo and had been sitting around the coffee table for hours, waiting to see what the interrogations revealed. But so far, nothing. Rick, also in a black tux, was in an office down the hall that had been turned into an impromptu interrogation room.

Earlier in the afternoon the four had gone down to the café across the street from the Hilton and had sandwiches and coffee, and then they'd all gone to the chateau to dress for Michele's show. Once they'd come back Michele had been coming and going in and out of Leo's office to check up on the progress of her show, dragging Daniele back and forth in an effort to maintain their identities.

"After all," Michele told her repeatedly within earshot of Jack and Rick, "it's your show."

The day-to-day access to the Eva facility was through the office building across the street from the hotel. Every half hour or so Michele would nod in the direction of the Eiffel and Daniele would say, "Think I'll go see how things are going. Wanna go Daniele?" "Daniele," of course, would always want to tag along – what choice did she have? – and they'd exit down the dozen or so broad steps at the front entrance to the building to go check up on the setup progress.

The show had exclusive use of one of the Eiffel's elevators to the first floor, with caterers, models, stage handlers, and Martin going up and down all day long. Martin's cell phone seemed to be attached to his ear, most often talking to Michele who kept her phone in her hand at all times once they were outside the facility.

They'd just come back into Leo's office and plopped on the sofa when Leo walked in.

"Anything?" Jack asked, his feet crossed on the table.

"Still nothing," Leo said as he strode over to the gathering at the coffee table.

Rick walked in a few moments later, paced over to the group and stood next to Leo.

Leo spoke directly to Michele, not covering for them anymore. "Maybe we should cancel the show."

"Cancel!" Michele said hastily.

Daniele still picked up the act, though she had grown weary of it. "Why would you want to cancel my show?"

"Extremely high terror threat," Leo said matter-of-factly. "We have no idea what these people are up to."

"But he's *here*," Michele reasoned. "He can't do anything now."

Leo had a pained smile, but spoke in a kind, fatherly tone. "These kinds of people don't work alone," he said. "They usually have a cell and a network. Believe me, there's more to this than this one guy, or even his cell that we raided. But we just can't get him to divulge any information."

"You ever think of using Eva?" Jack asked.

Leo focused on Jack. "Using Eva for what?"

Jack shrugged. "You know, for interrogation."

Leo looked intrigued. "What did you have in mind?"

The side of Jack's cheek broke into a devilish smile. "I can think of something."

Leo looked at his watch. "Twenty after," he said anxiously. "May already be too late to evacuate. And if we do, there'll be a panic. Let's give it a try. If I don't have answers before twenty till eleven I'm pulling the plug."

"Pulling the plug!" Michele said desperately. "*Why?*"

"I'm not taking any chances with all these people, not to mention the Eiffel Tower itself," Leo said.

"Well, I've seen the security guys down there," Daniele said. "They seem pretty normal to me, and they're checking everything that goes up to the first floor."

Leo nodded. "I've been in constant communication with them all day. I have an agent from the Secret Service running the operation. The local security is there too, but they haven't been briefed. Don't want to spread a panic. Even with all that, it just isn't enough. We don't have answers."

"What if there *are* no answers?" Michele asked. "What if they were just working alone?"

"Then we'll cancel the show for nothing," Leo said. "But I'm not going forward until I know what they were doing. Several men were already willing to die for their operation. I'm not gambling with people's lives, or with a French symbol as powerful as the Eiffel. You know what the twin towers did to us. Just imagine."

"Well don't they have bomb dogs or something like that sniffing everything?" Daniele asked.

"Absolutely," Leo said. "But in the best security operation it's possible to miss something. Something could slip through the cracks."

Michele got up and headed for the door, "Well we're going back over there, aren't we Michele? We're going to see if everything looks okay."

Daniele followed obediently. "Naturally."

As the door was closing behind them, Daniele overheard Leo ask, "So, Jack, tell me how you think we might use Eva."

Daniele and Michele came down the steps from the building and walked briskly to the end of the street where the park around the Eiffel Tower began. They could see Martin in the distance near the elevator signing something on a clipboard. Michele called his cell.

Martin handed the clipboard back to a truck driver and answered his phone as he headed toward the elevator.

"Martin Jackson," he answered in a singsong. Michele could see him over there with his hand on his hip, walking toward one of the tower legs.

"So how's it going?" Michele asked, holding the phone in front of her on speaker so that Daniele could hear as well.

"Oh, very good, very good," Martin said. She watched him disappear into the building housing the elevator.

"Anything, um, strange going on?" she asked, her high heels clopping on the pavement. "Everything normal?"

"What do you mean, sweetie?" Martin asked. His phone crackled a bit.

"You know, anything out of the ordinary?"

"Nothing," Martin said. "Everything's under control. Oh! Yes. Nice touch with the Benzes."

"The Benzes?" Michele asked.

"You know, the ones at each of the front legs of the towe…," he said as his phone went to static momentarily, "…ery classy touch."

"Who ordered them?" Michele asked.

"Someone named Mar…" Martin began, but the phone had gone to static again before she heard him clearly. "…ust signed for them. Somebody had to. Pretty late delivery, but they look great. Guests are arriving. Gotta go!" Martin said. "Elevator's here!"

The phone clicked off as Michele and Daniele walked under the tower. The elevator was halfway to the first floor by the time they'd reached the entrance to the building.

"Those must be the Benzes he was talking about," Daniele said, nodding her head toward the front legs of the tower.

"I guess so," Michele said. "But I didn't know they were part of the show."

"They really are a nice touch," Daniele said.

Michele stopped and looked at them. "They *are* pretty cool, huh."

There were two of them. One white and one black. E500 Benz sedans, each sitting in front of one of the concrete pillars on the Seine side of the tower on shiny chrome racks that lifted them two thirds of a meter off the ground. The cars were tilted forward and slanted in toward each other to give passers-by a better viewing angle.

Daniele was impressed. "Got to hand it to Martin, he does go for the details."

Michele was a bit miffed at that, considering that it was Daniele who'd given Martin her job. "They're nice," she said and took a closer look as they approached. "But look at them," she said annoyed. "They're not even the right ones."

"They're not?" Daniele asked.

"No, look inside. They don't have my designs in them." She looked a little worried. "I hope the Benz people don't notice the interiors. They spent a lot of money on my designs. This whole show isn't just about the Calvet Fashion line, ya know. It's about introducing the new Benz interiors," she flipped her brunette hair back, "designed by yours truly."

"Oh, don't worry about it," Daniele said. "Nobody'll notice."

"That's the *problem!*" Michele said.

Daniele surveyed the grounds. "Well there's no use hanging around here," she said. "Let's go back and see what's going on."

Leo, Valerie, Rick, and Jack were in the control room with Jean-Claude adjusting settings and typing rapidly on the keyboard when Daniele and Michele walked in.

"Here you are!" Michele said, but went silent when she saw Jean-Claude's monitor.

Gunter Hartmann, also known as Ghadir Mirsalim, his real name, was sitting alone in Eva's white chamber in an armless metal chair, blindfolded, with his arms stretched around the back and handcuffed. Wide leather straps secured his body to the chair.

"I think we're ready," Leo said, sitting to Jean-Claude's right.

Jack was sitting to the left of Jean-Claude with a small desktop microphone in front of him. "Shall we?" He turned. "Help me out here, Val."

Valerie was standing next to Rick with her arms folded, just behind Leo. "Eva," she said in French, "take him to outer space, moving toward the sun."

Instantly the view of the monitor changed, the white walls flicking to black, and Ghadir appeared to be floating in space, the sun coming ever closer.

"I'm not sure this is right," Rick said shifting nervously from one leg to the other, his hands in his pockets.

Valerie spoke into a two-way radio she was holding. "Take it off and exit."

A man appeared behind Ghadir and ripped the blindfold off, then slipped out into the elevator. Ghadir instantly pushed back against the chair with his feet, arching his back. His mouth dropped and his eyes went wide as he tugged at the handcuffs.

Jack leaned into the mike. "Ghadir! This is Allah speaking! You failed your mission and you must be punished!" He paused. "Anything you want to tell me?"

Ghadir squirmed, but kept his mouth shut.

"Ghadir, buddy," Jack said, "you're gonna tell me what I need to know or I'm gonna fry you."

They could see sweat starting to form on Ghadir's brow, a little drop trickling down his cheek.

"Ghadir," Jack said lightly. "What was your mission?"

Ghadir was silent.

"If that's the way you want to play it," Jack said. He palmed the mike and turned to Jean-Claude. "Take him closer to the sun."

The sun rushed toward him, growing in size until it began to fill the end of the room and looked as though it would surround him. Solar flares shot off to his right and left, his head and eyes darting back and forth following them. He was tugging hard at the cuffs now, his feet trying in vain to push the silicon chair back.

"Ghadir," Jack said softly, his quiet voice booming from the sun's surface. "What was your mission?"

The sweat was flowing freely now, so much so that it was forming spots on Ghadir's shirt.

Rick was anxiously shuffling his feet, scratching his chin and brushing his hands through his hair. "I wish you weren't here to see this," he said to Daniele and Michele.

Jack cupped his hand over the mike. "Can he feel the heat?"

"As much as we want him to," Leo said.

Jean-Claude turned around to see Leo. Leo nodded, and Jean-Claude typed a command into the system that raised the temperature about ten degrees.

"Is there a limit?" Jack asked. "A failsafe?"

Leo turned to Valerie.

"No," she said. "A scenario like this was never a consideration, so there are no safeguards. We could fry him if we want to."

"Good," Jack said and turned back to the monitor. "Take him to the sun."

"We shouldn't be doing this," Rick said uncomfortably. "This is torture."

Leo swiveled suddenly in his chair. "Would you rather he hit France?" he asked harshly, and then turned back and ordered, "Do it!"

"Eva," Valerie said, "put him on the surface of the sun."

Instantly the room was filled with bright orange-white flames, the monitor so dazzling that it made each of them squint. Jean-Claude slowly adjusted the temperature in the chamber up and up. It hit sixty centigrade according to a small window on his screen displaying atmospheric metrics.

"Comfy Ghadir?" Jack asked. They could all hear his snort echoing in the chamber through the speakers mounted on the ceiling of the control room. "Get used to it buddy, 'cause you're gonna be feeling like this for a very very long time you son of…"

"All right!" Ghadir cried, jerking his torso forward and back. "Please stop!"

"All right what?" Jack asked calmly.

"I will tell you!"

Jack turned to Jean-Claude. "Let off on the temp a bit, but let's leave him there in the flames."

Jean-Claude adjusted the temperature down ten degrees.

"What do you want to tell me, Ghadir?" Jack asked serenely. "What was your mission?"

"The…um…the," Ghadir started, but then seemed to change his mind.

"Crank it up," Jack said impatiently.

Jean-Claude instantly pushed the temperature to fifty-five and the flames rose higher.

"The tower!" Ghadir said in desperate agony, "the tower is the mission!"

"The tower," Jack said with a grunt.

"Yes! Yes! Please stop!" Ghadir pleaded.

Jean-Claude let if off a little.

"We *know* it's the tower," Jack said angrily. "What about it?"

"A bomb," Ghadir confessed. "That's all I know."

Daniele and Michele took sharp breaths. Rick crossed his arms.

"So there *is* a bomb?" Michele asked the monitor.

"Where's the bomb?" Jack demanded.

"I don't…I don't know," Ghadir said frantically. "That was not my part of the operation."

"What *was* your part?" Jack asked.

"The contract," Ghadir said hastily, "with Calvet Fashions. That was my only part."

Jack leaned back and cupped the mike. "That doesn't make any sense."

"Must be compartmented," Leo said, drumming his fingers on the desk. "They usually are."

Jack pulled his hand away and leaned forward. "Who should we look for?"

"I don't know," Ghadir said desperately. "That was my only part."

"What time is the bomb supposed to go off?"

Ghadir struggled against the handcuffs. "When the show starts. Eleven. Eleven o'clock."

Leo looked at his watch. "Ten minutes," he said. "No time to evacuate now. We have to find it."

"Why did you kidnap Leo Calvet?"

Ghadir's voice shook. "I don't know."

"Give him some heat," Jack said, and Jean-Claude obliged.

"To distract!" Ghadir exclaimed, sweating profusely now and pulling and pushing in anguish. "To stop you from looking! Please stop! It was to give us time to complete the operation! Calvet knew…he knew…" Ghadir's head dropped forward with his chin on his chest.

Jack leaned back.

Leo seemed to be struggling with his thoughts before he turned suddenly to Daniele and Michele. "You were just there, right?"

"Yes," Daniele said.

"What's going on?" Leo asked in earnest. "Anything out of the ordinary?"

"Not that *I* could see," Michele said. "But I didn't go up to the first floor this time."

Leo continued his grilling, "Did you talk to Martin?"

"Yes," Michele said. "He said everything was just fine. No problems. Nothing out of the ordinary."

"Everything is going as you planned?" Leo asked. "Nothing unexpected?"

"No. Everything's fine," Michele said.

Daniele's eyes became wide. "The Benzes!"

"What Benzes?" Leo asked.

"More Benzes…" Jack said lowering his head and shaking it.

"Well, there are two Benzes parked in front of the tower," Michele explained. "I think it was Martin's idea. But he got the wrong ones."

"What do you mean the wrong ones?" Leo asked in a severe tone.

"I don't know," Michele whined, giving up the pretense of being Daniele, as though her father was chiding her as he had when she was a child. "They didn't have my designs, that's all."

Valerie looked at her watch. "Nine minutes!"

Rick and Daniele flashed an alarmed look at each other, and then turned suddenly and ran out the door while Valerie helped Leo to his feet.

Jack yanked the headphones off and rushed across the room.

"Where's everybody going?" Michele asked.

"To the bombs," Jack replied. "Com'on!"

24

Jack had stumbled over something in the control room and was sprawled out right in front of the door with Leo and Valerie pulling him to his feet. He looked behind, but couldn't see what it was he'd tripped over, and didn't give it a thought as he rushed out into the hallway. They were running in single file when Rick and Daniele disappeared into the elevator down the hall. Jack sprinted to catch up, but reached the elevator just as the door closed. He tried to pry it with his fingers, but the car was already gone.

"Don't you want to go out the front?" Michele asked in a trot to keep up, Valerie just ahead of her.

"This is faster," Valerie said as she reached the elevator and waited, Leo coming up behind at a fast walk.

Jack stabbed repeatedly at the button on the wall, already illuminated. After what seemed like minutes, in fact only thirty seconds or so, the door finally opened. They could feel the heat on the opposite door emanating from the chamber as they all crowded in.

The door closed, Valerie pressed the "Up" button, and then they waited.

"How's the weather in there?" Jack yelled through the door.

"Really beautiful night," Michele said with a smile.

"Good turn out?" Jack asked amicably.

"Oh, hundreds," Michele said with glee. "The lights are twinkling and the moon is out."

"Good for you," Jack said, nodding with approval.

The door finally opened and the four of them were tumbling out of the shower stall of room 820 in the Hilton Paris, trying not to step on each other's feet. Valerie was the first out and ran as quickly as she could down the hall to the elevator where they had to wait for one of the three cars.

The elevator opened and they all crowded in again, Valerie getting shuffled to the back. The door closed and Michele pressed the "Lobby" button.

"See anyone famous?" Jack asked.

"Not yet," Michele said. "I'm kind of anxious to get there. It'll be starting any minute now ya know."

Valerie appeared even more nervous. She excused herself and wedged her way between them to the front of the car.

"Hope I get to see your designs," Jack said.

Michele was shifting behind Valerie next to her dad, saying, "I hope…," but then stopped herself.

Jack winked at her.

Leo was gulping air in the back corner from the double-time walk down the hallway.

The door had hardly opened before Valerie squeezed herself out, Jack fast on her tail. Michele and Leo were next and trotted along after them through the lobby. The same young girl they'd talked to twice before was at the reception desk.

Michele gave a smile and a little wave as she passed. "Remember us?"

"Are you live, or are you Memorex?" Jack asked as he passed the bewildered young woman.

Rick and Daniele had already shuffled through the oversized revolving door and were at the end of the street by the time the others had crowded between the moving glass panels and were tripping on each other through the revolving door. Leo was in the back trying to keep the door from giving him a flat, dabbing at his forehead with a handkerchief.

Rick turned to Daniele before they made the end of the street, and ran along side her for a moment. She slowed down to pull off her high-heeled shoes, hopping ahead on one foot at a time as she yanked at the heels, discarding them on the sidewalk, and then used both hands to cinch the skirt of her black sequined cocktail dress up around her thighs.

"I'll take…the far…one," he said breathlessly.

"Plan," Daniele said.

"Hope…the keys…are in them," Rick said sporadically as he

increased his speed and ran ahead of her.

Michele was the first through the revolving door and saw the same two doormen standing there. "Jerks," she said as she passed. Valerie and Michele had the same trouble as Daniele, though neither of them removed their shoes, choosing instead to pull their dresses up and take choppy little steps that were more like race-walking than flat out running, their shoes in a tap-dance rhythm.

They shuffled their way down the street between the tower and the Hilton, the seven story buildings on either side casting eerie shadows all around. The Eiffel Tower stood majestically before them, shimmering from top to bottom from the white twinkling lights. Rick, far ahead of Daniele now, had already reached the tower and had turned left under it as Michele and the others emerged from between the buildings and had slowed to a fast walk up the street and through the park. Daniele disappeared around the Eiffel's mechanical buildings and blew by the security guards who were watching with amused faces while the well-dressed elites scurried to make the beginning of the show.

Forty seconds later, Jack reached the guards. "Evening," he said with a nod as Michele, Valerie and he passed.

Leo had fallen behind, though he was walking with brisk determination. The three rounded the south leg and emerged into the vast clearing under the tower, where several hundred people were milling and standing in the center with cameras, gazing up through the middle of the massive girdered structure. By the time they located Rick and Daniele, Rick was already jumping into the car.

The keys were in it. Shocked people all around were watching him, and a soldier carrying an assault rifle was rushing toward him from sixty meters away, brandishing his firearm.

Daniele had reached the other car on the west leg and hesitated for a moment to look at Rick for direction.

Rick had already started his car. He pressed the window button and yelled out as loudly as he could at her, "River!"

She nodded, opened the door and pulled herself up and inside. "Oh good," she said to herself when she saw the key. And then she looked out across the grounds. "What'm I doing?"

The scattered soldiers, policemen and security guards were all in motion now, some running toward the action, some readying their firearms, and most talking simultaneously into their radios.

Rick's was the first car to leave its pedestal, engine revving and sparks flying as the Benz nosed into the ground and almost leaped off the front wheels on impact. A moment later Daniele's car did the same, her heart throbbing so hard in her brain that she actually thought her ears might burst. She followed Rick's lead and laid on the horn, blaring at the hundreds of people between her and the river. She pushed her window button and began yelling at the people to clear the way.

The soldier nearest to Rick leveled his weapon at his car and pulled off three rounds that impacted the windshield near his head.

"Oh no!" Jack said softly, rushing into the clearing under the tower as he saw the shards of glass spraying into the car around Rick's head.

Rick ducked down to peer through the steering wheel as he threw a dust cloud up behind him. The soldier was distracted by Daniele's car now and took careful aim at the driver's head.

Jack, Valerie and Michele were directly under the center of the tower, still hustling toward the action. Every head was turned in the direction of the commotion, with some already trotting away, looking over their shoulders as they fled. Jack slowed momentarily and twisted around looking for Leo. He spotted him, just next to the security station, and could faintly hear his voice.

The security guards at the station near the mechanical rooms had gone into action just as Leo was passing them. Precious seconds had passed while Leo, badge held high with one hand, explained to the senior man that the people in the Benzes were agents. "Tell your men to cease fire *now!*" Leo ordered.

The man in charge hesitated; a handgun gripped by both hands was aimed at Leo's forehead.

Jack had stopped and was thinking that he should go back and help Leo, but soon saw that it was unnecessary.

"*Now!*" Leo demanded, apparently not even slightly intimidated by the threat. "There are *bombs* in those cars! My agents *must* be allowed to get them away from the tower!"

The security chief faltered, and then lowered his weapon and spoke rapidly into a microphone pinned to his shoulder. "Hold your fire!" he said, glaring into Leo's eyes. "Do *not* stop the cars! Give assistance!"

The soldier had Daniele in his sights with his finger beginning to squeeze when the frantic call came over the radio.

"There are bombs in those cars!" The commander continued urgently. "The drivers are Secret Service agents! Clear a path for them to exit the grounds!"

The soldier's finger loosened on the trigger and he lowered his weapon. Immediately the security forces at the tower changed their focus from the cars to herding people out of the way.

The two Benzes were moving through the crowd as fast as possible, which was a shuddering, give it gas, hit the brakes, weaving and lurching race between the two to get to the street without hitting any of the people fleeing before them. Rick and Daniele both were blaring on their horns, while Daniele kept repeating, "What am I doing? What am I doing? This is crazy!" Rick could see the soldier that had fired at him holding his weapon with one hand while waving Rick on next to him with the other, shouting sharp orders to the crowd to get out of the way.

The people had scattered by the time they were thirty meters from the street, and the two drivers had a clear shot to the intersection near the bridge. Only they knew where they were headed, forcing the soldiers to improvise.

Rick jabbed his finger toward the river as he passed the soldier who had fired. He grabbed his shoulder microphone and clicked the button. "They're headed for the river! Clear the intersection!"

Another voice came through, "Where are they going?"

"Maybe Trocadero," the soldier said, referring to the museum across the wide bridge over the Seine from the Eiffel. "Just clear the intersection!"

"The river!" Leo's voice blared stridently over the commander's radio, indicating Rick's best route to minimize the damage from the blasts. Leo had come around the south leg of the tower with the commander and they were both craning their necks toward the intersection when Leo had leaned over and grabbed the microphone, speaking now into the commander's shoulder. "They're taking them to the river!" he repeated. "Clear the stairs!"

Daniele was passing a soldier and could hear her father's voice through the man's radio, causing her to take a momentary glance at the side mirror. She actually saw him distantly in the glass, shoulder to shoulder with the commander, the girders of the tower leg arching over his head, and she felt strengthened by his voice and presence.

Policemen and soldiers alike rushed out into the middle of the intersection and stopped cars, their hands and arms held up, shuffling defensively with their feet, and causing at least three fender benders at the suddenness of their actions. But their swiftness worked. As soon as traffic was stopped and the intersection hastily cleared, with cars jutting around it at chaotic angles, the uniformed men and women ran to the corner next to the wide stairs that went down to the river boat landings and commanded and pushed people out of the way. The stairs were ten meters wide – wide enough to make a clear path down the left side – with people scrambling up and down, vacating the steps in a panic.

Rick made it to the intersection first with Daniele pulling in a meter behind him. He gunned his engine, hopped the curb, and crossed the intersection, heading straight for the stairs. A kiosk was open on the sidewalk, selling tower souvenirs, and he just couldn't avoid it. He clipped the outside of the displays spread outside the small building, scattering little Eiffel Tower paperweights and cheap Parisian black and white prints across the wide sidewalk, with terrified onlookers screaming in rapid retreat.

Daniele had her own trouble. Trying to avoid the kiosk she came too far left and sideswiped the traffic signal pole, pushing it at an angle into the intersection. "Look out!" she yelled as several people had to scurry out of her way while the pole made a slow motion crash into the bed of a delivery truck sitting at the corner on the end of the bridge.

Rick's tires screeched when he reached the stairs, turning hard right and flying over the first few. The car jerked up and down when it hit, sparks flying, as every concrete step seemed to tear at the chassis. Daniele's ride was similar, overcompensating the recovery from the signal pole and crashing hard into the concrete wall next to the stairs on the left side. "Ah!" she screamed as the driver side airbags deployed, making it hard for her to use the wheel. She couldn't steer the car back to the middle of the stairs anyway, since the front wheels weren't making contact long enough to make the adjustment. So she just rode it out, the bag deflating next to her, and the concrete wall throwing sparks from the door across her face.

The bottom stairs were at a ninety-degree angle from the main stairway, with a wide concrete landing that Rick hit hard. At the landing he cranked the wheel hard left and floored it. The rear wheels spun and smoked but gripped enough to change the car's momentum. He was more or less in the center of the landing and had gained enough speed that the car sprung over the bottom stairs and hit hard again on the wide square next to the concrete wharf that ran along the river. When the suspension had stabilized the car, Rick hit the gas again and in a fog of screeching and smoke pushed it down to the left toward the bridge.

Daniele had lost most of her momentum along the rail, and was all the way to the left of the landing, next to the lower steps. When all four wheels were on the landing, she too gunned it and tried to spin the rear of the car ninety degrees. But she was already on the steps and had to take the bumping and bouncing ride down almost sideways. At the bottom, she was squealing and spinning in clouds of smoke just as Rick had done.

Crowds of people lined the bridge, and the masses milling on the square near the riverside road were awestruck by the intense moment. Valerie had been the first to give in and take her shoes off, with Michele immediately following her lead. By the time the two cars had hit the bottom of the stairs, the two women were at the intersection and had just made it to the rail in time to see Daniele's car disappear under the bridge. Michele, along with several hundred others, Jack included, having caught up to the girls when he saw that Leo was in control, crossed the street between the parked cars and made the view from the opposite railing of the bridge. Rick's car had already emerged and was speeding down the riverside road toward an opening between two boats about a hundred meters from his position.

Jack looked at his watch. "Oh man," he said uneasily, leaning over the thick concrete rail on his elbows and fearing that the cars would explode before they made it to the water. "Eleven o'clock."

Valerie had taken the route down the stairs and was hopping two at a time. She cleared the bottom and made the turn to where she could see the bridge just in time to see Rick's car pulling hard to the right, aiming straight for the river.

Rick was pushed against the door, his hands sweaty on the wheel. All four tires were smoking and sparking, damaged to the point that he had to struggle with the steering wheel to get the Benz to respond. It was floored again, and his heart pounded as he headed straight toward the end of the wharf and the river, between two long dinner-cruise boats full of people standing at the rails watching. The river rushed at him for two seconds and then he was airborne with a surreal tranquil feeling of weightlessness that seemed to last for an eternity. The car nose-dived and slammed into the water like it was cement, the hard jolt whipping his torso forward. He believed he actually saw the center of the wheel separating as if in slow motion as the airbags deployed with a bang, preventing his face from impacting the wheel while his eyelids involuntarily snapped shut.

Daniele had made the same moves, screeching into a hard right turn that directed the car to the river like a missile. She aimed for a point about five meters next to Rick's car in a desperate attempt to avoid crashing onto the top of him. The car wouldn't respond at first, and she clutched the wheel with both hands and pulled down to the right with all her strength to make the adjustment. Her efforts were only partially successful. Just before the car sprung from the pier it steered slightly right and she flew off and onto the right rear trunk of Rick's car with a sickening crunch.

Rick had been struggling with the door handle, but had given up on it and was halfway out the open window when Daniele's car hit. The impact jerked him up but the thrust helped push him out of the car. He was treading water, a feat that took more energy than he'd expected in his tux and hard-soled shoes, searching over the sinking top of the Benz to find Daniele.

He swam over the hood to her car. It was taking on water, but she was doing the same as he had, struggling to push herself out through the open window. He willed himself to her just as the car was going under. But Daniele's stylish dress had become entangled in the airbag and was taking her down with the strength of a spider's web on a frenzied fly.

"I can't...I can't..." she gasped. "I'm caught!"

Daniele's shoulders were going under when Rick saw where her dress was caught and just managed to clutch it with a clenched fist. But the car was sinking too fast. She struggled for a last gulp of air as she disappeared in a rippling pool with her blonde hair floating bizarrely peacefully before it too slipped under.

"Michele!" Rick called, and then sucked the air into his lungs twice, kicking and bobbing on the surface before he held the second one. He half-dove and was half-pulled by his grip on her dress.

Daniele was clawing in vain at the air bag, trying to free her dress as she faded toward the darkness. There was nothing else Rick could do. Wrenching at the fabric her bare shoulders emerged. He ripped again at the shoulders of her dress, tearing it apart as her torso started to slip out. He ripped at the front where it was caught, shredding it away from her body. He ripped it down the back and she was free, slipping from the material like a butterfly from a cocoon, and flowing out the window, being guided by Rick's firm grip under her arm. The sequins on her dress lost their glitter as the car disappeared into the blackness.

Valerie was running recklessly across the square toward them, her long tight dress ripped at the seams clear up to her thighs from her extended strides, while Jack and Michele stood in helpless horror from their vantage point on the bridge.

Jack was leaning over the top of the concrete rail, both hands gripping the opposite edge as though he was trying to pull himself over so he could somehow get to them and help them. Under his breath he was urging, "Com'on, com'on…"

Rick's lungs felt like they would burst as he pushed her to freedom with both hands on her waist. A moment later, Daniele's head sprang from the water, tilted back with her neck extended as she opened her mouth wide and took a frantic huff that wheezed loudly across the water. Rick had pushed himself farther down in his effort to lift Daniele, and kicked twice upwards as he pushed the air from his lungs and shot up next to her, seeming to fly out of the water. The sound of his gasping breath echoed across the still water, the hush of the crowd creating an eerie silence that made the desperate rasp of air rushing into his burning lungs shrill enough to hear from the bridge.

They bobbed in the water, searching the surface to regain their sense of direction before stroking and kicking hard toward the concrete steps that lined the river.

"Get away!" Rick yelled, stopping long enough in the water to wave his hand at the people on the boats. "It's going to blow up!"

No one moved until Valerie approached at a dead run and yelled in French. "There are bombs in those cars!" She waved wildly with both arms, signaling for the people to escape. "They're going to blow up! Move away!"

Aiming toward the steps, Rick and Daniele pumped the water hard
in unison as they swam the last few feet toward safety. Rick scrambled
the few steps up and turned to grasp Daniele's arm. They struggled onto
the concrete, pulling each other along arm in arm, grappling on hands
and knees until they worked themselves up to their feet and broke into a
furious dash.

Rick turned in stride, waving sideways at the people as he stumbled,
some still standing and watching as he urged them to get away from the
blast area. His arm had just made a sweeping motion toward the back of
the boat when both cars blew simultaneously.

The explosion knocked Rick and Daniele to the pavement and rolled
them over several times, arms and legs flailing while the pavement ripped
at Daniele's slip. The bow of the rear boat, and the stern of the front boat
seemed to lift lazily out of the water, followed by a massive mushroom
that burst fifty meters straight into the air, feathering out like a majestic
fountain as it rained in a perfect circle onto the boats, the pier, and into
the river itself. The boats were still intact, crashing down at first, then
bobbing high and low, sending rhythmic waves across the river before
settling down to a gentle rocking motion.

All Rick could hear was the blaring sound of a constant ringing that
sounded to him like a high pitched smoke detector.

The people on both boats had been knocked to the deck and were
slowly standing, soaked from the falling torrent.

Rick rolled around to Daniele and almost yelled to hear himself.
"You all right?"

She turned, rolled over onto her back, her arms spread out against
the cool concrete, and started laughing to the point that her tears were
mixing with the river water dripping from her face. Taking heaving
breaths that repeatedly lifted her chest she screamed, "What a *rush!*"

Rick leaned up on one elbow and started laughing too. "Look at
you," he said, trying to catch his breath.

"Another…" she gasped a breath, "…man…" her chest pounding,
"ripping my clothes off!"

"What?" Rick asked, still laughing, but didn't realize the meaning of
her words. "Man! That was intense!" He stood and took Daniele's hand
and pulled her up. He took off his drenched tuxedo jacket. "Here," he
said holding it behind her, "you should put this on." He looked up

toward the bridge. "You have an audience."

Daniele followed his gaze to see the lines of people crowding along the bridge and up and down the railing on the road above them, all cheering and clapping, waving arms and whatever articles happened to be in their hands. The roar of the thousand spectators slowly replaced the ringing in their ears.

"Feel like a gladiator," Rick said as Daniele let him hang the jacket over her white satin slip.

Daniele couldn't help herself as she turned around and threw her arms around him, her legs whipping up and clasping the back of his thighs, almost knocking him over as he staggered back a step. The roar from the crowds peaked again.

Rick embraced her as her legs slipped to the ground, and they stood holding each other while Valerie slowed, saw the two, and stopped thirty meters away. With a smile she turned and headed back toward the bridge, wanting to leave the lovers to themselves.

On the bridge, Michele grabbed Jack around the neck and gave him a tight squeeze. "That was *close*!" she said, her heart beating hard against his chest.

Jack took the opportunity to lean over and kiss her. Michele let herself go, the emotion of the excitement blending in to the emotion of the moment.

"Oh!" she exclaimed. "They're safe!"

Jack held her closer, kissing her on the cheek until he found her lips again.

Suddenly Michele's grip changed and she pushed back a little, her forehead down and pressing against his chest.

"What is it?" Jack asked with a sly grin.

She looked up at him. "I have to tell you something," she said. "I hope you don't hate me for it. It could change everything."

Jack smiled, doin' the wobbly. "So you have some secret to tell me?"

She nodded yes.

"So go ahead, Michele," he said, "tell me."

"Well, I'm not really Dan…" She stopped, his words soaking in, and then looked up into his eyes and saw the playfulness. "You mean, you *know?*"

"Of course I know," Jack said with a laugh.

"You knew I was me all this time?"

He nodded again, a wide closed-mouthed grin on his face.

She slapped his arm. "How could you know and not tell me you knew?"

"Hey!" he said. "Don't get mad at *me!*"

She laughed and pulled him close again. "When did you find out?"

"After you switched," he said.

"How *long* after we switched?"

"Pretty much right from the beginning."

"Well why didn't you say anything?"

He shrugged. "Looked to me like you were on a mission."

"Right…yeah…the dinner," Michele said. "Valerie gave us a mission."

"Seems to have worked," Jack said.

"But why didn't you say anything after that? Like last night, maybe, after the dinner?"

"And ruin your fun? Besides, wasn't it really about Rick and Daniele?"

"It was about *you*," she said, and admitted it with a grin. "And Daniele. And Rick. I couldn't marry Rick. We're not even engaged anymore."

"You're not?"

She shook her head.

A smile emerged on Jack's face. "When did this happen?"

"Oh, months ago. We both decided we didn't want to go through with it. He's just not my type. "

"And I am?" Jack asked hopefully.

She kissed him with a little peck on the lips. "We'll see, won't we?"

"Works for me," Jack said. "I'd kinda like to give it a shot. But…um…no rings or anything, okay?"

"Oh! *Please* no!" Michele said with a laugh. "I don't want one. Not right now anyway."

Jack let out a noisy sigh. "Whew," he said. "I was kinda worried about that." He gazed on Rick and Daniele below, clutching each other, and had a concerned look. "What about my son?"

"What about him?" Michele asked.

"Just wanted to make sure you were aware that I have one."

"Yes, I know." She smiled. "I'll spoil him. Can't wait to meet him."

"Really?" Jack asked. "You're okay with the fact that my time will be divided like that?"

Pulling his neck she kissed him on the cheek. "Why would that be a problem? If he's like you, I'll just love him."

Jack took a deep breath and touched his forehead to hers. "You're all right," he said.

"But slow huh?" Michele asked, making sure he understood. "Let's just have fun, okay? Nothing serious? Not right away, anyway."

"Right up my alley," Jack said with a broad smile. "No promises."

Michele rubbed her ring finger. "Honest? No rings?"

He looked in her eyes. "If it's meant to be, it's meant to be. But if it isn't, let's just enjoy what time we have and then let go if we have to. Deal?"

"Deal," she said beaming, and grabbed him around the neck again, kissing him passionately and repeatedly on the neck. Suddenly she pushed him back once more and hesitated, as though she just remembered something else. "There *is*...um...one other little thing," she said slowly.

Valerie had almost made it to the stairs when she saw Leo at the top. She stopped and smiled up at him while he stepped down the stairs to meet her.

Rick and Daniele were still on the dock, the crowds still clapping and waving at them like conquering heroes of an older France. They were silently embracing each other, but Rick was tentative, and had a slightly guilty look on his face that caught Daniele's eye.

"What is it?" she asked, vaguely shocked.

"I'm afraid I need to tell you something," Rick said.

She looked in his eyes, fearing that he knew.

"Yes?" she asked anxiously.

"I'm...um...I'm," he stumbled.

"What *is* it?" she asked impatiently.

"I don't know how to say it, now that I know what happened between you and Daniele."

She leaned back a little so she could study his eyes. "It's probably best just to say it."

"I, um, I thought I was in love with Daniele for a while," he said.

"There, it's out."

Daniele let out a gleeful laugh. "Really?" But then her smile faded. "You *thought* you were?"

"Yes," he said, "but it was just for a little short time. All day today, I've really come to know that it's you that I love. I guess I just didn't see it before. But right now, I'm so happy to be with you, and I'd like to think that our engagement is real. I know I already asked you before, but will you marry me?"

Daniele's smile was glued to her face like a mannequin, and she looked deeply into his eyes, almost in awe. "You really don't know, do you?"

"Don't know what?" Rick asked, his eyes wide and innocent.

"I *am* Daniele," she said.

Rick's eyes began to close, but were left with puzzled slits, his eyebrows pulling closer together in the middle.

"We switched," Daniele said in a hushed tone, lowering her head in shame. His eyes were penetrating, and now she was feeling guilty and stupid that she hadn't told him.

Rick's expression lifted and he chuckled. "*You're* Daniele?"

She nodded.

"When did this happen?"

"Yesterday," she said with a slow whine, then looked at him. "Valerie asked us to."

"*Valerie?*" Rick asked, his blue eyes looking dazed. "Why?"

"It was a mission. The dinner. She said I'd do a better job finding out if Father was alive or not. You know, 'cause I'm a prosecutor and everything." She broke his gaze, lifted her hand in front of his chest and looked longingly at the ring on her finger. "So when we went to do our nails we changed our hair color too." She looked at him and smiled again. "Not to mention the fiasco of trying to switch personalities."

Rick eyed her suspiciously. "So the last couple of days it was you, and before that it was you?"

"Yes," she said sheepishly, and gave him a weak smile. "You're not angry, are you?"

"Then it *is* you," Rick asked in a confused tone, "that I'm in love with?"

"Yes," she said, brushing her hand over her blonde wet hair. "I hope so, anyway. I'm so sorry we did this to you."

"But then," Rick asked nervously, "do you…um…love *me?*"

Daniele giggled. "Oh Rick." She looked deeply into his eyes. "You really are just blonde to the bone, aren't you?"

Rick smiled and lowered his head. "I guess that means you do."

"Of *course* I do!" she said and grabbed him around the neck, pulling herself to him.

They kissed passionately, the crowds reacting strongly again with cheers and clapping that they didn't hear.

Suddenly Rick gently pushed himself away, his hands on her shoulders. "What about Michele?"

"What about her?" Daniele asked, somewhat thrown by the question.

"What happened between you and Jim." He spun his neck slowly and scanned the crowds. "She's gonna kill you for doing it to her again."

"I don't think you need to worry about Michele," Daniele said knowingly and motioned toward the bridge with her head and eyes. "See?"

Rick looked up, searched the railing on the bridge, and found them. Michele's head was against Jack's chest, and when he saw them she waved.

"Michele and *Jack?*" Rick asked, staring in wonder as they smiled down at him. "I thought Jack was in love with *you!*"

Daniele laughed again and put her hand against his chest. "Oh Rick, sometimes…"

He turned back to her. "So how come," he said tentatively, "you're in love with someone as dumb – as blonde to the bone – as me?"

"I didn't mean that you're dumb," she said affectionately. "You're just a bit…um…*naïve* sometimes."

"Hmm," Rick said looking off toward the lights of the Eiffel. "Not sure that's any better."

She looked at him, her blue eyes sparkling charmingly in the moonlight, the Eiffel Tower lights glistening in them like shimmering flickers on the water. "Don't you *see?* That's what I *love* about you. It comes from a trusting, innocent good heart. No man ever did anything for me." She put her hand against his chest. "But you did."

"Yeah," he said, brushing his fingers through his wet hair. "What did *I* ever do for you?"

"You protected me," she said. "You held me when I thought I was going to die on that bridge, and you pushed me behind you just tonight when bullets were flying. And just now you lifted me from the water when I thought I was going to drown, and I know you must have been close to drowning yourself."

"But you did the same for me," he said remembering. "You were willing to die for me."

Rick's face blossomed into a disarming smile as he pulled her to his chest. He held her there for a moment before she turned and pulled him, starting to walk toward the steps.

"Com'on," she said. "Let's go see how Father's doing."

They walked along slowly, both of them leaving trails of dripping Seine water.

She slipped her hand around his back. After a few steps further she added. "You just happen to be a spy." She chuckled. "Liar. Clandestine. Ripping women's clothes off." She smiled up at him. "Typical man. Go figure."

Leo and Valerie, arms around each other, were waiting for them on the landing at the bottom of the main stairs. Jack and Michele had joined them, and watched the heroes approach in silence. Jack was wearing a shrewd grin.

"A job well done," Leo said and shook Rick's hand as they walked up the bottom steps.

"No group hugs, okay?" Daniele said. "I'm a little tired of the ditzy thing, and would just as soon go back to being my old sarcastic self."

"Oh gag me with a spoon," Michele said with a smile. "I thought you liked being me."

"I think I'm gonna prefer being me from now on," Daniele said, leaning against Rick's shoulder. She looked up at him. "Well, so what's next?"

"What's next," a familiar voice said, coming from the stairs above them, "is we tell you what really happened."

They all looked up to see Leo stepping briskly down the stairs wearing a white tux.

Daniele gasped and looked at her father standing next to her, standing next to Valerie, and then back up at the new Leo hopping the steps. "*What?*"

Rick looked from one Leo to the other and then around at the scene. "You mean to tell me this is all virtual?"

Leo had a smile as he approached. "All of it."

Daniele's face turned to confusion. "So none of this is real?" She pushed away from Rick. "Are *you* real?"

Rick pulled her back to him. "I'm real. You're real. I know you are. I can feel it." He looked at the new Leo. "But I don't know about anyone else here. So what's this all about?"

"About Daniele," Leo said and looked at her lovingly. "I told you I'd find out what was going on with you, one way or the other."

Daniele was in shock, trying to take it all in. "This..." she said, darting her head around. "The bombs...." She tried to push away from Rick again, but he held her firm. "The kidnapping...I thought I was gonna drown!" She stomped her foot. "Oh! How could you *do* this to me?"

"You wouldn't talk to me," he explained. "I had to know." He shrugged. "Sorry."

"But this!" Daniele stomped again and growled. "You!...You!..."

Leo's smile would not go away. "Are you telling me you don't love Rick?"

"Oh!" She said, and then forcefully calmed herself, looking at Trocadero across the river, at the riverboats, and then at Rick. "Yes," she said, gazing into his eyes. "Yes. I love him."

Leo shrugged. "Then why don't you just accept what happened and be grateful that you're loved?"

"By all of us," Michele said, and then tittered, "Wasn't it *fun?*"

Daniele put her free hand on her hip, the other still locked around Rick's waist, trying to penetrate her father with her eyes. "So you heard all that about Jim, didn't you."

"I'm your father," Leo said. "You could have just told me."

Daniele shook her head and looked away across the Seine, the crowds still watching them – watching her – though now she knew they weren't even there. "And then you did all this..."

"Hey," Leo said defensively, "don't blame it all on me. Most of it was your sister's idea."

Daniele looked at Michele in shock. "What'd *Michele* have to do with this?"

Michele had a naughty grin and lifted onto her toes and back down again, her hands clasped behind her back.

"She's the one who came up with this whole terrorist thing," Leo explained and looked at her playfully. "I just think she wanted to find a way to get to Paris for her show."

"So we're really *in* Paris?" Rick asked.

The other Leo and Valerie were still watching, with Jack seeming to enjoy every minute of Daniele's reaction to the revelations.

"Oh yes," Leo said. "We're in Paris."

"So there really is an Eva?" Rick asked.

"Yes," Leo answered. "And it really is networked with Eve."

"But how could you be so sure we'd bring them in…to…Eve…" Rick looked hard at Leo. "Bob knew, didn't he?"

"I asked him, and he agreed to help," Leo said. "So did Valerie. I couldn't exactly order them."

"So the door to the basement was no accident," Rick stated.

"Nope," Leo said. "But I could've shot Bob for the gas. Sorry about that. That was his way of being subtle. I just wanted him to leave the elevator open, but then he thought you'd suspect he did it on purpose, and, obviously Rick, you weren't supposed to know. He actually did kind of panic." He snickered. "And then he came up with that whole harebrained story about how he 'forgot' to close off the basement entrance."

"So how long have we been in Eva?" Rick asked.

Daniele answered. "Since we went into the elevator at the Hilton. We never actually left, did we?"

"That's right," Leo said, nodding with approval. "You've been in Eva the whole time."

"But we were eating, and drinking," Rick looked at the river, "and even *swimming!*"

"Pretty cool system, don't you think?" Leo said with a smile, as a grin broke across Valerie's face next to the other Leo.

Rick's frown turned to concern. "Don't you think this's a major security breach?"

Leo shrugged. "I'm sure I'll have to explain it to the National Security Advisor," he smiled, "if he ever finds out – Rick." He looked affectionately at his daughter. "But it was worth it."

Daniele was eyeing her sister with a mixture of anger and admiration. "So when did you come up with all this?"

"When Daddy told me, silly," she said with a laugh. "Remember the phone call I had before we went back into Eve? And I had to go to that planning meeting?"

Daniele turned to the Leo on the stairs. "That was *you?*"

Leo nodded.

Valerie chuckled. "I was so worried that you would see through Michele's plan." She touched her forehead. "We had so many things we missed."

"Like what?" Daniele asked.

"Like why Eva didn't know that Gunter and Marlene were registered at the Intercontinental." She sighed. "That one was so obvious. And why get fingerprints at dinner when I could have just had agents go to their room while they were gone. Or just get them off their butter knives. And what self-respecting terrorist is going to leave the keys in a car full of bombs? Things like that. Not to mention Michele's outburst that Leo looked so real when we woke her up at the chateau."

"Oh yeah..." Daniele said slowly with a look of revelation.

"Still think Rick's the one who's blonde to the bone?" Michele asked with a chuckle.

Daniele's eyes shot back at Michele. "How could you hear..." her mind was racing as her fiery eyes fell back on Leo. "You *told* her?"

Michele laughed. "*As if!*" she said. "Good ol' Robespierre told me."

"Loved that part," Jack said with a gleam. "But I thought Michele tripping me so you two could get to the cars first was kind of rude."

Daniele glared at Jack. "You were in on this too?"

"Nope," he said. "Along for the ride as usual. Michele told me on the bridge." He nudged Michele's side. "Go on, tell her about Jim."

"Jim?" Daniele asked. "What about him?"

Leo was gazing off nonchalantly in the distance toward Trocadero.

"Well," Michele hunched her head, and in a sneaky whisper said, "Daddy kind of found him. He's...um...in Eve."

Daniele was slightly amused. "In Eve?"

"Lemme tell her," Jack said anxiously, and Michele nodded permission. Jack's smile grew to downright evil proportions. "Bob put him on the far side of the Moon," he laughed, "and told him they'd let him off as soon as he found the golf ball!"

Daniele covered her mouth, hiding her laugh, bent over slightly at the waist.

"But it's okay," Jack said. "He has help."

"Help?" Daniele asked.

Jack rubbed his chin. "Yeah. Yoda, Bill, Oliver and Sherlock. They're having a tough time though."

"Oh, this I gotta hear," Daniele said with a grin.

"Well, Yoda's trying to get him to use the force and bring the ball to him, but that ain't happenin', Oliver's trying to argue Bob out of it, Bill wants to pay him off, and Sherlock's looking for clues in the moon dust with his magnifying glass and mumbling about it being too dark to see a bloody thing."

Daniele started to laugh, though she struggled to suppress it. She looked back at Leo, juggling feelings of gratitude and anger. "You…you…man!" She crossed her arms, but couldn't stop the emotions from brimming to her throat, her eyes tearing up as she held her outward reaction to a lighthearted chuckle. "Oh!" she said again with a frustrated laugh, once more stomping her foot. She uncrossed her arms and pulled herself to Rick, who pulled back, and she pressed her cheek and hand against his chest. Behind his back, she fingered the ring with her thumb, stretched out under her middle finger. And then she forced a squinted, repressed smile of a glare at her father. "You can get me out of here now."

"Ha!" Michele said smiling. "Still don't get it, huh?" She had a twinkle in her eye as she looked at the Parisian moon, and in flawless French commanded, "Eva, terminate programme."

The Eiffel melted away, the Seine disappeared into white, and even the water that Rick and Daniele were soaked with somehow slurped away into the floor, slithering down off of them like tiny snakes, making Daniele shudder with a moment of creepy fright. Even both Leo's disappeared, leaving Valerie standing with her hands clasped in front of her and her eyes rolled up looking self-conscious. Daniele and Rick were holding each other while Jack had an amused grin. Michele tossed one arm cockily around Jack's neck and put a hand to her hip as she crossed one leg over the other with her toe on the floor and leaned against him.

"Can we *please* go see my show now?" Michele asked. "Daddy's already there, probably making his speech right about now."

Jack smiled, peering into Daniele's dazed eyes. "Guess that answers the hair color question."

The End

ABOUT THE AUTHOR

Mike Johnson was born in 1955 in Los Angeles.
He received a degree in Biblical Literature from Point
Loma Nazarene University.

He currently manages a major, live fire Naval Training
Range on the west coast. He lives in San Diego, CA.

His first novel "The Altherian Code" was published
in 2001.